levon a

levona

J. D. RADKE

Bascom Hill Publishing Group • Minneapolis

BASCOM HILL
PUBLISHING GROUP

Bascom Hill Publishing Group
322 First Avenue N, 5th floor
Minneapolis, MN 55401
612.455.2294
www.bascomhillbooks.com

ISBN-13: 978-1-63413-858-1
LCCN: 2015917312

Distributed by Itasca Books

Cover Design by Alan Pranke
Typeset by MK Ross

Printed in the United States of America

Dedicated to August.

used not just herbs to cure the body, as I do, but animal parts as well, such as the horn of the white rhino and the claws of wild mountain tigers. Most of the medicines would be soaked in rice wine. The wine absorbs the properties, and then the sick can easily drink all those precious nutrients, both flavorful and powerful. That is how I started prescribing my medicines as well, in cups of wine, as you know.

Yet don't forget that even the Yellow Emperor was once a boy. He explores the ancient world. He probably gets into trouble often. He too tests boundaries and finally begins to write down his mistakes in the form of a medical theory. His body sometimes gets hurt. His friends and his family get hurt as well. Then we would do what all healers must. We try our best.

So, Dear Darling Jasmine, if you have come to the end of this *levon a* still thinking that I should be ground into fine powder and dissolved into the public drinking water for the health of the nation, so be it. That story I told you once of a man who does not die no matter what action is taken, you now know who he is and why he did what he did. The man without a heart who attended your thesis presentation in Hong Kong and was so proud of your use of complex statistics to prove that a single person can indeed make his mark on history, and also the man who gave his lung and stood by you in prison at Tu, the identity of these men you now know too. But alas, the man who stole your eye as a child, that was me as well. I am sorry, Dear Jasmine. He Song is an evil man.

When he died at the age of three hundred and thirty-three, C Y had one hundred and eighty living descendants throughout the land. This old medicine man is living with his twenty-fourth wife the day he passes. He maintains good eyesight until the bitter end. Strangely, his fingernails are uncut and stretch down onto the floor in tangles. What a long life compared to my own!

Lore has it he shared his secret of extraordinary longevity with a well-liked province official who had kindly taken the wandering doctor into his home just before a violent typhoon was about to descend on them. To most, C Y Lee did not share the closely guarded secret of his own longevity, but to this official who showed him such kindness, he advises, "Keep a quiet heart, sit like a tortoise, walk sprightly like a pigeon, and sleep like a dog."

By his tenth birthday, this likely ancestor of mine had traveled the entire Empire from Tibet to Manchuria gathering herbs. He spends his boyhood exploring the world and is an effective influence on others as a youth. Does he always know what he is doing? Can he foretell that he has so long of a life ahead of him? Maybe children all assume they will be here forever.

Because historical records show that C Y Lee was born in the town of Kaisheng, and since I don't know with any certainty where I, He Song was born, I will forever tell people that this town in Sichuan Province called Kaisheng is the land where I am also from. It is a rainy place of panda bears and the beginnings of great rivers.

Much further back, the Yellow Emperor was a long-distant grandfather to us all, both you and me. The Yellow Emperor's Inner Canon that will become the oldest record of medical theory passed down to us today is originally compiled during the first century BC. Many a medicine man follows his bible of truths, and my forefathers were no exception. They

Back in 1851, when Cixi was barely an adolescent, she was invited to participate in the selection of consorts for the newly coronated Emperor, alongside sixty other beautiful candidates. They stand in a line in front of him. The women wear the finest silks, and their hair is carefully combed and jeweled. At this early time, Cixi's prospects look dim. Her parents present a gift to the new Emperor when he takes their daughter away. The gift is wrapped in beautiful yellow ribbons around a wooden box. Inside the box is a golden rat, for Xianfeng was born in the auspicious year of the rat. The Emperor Xianfeng takes but one look at the expensive gift inside the box and sets it aside. The carefully crafted wooden box he never touches again. Still, Cixi is one of the few candidates chosen to stay in the Forbidden City. With time, she is placed in the sixth rank of imperial consorts. At that level, she keeps nothing of value to her name except for the wooden box that once contained her husband's gift. Cixi keeps it as a memory of her past. Everything of value in her chambers belongs to her husband the Emperor, and on his whim she could at any moment be hidden away or put on display. She feels bound by invisible chains to do his bidding, but that is better than being stored away and forgotten, as is the fate of many of his wives.

～ ～

But that dreadful Empress does not get the final word in *my* story. And, mind you, Dear Reader, please remember that most of the women in my tale are not like her. She is an example, not of women at their worst, but rather of a human, both man and woman alike, at its worst. She was a monster of an unusual sort that only extreme and unrestrained power can create. Let us go on. I want to end not with her story but by telling you instead about my own ancestors, the medicine men roaming the mountains of ancient China. I'd like to believe that one of these ancestors of mine was a common herb gatherer named C Y Lee who also became more of a health consultant in later life, and once assisted Buddha himself, to provide precious remedies when there was no other cure.

Dowager Cixi ousts a group of regents appointed by the late Emperor and assumes total control. She demands all the keys of power and kills for them as easily as it is to say the words, "So be it."

Unlike the many other women in the imperial harem competing for the Emperor's attention, Cixi was unique in her ability to assist the Emperor. On occasion, the Emperor Xianfeng requests that Cixi read proclamations on his behalf. When the Emperor is away, he leaves instructions for her to execute, and with time her voice begins to carry the weight of his own. Cixi becomes well informed about state affairs. This Middle Kingdom is a complicated empire with many players, but like any intricate clockwork, there is an order to the madness. She learns the art of state governing from her master.

She collected many keys over her time in the Forbidden City. Eventually the wooden box that sits on her vanity becomes full, and Cixi needs to prioritize which keys to keep and which to discard. The wooden box always sits there on her vanity table. It is a safe place for such an ordinary item among a palace of priceless objects. The simplicity of the wood box out in the open allowed nobody to notice it. If one were to snoop inside her room and see the box, who would care? It is just a box of keys. No meaning to them, no value. Still, when she is away, she locks the box and keeps the key around her delicate wrist.

Her rise from obscurity came with the birth of a child. When Courtesan Cixi's beauty catches the attention of the Emperor, and she is elevated to the fifth rank and given the title "Imperial Concubine Yi," she soon becomes pregnant and gives birth to the Emperor's only son. Becoming the mother of a prince elevates her to the fourth rank of consorts. When her son reaches his first birthday, Cixi's status is again elevated and she is given the name "Noble Consort Yi." This rank within the harem places her second only to the Empress. There is now just one other woman who stands between her and the Emperor!

In her womb, earlier still, this sense of past and future got more muddled, and I swam in an eternity, and it was heavenly. I feel warmth, and I feel protection. I feel life and love. I am never hungry. I am never scared. I swim. I grow. The bath sooths my pains. It is a happy time, perhaps my happiest time, right there in my mother's womb. There are people who wait their entire lives for this. For me, the real paradise is happening already before birth. Everything after these nine months will be a comparison to the good I once had.

~ ~

There is a curious beginning to our story about Emperor Puyi's evil grandmother, Empress Dowager Cixi. She's been the shadow behind the scenes. You've been wondering about her, I know.

Throughout her long life, she refused to adopt the modern Western models of government that would lessen her power. She supports some technological and military reforms in what will be called the Self-Strengthening Movement, but she still loses two wars against the foreign powers and has to pay back huge retributions in land and wealth. That is how the lands of Hong Kong, Tianjin, Shanghai, and many other cities were lost for a time to the foreign powers.

Empress Dowager Cixi consolidated her control over the dynasty when she installed a puppet Emperor at the death of her son in 1875. She is not the only woman to be in such a position at this time. Queen Victoria also lives large on the other side of the world. Each has a portrait of the other woman hanging in their private quarters, and they sometimes look on it as a reflection and ponder what a strange world this is.

With her husband Emperor Xianfeng's death in 1861, Empress Cixi's son became the Emperor Child, but since he was so young, she held his power as the Empress Dowager and ruled under his name. Empress

I do not remember the important details about my original family. I think I had siblings, but that is just a sense. It torments me to know that this memory has slipped from me yet I do remember our family dog, a wrinkled shar-pei that licks my face. Probably in my hometown it is believed that dogs scare away the evil ghosts, and so one is always kept close to my cradle. My father has a beard I have no doubt (of which I grow a perfect replica now on my own face). Let me look at a mirror, and let him talk to us here. Addressing the mirror, I now say, "Father." He smiles back at me. The face looks young, not quite thirty. The eyes are dark and true. He must be a medicine man. You see the yellow stains of herbs on his fingers. You see the blue stains of poisons on his gums between his teeth, for he tests many a curious mushroom and chews on many a poisoned leaf. In the mirror, looking at me, my father says to me, "You could have been a better man, He Song. Look at what you have been given. Look what you have done." The smile is still there. Why does he smile so? Is there love in his eyes still?

I learned some basic words as a young one before I went to Beijing, and I became aware of the many restrictions the world places on us as children. I come to understand how gravity works and that we are bound to the earth. I learn that things can still exist when they are no longer in view, and then "Peekaboo!" they can appear again. This makes me laugh. I can't get enough of it. It takes great strength to stand up and run. With trial and error, I learn that too. Falling sometimes hurts, but my mother, who smells of honey, is there now to rub away the pains when I cry. *Oh, the magic of my mother!* As an infant, I can see both into the past and future. Some people think that toddlers live in the present. That is not true. I see it all. Though I have a limited vocabulary, my mind is in touch with the whole span of my life as I will live it. My child brain is not bound by what you call time. I see a school girl in braids taking my child from me. I see my son The Monkey King later in prison asking me for all I can give. I see us all there at that wedding feast in Shanghai with the light dancing off the pool waters on the ninety-ninth floor of the Shangri-la Hotel.

Chapter 1

June 4, 1906

The Emperor has 413 million subjects.

I can only guess what my early childhood might have been and who my blood parents were. What do any of us really remember from that early age? Yet as we grow, we become the authority of that childhood story. Just as we all can only suppose what it was truly like to be secure in the womb of our mothers, we do our best to imagine it. Is it also possible to go even further back in our own story of ourselves to what it was like when all the senses came down to one single sense and our ears would only hear a murmur of the original Om? We will try. I will say that my story ends hypothetically, for I cannot yet tell this part of the tale with certainty. Still, *levon a* would not be complete if I do not try.

When I write of my early childhood, before my tragedy in Beijing, I want you to imagine that my mother is a young version of that kind old lady who once gave me the precious glass eye. Do you remember meeting her in Sichuan just before the televised speech to the nation about the panda bears? Maybe this is my own fantasy, and so be it if I am wrong, but she could be the same woman. She will be much older at the time she gives me the glass eye. I would like to think that it is the same woman. Yes, this is my mother.

The eunuchs strapped ropes around Puyi's body so more people could pull, and with concerted effort, he is finally freed but left with a mangled hand. Fifty hands take hold of rope to pull him free. Under the afternoon sun, only four minutes pass since the yelling begins, and then they have the boy again. He is safe, numbed and terrified, but no longer attached to the tree. One eunuch opens Puyi's clenched fists and sees his small finger is still there and parts of the others, too. How can the eunuchs tell the Great Empress Dowager of this tragedy? Of course, she must be told immediately. She probably already knows. Did she hear young Puyi's screams?

The curious boy to whom the Great Empress Dowager planned to bestow the dragon throne innocently put his small hand in a hole of an ancient cedar tree while playing in the Qianlong gardens. It is a bright, sunny day. There is no feeling of danger. Suddenly, the eunuchs hear the little boy's screams. Something is inside the cedar trunk pulling the boy inside. A hundred eunuchs come to attention, shouting and trying all that they can to pull the child out. *Why put his hand in the tree in the first place?* the older ones moan. A curious boy no more than three years of age is more than the old eunuchs can ever understand.

What they do not know is that his grandmother gave him a key as a test and he has tried that key on every doorknob and keyhole, and when the common locks failed him he moved on to the unsuspected. This bright, sunny day, he tries the key on the holes inside the cedar trees and something furry suddenly grabs his hand. Puyi screams. It is eating his hand. What a horrible feeling to be trapped while your fingers are eaten one by one.

My eyes are on the crabapple candy in my hand rather than my father's shoes, and when I look up, the shoes I am following are not that of my father. My father is gone forever. I drop my candy and run to catch up, but one alleyway looks like the other. I sit down crying when an old eunuch comes up to me and offers help.

I keenly remember not wanting to sleep the night before I lost my father in the streets of Beijing. I somehow know a dark day is approaching. Young children can sense their future. My father has some sort of business in Beijing, and we visit the city together. Since he is an herbalist, perhaps he has come to establish a distributor for his medicines. It seems unlikely anyone would ask my father to come such a great distance as their doctor, because there are already so many herbalists in the city. Although, the medicine my father practices is more ancient and of a nature that is quite different from what is typically available in the capital.

When my father took me on the steam engine to Beijing, I did not want to go. I feel the shadows of what is to come even then. I do everything I can to refuse. I hold my mother, who smells so sweet, tightly with my fingers interlocked. They both have to pry me, kicking and back arched. I will not say goodbye. I can feel this is the last time I will see her. I refuse to allow it, but in the end I have no say.

I cried and cried not wanting to go to sleep, refusing to let my father put me down, but eventually I could not help but fall asleep.

〜 〜

Back in Beijing, the original plan appeared to have been foiled but perhaps there was still a way. Events are all going as the dark Empress so carefully planned, except this one mistake. She sighs, and the eunuchs fan her with peacock feathers. "A boy cannot be Emperor if he cannot point," mourns the Empress Dowager Cixi as she ponders the news. They fan her as she thinks.

Before they cut off my fingers, tea was brought in and I drank. It calms my nerves. I fall asleep, but I have a dream that a large committee stands around scrutinizing my hands.

The eunuchs gave me a tattoo on my shoulder blade. The CGG wants to mark me in case they need me again. It is a strange tattoo that hides unless you know it is there. It looks like a cross. I remember not feeling pain when they gave it to me. At first it is a curious thing to me, yet being on my back, I will eventually forget about it. As a man, my hair grows over it and the tattoo disappears altogether.

They took me into a nice room inside the palace. The chair has a marble back. The window looks out into a garden with a waterfall. Birds are hanging in cages all around. I can hear the courtesans singing. It feels good here. I am not scared.

The palace had a color I had never seen before outside of nature: Mustard yellow. Yellow everywhere, the royal color. It is the color of the sun. I had no idea it could be recreated by man.

The quiet eunuch guided me into the Forbidden City through dusty underground tunnels after entering through the southern gate. There are rats, which scare me. I let out a cry. They are much larger than the black rats back home. My guide carries a ring of keys and a small fold-up map. Sometimes I can't see him in the darkness, but I follow the sound of his keys. He says the Emperor needs my help. "I am happy to help, sir," I reply. I forget about being lost, and my mind is consumed by the heroism of saving the Emperor, just as my father so often did for his patients. In the imagination of my child's mind, I mix herbal potions for the Emperor Prince as my father would certainly do. That is not what the eunuch has in mind for me.

I was snatched away from my father when I was trying to follow him through Beijing's hutongs but got lost in the labyrinth of narrow alleyways.

died. That old Dragoness would have no doubt done away with me using her bottle of cyanide. She did so to all men who came too close to the power of the Emperor (and murdered her own children who got in the way).

I knew games. We run through the halls, ignoring the chatter around us and focus on the fun of the chase until we are exhausted. Then I let him win. It is the rule I have come to learn, that you must always let the Emperor win.

We'd play hide-and-seek, and when I counted from one to twenty, it felt like an eternity. The first numbers go fairly quickly but saying thirteen, fourteen, fifteen, then sixteen, seventeen, e-i-g-h-teeeeen, those last seconds of counting last longer than the hours I stayed awake at night, longer than anything, and then finally nineteen and twenty. *Where did he go?* In twenty seconds, you can't make it farther than a few rooms, but if I start the search in the wrong direction that will give him even more time to lose himself deep in the palace.

The important finger, the pointer, healed up nicely on Puyi's hand. It looks entirely like his own. All of Emperor Puyi's orders will come from that dark pointer finger that once was mine. The others, especially his thumb, take longer to heal. They are puffy and pale. While his hand becomes whole, mine also heals, and I am none the worse for my missing digits.

〜 〜

When I awoke, my hand was bandaged and sore. A short, plump eunuch stands at my side and says, "Hello, my little man. I will call you He Song. The Emperor thanks you for your help. You were able to help him a great deal. The Great Empress Dowager has asked you to stay until you both heal to make sure everything is okay. For that time, you will be able stay in the palace."

They took my right thumb above the knuckle, my pointer finger, the tip of my middle finger, and the tip of my ring finger.

levon a

Heavens above. "My power must not pass to him. He would let the Empire fall through his hands."

As the Empress's time comes to an end, she can see the beginning of her life in daydreams. Cixi the baby, in these daydreams, can see her future death tomb and the moments that lie between and make up her life. The Great Empress Dowager Cixi's old dark eyes look into the eyes of that innocent girl she once was, and her soul remembers this meeting. She has known how her life would play out. In the back of her memory, there was that vision of the evil, old woman she would be, powerful and hated, looking back to her.

The Evil Dowager Cixi long exerted absolute control over the Forbidden City and all the Empire could hold. She began as just a consort among many, to please his Majesty, but with a talent for consolidating power, she becomes our de facto Emperor for decades, ending only with her last breath. The tides are changing on the world stage but she will not allow it in her Empire. The people come to her with what is called the Hundred-Days' Reform, but she rejects them all as dangerous. She places her nephew Guangxu under house arrest for supporting the reformers. The Council for the Greater Good calls a meeting, and, without them knowing, she sits in the shadows of their conference, watching and listening.

When we were given the chance to just be kids, ignored by the adults rushing around to please the dying Empress Dowager Cixi, Puyi and I got along like two peas in a pod. I hardly notice my missing fingers after a time, and he slowly grows accustomed to his. He has the phantom feeling of his old fingers at first, but eventually the new fingers have their own sense of touch and pain. In public, though, I remain mostly out of sight, or bow so deeply to the ground when in a crowded room that no one ever notices my presence.

Dowager Cixi probably did not know of our friendship before she the tears away. He is wearing a coat with seven yellow dragons. He digs his fingers into his coat pocket and pulls out a key. "Look, He Song. Long ago, my loving grandmother gave me this old iron key. Sure, you may take it and look. Grandma challenged me to find what it opens. What do you think it opens, He Song?" My eyes widen.

The Empress Dowager Cixi died in the Hall of the Graceful Bird shortly after she had poisoned a nephew she long despised and set into place everything necessary to install the three-year-old Puyi as the new Emperor of the Qing Dynasty. Her work is done, and it is time to go. She always knew hers would be a natural death. The pearl clicks between her teeth as she places it in her mouth and on her tongue.

Even past death, she wanted to control the Empire. The head eunuch looks at her as she says her final words, ready to carry out any order. With the Empress Dowager, there is always a plan.

"Listen carefully to these words. I have decided that my grandchild Puyi will become China's next Emperor. I have chosen no less than four emperors during my long reign as your Great Empress Dowager, and I have learned what the Heavens require of its messenger to mankind. This boy Puyi will do the job intended. The trees took away his hand, and we restored it. That is no small sign. I have no false reality of the dark world I leave to him. I know that the Empire I pass to my grandchild is weak from war and on the verge of collapse. But there may be magic in this boy!"

"Kill my nephew Guangxu tonight," she had said. Though she so often tries, she looks nothing like the goddess Avalokiteśvara when she says these five words. This old woman resembles instead the great dark monsters carved on the palace rooftops that I imagine could swallow a cow whole and spit fire. "Use the vial of arsenic I keep in my purse. I fear no retribution. Guangxu must die before I do!" She then raises her eyes as if talking to the

What happened to my parents? I was so young when I was brought to Beijing, I cannot remember my hometown no matter how I try. I just remember the most general things about my birthplace. Looking out from the palace and knowing I will never find my family again, out there in that ocean of four hundred million people in one hundred thousand villages… that is what makes me into the man telling you this story. The fear of being lost is always with me. I wish I could find my home, but I can remember nothing that narrows down the possibilities. My blood parents might still be alive when I am independent and old enough to look. The CGG will never tell me. China is a vast mystery. It is scary that when you are lost you will be lost forever, as I was. I think I will always be scared that it could happen again to me, so I do not mind leaving pieces of myself behind wherever I go.

Puyi was crowned Emperor with great lavishness. I want to tell you more about that day, but I do not remember being there.

I suppose I was not invited to the ordination ceremony. I do, however, remember all the preparations. The event took months of preparation, and stockpiles of wealth from around the country came by horse, camel, and automobile. What I remember most is that the Emperor was able to keep one of these camels as a pet. Huge caravans arrived from every part of the world.

The dead Empress Dowager Cixi was entombed seventy-eight miles east of Beijing, in the Broad Valley of Good Omens. The complex of pavilions that makes up her tomb is covered in gold. There is a lavish gate. It feels like a palace. A black pearl rests between her lips.

Emperor Puyi cried at the funeral of his grandmother, and on that same day he shared with me that most secret gift the Empress Dowager had once given him. His Highness is left alone to cry, but I know he needs a friend. I come into his chambers through a passageway that is only big enough for a child. "Are you sad?" I ask him. He looks at me and wipes

CHAPTER 2

May 1, 1908

China's population is 418 million people.

We are nearing the trunk of *levon a* if this story were a tree. Dear Reader, I have taken you from the tip of one of the upper branches, and from there, we have followed each branch inward. Each time a branch connects, you have seen that there were other paths, choices passed by.

When he was too young to govern, the Emperor Child Puyi took me to all the fascinating secret places in his palace, and I drew maps of our explorations. I often chase after him and find him hidden away in ceramic pots in the gardens or behind the large gargoyles on the palace rooftops in our wild games of hide-and-seek. We run around the grown-ups, making a mess of their order. His Highness would break this or that in his palace and then laugh about it. *Look how funny that flowerpot looks now, all shattered. What a mess. Call a eunuch immediately to clean up that mess!* The head eunuchs permit me to spend so much time with the Emperor because I am the secret nobody knows what to do with.

We would climb up the old cedars that grew in the Forbidden City gardens. Despite what happened to Emperor Puyi, he still does not fear the trees. From their branches, I look over the walls. I am curious whether my father is still out there somewhere. I have forgotten nearly everything about him and the rest of my family who were taken from me.

For those early years, I snuck out of the palace for a couple hours at a time to retrieve the common delights of the city and bring them back to share with the Emperor. He likes sweet and salty confections like twisted pretzels from Beijing's street stalls. Street food is such a different flavor from those fancy banquet dinners he has to endure every day. One winter our favorite treat is the candy-coated crabapples sold on the street side of Tobacco Pouch Road. I bring a dozen back so we can make a meal out of them. The crunch of the sugar coating makes us laugh. It crackles like firecrackers when we chomp down with our young teeth. Our smiles materialize like they are part of the crabapple. I have some control over the quantity I eat, but not over the smile they bring. It appears on us like magic. The magic of sugar.

time before Puyi startles me by saying, "Okay, we can go now." We never talk about it again. I want to ask him, but each time I do, he diverts our conversation to a different topic. Of course I will look for signs. The next morning I even go up to the drum tower to look for proof that he flew that day, and there I see small footprints on the tower's windowsill that could have been left by him. I wonder still to this day.

.

Before he made the attempt to do the impossible, he ordered me to try first. He is not very brave. Alas, a brave emperor might have changed this entire story for the better. But, he is who he is. We go together to the Hall of Everlasting Memory, and I do as I am told. I look away from him and focus on the project at hand. I need to raise myself out of the window. My body feels very heavy. I jump up and land back down. "Again," he orders me. I try swimming up. I try climbing the air. It is as if my feet are glued to the ground. "I cannot do it, Emperor. This is magic that can only be done by the Son of Heaven." Finally I say to him, "It is hopeless for me to go on. Son of Heaven, perhaps you will try?"

This was the Emperor Child I remember, making such demands of his palace staff. "He Song, I order you to fly," he says, ignoring the many complications, ignoring gravity even, not caring whether I get hurt in the experiment, just testing his own power over the world.

Early that spring, the Emperor Child Puyi would describe the recurring dream in this way. "I was in the Hall of Everlasting Memory and felt myself grow lighter. I set down my book and the toes of my shoes barely held to the ground so I pushed off and went through the window, swimming in the air, under the moon, past the bell tower, to the drum tower where I held on for a moment looking down below…"

That whole springtime, it was like a greeting we had with one another. I start by saying, "Son of Heaven, tell me of your dreams," and then he replies, "He Song, I dreamed I was flying again. Do you think it is a sign?"

through me. From my cupboard I take the paintbrush and ink and a brown piece of rice paper folded into a size that fits into my pocket.

The door unlocked with the combination 18-1-20. The map is here. The combination lock falls to the ground. I never use that sort of thing again. *I will stick to using keys from this day forward!*

For hours I tried to unlock the cupboard to retrieve my maps of the palace, but what was that secret combination? The new style of lock felt so convenient until today when the numbers escape me. It would be far better to use keys than combination locks. Memory is nothing like actual keys. The precious maps I made all lie inside. I want to get at them. Is the combination, 7-15-4? *No, it is not.* Is it 11-5-25? *No. What were the numbers? What is the order? I cannot get into my own cupboard.* I kick at it.

The night before I slept on my back there in the palace with my arms stretched up behind my neck. There are always sounds at night, whispers of the goings-on. Nonstop cooking. I can smell tomorrow's breakfast before I go to sleep. I think about an unexplored section of the palace. It brings good dreams.

I said things to Puyi that I felt were important. I say nothing is impossible. He doesn't listen to most of my words, but he is the Emperor and I feel grateful that he hears my words from time to time.

I told him he should fly like in the dream, and he tried to fly that June. The Emperor Puyi shows no sign that he fears failure, but I suppose he is terrified. "I will do it," he says, then hesitates. "He Song, I command you not to look in my direction." So, I turn around and do not look. I close my eyes and wish that he will be able to fly. I believe in him. If that is the recurring dream he has, then that is what he is destined to do. I hear him set down his scepter. I hear him removing his heavy garments. And then there is quiet. There is a breeze I feel. I keep my eyes shut and wait. It is a long

~ ~

In those days once upon a time, the palace grounds were immaculate. Every wall is painted fresh. The rooftops all have new glaze. Between each cobblestone there is a perfect space of dirt and not a single weed could take root there because the eunuchs' eyes are vigilant. Their long fingernails are perfect to pluck those weeds away.

I remember that summer before the Republican Era first began to take hold, before the warlords broke the Middle Kingdom into their own little territories because the Child Emperor Puyi did not know how to wield the Heavenly powers his grandmother had given to him. Instead of ruling over his Empire, Puyi plays with me. He dreams about impossible things. Under the cedars in the garden, Puyi tells me that he has many dreams of flying. He says those dreams of flying make him wonder whether that is what Heaven requires of him now. Should he attempt to fly? It would no doubt prove the validity of his claim over the Empire. Of course we have all heard the old stories of emperors who wielded superpowers, like body transformation or flight. It is after this particular dream when I begin to interpret Puyi's dreams as his trusted advisor. He listens to what I say and hangs on to my words, so I speak slowly and with great effect. I try to first see his dream in my head and then imagine it going on further, and then I tell him the conclusion that appears in my mind. It is similar to when we would play our childhood games like hide-and-seek in the storerooms or go on treasure hunts in the catacombs. Then, too, I would carry that imagination even further, and all the while tell Puyi my fanciful ideas, such as the feeling I have that while exploring the Forbidden City we are actually entering the soul of the earth, and in our games might do the planet a great good or great harm. My interpretations intertwine with Puyi's own dreams, and I would say it affects his perception of reality.

With my map of the Forbidden City one June day, I went out exploring on my own to see what I could find. The rush of exploration runs

It allows them to use me in the future if the Emperor should ever need another piece of flesh.

This palace always felt like a giant stage. There are curtains on nearly every wall and men hidden behind the curtains. I sometimes pull random curtains aside and see an old eunuch there fully exposed. He looks at me harshly and then pulls the curtain back as it was. I don't know how I feel knowing there are eyes and ears ever present. I never feel a need for privacy. Let them hear. Let them look. I really don't mind. Of course that goes for you, Dear Reader, as well. I let you sit there behind your screen as a silent observer. There are fans in this place made of peacock feathers. Eunuchs stand by, and their sole purpose is merely to move the peacock feathers up and down to create a nice breeze in the summer months. Music is everywhere. Your ears need not ever grow bored. Eunuchs play stringed instruments from side rooms, and the notes flow through the vents and windows, spill into the gardens like oxygen. The Forbidden City can be a very comfortable place. I carry a peach blossom fan of my own. It is made of thinly carved and scented wood, and it folds into a small piece that fits neatly into my pocket.

Puyi was carried around in covered chariots. I almost always walk. Occasionally, I am allowed to ride one of the horses but not today. There is such a crowd of eunuchs surrounding the chariot. A boy my size cannot see over the heads of these adults. I only see shoes and robes. They all think the boy emperor is inside the chariot, but they are wrong. With all the commotion Emperor Puyi snuck away. We are in another part of the palace playing with the one camel Puyi keeps as a pet that I do not ride so much as climb while it tries to knock me off its back. The camel reaches for me with its long, scratchy tongue, and when I finally land on the hard ground, the camel spits on me. A huge wad of spit lands on my robe. And there, another lands on my hat. And another. The camel spit is full of seeds and smells. It stinks like something rotten.

shows. The stage is a small mobile structure made of painted wood. Red curtains pull back on a drawstring. My heart thumps in anticipation of the show beginning. Our favorite puppet show is the story of The Monkey King who long ago brought Buddhism from India to China. There was a pig in the story that I liked very much, and I sometimes take the pig puppet to my room afterwards to play among the palace shadows when I am alone. I pretend the pig was a great hero that could tame each shadow and make them his pet. His scheme was to eventually have an army of shadows, like the ninja.

The Council would meet in various venues of the Forbidden City. They were once members of the Righteous and Harmonious Fists, who had warred against England using old magic and almost won. This time they choose the Hall of Supreme Harmony as their meeting place. I hear whispers among the staff whenever the CGG meets to decide the good of the Empire. It all comes to my own ears as hearsay, but often involves the use of the Ninja in covert operations. It spurs exciting dreams for me at night.

The CGG called me to the Room of Tranquil Longevity one night before the winter winds came. It is late at night, and the Emperor child is asleep. They ask me about Puyi's studies. I say that his calligraphy is better than my own. They ask me about my hand, if I know why there are fingers missing. Can I remember a time when my hand was whole? I look at the man who asked me this. This is the same eunuch who first brought me into the Forbidden City. His eyes beg me to answer him, here in front of his peers, that yes, I remember. I do remember, but I refuse to cooperate. I look away, and I lie to him. I say, "No, I think my hand was like this from the start. I am a mistake of nature. Fortunately I still can serve our Lord of Ten Thousand Years as a less than complete man." I look around at the eunuchs. Compassion forms in their eyes. Perhaps they will not kill me after all. I fool them at least for now into believing that I do not remember. The Emperor is now healthy, and there is no need for me anymore. Although they could easily do away with the secret, they will choose another option.

to his death. "Why didn't he hold on?" Emperor Puyi asks me to interpret the disturbing dream for him. "Your Majesty, perhaps the dream means the people are not ready for you to leave the tower. Perhaps the proclamation must allow your subjects to keep the faith that, come what may, you will continue to be the Emperor."

Puyi could have anything he wanted within these mustard walls, but his magic did not extend outside of them. He is not allowed to leave. Eunuchs will give him everything he requests. He can eat the most precious foods. He can destroy a painting that is one thousand years old by paining his name and silly cartoons on its paper, and they will not stop him. But the eunuchs do not allow him to leave. We search for that key together, the one that allows escape, and that is probably what led to our obsession…the game of opening hidden doors.

Up to this time, His Majesty and I made the most of windy weather by flying kites. We cut out long lengths of rice paper meant for calligraphy classes and fasten them onto light bamboo rods. Our kites fly up over the brick-red walls. The kite tails resemble the queues that wag behind our necks. Our foreheads are cleanly shaven, but the queues of black hair hang long behind us and are whipped by the wind. Our kites fly so high above the city that everyone in Beijing must see them. I wonder whether kids on the other side of the wall would watch in anticipation and form teams ready for that moment the kite is released, so they can track it down and take it for their own. You see, Puyi always cuts his kite free. Sometimes it is a result of our strings getting into knots but most often we are just finished playing, so rather than wind our creation up again, we cut our creation free. He watches it go up into the sun and get smaller until it becomes a speck and then disappears. We stand in the Southern Three Places with our spools of severed kite string. Puyi looks from the sky to the walls, turns, and runs off. I stand there, wondering if I will ever be free.

The eunuchs who cared for the Emperor Child often put on puppet the yellowing of your old hair! It includes the yellow beams of light that fall onto you in the morning. His proclamation goes something like this. Remember he is very young. No one so young should be expected to govern. He says, "As your reigning Son of Heaven, I ask all true subjects to go out of their way to preserve the color yellow for the Emperor only. Only I, Your Emperor Puyi of Ten Thousand Years, am allowed to touch the color to skin. If the sun gives off yellow morning rays, you must avoid them. You must never look directly at the yellow sun, just as you must never look at your Emperor in the face. If your teeth should yellow, you must remove them. If hair yellows, you must cut it off. Yellow paint is a criminal offense unless it is used inside the Forbidden City. For all this, remember, is important to show your respect to the Son of Heaven."

Every word of this proclamation had been carefully written by Puyi himself. Some of the words are a bit extravagant for a child and this is likely the first time he uses them in a full sentence. Emperor Puyi takes a full month planning it. He writes and rewrites the proclamation until he is completely satisfied. He has dreams about the changes it will create throughout his Empire. When he looks the paper over, I can see the pride beaming from him. The eunuchs at first say this issue is not important and should not take up our time. The Middle Kingdom recently lost two large wars against the foreign powers, which resulted in lost land and naval capability. Hard-hit farmers require something better than proclamations about the color yellow. They need to be out there under the yellow sun sowing their seeds. Yet, Emperor Puyi insists that the imperial proclamation be his own, and the eunuchs finally agree to pass along the decree to every official in the Middle Kingdom. Puyi has a dream that night that he is climbing down a tower toward safety but there is a little child, not more than two years of age, hanging there on the same ladder. In his dream Puyi shouts to the child to hold on tight. Emperor Puyi will get himself down to safety first and promises to himself that he will have his eunuchs come back up to save the child. But it does not happen that way. The child just lets go. The child in the dream releases his tiny fingers and lets himself fall

CHAPTER 3

April 24, 1909

China's population is 421 million people.

I n the beginning, Puyi the Emperor wanted us to look into his eyes. The child does not want us looking down. The child wants to be our equal. Of course he does. Wouldn't you? Puyi wants to be free and to play and be like everyone else.

Before warmer weather came, the blistering wind blew through the palace grounds. It finds us, even behind the walls deep inside the buildings. There are stone guardians at each door, but they do not protect against the wind. A stone lion is at each side of a red door where I eat my meals. Other doors have dogs and fantastic beasts guarding them. All are made of stone. Some are as large as a horse.

Puyi would wear a dragon coat with sleeves so long his hands remained hidden. I rarely ever see those fingers that were taken from me.

As Emperor, Puyi was so young, and the country was in such need of an experienced leader that his influence on the Empire was minimal, if nonexistent. I remember one proclamation to everyone in the country that he is the only one who can make use of the color yellow. This went beyond just the wearing of yellow, which emperors long past have insisted be the case in the Middle Kingdom. That is an old tradition. Only emperors wear yellow. Puyi's new proclamation includes the color you paint your boats. It includes the yellowing of your teeth, yellowing of your eyes, and

Outside the gates of the Forbidden City, the new culture movement was in full force. Students of Beijing are demanding that science and democracy replace the outdated philosophy of Confucianism. I see students burning Japanese goods in the public squares. This is to protest the treaty of Versailles that allows Japan to encroach on more Chinese land. The Shadow is growing. These protesters can feel it on the horizon. I understand none of it, though. I don't care to understand

We opened the room on a Sunday morning. Sun was streaming in from the well hole above. There was water dripping down the walls. I held my breath. The key fit!

I think Kublai Khan took the famous ark from Mesopotamia when his empire extended to Europe and the Middle East, connecting the East and West, ages ago. Someone eventually placed the ark here, deep below the city. Until we disturbed their peace, the two cherubim of glory have guarded the two slabs of stone that lay inside.

This day concluded the game that had entertained us for many years. Cixi's old key is heavy. It has teeth the shape of crescent moons. The two of us will make a grand game of trying every lock and learning all sorts of new things about the palace. Emperor Puyi discovered early that some rooms that should have been filled with treasure lay empty and others that should have contained ordinary things instead contain extraordinary treasures. We find rooms filled with bodies of those Puyi's grandmother has murdered. We take an odd fascination in the bodies. Who were they? The Grand Empress Dowager had killed even her own children when they stood in her way. In one of these rooms resides the ark of the Covenant none knew was there. It is a box four feet long by two feet wide. As young boys, we were not educated in the Jewish, Muslim, or Christian traditions, so we will not understand what we stumble into.

Of course there remained many secrets for future generations to discover. I suppose there is still one room that contains spools of kite string tangled in knots on the floor. I know this place. When the knots become too bothersome to manage, we cut the kite string and let our kites fly free. We leave the remaining knotted string in this room of our knickknacks. Just before I go out to the courtyards, I pull back a curtain that covers a mustard-colored wall, and there is nothing behind it, just a wall in need of fresh paint.

it. Now this box has a new significance. The child is me. This box is my obstacle to overcome.

Emperor Puyi showed hesitation at the entrance to Khan's room, which I will later respect, but I ran right into the unknown darkness and disappeared. My eyes adjust. There are many treasures, but I am drawn to a box of wood with gold overlay that is just big enough for me to crawl into. Atop it sits a gold crown and other figures. I lift up the lid and look inside. *Well that is disappointing.* There is nothing there. I then get it into my head that I must crawl inside the box. *I will jump out and surprise Emperor Puyi!* It is a perfect size for me to hide. I lean my head against a tablet of stone. The last thing I hear is Puyi's footsteps coming closer. The lid slams down on top of me.

I did not know what the Mongolian script meant, but when I found a passageway that led to the old library of a Buddhist monk. I showed it immediately to Emperor Puyi. He was as excited as I was and thought we should take the wrought iron key with us. I hold a candle and Emperor Puyi holds the key. Puyi can tell it is Mongolian script because it has a sword running through all the letters. He says the Mongolians were great warriors who conquered almost the entire world, except of course the Americas. This door we find is hidden deep, behind many other tricky spaces. There is what looks like an abandoned kitchen, and it takes us a while to realize the sink lifts up to reveal a passageway. This passage leads to the Buddhist monk's library and then down a stone staircase that winds three levels with a well hole way up above us providing light. There at the bottom by the water source is a door with Mongolian texts. None of my keys fit in the keyhole, but Puyi has a special key he can try. It is a key he has tried ten thousand times in ten thousand different locks in this palace that stretches forever. It is the first key Puyi was ever given, and it was given to him by his grandmother Cixi long before he was picked to be her successor. But she never explained why. She gave him the dragon throne on her deathbed, but long before the ceremony of ordination she gave him the wrought iron key.

almost trapped forever inside because the cherubims of glory held down the lid so tightly over my head and, as the Emperor Puyi retells it, refused to let me out. Inside that box where I am hidden, it is a good thing I feel a gold pot down by my feet because I strike with the rod against the pot, making it ring. This time the Emperor will hear. It rings through the small space where I am hidden. The oxygen is getting thinner. How long have I been trapped inside? I now hear Puyi trying to open the tabernacle. It stays locked so he pushes the entire chest off its pedestal onto the floor. Down on its side, all the contents spill out, and I run away. I will not stay in the room a moment longer. Fear overcomes me. I run out the door and into the light. Emperor Puyi runs after me to catch up. Once outside, we both laugh, relieved to be in the light and so proud of ourselves to finally have solved the riddle of the old key. I feel the stickiness of manna in my hair.

An old box sat there in a forgotten room with a boy inside.

Trapped, I tried to push the top open but it was too heavy. My arms are not very strong. I wait for Emperor Puyi to find me. *Golden box, why do you keep me away from my friend?* Not to worry. He always finds me when we play hide-and-seek. This is no different. To give him a hint, I hit a rod that I find within the darkness. I hit it against the side of the chest. I am afraid he cannot hear me, and I try to lift the lid a little but it does not budge. The longer I stay, the more content I become to just stay there inside the golden chest. Perhaps I will take a nap while I wait.

Looking back at it all with hindsight, I wonder now, what was this thing? Is it mankind's attempt to separate creation? Does its identity come from what it keeps out or from what it keeps in? Is its present location important? Some elders might say no, it is the history that matters most. Children might define it by its dimensions and wood structure. But to me none of that matters in a dark, forgotten room. Inside of this box there are musty air and slabs of stone. Forgotten here in this place and time, I suppose this ark is not even a box. It is nothing…until a boy gets into they called the CGG meeting, to discuss the implications of the storeroom, but in doing so they take the opportunity to whisk me away to the South. At least they vote against throwing me into an abandoned well. I somehow suspect that option is considered.

It was a wonderful game we played as kids that led us to Khan's secret room. We call our game The Mystery of the Wrought Iron Key. Whenever we would say the long name, a smile would appear on both of our faces before we got to the word *key,* and something inside us would bubble over causing us to run around the room, chasing each other, laughing. It is the spirit of exploration that drives us. The game originates from the frustration of Puyi's grandmother and takes on a wonderful life of its own with us as we continue the search she once started. We roam everywhere testing this last iron key of Cixi's collection that, at least in her lifetime, never found its correct lock. For those early childhood years, I feel compelled to find out what it could unlock. Our imaginations often go wild about unlocking hidden worlds full of ninjas or pirates, and the hunt encourages us to explore new parts of the Forbidden City. We were always looking around and wondering what corner had not yet been checked. The game lasted years and then finally we found it!

Our adventure occurred in a room with tall ceilings, deep under the city, that had been lost to the world above for many hundreds of years. We see Khan's markings on the outer door and inside the room itself. This is one of the old places that predates the Forbidden City. We are down in the foundations that were built during the Tang dynasty when Khan ruled the entire world. Black walls have Mongolian writing in silver and gold that looks like a single vertical sword that curves and circles, jutting out on either side. It is a unique style of writing. The letters look like swords, and the words they form look like a battle scene of swords. As a future calligrapher, I cannot get that style out of my head, and it becomes my own style.

We ran from that room in a joyful panic, laughing about how I was

Is it any surprise that I am shaking as they escort me away? I am ever so surprised when they open the main city gates for me. I do not see the key that opens the gates. For all these years I have never laid my eyes on such a key. It was opened before I got to the door. The door had been open already. I am given instructions to wait here, at the doorstep, for a woman who will take me to my new home.

Emperor Puyi told me he heard rumors that a decision would soon be made on what to do with me. "You can't stay here," he says, matter-of-factly. We are so proud to have found the room of treasure and we whisper about it as a secret between us. I am sure the eunuchs hear our outrageous tales. Do they believe us? Do they care? Have they gone in search of the mysteries as well? I remember the beautifully cut jade in the hidden storeroom, as well as exquisite jewels, but truth be told we are not eager to find it again. Initially, we do have our laughs about how scared we both were. We are so dirty by the escape, and we tease each other about that. I joke with Emperor Puyi about how I had become trapped in the golden chest. Yet, in saying it, I wonder whether I really was locked inside and how I was finally rescued by him. He claims that the gold angels had come alive while I was inside, and with wide wings fluttering around his head, they prevented him from approaching the tabernacle. He tells me there were many precious objects in the room, including jade unlike anything he has seen anywhere in the palace. There was a set of jade rings that he fancied to grab if he should enter the room again. At first, Emperor Puyi lets me see the key again. But eventually that memento of our adventure disappears from view and will end up in his Empress's collection. Will they now send me away? Puyi tells me I can always keep my valuables in the royal storerooms and for as long as I wish. He assures me that no matter where the CGG sends me to live the rest of my life, the Emperor will call me back when a visit is due. "You are still my servant, He Song!" I nod. "I am, Your Majesty. I will come when you call for me." I start to hear whispers around the eunuchs that the palace children found something new that they never knew existed, but neither of us are questioned directly about Khan's room, and perhaps that is why that goes right back to the beginning. He says it is a way to determine The Lord of Ten Thousand Years' present health and future needs. He never asks Emperor Puyi, "How are you feeling today?" The Emperor Child might not know the correct answer. It is better to have an experienced old hand determine the answer. This man is a longstanding member of the CGG. But nobody looks at him as he speaks. Eyes are all on the Widow Du. The chamber pot sniffer says, "The Lord of Ten Thousand Years has benefited from this boy, He Song, and may with time require his company again, so we cannot dispose of the boy permanently. Still, He Song cannot live here as he grows into adulthood unless this becomes his home. It is a problem we have created for ourselves. We need to find a home for this brave child with the ruined hand." It is tradition that the CGG refer to the reigning Emperor as The Lord of Ten Thousand Years. Some members in the room wear colorful robes and have long braid queues that go down past their feet and form a small mound by the legs of their seats, but there are a few present who keep hoods over their faces.

She had walked into the meeting hall without an escort. She knows her way throughout the mustard-colored hallways of this secret city. The red doors open before she knocks. Curtains hang everywhere. Behind every curtain is a eunuch listening and watching. She knows all this. There are five thousand eunuchs in the capital altogether. Some of them are a part of the Council. Others refuse to join the CGG and will at times go against its wishes. They all have a role to play in the life of The Lord of Ten Thousand Years. But of the many men and women who reside in this forbidden place, I think none can compare to the mother who had arrived that morning. She is unique. The air even smells different today.

The Council called this meeting one month after we found Khan's storeroom. This is only the second occasion the CGG has met with me after my surgery. Before the meeting with the Widow Du, they call for me and tell me I must prepare to leave the Forbidden City immediately. Is that not their style always? I fear that they will lock me away in a room somewhere.

Childhood for me was mostly good, and I went unnoticed by most people in the palace before the CGG sent me to the Widow Du. She came to Beijing herself at the CGG's request.

That day I left for Hama village, I saw a giant kite as my train left Beijing station for the South. Riding the train is very exciting and I feel the engine grumble like a volcano as it slowly picks up speed. Out the window I see the paper kite that Puyi and I once made together stuck high up in an elm tree. It looks beautiful up there with its tail tangled around the branches like it is part of the tree, almost as if that is how a tree should look when its flowers are in bloom, with a gigantic paper tail streaming over its branches. I would like to tell the Emperor that I saw his kite. It is still free of the city walls. And, look here, so am I. I have been freed as well. I am free! To where will this great steam beast take me? I wish for home. Will I miss the palace? I look over at the Widow Du sitting beside me. She is mysterious with her long flowing hair. Long fingers are gracefully folded on her lap. She looks at the kite in the tree as well and smiles in my direction. "Beautiful kite," she says to me.

The Widow Du stood tall before the Council when she agreed to take me under her care. "I will take He Song." There is a murmur of consent in the room, that this is the right choice to place the child under the woman's care. It is an early morning meeting, and she had only just arrived in the Forbidden City by overnight train perhaps an hour before. The Emperor and most of his staff are still asleep. She repeats, "I will raise He Song for you if that is your wish. The women of Lake Lugu will continue to support The Lord of Ten Thousand Years in any way we can, but let there be no mistake, there is a price. The Council must respect our ways and allow us to live as we do."

The man who sat in front addressed the Widow Du with their request, reading from notes he scribbled in advanced. He is the eunuch whose job it is to smell the contents of Puyi's chamber pot each day, another tradition on my pad that, "This is now a perfect spot to spend one's day at study or at rest, now with the small crooked pine I transplanted here." *I wish to designate this as the place where I want my remains to be buried someday. My children and grandchildren, take note!* That crooked tree continues to grow healthy by the stream.

When I entered the Widow Du's household for the first time, it all struck me as oddly familiar. Just like the organizational structure inside the Forbidden City before the Empress Dowager Cixi passed, this household is centered around a woman. Men are just on the periphery. They come and go. None are allowed to stay. The Widow Du shows me my bedroom that I will share with my brothers, Cloudy Sky and Spring Rain. Their surnames are not Du, and each child was conceived by a different father who they rarely see. They are excited to have a younger brother. It wasn't long before we were wrestling in the backyard. Out in the backyard, with vast valleys framed by mountains, it feels somewhat like the Emperor's manmade palace, although of course this place of Peony's is far older and not the creation of man. Later, when the Widow Du is away, Cloudy Sky takes me into his mother's bedroom. The room has rich woodwork and piles of pillows and blankets. On the vanity is a photo of the Empress Dowager dressed up as Avalokiteśvara, the Goddess of Mercy. Cloudy Sky tells me that the deceased Empress was a devoted Buddhist. The photo has the Empress sitting on a barge in Zhonghai. The Widow Du lays out freshly cut wildflowers in front of the photo each day.

Yes, the eunuchs stole me from my family, marked me, and sent me far away to the South. In the South, I suppose I will be free to leave the Widow Du's household to find my family again but where could I look? The Empire is too large! There is no way I could know where to find them in the sea of small villages, large families, and the vastness of land.

‿ ‿

to tell me the names of these other weeds. I bet you don't know where they grow and what uses they have to the Yi. My mother says that your people used to know of the old medicine that grows in our hills." He turns away, but I set another bait, "Those plants over there. Are they weeds? Tell me their value to you. What do you know?" The Yi boy is about to pay me no mind as only a stubborn child will do, but then there is a wind that blows down from the Jade Dragon Snow Mountain and sends a shiver down his spine. He reconsiders me standing there on the ground, wearing my fancy Beijing shoes. He hops off his horse and puts his hand on my shoulder. "That is hog's wart. It is poisonous. But that fern over there, dog spine, it can be used to numb any pain. I see you have purple sage, honeysuckle stem, dill seed, pig's fungus, and cow's knee." I listen to his talk.

Back home, my foster brothers and sisters had asked me from early on the obvious questions that little kids will wonder. The life I have in Beijing is so different from the one we live here in the South. "Does the Emperor ever use the toilet?" one asks. "Yes, I suppose he does," I say. I tell them that at those times the Emperor calls for four eunuchs to stand around him holding large blinds. I cannot see what he does, but I know that there is a chamber pot there inside. The chamber pot is later examined by one of the palace staff before it is taken away. He scoops the fumes with his hand, bringing them up toward his nose and inhales. It is a very prestigious position to hold in the hierarchy of eunuchs that serve the Emperor. I add that this same eunuch is on the Committee who sent me here to you.

As a small child, I fixed nature so it looked better. In other words I want the world to look more like the palace grounds. I make a flower garden at our house to try to replicate something I had seen at Emperor Puyi's palace. There are no other flower gardens in Hama village other than ours. Sitting in a garden, with natural water flowing nearby, it feels so perfectly Taoist, but no…it is not yet right. There should be a pine there to provide balance. I know the perfect pine. Can I get at it? Yes. I plant the pine. Then, I sit there all afternoon reading my field manual on herbs, making notes

He believes in the university education he could obtain someday in Beijng if he can pass the local exams. It doesn't matter who you are, if you pass the exams, you may go to university. That is true freedom.

That grand old tree stump beside the bridge where I first sold my potions was a central location in Hama. The stump bears three hundred and twenty-one rings. Its bark is thick and its roots are long and deep. Someone occasionally trips on a root if he is not looking. Even with my blanket laid out, there is still room for others to play chess on it in the sun. I dry my herbs there. In front of me there are two main paths going through the village, and the tree stump intersects both paths. Old people walk around the tree as they did when it was a living thing because they are used to that. Before a windstorm leveled the tree, it was indeed grand. I am told leaves of every shade of yellow floated down in slow motion from high above, slow like cottonseeds. I am told its canopy was a cathedral for the migrating birds. This is what the Good Doctor tells me one day when he sees me drying herbs on the stump. Now, kids like me hop over the stump without thinking anything of it. We don't bother walking around.

The Yi boy would come to my blanket on the bridge to buy liquor and tobacco, and he was only a customer until that one time he surprised me with something new. That day he says, "How much would you sell that for? My dad will attempt to plant it." I look at where his finger is pointing. It is a weed mixed into my herbs that I mean to discard. "What on earth will you do with this weed?" I sniff. "You can have this weed for free. Whatever you do, keep the seeds out of Hama!" I say. He sniffs at my ignorance. Today will be the day I learn about a weed's role in medicine, and I will also learn that a little Yi boy can know more of the old lore than anyone in Hama village. The Yi boy puts bits of the plant in his mouth. He then gives me a taste of the weed and asks if I feel a numbness or taste bitterness, or more rarely, sweetness. "Now crush it," he says. I smell the crushed powder. He is at least three years my elder. He turns to go. I shout to him, "Hey, boy of Yi, before you gallop off on that silly beast, I dare you

levon a

CHAPTER 4

July 4, 1913

China's population is 437 million people.

I respected my foster family and made many other friends in Hama village, but my greatest teacher for those first years in the South might have been that Yi boy who came down from the mountains. Something about him reminds me of the Emperor. I wear my hair in a queue, my forehead shaved, as is custom. He, however, never shaves his head. It is all great curls that resemble the horse he rides. These people of Yi are horse people, nomads, and hunters. There is something wild about them, although their lineage is ancient and respected. Long ago, they had great armies that provided our region with strength and security.

I sometimes wished I could copy this young boy's strange habits, and that made me peculiar because most people of Hama paid no notice to the Yi. I learn the medicine in nature. He is just a boy but older than me and with knowledge to share. I am learning from those ancient Yi people long before him, who moved up into the hills long ago with their horses and live in relative seclusion to maintain the old Chinese traditions in ways we villagers have not. This boy is a carrier of that tradition.

The Yi boy talked of escape from the mountains where he was born. He is never satisfied with the mountain ranges around Hama. Time and time again, he packs his few belongings to go away, but he never makes it far. His horse slows. He just sits there staring in the direction of the fading light beyond, knowing the direction but still hesitant. He doesn't go.

meeting place for secret endeavors. Homeless travelers sleep beneath it in a boat, its bow half in the water half on the muddy embankment, rocking gently with the water. I usually have a few jars of rice wine there, one with mushrooms soaking and another with a full snake wrapped inside, its fangs outstretched. This one is merely for effect. I never prescribe the snake wine to anyone for fear I might poison them. The Widow Du gave me advice that I always follow: "Try it all yourself first and if you don't, don't you dare give it to a patient." I am not yet willing to try the snake wine.

book. It is written in French. I flip though it but the words mean nothing to me. I put it back into the soil.

I often saw my aunt at the end of the day when I came back into town after hunting for new herbs. She is indeed an ancient woman, brandishing a long fighting sword that dances in the last light of dusk. Does she do this routine with the sword, so elegant, to stretch or to exercise, to meditate, or is it training for war? I hold a suspicion it is the latter. My foster mother often suggests it is none of these reasons. She laughs at me when I think of her sister as a warrior. "Foolish little one. It is just to pass the old magic on to others, the children like yourself who cannot help but stare. Some will remember this so it is not one day completely forgotten."

In her presence, a fresh wind always blew over your body. She is held in awe by the evil old hags in our village. They gossip nasty things, but never when the white-haired sword woman is around. She taught Peony how to dance with a sword, and I see them practicing in the early evening. There are times when a piper plays a soft tune to melt over their stretching movements. The silver swords of fifteen women are all there following the white-haired woman's lead, including the old aunts and my siblings, pulling back, balancing, lifting, and striking together in choreographed exercises. This white-haired sister of Peony is a tall woman until you come up to her and are forced to accept that you are looking down into her marble yellow eyes. She can sing shrill tunes of Chinese opera during the day. With a fan she can dance as fine as with a sword. Town legend has it that she can kill with a paper fan alone.

Years before I set up my early medicine shop behind the Widow Du's house, I first started off selling medicine from a simple blanket laid down on one side of the town bridge. My dried herbs and potions lay on it in careful rows, all for sale. The bridge at the center of Hama village is a to the village regularly to sell mountain herbs I could not possibly find on my own, and I often buy the entire lot not knowing what to do with half of them.

Not long before I started purchasing medicines from the Yi boy, we talked about that phrase his grandmother repeated to him before she passed on. Like my foster mother, his grandmother knew how to read and had scrolls hidden away because she remembered times when the people burned old literature. "Education will give you wings," she would say to him. "Hard study begets freedom." The boy swore to his grandmother that day that he would not forget her good advice. His grandma said she will find him even after death, and he will not be alone.

While the Yi boy yearned to escape his nomadic life, I was content exploring the world under my feet. I experiment with ways to find fresh patches of herbs. I blow a dandelion stem while standing on the spent patch of herbs to see where the seeds will go. They float up over the bushes and down to the riverbank. The birds are feeding near the herb patch. I need to discover where they go to poop. There will undoubtedly be a fresh patch of herbs growing there as well. I pull out a bright red thread from my sweater and lay it out there in the open beside the birds. I know they will want to use the soft thread to make their new nests this spring. A bird flies off with the bright thread. When I later find it woven into the bird's nest, I will know that a new cluster of herbs will soon appear just below it or nearby.

There was an old burnt-out temple in Hama that I often walked past before getting to the lower river's edge. A charred stump remains there where a grand tree once stood. Fire and new growth. That is what I think of life. I learn that going back to the scene of a forest fire is worthwhile because the following year the place that was once black will be full of green. New herbs of all kinds that were long lost appear in that charred field. All sorts of new life will grow. Digging around I find a leather-bound is too young to appreciate it. Alone by the fire, he blackens his needle. The needle the Yi boy uses is from a porcupine burr that I had once given him from my own stockpile. I use them as a remedy to treat heartburn. His jar of ink comes from crushed berries. He writes the tattoo first on his wrist. He presses deeply with the needle. It says "studious knowledge seeker" to summarize the saying his grandma would recite. He wants it to continue to inspire him to work harder, to get a good education, and to make something of his life. He wants it to remind him each time he is tempted to while away his days on horseback rather than study for his exams. Every time the temptation to escape should tickle his imagination, he will look down at his wrist and know that true escape will come only after he gets a proper education at a university. The Yi boy knows this is the right thing to do. The next day, he looks at his wrists and cries. The design has nearly faded away.

The Lugu Lake region has a matriarchal society and such things are rare in the world. The women run things here and encourage the men to leave home. My foster mother says to me early in life, "Runaways, the lot of them. You will be too. Look how they stare out the window all their lives. They run away when they get to be of age. Most never come back."

The Yi boy also wished he could travel beyond Jade Dragon Snow Mountain and the other peaks he could see and let his adventurism get in the way of his studies. He considers galloping onward, southward, to the tropics of Vietnam and Laos. The boy sometimes starts off in that direction with his borrowed horse, yearning for those adventures, but then remembers his arithmetic homework left unfinished. Going away would mean not completing his schooling.

Before his daring tattoo, the Yi boy would be so shy when he visited our town. He feels that the village people always stare at his long toes. Actually, they stare because he rides a horse in sandals. *Who does that? A strange boy indeed.* But he is one of my best friends in Hama. He comes in recorded all the strange traditions of this valley and the surrounding mountains. She takes out a handmade book. She browses it for a moment and then settles down on a page. She turns the open book to the Yi boy so that he may see the drawings while explaining, "The Yi man has always believed he must have a permanent marking on his body. When boys of your clan receive their first tattoo, it traditionally marks the day they cross the threshold into adulthood and become a man. I believe it is done for many reasons. Tattoos signal to other tribes that this individual is Yi, a roamer of the world. But more importantly, the tattoo marks one's soul so it can be distinguished after death. The Yi people of old feared becoming lost after death. It was believed that you can only recognize another man's soul in the afterlife if his body had been tattooed while he was alive. Thus, every Yi man wears his own tattoos proudly in life. I would say it has become less common in modern day, but that was the tradition of your people." She looks at the Yi boy standing there in her sitting room. Shadows always hang on his cheeks, down his neck. He is becoming more hairy. His eyes have turned a more smoky black than the dark jade color she remembers them once being. He still never wears shoes, even now here in her home. Just sandals sometimes so you still see his hairy toes. Even on horseback he goes without shoes.

I brought him to my foster mother because I knew she could help. "Tell Peony how you did it, how you chose the words from the saying of your dead grandmother and the method you used to make the marks on your wrists." Then I whisper, "You can tell her you got the porcupine quill from me. I don't mind." The Widow Du looks down at the Yi boy's flushed attempt at a self-made tattoo. "Don't tell it to me here. Let's go inside," she says.

A week before coming to us for help, the Yi boy made a bold attempt to do it himself but without great success. He knows something of the tradition already because his father, his uncles, and others in his clan have tattoos. They have never shared with him the deeper meaning, thinking he

But Puyi and I became childhood friends after the horrible day of the surgery, so let's not race to that story yet. I want to first tell you about the amazing years that followed. I suppose I am kept around the palace mainly in case there is an infection against the transplant and my blood is needed. You could say I am like a walking blood bank and organ donor to the CGG. I didn't know that, and neither did Puyi, but that is probably all it was. This must be why the Council for the Greater Good kept us boys together during Puyi's early years as Emperor. Puyi gets used to me. There had been no other children around. When I officially leave the palace, he has his own reason for keeping a close rein on my comings and goings. He needs a friend.

~ ~

"Now this tattoo here cannot be taken from you," Peony said while needling the skin of the boy's wrist. "I still remember when the Yi men would come down on horseback to Lake Lugu when I was young. Their bodies were covered with designs so indelible that they'd say they could be seen even after one's death." She finishes the final tattoo and says with a smile, "There. This will always exist because it is here now. It is a permanence that the future cannot steal from you."

She wrote the third design after finishing the phrases, "Education gives me wings," and "Hard study begets freedom," on his lower arms. He smiles proudly. "Widow Du, please add the word 'Strength' as well," the Yi boy asks of her. Peony looks him over like she has only just met the lad for the first time, sighs, and then takes out her brush, dips it again, and adds the word near his wrist. The needle presses the word into his skin.

The Widow Du introduces him to the old Yi ritual when he turns thirteen. Although she is not of Yi blood herself, by default my mother is Hama's local historian. She is the only one in our simple community, other than the Dongba priests and Buddhist monks, who has meticulously playing a game hiding walnut shells in some of the dishes and guessing who would break their teeth. Puyi, of course, hides the shells. My role is to find the broken teeth. The anticipation is too much. I can hardly touch my food as I look around the room. Then, I hear a yell. I report everything back to Emperor Puyi in great detail on who broke his teeth and how it was done. I don't care for the eunuchs all that much. They are snotty and full of rules. The eunuchs treat me as a son they are not allowed to beat so I get away with more than you'd expect. I am an exception to all the rules, because I once gave my hand to the Emperor, and that changed everything.

You see, even at that time I had only a few fingers left on my right hand, and that abnormality goes back to when I was very young. The fingers were removed when I was perhaps three years old, and that is my earliest memory. I will save the full story for when the time is right, but for now you might as well know those fingers are now on the Emperor's own hand. It is his right thumb, his pointer finger, half of his middle finger, and half of his ring finger. Four in all that were once mine but now are his. The bone and skin and muscle were originally my own but once stitched onto his hand, they grew along with Puyi like they were always his body, and he soon considers it so. When his mind says to the pointer finger "point toward Nanjing!" the finger does as Puyi commands of it. If my mind were to ask the finger I lost to do anything—"Stop, no!"—I would feel like it too was listening but then I would look down on my hand and see it is no longer there. Those fingers are gone and do not do my bidding. It is a phantom feeling that they say all amputees have. They feel ghost limbs that are not there. I look over at Puyi's hand whenever I get a chance, although it is often covered with heavy silk garments, and it would not listen to my mind. The fingers now belong to him.

And so when we will in the future hold hands that time I help him escape the Forbidden City, lowering him over the wall, it is a strange feeling indeed. It will be the first time I ever touch those fingers on Puyi's hand.

levon a

all spent, although some colors hang on. The sun lowers down through those reds and yellows and oranges and lights them up like lamps. The ground is awash in color from fallen leaves. Broad leaves of vibrant colors fall beautifully into piles on the ground and do not yet brown; the sun treats them kindly. The leaves crunch as I walk to the train station. Then, I am home. I stay in the Southwest. Puyi remains in the North. There, we wait. They day comes and passes.

For this latest visit and consultation, my reward from the Emperor was an unusual key. Emperor Puyi must still remember our early childhood together. We have been playing a game of keys since we were kids and this one in particular will stump me for many years. After the Emperor escapes Beijing, still far in the future, I will not return to the Forbidden City for many years. It will be hard to find the lock for this key he gave me, because the door is so cleverly hidden in the shadow of the drum tower. Unfortunately, by the time I finally open the tiny door to a room the size of a broom closet without a window, far into the future, it will be completely emptied out except for dust. I wonder what it is that the Emperor keeps inside at this time when he gives me the mystery key. I don't ask him when I accept the gift.

Compared to my freedom in the mountains, Puyi's life was often drab. The ceremonies reach far beyond our attention span, keep going past the unbearable, and then further into the day. It is not uncommon for the Emperor to fall asleep and have to be nudged back to attention. Fortunately, we are able to make up games. Perhaps one of the greatest gifts I give to the young boy, even better than my hand, is to be the only other child there in the entire lonely palace, to play together. My favorite game follows Puyi's dinner. The Emperor is always served three hundred separate dishes, of which he only eats a few bites in a quiet room alone. Where does all the succulent food go after that? The eunuchs in the palace have a grand feast of the leftovers. There is an abundance of wine and song. It is wonderful. One day, I tell Puyi that all of his leftovers are being eaten by the staff, so we start hands pull at his throat. The Widow Du looks at the dead man and then at the remaining medicine that had been prepared by the Good Doctor. She pours the remaining liquid onto the ground. Eventually, the rest of the family recovers. Her late husband she buries in the backyard under a great elm tree. After telling the story, something lifts from her eyes. Better now that she shared it with me. "Thank you, Mommy," I say. "I think I know you a little better now." I do not press her for further details. I am happy to have gained her trust. How sad that day must have been for her, watching her husband die so violently as he did.

～ ～

The Forbidden City had even deeper secrets than my foster mother. Yet I could not help but love both. Maybe the darkness inside them makes them even more captivating. Weeds start to form between the bricks on the walkways in front of the Hall of Supreme Harmony. They distract the eyes. Some weeds flower a purple color. It clashes with the mustard yellow and the burnt red of the buildings and the white cobblestone of the grounds.

The Emperor Child had so many strange dreams, and why would we not think each dream could hold a special jewel of meaning that, if properly understood, might change the world? The Emperor tells me one day when we are sliding down the grand staircase banisters that he thinks he knows the day that the world will end. We prepare for that day together. Who's to say he is mistaken? We might as well take it as fact and prepare as best we can. What needs to be done before that date? Surely, all scores must be settled. There should be no loose ends. Knots need to be tied firm. The end of the world will not go easily. "I will not stay for it," I say to the Emperor. "I am needed back with my foster family in Hama." I would not stay here another winter for all the gold in this palace. Not, certainly, if these are my last few months to live. The Emperor Puyi says he never intended that I stay at the palace for the end of the world. I may go. The doomsday date in his prophecy is May 4. I leave in the fall when the trees are nearly

levon a

developing, and the people busy themselves with the day-to-day grind. Peony's home and business develops faster than the average household, and laughter is often overheard by those walking by. What is her secret? The medicine shack of the Good Doctor doesn't expand in line with the local economy. Sometimes I feel his shack is actually getting smaller and more makeshift. I think it is our courage that makes us succeed. Peony often ruffles our hair and says to us, "It is never too young to learn courage." We laugh. Courage even shows itself in tangles of our hair.

Peony explained to me one day that real healing involves learning one's stories, and then she shared one of her secrets with me. I want to become a better medicine man. She tells me that a healer must know the patient's history before giving a prognosis. I should go into my patients' homes when I can. I should look at how they live and assist with the cooking. I should ask to see the recipes that were passed down from their ancestors. I should then teach them to add new herbs in their soups and meats. Mother is wise. I scratch at my tangled hair and I say, "I understand but…" There is a pause. "But what, Little Bean?" I take a breath. "Mommy, *you* never talk to me in that way. I don't know anything about your story." So she then tells me the story of the man she once married. He is handsome and proud. Shortly after the wedding ceremony, an unusual disease spreads within the entire Du clan. The Widow Du tells me she believed then that it was caused by an imbalance in the clan: namely, this husband she took in. He is trying to take the lead of what is meant to be a matriarchal household, which had for generations been a matriarchal system here at the shores of Lake Lugu. Was her husband the cause of the clan's illness? A blind fortune-teller she consults agrees with her worst fear. Her marriage is the cause! The Widow Du's husband then falls seriously ill. That is why he is the first to drink of a unique concoction of boiled rattlesnakes and honey. Peony is in an early stage of the illness, making it easier for her to bear, so she lets her husband drink first. Her children are young and strong, so there is less fear that they will die. They all let the man of the household drink first. He quickly dies in violent spasms. That is the end of her husband Du. His including my silly boys," she says to the neighbors. Her jokes often have to do with mislabeling. When we are in trouble she will look at us sternly and ponder, "Aren't you those children from the Yi tribe up yonder? You are not my children." I will say, "No, it's me! I am not a Yi, Mommy." She refuses to listen, "Go, off now and ride your horses away! Bring back my boys before dawn tomorrow or you will face the wrath of an angry mother!" We look at her on the porch and crinkle our eyes so they twinkle. Peony smiles wide with lots of teeth.

"Come in," said the Widow Du one day. There is a knock at our door causing our laughter to be hushed. We all look outside. There stands the local inspector. He must be here on bureaucratic business. Taxes are due. New rules are now in place. The man at the door will be given a handmade cigarette. I start rolling a special one made with itch weed and garlic leaf. We all wait in eager anticipation to witness the result!

Before the knock at the door, we had been playing what should have been an outdoor game in our dining room. Our tables and chairs are all upside down. I am sliding down the side of a table, laughing.

One chair had already fallen over and carefully the Widow Du placed her other furniture on their side or upside down and in reverse. We are making a children's park of slides and obstacles in our house for the day. Sorrow cannot remain here. Our eyes grow wide in wonder.

Earlier that day I had accidentally tipped over an antique table of great value. *Bang*, goes the wood frame. *Wobble, wobble wobble wobble. Maybe I can save the marble inlay before it. . . . smash! Oh no.* A thousand pebbles now litter the floor. My mom stares me down. There is a flash of a memory that floats over her face. A tear forms. She then smiles everything away like magic and says, "Little Bean, let's play!"

The others in the town did not live like we did. Hama village is old bridge, and in the trees. Inside the paper lanterns are candles made of beeswax. The Yi boy waits in great anticipation because he turns sixteen this year.

There I was, a mere boy ready to inherit the title of town doctor from a long line of healers stretching back to myth, about to turn another year older. My child's shoes from Beijing no longer fit, so I finally settle for sandals of lesser quality. At times, like the Yi boy, I wear no shoes at all. As a medicine man, I do what I can for the sick villagers based on memory, local folklore, and my own imagination. Courage I gain from Peony helps me to push forward. She watches me work from our back porch, and I feel her love like one feels the sun.

I did want to cure, as do all doctors. But I didn't see things like we do today.

There were lots of joking and giggles with my siblings before we went to sleep at night. I whisper about all the illnesses I have seen that day in great detail, and they laugh at the warts and pains of our neighbors, my attempts at treatment, and how my medicines so often backfire. I have fun experimenting. Each day presents new problems and for remedy I have a palette of colors around me drying on the dirt floor of my shed. These are dried herbs of every sort. Everything goes into my mouth first, to taste, and then I spit. My hands are forever crusted with dirt. The jokes I tell my siblings at night have to do with discovery through mistakes. Too much tree bark in my potion prevented our local miller from pooping for seven days but now that I got the formula right his body is now in balance. After rushing to the latrines he came back to our home smiling with a sack of fresh flour. The talk about poop makes my brothers laugh. We all fall fast asleep.

My foster mother was the instigator of this playful attitude we harbored as children. Peony has fun with life. No matter what the tension may be, she can find a joke that will provide release. "I let most things fly,

Seeking it out prevents us from becoming idle. We do not settle for what fate prescribes. This reminds me of a conversation with the Yi boy that needs to be retold somewhere in this story.

I felt I knew a lot about everything, having the trust of The Lord of Ten Thousand Years and living here in the House of Du, which was the epicenter of knowledge in the Lake Lugu region. Sadly some of that feeling of control is taken from me when the Yi boy, whom I admire, challenges one of my most basic assumptions about life. What is that assumption exactly? "They say this is always so" is a phrase I liked to use at this time. I have taken many things as fact until the Yi boy hops down from his horse and challenges me on what I assumed is true by saying, "Who are *they*?"

How did those conversations go? I know it happens when we are both riding borrowed horses along a dubious path of steep ravines with willowed meadows far below us. Did I ask him about his allegiances; is he loyal to our Emperor Puyi or the newly elected president? Or did I ask him whether he was truly Chinese since he holds no allegiance to anyone? Or did I ask which side of the national boundaries in the Golden Triangle of countries, through which our horses are now wandering, did he call his origin and his home, for he showed no preference for China versus Vietnam or Tibet? "They say you need to pick a nationality today," I say to the Yi boy. "Who are *they*?" he replies. I feel an earthquake under my feet when he says these three words. It happens again when I ask the Yi boy about having a home or a goal. "They say you should be in school until you are at least fifteen," I say. "Who are *they*?" he replies. Another time, teasing him, I say, "They say you should sleep indoors, not in a tent strapped on your horse." Or, when I say, "They say you should value the life of a man more than you do this horse." Always he challenges the source of these assumptions.

It was Chinese New Year, and everyone in Hama turned one year older on that day. We hang red lanterns around the main street, over the to go. Eventually, that new spouse of yours will also get old and frail and die away. I will be there then, and if you need me, I have more to give. I did not mean it at the wedding when I said this is the last. It was spoken out of emotion. The truth is that I am here for you, and if it is a revolution that you need in this new Middle Kingdom, then I will help you, to whatever path that brings us together.

Good, now that's been said. Let us continue with the story.

As I have said, decades before my successful medicine shop in Shanghai, I ran a much smaller medicine shop in this little village called Hama deep in the mountains. I wonder if it is still there today.

I would wander down the river valley to see what plants had been sprouting on their own. The valley's climate changes with elevation, and certain herbs poke through from the rocks as I get down closer to the riverbed. As I get lower, the air gets warmer, cactuses grow, and I need to shed some of my extra clothing. I leave the sweater and jacket on the trail and will pick them up on my way home. I collect the herbs in my pockets, pulling them by their roots. Some of them will be dried. Others will be planted in my garden plot behind the Widow Du's house. I want to someday cultivate patches of precious remedies in the fields of Hama. This aspiration is the beginning of what would become my shop in Shanghai. I find that there is a bit of poison in all medicine, so it becomes my doctrine to always look for the balance. I add an antitoxin or something with healthy vitamins when the key ingredient is poisonous. Cinnamon bark is a favorite counterbalance of mine as a youth. Eventually I grow addicted to its scent.

It isn't real medicine, you say? Yes, but there are no alternatives in Hama village, just the old Good Doctor who practices more of the same. It may be that my search for the magic herb or mushroom is more important than the mushroom itself. The traditional medicine gives us an objective.

CHAPTER 5

February 4, 1917

The Qing have ruled for 273 years.

China's population is 457 million people.

Age fifteen is when I began to feel the presence of God. The moon follows me home always. I lose sight of it at times, but it is there somewhere behind me. It is a spotlight in the night. Over the rice paddy fields, the moonlight shines and catches the horns of water buffalo. Their horns shine in crescents of blue in the rice fields. When the moon is present, all the other stars tend to fade. Sometimes they become invisible in its heavy light. Only Venus can still be seen.

I suppose this is as good a time as any, now that we are in my early childhood and nearing the end of *levon a*, to tell you, my Dear Reader, why I am writing this. I am writing this for you, Dear Jasmine, so you know the full story someday. In a way, this is my gift to you rather than those imperial jade rings I presented to you and your spouse. I am sorry, by the way, for suggesting your lovely spouse is less than masculine at the beginning of *levon a*. I am sorry for making light of your other lovers. I am the storyteller after all, and I admit I have the jealousies of any man. I took some creative liberties in the details of your wedding because, yes, I still want to be yours. I am sorry if my words have stung.

I should apologize for my son's part in spreading H1N1 at your reception, but I suspect it only kills off those in our circle who really need

"How goes your health this season, old man?" I said when I first saw him that spring afternoon.

Ahh, memories of these first patients are so vivid to me today. None of them are living anymore, of course. It feels good trying to help them. I fill a need and, well, I do my best.

Don't get me wrong. I can understand Jasmine's modern-day argument that traditional medicine is bad for society. It misuses resources and gives the downtrodden a false hope. Even the Good Doctor's concoctions are based mostly on fairytale, I'd be the first to admit, and here I am a boy trying to follow his lead. The real stuff, passed from doctor to apprentice for at least two thousand years, unfortunately becomes lost to the Middle Kingdom shortly before my own story begins. Sure, I might be recovering some of the traditional lore when I am young, but being young I tend to explore and discover things on my own.

rattle him up from behind. *Are the women on the porch suggesting that I am an alcoholic merely out for more? Focus. I must keep it humble and on topic when talking to the doctor*, he thinks. He says to me, "Uhh-mm. I am having a problem with the lungs as of late," and to my mother he adds with a wink, "I am here for a different reason today. Dampness and tired limbs." He chuckles. *I can't help it. She is so beautiful.* Tensions brush away. We are forming a bond of trust under her watchful eyes.

After my mother said her piece by calling the Clockseller a drunk, it wasn't that I didn't think the man wanted alcohol, but I wanted to try to heal him, so I said as much. "You have come here for liquor and mushrooms, old man?" I said this in a way that was gentle, to ease the insult. The tone wasn't so insulting at all. It was more like the two of us were in on a secret joke.

"Soaked in wine. I dare say!" is what the Widow Du actually shouted when she overheard us in the shed. Then she coughs a fake cough. She and her sister laugh together. Though embarrassing, I cannot control when or how Mommy expresses her strong opinions. I ignore the breeze carrying her words.

Before her rude interruption, the Clockseller was talking to me about past medicines he had been prescribed by other doctors for dampness over his many years, and I become increasingly aware of the true nature of this rough peddler's illness. He says to me "Why, surely, all true medicine is laced in rice wine, as you must know," while eyeing my wares in the shop. Yes, it is true there are vats of rice wine in the back of my shop. We herbalists traditionally use wine rather than hot water to soak up the nutrients of our herbs.

The lazy Clockseller, unshaven and dirty, was startled. He is scared perhaps. I am so young, but then everyone looks young to him. Am I too young to be a doctor? His hesitation makes me hesitate myself.

out the porcelain comb that holds up her hair. It comes tumbling below her shoulders thick and lovely. Her breasts are firm and point slightly upward. Everything becomes silent. Conversations are forgotten.

The Widow Du let me set up shop in our back garden shed. I have only a handful of regular patients. One is the lazy Clockseller of Hama who thought he had come to the other doctor's clinic for the first visit. He will soon become dependent on my cocktails and elixirs. This Clockseller is not the same man I will befriend later in Tianjin, but he is a Clockseller and a lazy one nonetheless.

When she was sitting on the porch, she would often shout over to me while I worked in that shed. I can hear them on the porch. She would say, "In medicine, the Yang is never held constant. Finding where the imbalance is inside you is a tricky trick. It's a slippery slope. The Good Doctor surely does lack many of the old texts, but he tries the best he knows how. What more can we expect? I will teach Little Bean the texts when he is older. I will need them both to keep this complicated body of mine beautiful and ticking as it does. So, I must do my part, too. I need to teach him to become that doctor I will someday need."

Earlier, the Second Sister of Wu argued that Hama's Good Doctor would try to do his best, but his medicine lacked substance. "The good texts were lost, the tradition is all but vanished, and so we are left with the modern to meet our most primitive needs. He does try his best, the Good Doctor." The white-haired Second Sister of Wu smiles while she speaks, causing most of her creases to unfold like a paper fan across her blue-white cheeks.

I worked hard in my shed giving my young boy's version of a prognosis to the next patient in line. The Clockseller tries to ignore my mother's insulting tone and focus his undivided attention instead on me (he doesn't remember the Good Doctor being so young!) without letting the women very bottom of the river valley take me all day. I am so thirsty sometimes, rationing my glass jar of tea. A small sip runs cool down my throat after swishing it through my dry mouth.

The herb hunt always began with going over the town bridge, but the direction then varied with unexpected surprises. I walk over the old stones, a dozen times reorganized when they have fallen apart from war or earthquake, and pieced together again for more than a thousand years. Hama, the river, and the bridge have all been here for that long. Old lichens hold on to the rock. The dependable rocks forever stay by the river, under the shade of willow trees. There is mud between my toes. The red clay hardens there. What was first cool and slippery becomes hard and painfully dry and flaky. I find a dead wild dog. I dig at the corpse with a stick so that I can take a bit of bone. I wipe the blood off with maple leaves. When I get home, I drill a hole into the bone and pull out another string from my sweater. The charm will be tied around a baby one month after its delivery. We will also string hot pepper around his cradle. It is a bit of old magic.

There was much magic in Hama at that time. I remember seeing the Widow Du practicing with her sword in the morning light. When I approach, she says to me, "It is Yang, my dear Little Bean. Yes, and too sharp to touch. You mind your mommy, Little Bean. Yes, that blade is indeed Yang. The Yellow Empress, she merely borrowed the idea of Yin and Yang from The Monkey King. The Buddhism she taught our people was founded on the principle that humans can only become balanced by comparison. Yin and Yang are completely relative. The Yin is only defined after you categorize the Yang. It is a shifty business. In my case, Yang is the warrior's sword and I balance my body against it."

The Widow Du caused all sorts of mischief in and around our little town up until her untimely death. If men begin to talk politics or philosophy, she will say, "That's all a barrel of monkeys! What do old men know anyway? Little, very little, I say! Let me prove it right now." The Widow Du pulls my foster mother for a pain in her lower back. "Let's just not tell anyone about this," I say quietly to the dead cat. I dump out my potion and give the remaining twig to the Good Doctor. "What is it?" I ask him when I enter his ramshackle office. He gnaws on it. A wild version of necklacepod perhaps, rather than the domesticated?

"The roots of the wild varieties are shorter," he says, consulting an old book. "Ghastly! Throw out that dark potion. It's poison, Little Bean. Pick me real Sophora, and I will pay you a nickel. I am indeed running low in my supply. The right plant next time."

Yet, I was carefree. While I am alone in the mountains, I try working on a song. Fitting different melodies to these words, I bellow it out and hear my echo come up from the valley:

Alone on a mountaintop I search
for herbal remedies to cure
the Son of Heaven's future ills
so that He may rule us with a steady hand
alone from his Forbidden City far away…

One day, I took along my siblings to the peak of Jade Dragon Snow Mountain so we could fly kites. The kites came from my last trip to Beijing, as presents for them. One after another, they rise into the air. The string snaps. We run after it.

Another day, my Hama brothers and I tried to catch a wild turkey. For a long time, we had tried to hunt without much success. On this occasion, we bring lots of supplies, including twine, rubber binders, metal hinges, kitchen knives, and screws. We have no gun. We are not allowed to use our mother's sword. We turn it into a contest and the winner gets to eat the neck. We will smoke it with salts. If we catch it, our family can eat it all summer with pumpkin and greens.

I walked far for certain herbs I thought I needed. The trips to the by the three local scavenger ladies, old hags, and I hated them. My legs are not quite long enough to outrun them, but give it one more year and they should be. The old hags are the gossipers in our town. They talk about Peony, and about me and my hand, and always cause a noisy ruckus in the forest. They are rivals of mine and sell the herbs they find to the Good Doctor. Fortunately they are also rivals among themselves. If it were just one of them after my herbs, they might succeed in finding my secret stashes of plants in the forest, but because each is trying to put the other two off my scent by creating diversions, I have a better chance of evading them all. One old woman has a semi-domesticated squirrel monkey that is able to create misleading trails. Another old woman tends to aggravate snakes as she passes so the others cannot easily follow. They all follow me because they know I have found the Artemisia wormwood. Muddy-faced children are also curious observers of the treasure hunt and the chase.

I sometimes needed my younger siblings to guard the wormwood from those terrible ladies and the wild monkeys. Payment was usually in wild strawberries, which I'd pick as I wandered. My little brother tries finding the value in the plant, tasting the leaves themselves, making a Hmong headdress out of the stalks, but he does not understand. I roll my eyes. There is no value until it blooms, and yet I need to guard this patch. One day I grow so fearful of its discovery that I take a stalk home with me that I plant in our garden. That's the day when the first frost hits the northern tier, but the stolen bush is safe. I replant it lower in the valley.

There were frustrations. The patch of Sophora's root closest to home never looks healthy and, sure enough, does not bear fruit this season. What is growing around it? It must be a parasite feeding on the root. A wilder version of it pokes out of Dragon Tongue Hill with many stems. But is that the right herb? A dead mouse rots nearby. Maybe this is the wrong plant after all. Instead of asking the Good Doctor, I first give it to a stray cat that violently dies four hours later while I am boiling the same plant to give to the Clockseller; my aunt, the sword dancer—none of them have fun like my foster family and I do under the roof of the Widow Du. We are like free spirits. We live life. I learn early how to crinkle my eyes to make them twinkle. The Widow Du smiles wide with lots of teeth and does the crinkle to her eyes as well. She taught me that. She teaches me well.

Peony taught me her form of calligraphy, which became a valuable complement to what the eunuchs taught at the Forbidden City. The two are so unalike. The Beijing style is tight and strong and based on rules. The feline calligraphy of Hama flows like silk, loose. Her poetry climbs up the paper like a vine, takes hold where you thought no line could go, and reaches and blooms. The letters swing and swerve. My own style became a combination of the two.

Hama was developing as fast as my little body was growing. After the fire to our barn, our new expanded barn and surrounding farmstead increases in size and develops faster than the average household in the village. I am not satisfied. I walk the land with lower lip sticking out in a frown. Things would be great if only more of my domesticated herbs would bloom. I need more sagebrush and wormwood. I want to be ready to heal us, whatever may come.

For those early years, I was a scavenger of wild herbs, more dependent on dumb luck than skill, but I did have skill, and with time I developed a system of finding things within the wilderness. Down by the banks of the lower river is one of my favorite spots for gathering. It is a place I've known about for years. I first harvest the plants here where the air is warmer. Next, I go beneath the great elm tree with the nest. A red string is woven into that nest, and it is that red string that flags the tree for me year after year. Otherwise it is just one of so many thousand large old elms just on the border of Hama. Beneath that nest is my best patch of Cuscuta.

When I went on my long hikes as a kid, I expected to be followed waited outside the school gate the entire morning and afternoon, nervously eating steamed bread. All his siblings are there. Each came on a horse.

ⸯ ⸯ

I was confronted with some of the false promises of our herbal medicines early on in life, even before the death of my friend. My patients catch on eventually as well, and even Emperor Puyi grows suspect, but I probably know most of the failure of my herbal potions even before my patients have formed their suspicions. Without a doubt I know early on that the old Good Doctor's medicines do no good for me. But there is no alternative to the Good Doctor in town except for those scary vials of antibiotics brought here occasionally by the Christian missionaries.

But thinking about it all backward, I do see times when our natural ways of healing did surely cure the body. And so where do all my mistakes originate? It is hard to say. That is partly why I tell this tale. I did want to cure them, as do all doctors. But I didn't see things then like I do today.

There were lots of jokes among my siblings late into the evenings about me trying to become a doctor. They say, "Little Bean is always having fun through experimentation. Everything goes into his mouth, to taste and spit out. Look at those healing hands crusted with dirt. I would not dare take his potion. Come here and smell it. Doctor He Song, ha ha!" I laugh with them. They love me, though they tease me. There is support just in the fact that they notice me in this household of so many.

Despite the jokes, my trial and error did lead to discovery. The Widow Du is supportive of her little doctor. Her demeanor is to nourish the sprout and let it grow. Rather than control and create tension within the house, she prefers releasing tension in herself, in her home, and in the world. Peony will let everything fly, including her boys. She encourages me to go out and explore. The others in our small town—the old hags;

the academic tests. Never before had anyone from his tribe attended a university! After all the trips by horseback to attend school, it now comes to this. *He passed!* The Yi boy shows me the letter. I tell my friend that I am happy for him. It will be nice to have someone else I know in Beijing. We can take the train up there together. If the Yi boy attends university, perhaps I should try to do the same?

The letter was scheduled to arrive in Hama ten weeks after the exam, and every day the Yi boy was convinced he failed the test and would be rejected from university. I deliver this letter. I am doing a favor for the usual postman who is too busy with his farm to go all the way to the Yi's camp. I don't normally deliver mail, but the Widow Du insists I help my neighbors when I have the time. I first deliver a letter to another house. It is an old family that lives right on the river and whose goat happens to be delivering a kid just then. I take hold of a rope and help pull the bearded kid into our world. It is fun to see the new breath of life. It makes me laugh to see the little thing try to stand. The kid gets to his feet and gruffs as I walk up the mountain to where the Yi people live.

The examination was held in a larger town a day's ride from Hama village. "You may begin writing," the teacher says. The Yi boy tries to close out the world around him. All the other children fidgeting in their chairs around him are not his competition. None of them will likely pass. He will not let the distraction prevent him from competing with the millions of children taking the test under the gaze of their tutors in private rooms. He looks at the tattoo on his right wrist. It says strength. Then he steps into the vivid part of his mind. He looks at the tattoo on his left wrist. It is the ancient word for knowledge and hard study. Inside the classroom, one child is overly hyper from taking some fresh ginseng that morning. His knee bangs against the desk. The Yi boy pays him no mind.

The Yi boy's mother and father came down to the school building on their large, gray steeds, carrying their young son's books for him, and

"I see in your file that your test scores were superb yet, tut, tut, tut. Those dark tattoos on your arms are unacceptable." The Yi boy starts to cry. He wants to say something but his voice cracks. They look at one another for a moment. The boy finally swallows and says to the medical examiner, "Help me, sir." The man frowns. "It is a shame, I cannot lie. Rules are rules. Not knowing the rules is no excuse." The gray-haired examiner thinks about what he just said. He thinks about his own life, and then, before the boy gets up and turns away, he adds, "But, let me do this. I will have you repeat this medical examination in six months' time. Your academic scores remain valid for that period. Meanwhile, you must take measures to remove those tattoos." The old man gives the boy a copper coin with a square hole in the center, a very common coin that holds little value because it was minted long ago. He whispers. "Listen now to what you need to do. Scrape this coin against each wrist four hundred times. That will remove the skin. Wash it with soap, bandage it up, and change the bandage regularly to keep the wound clean until a scar has formed. It will hurt. If there are still remaining marks of a tattoo, carry out the entire process again in two months time."

Was there more to the story? Yes. There is a letter of acceptance, along with the notice that a delegation from the university will arrive to give the preliminary medical screening required of all new students. *Congratulations, child!* The Yi boy can't help but smile that week after receiving the acceptance letter. He can taste the future. The Yi boy looks out into the mountain ranges toward Tibet, where the sun disappears every night, where he has always wanted to venture. He wants to feel the sunlight on the other side of the mountains someday. A long road; impossible by foot. He first needs his own horse. He wants to escape his family's nomadic tents. Even the horses tie him down somehow.

The Yi boy opened the acceptance letter with a huge smile. It is a surprise like he had never had in his life. There is no thought of the tattoos on his wrists when he opens his letter. He can't believe he has passed

The Yi people rode Ferghana stallions down from their mountain camps to trade goods with us in Hama village. That Yi boy who became my friend rides a borrowed horse from his uncle. He is probably not as in control of the horse as he seems to be to me. The people of Hama do not know much about horses. It takes very little to amaze us. The other Yi people snicker at him, though. When there are new smells in the air, his horse suddenly turns around on his own, ignoring the small rider. The Yi boy sees the branches coming at him from ahead and ducks rather than steering this loaned horse. The horse is looking for eggs. Does every doggone tree have a nest? The horse stops to sniff at the sparrow eggs. "Go!" commands the Yi boy while pressing his heels into the horse's rib cage, but I just laugh at the two of them. I guess I realize that he is not in control, but I couldn't admire him more. He rides a horse! *Not only that, he knows the nature of Lake Lugu like I only wish I could.* He is starting to teach me what he knows. The Yi people are rich in oral lore about the land. I encourage the Yi boy to look for the old lichens, moss, and mushrooms that are in the old stories so he can trade them to me for blankets. It's fine that the horse wanders in the trees. If they find lichens and mushrooms today, I will make these things into medicines.

I did not say much to him when I saw how weak the Yi boy had become over the last week. I just spat. There is something unbalanced in his blood but I know not what. I am so young. I want to become a doctor, but I do not know much about real medicine. I show him compassionate eyes, and we say very little. He wipes his sweaty brow. He brings me Sophora root and Cuscuta seed, and I say thank you. His wrists have finally healed. There are scars still but the tattoos that once dirtied his body are gone. I can remember the Yi boy's bloody wrists when he removed the tattoos.

Months before, the Yi boy was told that, although he passed the official state examination to attend university in Beijing, he had been disqualified because of a technicality: the ethnic tattoo he applied to his wrists as a young child was not allowed in the classrooms of Beijing. Body tattoos are not allowed in the classroom.

great leader for our Republic. The Yi boy simply says to me right now, not knowing the future, that he perhaps can meet me in Beijing if I stay there long enough for the new semester to begin. "I will try," I promise him. He perspires little beads on his forehead. I should put more effort into healing him, but my mind is on the new letter. I am needed in Beijing.

It was rainy season in Hama village, and the Yi boy rode his horse back home in the storm the fortnight before. The moss is cool and slippery. He will make a fire to boil the herbs I gave him if there is time before bed. He sees a dried snakeskin on the floor beside his pillow. His uncle tells the story of a snake causing trouble today and thinks it is time they move camp to another location. *The snake must have shed its skin,* the Yi boy thinks. He looks at the translucent snake lying there on his floor. *It is just skin.* He adds the tail to the brew of herbs thinking about how I had offered him a sip of my rattlesnake wine once when I noticed he showed signs of a coming cold. That was nice and healed him then. This might help him now. The water boils. He drinks the tea and goes to sleep.

My mind changed ever so much during those pre-teenage years. I am no longer that quiet introvert that nobody notices in Hama. I am instead growing into an extrovert that people come to for company, for herbs soaked in wine, and for my advice. I do admire the Yi boy's attempt to leave his happy life in the mountaintops, to want more, with an ambitious plan cut deep into his skin. He wants to become the first in his clan to attend Beijing University. He has already passed the exam, beating everyone's limited expectations. Now it is just about finances, which, as a child, doesn't seem like a big obstacle. I can be like that too one day, I think to myself while doing my daily chores in Hama. I consider letting my hair grow long on my forehead, showing that I am in control of my fortunes. I am the only person of this village to have been to Beijing. I know things. I often take out those tight shoes of the capital but they pain me just walking around my foster mother's house. Still, I keep them shiny.

for any failure the Emperor might display in class, and when I am not there, and there is no other person in the vicinity to blame, to just go easy on Puyi and ignore the mistake. Unfortunately the substitute wasn't told this or thinks it is best to teach in another way. The eunuch frowns in the direction of the Son of Heaven. He shows no fear. Emperor Puyi frowns back and subsequently commands this eunuch to drink his ink. "Drink it!" he says to the teacher. The eunuch looks at Puyi and the ink on the table. He puts the bowl to his lips. The black ink slides down his throat.

I looked out the window of the train heading toward this boy and his palace of illusions. The steam whistle blows. St. Paul's wort spots the surrounding fields as I cross this vast countryside. It pokes out from the cracks in the stone bridges and blankets the tiled roofs of the houses. The leaves are fleshy and flat except for the stalk of its flower. At times the train moves slow enough to see such details. What a nuisance it is! To remove a St. Paul's wort, the Widow Du taught me when I was maybe ten, you must pull hand over hand, tugging first on the reddish-purple stalk. Branches radiate from the stalk that are fleshy but firm. There is a determination in the weed. Its dusty yellow flowers are surrounded by a star of spiky leaves. Sitting in my seat I hear bladed wheels scrape against cast iron track. I think about weeds, and as I do, my friend back home dies from the flu. I didn't know he would die from it. Who dies from the flu nowadays? I will not think of that Yi boy for the whole train ride north, nor during my time at the capital.

It was the sick Yi boy who handed me the Emperor's yellow envelope that morning, and that was my final farewell to him. It is one of the Yi boy's part-time jobs to deliver our mail so he can earn pocket money to subsidize his studies when he goes to Beijing. I take the envelope. "I must be needed in Beijing!" I exclaim happily, and I tell him farewell. I can tell that he is ill, but I am not concerned. I certainly never imagine he will die. Had this boy been given a formal education, I believe he would have become a

The Emperor's finely embroidered dragons flapped from his back as he ran down the long hallways. His forehead is always cleanly shaved. A thick braid dangles down his back. I have a similar queue. My head is also shaved. I am often running after him, or somewhere a few steps ahead. We are playing one of our games of imaginary war. "The white ninjas are after us!" We pull back a curtain. There we find a eunuch hiding, but to our imaginations he is a ninja. Ah, we need to go a different way! There are so many ninjas hiding behind the curtains. "Run faster, my Emperor," I call out to him.

Once, we hopped over a eunuch dead on the marble steps, his mouth black, really and truly dead lying there in the open. We are in the middle of our imaginary game and so pay the corpse in robes no mind. I leap over it, not worried that he is dead. The dead body becomes part of our play, and we imagine it proof that the ninjas are here. The reality of his death is not our concern. The eunuchs are simply here to serve the Emperor Child, and how dare he die like that and became an inconvenience, lying in our way, where we need to step around his flesh! Their role in life is simply to serve. Emperor Puyi thinks in this way. I share the view.

I believe that the important questions in life are not, "What is going to happen?" We know that immediately. The real question is always, "Why did it happen in that way?" A much more interesting question, really.

In this story, you notice death first, then find its cause a day earlier. It is now the day before we run through the palace halls playing ninja. In an unusual course of events, Old Teacher Jaw is away on an errand for the CGG, so cannot teach his usual lesson to the Child Emperor. Emperor Puyi is in bad spirits because I am not invited to the writing lesson. Who will take notes? They practice calligraphy together, this soon-to-be-deceased substitute and the Emperor Child. The eunuch scolds Puyi for how he draws his letters. "That is the wrong order," says the teacher. But the student roars back, "That is not how it's done here!" The protocol is to scold others and I know not of those. If our teacher knows of them, he does not share the information with us. Eunuch Jaw allows me to sit in on Puyi's astrology lessons because I carefully write down notes that Puyi can then review. One day, there is a very old eunuch, a visiting scholar who was filling in for Jaw, who says to us on a cold October night, "Venus is the star of sympathy and is responsible for the morning dew." This lesson strikes me as unusual because the Five Stars that include Mercury, Mars, Jupiter, Venus, and Saturn have always been treated as a group that should be considered together. *Dare I think of Venus as a power on its own?* The old teacher goes on. "I will show you how to track Venus through the seasons. Time can be kept using its eight-year cycle across the sky in line with the moon. Watch just before sunrise, or at dusk. It will be the first brilliant light pulling up the sun." That strikes me as something to write down and remember.

It was Old Teacher Jaw who first taught me to write fine calligraphy as well. If I am to take good notes it must be done in a beautiful and steady hand, Old Teacher Jaw tells the CGG, and they all agree to let me take classes alongside Puyi. Teacher Jaw tells me that each letter of the 50,000 words in the Chinese alphabet I need to practice no less than one hundred times. A stroke of a letter carries the weight of that letter, so I learn. If even only one stroke is weak, the structure of that word falls apart. That is what Old Teacher Jaw teaches me, and repeats again and again. Some of the eunuchs I hate, but this teacher I will miss dearly like a father.

Calligraphy of that time was so different. We write not left to right. Instead, we write each word right to left. You write not from up to down but instead you write and read from down to up. Each character has a special order for each stroke that I must carry out in the absolute correct order or else the word becomes unreadable to Old Teacher Jaw. "What is this scribble?" he asks me, confused. Old Chinese is a strange system that few can read. I am privileged to learn the code. I am reminded again and again that I am very privileged indeed.

successfully. First, I kiss Belle's friend. She is a beautiful girl named after nighttime snow. The feeling of my lips touching another pair of soft warm lips is surprising. It tingles my entire body, and the touch remains on my lips even after the kiss is done. The touch holds on somehow. We spend that entire day playing in the backyard of the Widow Du's house under the big sugar maple. Mother is not around that day. We are on our own.

Mother and I never told my sister or other siblings about the Yi boy's death because we knew Belle would take it badly. While she dreams of his love, he is actually rotting in the ground. His funeral was performed in the hills by his tribe while I was away, and nobody in Hama took notice of his absence, and Belle never finds out. The Widow Du tells her daughter that the Yi boy has gone away early to university in Beijing. Why not tell her the truth? I do not know. It sometimes causes too much pain to say the truth. Never knowing he is dead, Belle gives me things she knitted for him each time I travel to Beijing. "You will see the Yi boy, will you not?" She asks me with red cheeks. I say I will try but then give the gift to someone I meet on the train.

⌐ ⌐

When I was twelve, it was the eunuch named Old Teacher Jaw who taught me how to read the stars. Emperor Puyi has many marvelous telescopes in his quarters. It is a collection from every part of the world and goes back many centuries. He has the same model of telescope that Christopher Columbus used to find the New World. He has the actual telescope Magellan used to navigate around the Cape of Good Hope. It was given as a gift. All the old explorers used telescopes to find the Middle Kingdom and trade with the emperors of old. Europe wanted our herbs and teas. I walk under a telescope that weighs at least two tons and reaches the span of the room. It is oiled so well that it moves easily with the brush of my hand. At one time, this was the finest collection of astronomy equipment in all the world, but I suppose there are now more advanced telescopes elsewhere, although Puyi this time. He writes, *I am thinking about a room we discovered long ago. It is on the edge of my memory. I am in need of your old maps, He Song!* I could think of many such rooms, full of fascinating things. We once found a room stacked full of bodies, those who posed a threat to the old Empress Dowager Cixi, Puyi's grandmother. There are so many skeletons stacked one over another. There are rooms of amazing treasures in that Beijing stronghold. One room holds a golden chest that I crawled into and almost became locked inside! It will be interesting to see whether we can find that one again. It was such a strange place. I remember the box smelling like sweet honey. I have had nightmares since then, with the helpless feeling of being trapped inside that dark space.

My foster sister for whom I had the most affection among my siblings was just a few years my elder. Her name is Belle. She is beautiful in every way. When I think of her, it is with sun on her face and a lovely smile.

My sister, Belle, fell in love with the Yi boy, although as far as I know she had only ever set eyes on him from a distance. I overhear her telling our mother that she dreams of being with him at night, galloping the surrounding mountains on his brave horse. One day, Belle and her two best friends decide it is time to practice the art of kissing. I become their practice doll for the experiment. I have no choice, Belle explains. I must do as they say. The girls first dress me up into that man they think is most becoming. They clip my nails and wash my hands, face, and feet. It takes some time to get me looking good. They comb my hair and even cut it into a new style. They sew me a new shirt. It is just my sister Belle and her two friends here this fine summer day. They each have their own ideas of what qualities are most handsome, and eventually they come to a consensus. I now look good enough, they agree. Now, as their rag doll, I must attempt to kiss each of them in turn. Each time I do, the girl I try to kiss pulls back and giggles. She says she is not in love with me. She says to go away, but that is not the end. The test is to win their affection and get a kiss, and I have somewhat of an advantage because they all are eager to practice. I learn to play my role focuses on the tones of your voice, not the content of your words. Don't worry about what you say. Focus on how it is said. When hungry, her nose can hunt through our thoroughly combed garden and still she finds parts of plants that are digestible. It is a nose that is sharp like a hound's. With these traits, she keeps this large household running in a controlled chaos. She must have seen me in the woods and, before yelling, went into her study to write a note to the Good Doctor. Let him be the executioner.

She was not my true birth mother, but was the parent I was given at this stage of my life. She makes me a rebel of sorts, because in a way that is her lifestyle. There is no taboo that she does not test. I remember a time when the Widow Du passed out to unwelcome visitors cigarettes that would make grown men fall asleep. She hates smoking, but the usual custom is to offer your guest a cigarette. I helped her make the secret powder with a unique mix of mushrooms and herbs. Other times, she would literally tickle grown men into submission, even elderly men, until she got the answers she required. A permit is needed, you say? The Chinese warlord bureaucracy that frustrates others in the village, all the would-be-impossible scenarios that were part of daily life here, she would simply resolve with an unrelenting tickle until the recipient yells, "Okay, okay. Stop!" Of course, we kids get tickled too, especially when we are close-lipped on a topic she finds important. Can an adult really act this way? The answer is yes. Yes, she can.

To the women in her family, the Widow Du would advise never to marry. "What's the point, dear? Men of this day and age are interesting but a few hours each week. If you spend any more time with them, they begin to smell like rotten vegetables. And they become soft too." She says this, yet her income is based on the sale of wedding blankets.

I received another letter to go to Beijing, but there was an earthquake that tore up the railroad and prevented my immediate departure. The letter calls me north, but I must wait. I wonder what the Emperor needs of me

To get to the Good Doctor's shed, I walked over that small river that flows clear mountain water through the center of our town. The chamber pots from the night before lay out there drying. Women are washing clothes in the crisp water now. Some homes built right up against our river have their own stone platforms on the back porch where residents can wash clothes and vegetables, and the pots and clothes are drying there in the sun. I cross over the river using the old stone bridge. As I cross, my fingers feel the ancient script of Dongba carved deep into the pillars of the bridge. Reaching out on all sides of me are hills and valleys thick with trees and the shadows of great mountains. I wish I were older. I am angry at being punished in this way. *Why must I drink this man's potions?*

The Widow Du was furious when she saw my misbehavior that afternoon and, with a look that could kill, sent me immediately to the Good Doctor for my punishment. I am caught playing with her sword in the woods. I don't think any of her other children would have dared. I know we were not supposed to touch the sharp blade, but I do it anyway. I fantasize I am a great ninja and that I had to save all my sisters from a great sorcerer. What else is there in the house that could defeat the sorcerer? I had no choice. I am creeping around the base of an old pine tree and then feel a hand on the back of my neck. I try to swing my sword but it does not move. Someone is holding the blade. I see the blade fall into its sheath, and a note is handed to me. The Widow is there, and she has the broadsword back in its sheath, back in her possession. The hand I feel on the back of my neck is hers. The note I take from her, folded twice, says this: *Dear Good Doctor, He Song has been out of sorts today and will need a strong three-day dose of your medicines. I suggest something bitter. Sweet Kisses, Peony.* The writing is in fine calligraphy. The note crumples in my hand.

Growing up it was important to know that Peony's sensitivities were triggered internally. When angry, she notices only the visual. No sound can penetrate her mind when she is angry. There is no need to say a word on these occasions. I learn to just stand back. When compassionate, Peony itself. I am after this special mushroom today that will only appear in the first part of April. It's a brilliant day. No one in the village yet has that flu. It is festering other places.

The water buffalo I will take for my own belonged to a young family on the other side of Jade Dragon Snow Mountain who thought his care could be trusted to others. The neighbor who is asked to watch over the buffalo while the owners go away on a long journey assumes that the family will bring the beast over before they leave. When they never come he assumes he no longer holds the responsibility to care for the buffalo. In the neighbor's mind, either the buffalo has gone along with the family or another caregiver was found. But the situation isn't sitting well for the buffalo, starving to death and tied to a rope in his backyard pen. He has never been tied up for so long, and he is very strong. When the ton of flesh gets hungry and thirsty enough, he frees himself and goes on his own, spending most of his time soaking in the rice paddy fields, but eventually goes hunting in the hills for his master or perhaps a mate.

〜 〜 〜 〜 〜 〜 〜 〜 〜 〜 〜 〜 〜 〜 〜 〜 〜 〜 〜

I learned from the old doctor that there is a bit of poison in all medicine. *Always look for the balance where you kill the bad but not the good. Sometimes two poisons can cancel each other out.* I often see the old doctor overestimate the toxin because it depends on the individual plant, its age, and freshness. Is that why most are dried, just to be confident of the dosage? "Yes," he says. "That is true. You never know for sure."

"What did you break this time, Little Bean?" the Good Doctor asked me, taking the note from my hand, smiling down at me. I hate that name, Little Bean. That is not who I want to be. I demand to be called Doctor He Song, and, looking into that old man's eyes, I know I will soon rival him with my own makeshift medicines.

an herbalist. Look at my right hand, the three dirty nails. The other nails remain clean far away in Beijing. But I do not think much of the Emperor when I am away. As I farm, I grow accustomed to spitting in the mud. *Oh, the bad habits I have picked up from the locals!* I use the public pipe in our village whenever I can, and that is why I cough heartily out here in the open field, and then spit. The tobacco from the public pipe soaks into me like water does a sponge and stays with me throughout the day. A water buffalo helps me till the land.

Once when working the garden plot on the edge of town, I came across a water buffalo that I knew didn't belong to anyone, or so it seemed. It is such a large animal to not have an owner. A guilty look plagues his big black eyes. Ears are lowered. "Where is your owner?" I ask someone on the road. The kid knows. "Well, come with me, and we will return this old fellow." We arrive to find the house totally empty. It is a mystery why they had gone and where. I look around the old house and leave a note about the buffalo. I write that I will take care of the beast until they return. The buffalo's strength cuts down on the time I need to work the land. I have extra time now that can be spent as I wish.

There were layers in everything. The grasses. The bushes. The sky. The air. Can I see the air? Grab it, no. A big inhale. Yes, I capture the air. I blow it out of me with a yodel. And I breathe it in this time through my nose. It smells like everything around me. It smells like the colors and the sounds and the moisture.

Going out in the mountains searching for herbs in broken shoes was my daily routine back then. This is my life in the south, with only occasional ventures to Beijing. As I walk, I stop to fix the strap of my shoe with a natural twine I make from grass. I start a small fire to cook the potato I have in my pocket. I find large pinecones to add to the fire and will eat the seeds when they are roasted. I see now that the search for the mushroom the elders call Spiritual Mushroom was more important than the mushroom

I brought my medicinal herbs to Beijing soaked in jars of wine, and we drank it all in a single day. My formulas mixed mango leaves, pumpkin root, thousand-day flowers, cattail pollen, peppermint oil, and black fungus. Those who have never become drunk with an emperor before will never know the fun it can be. My medicine may be doing him some good, but the liquor itself is a medicine too. Being included in his indulgence allows me to heal as well. I long for my childhood friend.

The day before, I had arrived by train. I hail a cab from the central station to see Emperor Puyi at his palace. During this unannounced visit, I notice guards with a new type of uniform at the palace doors, but they are not the usual imperial guards keeping the public out, as tradition requires. The new guards wear the white uniforms of General Sun and are placed at each gate to keep Puyi confined to the palace. They allow me entrance. I report the guards to Emperor Puyi, and he is not surprised. He shrugs. We first talk about his newest cars imported from Detroit. Buicks. They are beautiful cars, and we just sit in them. Sometimes we drive around the courtyard. He could never leave the Forbidden City so there is no need for a car other than to collect it and dream about the future. Puyi shows me a new car given to him by the Japanese delegation, and we take a spin around the courtyards. While he drives, he says to me, "China has suffered from the disasters of democracy, and apart from a selfish minority, the great majority of the people loathe the Republic and long for the Qing Dynasty. That is the truth of things."

〜 〜

Before I was even in my teenage years, I trained to become an herbal doctor. In Hama village, I have daily chores in our family's garden, and so adding more and more herbs to the mix is an easy way to learn. The normal vegetables we grow are corn, potato, some sunflowers, and red hot peppers to keep the family fed. I have dirty nails from digging in the ground all the time. Having dirty nails is a mark of the trade of both a farmer and

Because that old emperor, my husband be,
was born in the year of the rat.
Tatat tat tee.

The officials were so pleased with themselves, patat tat tift
that they first showed me their expensive gift.
"We spent so much money on it," they all said, badad say da dad dad.
I was delighted, but then suddenly very sad.
With puppy dog eyes, I whispered in their ear, sssi shee shoo sooon

I whispered, "Did you know that my birthday will be coming soon?"
"You deserve a golden gift as well!" baddell dell lee
the officials all declared right there to me, meteeb tee teet
bowing low to my small feet.
So I then add…. sockock dock toxx
"Surely you know," sodox toxity tocks
"I was born the year of the ox!"

I guess it doesn't seem as funny now in my retelling, but at the time the thought of those poor officials in days gone by trying to gather enough gold to make a life-sized ox for this now wrinkly, ugly woman seems utterly hilarious to us. He laughs and she laughs and I laugh. The other ladies try not to laugh but they join in.

I started to notice the weeds growing between the cobblestones of the vast courtyards of the Forbidden City around that time. I don't think of it as anything negative as of yet, but things are indeed changing. It feels as though my mountainside world of Hama is following me here when I return on these visits and is encroaching on these vast courtyards of brick behind high walls, which as a younger child seemed so pristine. Perhaps the seeds of wild plants fell from my coat during my last visit? No, it is more likely just the wind. The eunuchs no longer tend the grounds as they once did. They grow lazy and depressed because there is little hope that the Empire will be restored. They begin to see that the Emperor and his city are merely a mirage.

Emperor of my poor treatment by his eunuchs, he just shrugs it off. He commands his senior eunuch in the households department to give him what I stole so he can see what is at stake and judge my punishment, for he is the Emperor and should have the final word. The eunuch picks up what I stole and puts it into the hands of the Son of Heaven. This eunuch has a long beard extending down to the floor, and his eyebrows are extremely long. *How old he must be!* I would guess he is older than rock Everything sags when he scowls at me and then releases the jade carving of a seven-headed dragon to rest in Puyi's hand. That is what I stole this time. Emperor Puyi, however, shrugs it off when seeing it and says to me, "He Song, I give you this jade. Remember my kindness." Still, getting caught earns me the name "Little Jade Thief" among the elders in the Forbidden City. Like I have said before, the eunuchs were no better.

Drunk off the rice wine I brought from the south, Emperor Puyi and I caused great havoc in the courtesan chambers early on during that particular visit when I stole the seven-headed dragon. We were teenagers after all. This distinctly feminine section of the palace would remain a great mystery to me. The women live there now as courtesans because they once were the wives and lovers of emperors long past. Something about them scares Emperor Puyi, and he usually stays far away from that section of the palace. However, today with me there he has an accomplice. We go there together, right into the courtesan chambers. Puyi demands all the courtesans gather around and entertain us with dance and song. Both of us are drunk, so it does not take much to amuse us. I suggest that the women try to make us laugh, so Puyi decrees each lady must come up with a funny joke. As it turns out, these are very funny women, or so it seems to us. The funniest of them told us this joke in an old form of rhyme:

> *Once I remember ages ago, a yo ho ho, a diddley dee*
> *a group of officials pooled their resources together to give His Majesty*
> *a fine birthday gift, budum boll old duddold doo sold*
> *The gift was a life-sized rat made of solid gold!*
> *Why a rat? patat tat tat?*

Rather than being invited to the event itself, I was requested to come this time to interpret the signs leading up to the wedding ceremony. So the balance of the sun and the moon is not disturbed by any disgrace caused by guests, and thus our Emperor and his wives will be able to stand there above us with pride and without fear on their wedding day. Though I never say it to anyone, from my point of view, I come to the Forbidden City to play, not work. I try to come in unannounced and meet as few staff as possible. I understand the Emperor to be desperate to consult his numerous oracles to find hope in the situation into which he was born. Emperor Puyi says to me again this trip, "I will not stop until I find a good omen. Look at those skies over there, what do the stars say tonight?" If that produces nothing, he continues to push by asking, "Tell me where old Turtle goes this season? When will good Venus come our way again? I need something positive so I can sleep." I do my best to assure him the wedding will be fine.

Since I had moved away, the Emperor usually paid me for my travel expenses and council with his stored treasures, although I needed none of those riches in my simple life as a young man way back then. He pays me too much and what does he get in return? The Emperor doesn't mind my failures as a self-taught herbalist and at best a mediocre friend. He says as much to me on many occasions. He is perfect. I am not. We know this. Yet he still calls me back.

In earlier visits to Beijing from my home in the south, I was given free rein in the palace stores, which allowed me to take additional trinkets here and there for myself, as did all the Forbidden City's staff. I will freely admit that there is a time when I am caught red-handed by the senior staff. As punishment, the head eunuch forces me to spend a night locked in the garbage cellar with the company of rats and rotting leftovers. It is cold, and the eunuchs keep me locked there alone until late the next morning, hearing me pound at the heavy red door the entire while. "It is your punishment for stealing the jade," they say through the keyhole. The crawling darkness terrifies me. "I am only a child! Let me out," I say. When I later tell the

CHAPTER 6

August 1, 1918

China's population is 462 million people.

In contrast to Hama, Beijing was a different sort of forest. To escape all the pageantry of servants and officials in those early days, I escape to The Quiet Gardens as often as I can during the months that I reside there.

I came here for a wedding. Staring up at the crookedness in the branches of the Forbidden City's gigantic cedars, lying on my back in the grass, I can follow time back to when there must have been a severe storm breaking off limbs—six, seven, maybe twenty years ago—and I see it wasn't even the first time it was damaged. There are signs of breaks even earlier by other storms going back centuries. I think I can remember a violent storm years ago, and the trees now look better for it today. The main branches fold back into interesting angles from the wind then continue on in the direction they had first intended. They were minor branches before the storm and have since taken over a larger role in the life of the tree when other branches were forced off.

The quilted blankets the Widow Du sent me to give His Majesty as wedding gifts have worked their magic in a section of the palace where I have never gone. The Emperor is happily occupied with not one but two lovely new wives, both lying on their own blankets of magic. I think he likes being married. I think I may like it someday as well. But today, I am content looking up at the trees from below. The wind blows through their millions of needles. Shadows dance down to me.

Good Doctor to Peony. "It is possible that one of the higher bushes might be ready. But if I pick too early, there is not enough potency to do you much good. It is like an unripe peach. An extra day can make all the difference." She shakes her head. "No time to go, and I am not feeling well. I have to finish a wedding blanket today. Do you have anything lucky for me to put inside? Here, take Little Bean with you as your apprentice." I squirm. The Good Doctor wants to keep the conversations going. "The rumor is that you always braid in a strand of your own hair. Is that true, Peony?" She blushes crimson. "Of course I do. I must. It is custom. But perhaps I will break tradition just this once." And before he can even react, she grabs for the three curly hairs in his large black mole, and tugs them selfishly out and into her little handbag. "Please keep me updated on the herb's progress, Good Doctor. And thank you." The Good Doctor, bedazzled, sits hunched on his porch, rubbing his left cheek. "Lugu women. Humpf." He then looks at me, still standing there. "Healing involves emotions, Little Bean. It is not just about herbs."

Many hours before, when the morning sun from the east was first in my eyes, it revealed monkey tracks. At the crack of dawn, I wake feeling a new determination that I can find the medicine she needs on my own. My memory contends that the Green Dragon Pinellia has bloomed all around in great supply in years past, just not now. There is this one place I must look first thing today. The hike is fast, and I get there as the sun begins to rise. My eyes need to adjust. Light is everywhere. At first, I can only see bright white light around me. Then I see the plant… and the tracks. One of the herbs indeed blossomed overnight, but a monkey has already eaten it. The squirrel monkeys always do things of that sort then laugh at me in spite. I contemplate bringing the full-bellied monkey home with me, collecting all his poop, picking out the seeds, and planting them near our doorstep. Someday I will domesticate the wild herbs to grow in a more convenient place.

The Good Doctor went up into the hills alone that afternoon, and then I met up with him before long, but even our joint efforts could not turn up any Pinellia bulblets ready for harvest. I first make arrangements that day for my train ticket to Beijng when he sets off after lunch. There is light rain in the air, and a chill of the season to come. One bush the Good Doctor comes to is covered with worms. "Oh, you devils!" he exclaims. He presses their bodies until they burst, then wipes his hand on the earth. They had begun to eat the herb, and he can see a sack of eggs, which he presses his cigarette into until it smolders. His face turns red with anger. Then comes a chill of confusion and fear. He walks quickly, almost at a sprint to the next bush farther up the hill. Very closely he examines each leaf. Never had he noticed how yellow the veins are, how flatly they widen into the stem in an intricate pattern, resembling a stitching he had once seen on a native headdress. "What are you doing, Doctor?" A high-pitched voice startles him from behind. I am trying to learn, but this old man is so boring to me. I say, "You haven't moved for almost a quarter of an hour, Good Doctor. I thought you might have fallen asleep. I almost fell asleep watching you." Then I laugh at my own wit (of late I have become convinced I am the funniest man of this century), with my nose tilting high, making the old doctor laugh in turn. We try another location. After many hours of tenuous climbing on rock cliffs, I can see the herb only meters away, but there is a ravine between us. The Good Doctor tries to grasp at the herb with a stick. I try to swing a rope. Both attempts fail. It is a little too out of reach from here, so tomorrow I will have to hike the half day it will take to go around and down into the gorge, across the river, through the thicket, and back up and around to the other side. It can be done but not until tomorrow. By the time we get home, the sun is going down into the western sky, shining right in my eyes.

Earlier that day, the Widow Du pressed the Good Doctor to try harder. She knocks with her fingernails on his medicine shop door and yells in, "Can you harvest today?" Through the cracks in the wall, her shadow pulls long lines onto the dirt floor of drying leaves and flowers. "I would be happy to have you accompany me to have a look this afternoon," replies the land's long-strung scrolls. This real medicine of the Middle Kingdom is refined, tested, and retested, all the way back to the Great Yellow Empress herself, who first wrote down the words, 'A body is divided into the Yin and the Yang.'"

Everyone in the village was entertained by the stories told on our front porch.

~ ~

At the very beginning of my tale to you, when we were with Jasmine at her wedding in Shanghai, I may have appeared nonchalant as your narrator about the virus that ran rampant in the kitchen of the Shangri-la and among the wedding banquet guests. It is because I have seen it all before, and the truth is that the world survives. It will be nearly the same strain of flu in 2016 as what is causing our flu pandemic a hundred years before.

The herb we thought we needed to cure the Widow Du, called Green Dragon Pinellia, only bulbed in late autumn in Hama, but its rhizomes withered the instant of the first frost, making it a long-awaited but difficult to harvest bit of magic. Every day, the Good Doctor would go check on its progress. There were three reliable patches that he knew of growing in the forest, each growing at slightly different elevations, making it possible for either the lowermost to escape a freeze or for the uppermost to gain enough additional sunshine over the summer so that it could bloom in advance, all depending what the weather brings us this year. In addition to these groves, I knew of single plants that sometimes sprouted on Five Dragon Hill, which I would mark with blue marble rocks. This year, the chances seem good we will get an early harvest. Yet, this year, the need is also dire. So many people are catching the flu that five people already were prescribed the needed medicine, and the Good Doctor's stockpile has run out. It feels likely that others in the community may soon have the need as well. The Yi people in the mountains are said to be dying from the summer heat left and right.

The Widow Du had been telling us stories of old medicine, causing my baby sister (not by blood, but I regarded her so) to chime in, "Oh, the Yellow Empress! Did you know her, Mommy?" from under her mother's arms there on the front porch.

The ears of a white-haired woman pricked up, as neighbors often listened near our porch to pass the time. This passerby, a relative of ours, says to us from the steps, "Oh, what a powerful notion. Yin…" The Widow Du cuts in, adding, "…and Yang. Yes. Absolutely, it is. Absolutely. Your sword is Yang and the weight of your forearm is Yin. I saw you practicing this morning, Good Second Sister of Wu." The passerby blushes a soft crimson from her crow's feet down to her slender neck and perhaps farther down, even, to her toes so unaccustomed the white-haired Second Sister of Wu is to fine compliments and attention. We normally do not see her. The Widow Du continues by saying to her sister, "What this town has lost in medicine is perhaps being rediscovered in your study of swords and tai chi." Then to me she says, "Little Bean, you pay attention. I cannot think of anyone so in balance with a sword." The white-haired woman pulls the blade up from its sheath and looks at its edge. We all look. The Second Sister of Wu says, "Oh, you shame me, Sister, with the undeserved compliments. I am afraid you exaggerate so as to make a warrior out of a dilapidated old hag," then adds quickly, "but surely, I could defend our grandchildren if put to the test." I enjoy the talk. Hearing the banter about swords, I remember when we were young and would not quiet down for dinner's grace. The Widow Du pulled the long sword from a yak-leather sheath that was kept under the window in our kitchen, and how it rang! I remember it shining a bluish brilliance like the moon. But she never let us touch it.

My foster mother had been saying, "Just consider for a moment, Little Bean, the thousands of years of study done by our foremother and their foremothers. It developed over some ten thousand years. More, I say! And, it was passed on by generation to generation in rich poetic language— as morning dew accumulates on old bamboo—added with time to this

It was the way my foster mother liked to tease, but she did intend to marry them off as quickly as possible to women who were much older. It will not be a legal marriage until they reach the age of twenty-two, but nevertheless it could be a recognized marriage in our town, wedding blanket and all. *She will not have a chance to arrange my marriage,* I promise myself. I will leave town.

I often thought that the most fascinating aspect of this woman who took me under her roof was her chosen trade. She makes wedding blankets. They are of a special quality. Two of them were even given to Emperor Puyi himself when he married, but it is too soon to tell that story. She would write code in the wedding blankets and hide others possessions inside to bring luck. There is only one house in town that could potentially rival the quality of blankets that our house is able to sew. Recently, the Widow Du intentionally (though she denies it) dumped soup on the dress of that rival family's matriarch. When that soiled dress is later hung out in their backyard to dry, the Widow Du sends one of her daughters to steal the garment right off the clothesline. Then she cut it into squares and uses the pieces of cloth unabashedly as material for her final set of blankets.

Although the Widow Du's fever would not break, she refused to look ill as she talked to us on our porch just days before her death. I dry the herbs I found along the mountain banks. I have been searching high and low for that one herb that the Good Doctor thinks will cure her, but so far have not had any success. "I am no real doctor, mother," I say to her, while she insists, "Hogwash, Little Bean. Why haven't I gone to the city hospital for a good seven years, and only send you kids to the Good Doctor for your punishment? Modern medicine is just a lot of hocus pocus, that's why! Honestly, Little Bean, you could be a great doctor if you try. I know you want to become better than the Good Doctor down the road. I think you should set your sights higher!" Something makes me look up, and the sky is as blue as ever.

me any differently from her birth children, that is to say, no different from any of the sons. The daughters, of course, receive special treatment because that is just the culture of this unusual place where the CGG has sent me to live. To punish our naughty boyish behavior, she would often send her sons to the town doctor where we would be forced to drink every drop of whatever the Good Doctor prescribed for the next three days. The Widow Du's given name is Peony. Peony's lifestyle and intellect are at a higher plane than anyone else in the small mountain village, and she is well aware of that. We all know it. Of all the other men in town, I think she may like our old town doctor most, and therefore trusts him more than she should. It's as though she finds his faults attractive rather than repulsive (as I do!) and would ultimately forgive him for any wrongdoing (while I keep tabs!). Peony is a forgiving person. The best example was her ability to forgive a neighbor for accidentally burning down our barn. That time she simply said, "Ai ya, humanity!" then grabbed her saw to begin reconstruction. I do admire her for this. We children laugh about that story sometimes.

I noticed a drop of blood drip down from her ear before she wiped it away. Seeing her ill is strange and out of character. Most men were clay in Peony's hands, awed by her as if she were a Beijing opera star. The smell of her buttery walnut skin gives an instant erection. The luckiest of the townsmen tie locks of her long hair around their bedposts for good dreams. The wedding quilts made and sold by her daughters also contain a strand of hair from Peony. This is well known. When a daughter hints that a strand of her mother's black hair is sewn into the inside, her quilt will sell faster than pan-fried hot jiaozi.

"I have given my books to the library and plan on selling everything else in auction before too long," she told me in those last days we were together. "I will keep the house but put the farmland up for auction and perhaps my boys as well. Who needs sons when you already have a houseful of such lovely and competent daughters? I am sure that in this town I will get twice what they are worth."

finally dies, and so I, only seventeen, would have inherited the title from a long line of healers stretching back to myth, if I were to return. As their doctor, I would have done the best I could based on memory, local folklore, and my own imagination. Love for the Widow Du might have encouraged me to push on and make medicine a lifelong career. Unfortunately, she dies from the bird flu. That is probably why I never return.

✓ ✓

Except for those special occasions when I was helping His Majesty at the Forbidden City, I lived in the house of the Widow Du on the banks of Lake Lugu. I live with her until I am seventeen.

She wrote a letter before passing. She writes it on beautiful paper with her black calligraphy ink. It is days before the fever finally takes from us the finest lady Hama village had ever seen. She writes: ˙

To all my children,

Life has been a blessing to me. You are now my legacy.
Never mind my assets, the house, and the things we keep in the house. I will die owing more than I have. It is not worth any of your time to find value in any of those things. Let those things be. The villagers may take what they can. I have moved all our books to the library. The rest may rot. My obligations die with me.

When I am gone, there is no reason to stay in Hama, my children. Don't try to maintain our old home. It was a special place for us, but that time has now passed. Life cannot be as it once was. Please just go, and fly away, my young birds!
    With Love,
    Mother Du

As my foster parent, she was firm but fair. The Widow Du never treats firecrackers. Before that, my first field manual was found stored inside this very jar hidden in the Widow Du's dusty attic.

I tried not to smell the harsh chemical entering our traincar through the windows. I remember reading of spills not long ago on this area of the tracks. They say it will probably be decades before it completely clears itself away by rainwater running into the rivers. Chemicals can be both good and bad, yin and yang. Good thing we don't drink it all our lives, though. *Good thing I grew up on fresh, clean mountain springs,* I tell myself. "In Beijing, just drink the beer," is the advice my foster mother always gives me when I take these trips. Tea is meant for home. Don't trust the water in Beijing for tea.

I missed Lake Lugu already. This is just the start of a long trip north.

The H1N1 strain of bird flu started to take hold of our mountain community on that wet fall day when my train departed for Beijing. The village paths are smooth and slippery. The slipperiness is a mixture of cool weather and an algae that grew overnight. Down the dog slips. Walking toward the station, I also twist an ankle and will now have to hobble around. "Shit!" I shout out. I have the yellow letter secure in my hand as I get myself back on my feet. I see, across the road, the Hama Clockseller slips holding his bottle, and now broken glass is all around.

Someone then steps in the glass. A whole herd of goats slip, some falling into the river that flows through our little town. The shepherd is there gathering up the mess, pulling goats from the river. But before he goes on himself, he takes handfuls of dirt and spreads the textured pebbles across the stone bridge. The bridge likes the dirt it collects over the years, eventually pushing down into the edges of the riverbank. Today begins that time in local history when the people of Hama village become so extremely ill that I suppose many will wonder if this is truly the end. It will not be. I will be away, yet I am sure most of the villagers make it through fine. The old Good Doctor window, cooling down both the cough and their tempers. "There is heat in the leaves," I say to the woman who also complains of chills. I am referring to the tea leaves I put in her jar. Perhaps she caught my flu bug breathing my air yesterday and the day before. I also dig out some pills made from crushed mushrooms and put two in the passenger's callused hand. "Here," I say. "Take these right now, and I will write you a prescription of herbs to take for the next three days."

Those poor souls who dreaded conversation with other passengers. Stare ahead and look at no one? That becomes impossible when hours turn into days on a long train ride north. We talk about the taste of the water. Again and again, the same conversation. We talk about the taste of the tea.

Early on, I gave a hand-knitted sweater wrapped in red paper to a lonely old man who sat two rows away. "It was hand knitted by my sister," I say to him. He unwraps the paper and tries on the sweater. A small photograph falls to the floor. It is a picture of my foster sister, Belle. I pick up the photo, kiss it, and walk back to my seat.

The water on the train did have a metal taste. Iron? The minerals are different here in this middle region. I could never get used to the drinking water in the north. "Please hand me some tea leaves," the woman next to me says. The glass jar is stained yellow in various rings where a dark tea once rested for a time, perhaps long ago, testimony that soap is not regularly used in the washing of these vessels. We just rinse them between uses. The glass is clear but distorting. It makes my thumb look bigger than the rest of my hand as my strange fingers wrap around the side. It is an optical mismatch. When sipping from the jar, my bottom lip and unshaved chin are similarly distorted. The cap is of thin metal with a plastic seal. Words rise from the smooth glass, telling the name and place of manufacturer. They feel good under my fingertips. My mind wanders. My fingers find the words now and again. In my mind, I can follow this jar to its origin. I remember that before it becomes my tea jar it stored my gunpowder for am just a teenage boy. It is from this place the steam engine now takes me northward to Beijing.

The train ride from my home to Beijing was always a hassle, and this final trip was no different. I have trouble in the rocking toilets, spraying piss on my shoe and not flushing properly. "Fuck," I say. "Fuck this train!" I say again. Someday I swear I will only walk the land. I am not able to wash my hands properly. There is no soap. In my carriage seat all I have to keep myself sane is a two-jin bag of roasted sunflower seeds. I am constantly spitting the shells onto the floor to keep my sanity intact on the long ride. Most of the other passengers do the same. There is a blanket of shells on the floor. I fill my tea jar with hot water every half hour trying to keep warm and peeing it all out every hour like clockwork.

As my train moved toward the Forbidden City on those old steel rails, my pocket watch slowed down. Time becomes irregular and sometimes it outright stops. Is it the watch, or is it Beijing warping reality? I feel my breathing slow. I feel the heart in my chest beat more slowly. *Pat. Pat. Pat.* I massage my sore ankle.

"Thanks, friend," one passenger said to me after I defused a potentially explosive episode with a cup of my special Yin Qiao San tea. Soon everyone is back to sleep. I drum up business on the train. I find that new patients are potentially everywhere, especially in these train cars. There are those who are already sick, there are those about to become ill, and there are those like myself who are just recovering from an illness and will need medicines to regain strength. All of us need healing of some kind. For other doctors, it could be a way to make money, but my wild herbs are virtually free so I never charge very much.

At midnight, one passenger beside me began coughing and could not catch her breath. Passengers on nearby beds put pillows over their ears. When the coughing continues, they sit up and share cigarettes near the because I often bring in a suitcase full of rice wine mixed with herbs that the Emperor and I drink at each reunion. When the Emperor is drunk, a bad situation becomes worse. They have good reason to keep me away.

I was called to Beijing this time because of the great fire that destroyed his Palace of Established Happiness. Puyi fears that it may have been started by the Heavens themselves, and he requests my help to decipher what needs to be done. When I arrive, there is a great speech underway. There are ten thousand people in the square. The eunuchs alone are three thousand men. It takes this many staff to keep such an extravagant place running. The head eunuch is addressing what has been lost to the great fire. Dozens of warehouses full of treasure and art are now ash. He has lists that take forty minutes to read through piece by piece. Emperor Puyi may have been crying. I had assumed he didn't care for anything that had been lost. The proper courtesy is to look down whenever he is present, but I always look him right in the eye, and this time, to my surprise, I see his tears. A fire had burned part of his castle. Why was it started? Who is responsible? Is it people from the inside, his own eunuchs? Is it the warlords on the outside who wanted him dead? Or, did heaven indeed start the fire? Puyi interrupts the list of lost items and says, "It concerns me little what has been lost in this fire. The important thing I want you to find out is how exactly it was started. I will not allow this palace to burn away. This is my home."

For years, I took the train back to Beijing whenever the young Emperor requested my presence. He need only send a letter and I drop what I am doing and take the next train north. The latest letter rests in my hand. The contents of the letters rarely hold much meaning. The fact that a letter arrives addressed to me on imperial yellow paper is always the signal that I must return. Early on, the Council for the Greater Good arranged a regular home for me in the Himalayan Mountains of the south under the roof of a generous foster family where I try my hand at medicine as a village herbalist. It is in this little Hama village where the people eventually call me Doctor He Song (imagine that!) even though I yet. I can first brew him a pot of the Himalayan pu'er tea I have brought from my home before we get into a true conversation. I feel frustration, but do not allow it to control me. The frustration is not really directed at him for being self-centered, but instead at everything around him. I feel the weight pressing down on him from his staff and his wives and this old, old place. So, I spontaneously say, "This fire to the palace storerooms is a clear sign! It rang through the entire countryside as my train approached your holy city. Even in the high Himalayas I felt its rumble. The fire is telling us…" Pause for effect… "Don't ever blink your eyes! From this day forward, it is unlucky for any of us to blink our eyes. To blink is to die." I proclaim this as if it were now law. "This powerful omen is sent from the Fire Dragon herself in the Heavens. We must be vigilant. We must never blink!" If it were a different group of people listening, perhaps they would stay more on their toes because of my warning. But I never expect that of them. I have known these people long enough to assume they will merely be intent on keeping their own eyelids from blinking. They will become so focused on battling against their eyelids that they will become less vigilant of their surroundings. Meanwhile, I know Emperor Puyi hears nothing of what I have just said. Yet his automatic response is a firm, "Yes." That puts it into law. *Thank you, my Emperor.* I hear Empress Wan Jun cough from the adjacent room, so I am assured she and his Majesty's second wife, Wen Shu, have their ears pressed against the thin walls. The Empress Wan Jun (who you know as Elizabeth) will become so engrossed keeping her eyes open that for weeks she will not blink her eyes. Many eunuchs follow her lead. This allows me the freedom to plan Puyi's escape. I need the wives and the servants out of our hair for a period of time, and keeping them focused on this task is just the thing. A senior scholar in the palace eventually proclaims that the opposite is most certainly true: blinking will scare away the evil spirits, and our blinking habits go back to normal.

I tried to meet with Puyi in person upon my arrival, but the eunuchs intervened, insisting that the Emperor was too busy to see me. His eunuchs act as another wall. I suspect the eunuchs do not want me to see him believe in his magic and his inherent power. The eunuchs who stay on staff believe as well. His wives try to believe.

Because I helped Emperor Puyi regain his lost fingers as a child (an important event we will certainly get to), he has always regarded me as an imperial oracle, and by his teenage years, occasionally wrote to me over the thousand-mile distance between us requesting that I return to Beijing for a time to decipher various omens he and his wives found in their sheltered day-to-day life, both the good and the bad, in his ever-more reclusive Forbidden City. Some of Emperor Puyi's eunuchs encourage him to be overly cautious of the bad omens and rush these letters to me. However, other eunuchs on staff in the Forbidden City are not supportive of the Emperor reaching out to anyone on the outside, and they destroy his letters. Some letters slip through. I am always happy for the communication and for an excuse to visit my friend. I feel proud of my contribution to the Emperor's health and well-being. Deciphering omens, however, is not my calling, though I never admit it to him. I sometimes even go so far as to play with his naive trust in me when I have no idea what a true explanation might be. You see, I don't ever say I do not know. Not as a young man.

The final time I came to the palace at the Emperor's invitation, I was just recovering from the H1N1 flu, but on my arrival Emperor Puyi noticed nothing about my own poor health because his mental state of depression was so severe. *There no longer are 999 buildings*, the letter he sent to me read. The recent fire destroyed forty buildings at first count, a sickening and unlucky number. When my appointment with him finally arrives, I have so many things I want to say. I know both Empresses and his senior eunuchs are listening in on my every word from the adjoining rooms. So, I take pause. *What is the point of saying anything of substance right now?* I see as well that the Emperor is absorbed in his own thoughts and will not hear a word I say to him. His look is of a dazed and tired old man, and sad. I rushed here to Beijing, as I must, because he is Emperor and the Emperor is in great need, but he is not in any condition to listen and I will simply hail a cab to take us to the nearby train station. An hour later we will be on a train to Tianjin. I smile. Nobody will notice we are gone until long after we cross the border.

Very early that morning, the chirp of a cricket echoed over the building roofs. The air is so peaceful in this place. Still, after all that has happened to Puyi's empire, this palace air feels sacred. Of that, no one will dispute. This is indeed where the center of the universe sits.

It was the Emperor's pet cricket that gave me the plan for escape. The cricket is singing from within its small walnut cage, which causes me to wonder what would happen if I were to open its cage. Surely the cricket would venture out, but where would it go? It would hop off in search of other crickets but where would they be? The free crickets would sing to him from the open fields. The pet would follow the vibration of their song to the fields beyond.

The Emperor and I were in the drum tower looking out across the city when we decided it needed to be done. I say I can arrange it when Puyi says to me, "I yearn for freedom." I understand; he is trapped here. "The stars are right, Emperor. Let's go." His life has been that of a genie trapped in a lamp, although the lamp has many rooms. Emperor Puyi is just eighteen at this time. He already has two wives and a vast fortune. His power and wealth are all relative, though. If there is nothing on which to spend your money, what is wealth? If nobody acknowledges you as Emperor, what is power? If you do not have freedom, what is the point?

I called him Emperor, although much of modern China disputed his authority from an early age, and Emperor Puyi had long been living in a kind of fantasy, in seclusion, thinking he had a magical effect on the world that only he could see. I admittedly also believe it to be true. For instance I have seen him wish for rain. The clouds came and it did indeed rain. I

91   levon a

future attack. Emperor Puyi, his wives, and I are of the survivors from an earlier time.

The day of his escape, Emperor Puyi led everyone to believe that he was watching a film in the Hall of Supreme Harmony. It is midday. The sun shines brightly. The sky is blue. General Sun's Republican guards surround the Forbidden City walls but do not try to enter. General Sun is content to control the outside. Some of them show symptoms of the flu. Some of them have just recovered. The trick is to get past these guards.

We followed the rats out. Our plan is not what anyone will expect. We will use the rat packs as our secret collaborators. I learn that a cook had captured a docile brown rat the day before in the imperial kitchens. I now tie a collar around its neck. I have my foot on the tail and another pressed down onto his body so he cannot bite me. Now the collar is secure. "Take us to freedom," I whisper. It seems to understand. I follow the large rat, and the Emperor follows me. The rodent is as big as a Shih Tzu and tugs at his new leash. It does not like the scratchy pull of the leather so I let it out a little bit longer to about five feet, and with time, as we step into the shadows, the brown rat allows the leash's unnatural pull and ignores our presence. It wants to get away from here as much as we do. Somehow the kitchen rat has a sense or a memory leading him to where the others in his pack go during the day. That is our hope. Who knows what senses it uses. Is it smell, or is it something we have no words to describe? Immediately, we leave the bright gaze of the sun beside Longevity Kitchen and delve into the shadows. The first few passages I know well but the rat takes us to other passages in complete darkness that I never knew were here. This is when I learn that there must be at least two more levels of underground tunnels beneath the city that I have never explored before. It is as if some of these places only materialize for our sole purpose of escape and will seal up again once we pass. We travel in the pitch black for miles toward the Temple of Heaven five miles south of the palace. What luck that would be to come out in the middle of Beijing's city streets so far outside the palace wall. Puyi

CHAPTER 7

March 18, 1921

China's population is 474 million people.

The dethroned Emperor Puyi finally escaped Beijing's Forbidden City. It is the first time he leaves the palace since ascending the dragon throne as a toddler. For the past decade or more, the grounds act as more of a prison to him than a palace. He is ready to leave. Our escape plan is simple enough. There are only four known exits to the Forbidden City, and each one is heavily guarded at the outer doors by the enemy. To find that secret exit that remains unknown to all, we need to have an outside collaborator, a nonhuman. We do not tell Emperor Puyi's eunuchs or his two wives about our plan. To them, this is a normal day. They will follow us later when the coast is clear. Emperor Puyi takes my right hand and I lift him over the final wall, and we are gone.

Part of our success that day was due to a second wave of the ravaging flu that had recently killed healthy young adults around the city. The Republic's government is not concerned about the young Emperor's activities right now. Officials are instead worried about the health of their own families and themselves. This new bird flu kills its victims through a cytokine storm. An otherwise healthy immune system will overreact to fight a virus so that the body burns itself up. Sadly, this happens to one out of ten in Beijing. Their bodies burn to death trying to fight off the flu bug. The severity catches us all by surprise. Five million people die in just fifteen weeks. Everyone catches it eventually. I had caught it before. Those of us who are lucky enough to recover are then immune from any is opened with dynamite. Two dozen Kuomintang soldiers remove jewels from the cavernous rooms even before General Sun arrives. Everything is stripped down so what began as a palace looks more like the tomb it truly is. Chisels echo in the darkness. These precious jewels they take weigh on the soldiers' minds. Never before have these men touched such things. Each soldier believes he will be able to keep some of the wealth to take home, because there is more than enough for all to share. But can they trust their wives with such valuable things? Their neighbors will talk, and robbers might try to steal them. What a burden it will be to be rich.

I wet the ink, gently grinding the ink stick on a large, flat rock. The ink stick moves in slow circles. The water turns black. She does not look in my direction.

"I want a poem," Elizabeth said to me. I take out the long brush with stallion hair wrapped tight into a bamboo handle. It is wet and soaks up the ink.

"Tell me first where is the Emperor Puyi," she had first asked but I could only guess. "Isn't he with Courtesan Shu on an outing? I remember he had promised her an outing at the park."

I was a bad friend that day. "What shall I write, Empress?" I say when I enter her room. I can see there is something else on her mind.

⌐ ⌐

Where the black pearl came from was of no small consequence.

While Emperor Puyi was living in exile, the tomb of his grandmother, Empress Dowager Cixi, was broken into by a rotten Kuomintang general named Sun. The tomb sits just outside of Beijing, which is territory held by the General so he feels it is his right to pillage.

Sun thought there was a floral smell floating out from the Empress's coffin until he took hold of the back pearl. His heart beats heavy. Empress Cixi's corpse is still intact as if she had died only yesterday. In her mouth rests a massive black pearl. It was placed in her mouth at the time of her burial to prevent the body from decomposing. It pops out easily. General Sun takes up the corpse of Puyi's grandmother into his hands, stripping the body of its jewelry, and throws the old woman's body onto the floor.

The interior to Empress Cixi's tomb was finally revealed. Its entrance isn't anything unusual. I figure its lock may fit a key I saw once in the old days. The silver key used to hang from Elizabeth's thin wrist when she lived in the Forbidden City. "The box contains only keys. I like to think of the young Cixi hiding away each key, one by one, as she finds them laying around the old palace. It was a collection for her, like I collect jade. She found them on the floor or lying on tables, but that is not all. Before putting them in her box she would try to hunt down the locks to which the keys were made. She did so by patient trial and error to see which key would open which door. She had so much time on her hands, why not explore? Eventually, Cixi matched them to many of the doors in the palace. You know, Cixi came to the palace much worse off than I was. She was but one of eighteen wives to the reigning emperor at the time and was essentially his slave. Instead of giving up, she collected these keys, one at a time. I think it gave her hope." I want to know more. I can think of nothing but the keys and the box. "Cixi became a powerful empress with time," I say. "One can't help but admire her."

I cleaned up the remaining ink with my handkerchief, and she thanked me with a nod. The calligraphy ink that was still on her forearms is wiped away. I fold up the spotted handkerchief. I pack it up with my other supplies.

I was in Elizabeth's dressing room when she asked me to write some calligraphy, and then more. The rice paper I laid out is secured by beautiful jade stones on a long table. The sun is setting and through the window is a light that only comes on rare occasions. It floods onto everything in the room. I write with the brush, "If we join our hearts in this hour of gold, to the end of time our affection will hold." They are the old words of Qin Guan. She allows me to kiss her neck. I undress and give her a moment's pause. She kisses me harshly, almost as if she were going to bite. Under her breast I find a tattoo. Strange, isn't it? It is the Emperor's name there in ink, *Puyi*. "We all must have this done. It is tradition. Take me, He Song." She lies on top of the calligraphy.

from the dead to haunt him and all his descendants for failing to protect her body. Puyi says as much to me. I go to his office in The Quiet Garden to discuss what this all might mean. I say to Puyi, "Emperor, we can only suppose that this is a sign of how little power the house of Qing still has in this country, and it forebodes that it is not only your own legacy that is in peril but the legacy and graves of all the emperors and empresses."

~ ~

Elizabeth, too, would not stop blinking her eyes when she read about the raid of Cixi's tomb in the daily papers. This is about the time when Elizabeth grows so attached to her jade hand mirror that she will never let it go. Even in sleep, it remains tight in her hand.

I was left alone with Elizabeth the day before. A novel is by her bedside. "The mystery is about a murder of a beautiful movie star," she whispers to me. "The police don't know how the murderer did it, but I suspect I know how it was done. Poison! There were little bits of hidden poison in her food. The murder is a conspiracy of her family who all wanted her dead before she can turn old and age spoils her legacy. The police captain might be involved in the coverup, so the facts do not add up yet. Still, that is what I think happened. I have just ninety-seven more pages to go before I know for sure." She keeps her eyes closed and spits at the word conspiracy.

"What is happening now?" I asked because I wanted to talk, and the novel was an easy subject. She recently read some pages so will have something new to say about it.

It was an evening when we were most intimate. I try to go out. She looks to me and says, "Come here, He Song." I see the box of keys there on her dressing table. Elizabeth sees my gaze and says, "The box once belonged to the Empress Dowager Cixi. I have heard tales that she kept it in her private chambers of the Forbidden City before she consolidated her power." The box in his hand. Now Chiang will listen to Sun's ambitious military schemes. The pearl glistens in front of them as if it is wet.

~ ~

Meanwhile, I did as I was told and traveled to the Shaolin Temple for six months of training. I take the train and travel in disguise, wearing just the simple robes of a monk. It is at this ancient temple in the Himalayan Mountains where I learn the art of qigong, which will become a lifelong mantra. Puyi thought Shaolin's mysteries might be of some use to him in the years to come. It is said the monks even know how to fly and have other magical powers.

Before I departed, the Emperor said to me, "I command you to go to the Shaolin Temple on the next train. Perhaps there is magic there that we can use in our fight. Give the abbot this letter and bring me his response after your study is complete." The envelope has the waxed seal of the Emperor. Although his request comes out of the blue, it also comes as a relief. I love my life here, yet I need a break from Tianjin, I know that. I have grown envious of others who travel. I am still young and in need of new adventure.

I was not sure what Puyi had in his mind that day he sent me away. He looks out the window for long stretches of time, minutes that feel like days as the clock ticks on the wall, and I think he might jump out of that two-story window onto the concrete below. The Emperor pounds his fist on his side table, shaking his teacup. I take a sip of my green tea. Again, he hits his fist against the table. It is red with burst vessels, and he hits it again.

The desecration of his grandmother's grave greatly disturbed Puyi. Empress Dowager Cixi held power for the greater part of the nineteenth century, and she of course was the one who designated him to be the next emperor at her death. He feels now that the ghost of Cixi will come back

While we were living as expatriates in Tianjin, which was controlled by England and others for decades, the Chinese generals and warlords lived in an extravagance of their own across the border. Chinese government and the high social life of the generals and their families center around the city of Nanjing to the south. Here in the Grand Hotel in Nanjing, a large stringed orchestra plays now for an elegant ball. Many Americans are here tonight in black ties. But look over there at Madame Soong Mayling. She is everyone's darling. Madam Soong Mayling is a Christian and is college educated. What could be better? She and her husband dance the waltz with such even grace. Her gala shoes are ornamented with a large black pearl split in two. Everyone in the hall knows the story of those shoes. It is spreading through the ballroom like a grassfire. The cobbler told the story, and no one dared believe it until tonight. The shoes are a gift from her husband, Kuomintang Leader Chiang Kai-shek.

Leader Chiang had split a black pearl into two halves to have it set into the custom-made pair of high heels for Madame Soong. The heels are of the loveliest pink leather. The pearl halves are perfectly set. Lovely. There was nothing like it before.

"Thank you for this black pearl, General Sun. It is indeed Cixi's pearl. That carries great meaning. I will have it ornament the gala shoes of my Soong Mayling."

Earlier, Kuomintang General Sun Dianying held out the gigantic pearl to Kuomintang Leader Chiang Kai-shek in a silk handkerchief. Sun notices that he finally has Chiang's full attention, and that was the intention of his extravagant gift today. He may have kept the pearl for himself but he needs Chiang to accept his proposal for a strong military response against the foreign aggression to the north. Chiang is amazed by the pearl of Cixi

Those preceding weeks, I noticed scratches on doors throughout The Quiet Garden, but I did not understand the cause. Elizabeth must have tried to use her keys on all of them. It would be better that she not have them anymore, the burden. Her insanity came from other things. Perhaps it is her husband, Puyi's, favoritism of his other wife, perhaps it is the opium supplied by their friend Yoshioka. Yet, the keys are dangerous in her hands. She might stab us all in the night.

Those were hard times. Elizabeth smokes her opium-laced cigarettes while strolling the gardens with her camera. The Emperor drives up in a new car with Courtesan Shu at his side, and she snaps a photo. Elizabeth was originally from this port city of Tianjin, before she was sent to the Forbidden City in Beijing to become Empress. She loves being back here again and hates it as well. Puyi allows her to buy clothing and jewelry in excess, which makes Courtesan Shu immensely jealous. The second wife can complain all she likes. Sure, her husband will try to compensate by buying things for each, but it is never enough. Elizabeth knows that the second wife will eventually demand a divorce if pushed, so push she does. She talks this over often with Yoshioka, whom Courtesan Shu utterly detests.

There are many such stories of Wan Jun and Wen Shu, or, excuse me, I should be consistent and say the Empress Elizabeth and Courtesan Shu. Elizabeth fears bad omens most, and not being able to use her keys strikes her as such an omen. Courtesan Shu fears Elizabeth more than omens. All she really wants is to be treated equally by her husband. The Emperor does love Courtesan Shu, but does not dare give her the most attention because her nature is not as forceful as Elizabeth's. It is far easier to comply with Elizabeth at the expense of the other. And, with this tension, we all sit in The Quiet Garden. I am there, of course, to entertain the other woman.

Puyi summoned me back from the Shaolin Temple for that purpose. The one who gets left out today can be entertained by He Song. Puyi goes into the other room with one wife and leaves me here to entertain.

them. These are now mine. I take the box and its contents, and with those keys came the treasure beyond my imagination.

I will always remember the day Elizabeth hallucinated, believing she was in the Forbidden City again. We are in The Quiet Garden, our temporary palace in exile.

I remember it partly because that was the day she gave me the keys I will eventually strap to my waist. "No!" Elizabeth pushes the pile of keys toward me with her feet. To her, the keys are now spiders. "Get them away! Take them, He Song." I collect the keys into the box again. I take them away. Elizabeth will never ask for them again.

Infuriated, Elizabeth dumped the wooden box and all its contents onto the floor. Keys collide, ringing down the hallway.

She was so frustrated, and I saw the frustration building into something lethal, trying one key after another to get into her room at the The Quiet Garden. "None of them work here," she exclaims. "Damn it all." A key is jammed into the lock. It will not turn. It will not release. It is trapped in the door's lock. I say, "These are keys to the Forbidden City, my Empress. They do not work here." Elizabeth will not come to her senses. The ash from her cigarette has grown long. "Guards, call the guards!" What should I say? "Elizabeth," I protest. "The guards are not here. We have just a few servants. Let me get your husband."

Earlier she had a heated conversation with Yoshioka, but when I came into the room he slipped away. I guess he said the same to her. These imperial keys do not work in Tianjin.

When I arrived, it looked like a lion had clawed the door. Hers was an ongoing illness. The keys scrape into the wide wooden doors like claw marks.

add in purple perilla fruit. It feels like a drinking match at times. "What do you got for me today, young Doc?" He looks at the color of my potion, this time a semitransparent gold, and says, "Cheers!" I respond, "To health!" and he takes a swig from his medicine bottle.

When I first met Mr. Dingding Lee, he sold his wares on the roadside in the shade of a Camphor Laurel. At that time, on that day, long past, he has twenty watches laid out on a blue wool cloth. When I ask what time it is, Mr. Lee looks at his own watch rather than his merchandise and states the time down to the second: "It is 2:34:55…*exactly*." But that isn't correct. He's fast. Some of his clocks are unwound and stopped. All tell different times. It is hard not to stare at his face. I like him. He makes me lighthearted. He has three hairs at least eight inches long that come out from a black mole. His eyebrows are knotted and fall to the upper edges of his eyes. His nose hairs, too, are protruding, as is his silvery ear hair, and it all continues to grow as long as I know him.

⌐ ⌐

Taking the tea I poured, Elizabeth had said to me, "I trace my lineage back to the Qianlong Emperor. He was the sixth Emperor of the Qing, born in 1711." Elizabeth talks of those times as if dragons still roamed the land and emperors could move the stars. Her eyes look sleepy. The tea is having a calming affect on her. Pity it does not last. She looks up from her teacup and she spits. She spits and blinks at whatever she thinks is unlucky.

I took the keys, one by one, and placed them back into the wooden box. The dragon key is there. There are large iron keys familiar to me from my time in the Forbidden City. There are keys to the secret chambers where Puyi and I had played hide-and-seek as kids. *There are keys to the storerooms. What an amazing collection this is.* What good are they now? I see why Elizabeth casts them away. Good for her to get rid of this weight. I will take

Years earlier, but still in Tianjin, I looked up at the clock on my wall. It is the clock I purchased from Mr. Lee. That clock has an attitude of its own! It rings at odd times. It either speeds up or will stop. *Hasn't it been 4:00 p.m. for a long time?* I look out the window, and there is a bright moon and stars.

Let us go back a few more years, when I healed the Tianjin Clockseller. This is why he calls me Doc. I am, after all, a herbalist.

Mr. Lee did as I prescribed, left town and returned anew. He returns to Tianjin with amazing new clocks nobody has ever seen before. Mr. Lee is still as sensitive as ever to the tree pollen in the air, but with such better things to sell, he is happier now and gets by. He sells his wares so well, he quickly moves from the street corner into a rented showroom. The annual trip abroad will become routine. He plans to go during the most heavy pollen season, leaving the shop to his wife and kids, and he will take long excursions during this time to build up his supply. He goes to the Middle East and perhaps as far as Istanbul.

His problem was midsummer allergies, before he started to travel. When a person is allergic to the environment around him, he must change his environment. That is exactly what I tell him as his doctor. His nose drips onto his mat of watches. How pathetic he looks. Only the poor and homeless bother to look at him and his things, and they are not customers. I prescribe a vacation.

I provided him with herbal remedies before he took my good advice. The prescription numbs the body to the environment, with liquored medicine and yellow mushrooms. During his highs, he is deadpan philosophic. During other times, he is quiet. But is that the best prescription? The real prescription ought to engage the body, to fire it up, and fight back. I try that approach for a while. Each day I actively give him stronger, more potent brews, such as the arrow shaft yellow hemp tonic. The effect is less than satisfactory, so I make no profit with customers like you. Goodbye, sir." And he falls back into his open-eyed sleep until the potential customer leaves empty-handed.

~ ~

The Empresses and their Emperor had such a strange relationship in Tianjin. Elizabeth demanded total attention. "I was just going out for a drink with her, darling," he would beg, and she would cut him off saying, "I know you gave her that jade pin. Where is mine?" He huffs back, "Of course, I have one for you as well, my sweet Empress," and he pulls out a pin almost identical to the one he had recently given Courtesan Shu. She softens immediately and melts into his arms. He kisses her. "Empress," he says. "I feel that I don't make a real impact on the world." She looks in his eyes and replies, "Most people don't impact the world, your Majesty. I don't feel my life makes a real difference on the world day-to-day." The Emperor stops wallowing in his self-pity and looks at her fine cheekbones, strokes that young white skin, and says to her, "Empress, you make a difference to me each day."

The three of them somehow found ways to get along under that single roof, but it could not last. "Why are you crying?" asks the Emperor to his lesser wife. She says she is just blue today. "Blue as the sky." He pulls out a stunning jade hairpin. "This, darling, is just for you. Your happiness is my happiness. Don't cry."

Alone in her room, the Courtesan Shu was thinking about her life here, and of her past life as his Majesty's second, but more lovely, wife Wen Shu, living in the Middle Kingdom's capital. She so misses the palace. If only that past could be her reality today. The day-to-day of Tianjin feels fake. She refuses to live in the moment. She doesn't know why. It is only the memories of the Forbidden City that feel real to her now. She must find a way to make life feel real again.

watches were often art deco and filled with rubies and dozens of diamonds. They are eighteen-karat gold with thick, soft gold chains that hang loosely like scarves on their wrists.

The Emperor preferred pocket watches before moving to Tianjin, but now we are all on the wristwatch craze. I carry a pocket watch as well for sentimental reasons, but there is always a watch on my wrist for show.

When I entered the store that morning, the talk began. I love the showcase of faces lined up in front of me, behind clean glass. He says, "Emperor Puyi might be excited about this Swiss Minerva Chronograph. Please, you can take it for him to try on his wrist. No need to pay now, just take it. It is something truly unique. There is a stopwatch inside the chronograph. He could use it at the horse races." I am eyeing a Gruen tank-style watch in the case. The hands are painted with a luminous green for telling the time at night. How modern! Mr. Lee goes through his list, saying, "Let's see here, Doc. The Rolex is done. It works like a charm now. The wives' Omega and Tudor still need some work. Come back later this week for those."

When any customer bought a clock, Mr. Lee made reassurances about the quality as he wound the back. He pulls up his sleeves and adjusts the hands, and shines up the glass with nice linen. The curious passersby without an appointment must wake him up to make a purchase. Even when his eyes are open, he is half asleep. At first he refuses to acknowledge the customer's desire for a purchase. It takes some prodding on behalf of the buyer to look into his backroom stock. "I will not sell. That one is not for sale," Mr. Lee will say. For something that surely has less value, he often says, "I cannot accept such a low price. That's ridiculous. Go away!" And then, "Tell me, son, you can go all the way to London and get a clock exactly the same as mine at a higher price. Plus, let's see, add five for transportation. And the extra hassle. I changed my mind. My new selling price is five more yuan than before." I remember when I was that customer. Am I a fool? Yet, I want what he sells. He knows this and insists, "I will a problem for many years. He still doesn't remember my name, so he just calls me "Doc," but he registers my face and knows my close acquaintance with the imperial family.

Mr. Lee said to me, "I am here for your business, Doc. Seven days a week, day or night. I never take a holiday." He winks at me. We both know this is not true. His success comes in part because he does take holidays. His voice is a color: dark red cherry, very near black and sometimes slightly violet. The volume of his voice is always three notches below what is usually considered normal.

I dismissed his gossip. He pries by saying, "I heard from the staff that Empress Elizabeth found out about that stunning Bulova for the Courtesan." I convey no information on my face. "He will just give the watch to Elizabeth instead," I say. I check my pocket watch. "It seems this one slows down on me and skips an hour every couple days. Can you take a look at it, Mr. Lee?"

He and I had the normal disagreement about quality before that. The Clockseller disagrees with me, saying "My wares are the most beautiful timepieces on the continent. You find me something more lovely." Tugging on his mustache, he says, "Is there anything else, Doc?"

Every visit, usually before money exchanged hands, I made a point to tell him that, "I feel I am often returning your clocks to you to fix again and again. Not that I mind your company, Mr. Lee. You are an amusing man. Your watches, though, are not of the best quality." His daughters, Summer and Mercy, walk into the room eating ice cream.

Mr. Lee's eyes sparkled. He knows we cannot resist his wares. His eyes are wet and ever twinkling, even when gazing forward. The lobes of his ears sink down like heavy dewdrops, stretching his ears to an enormous size. It is not the time keeping we are buying from him. It is the art. The wives' down to the smallest parts, fully disassembling and reassembling it gear by gear, before ever going so far as considering a refund to a customer. Yet despite all his tune-ups, oiling of gears, replacements, and the months upon months of back and forth from the shop, he never gets them running completely right. The clocks themselves are always so stunning that you cannot let them go after you buy them. The time isn't exact. Sure, there is a good argument against keeping it, but I remain a loyal customer. The clock is so lovely anyway, hanging there on the wall or on my wrist. What's a few minutes difference, here and there?

Mr. Lee was born with teeth. That's true. Everything about Mr. Lee is slightly ahead of schedule. I suppose someone who is truly unbiased would categorize Mr. Lee as one of the bad guys in this city's underworld, but his maverick nature is mostly due to timing rather than choice. He just doesn't fit in properly in the 1930s, and I suppose our long acquaintance didn't help his karma, although, I daresay it did help his career. Where have all the good watchmakers gone in the world? As kids we were told that Confucian expression, "Lee is everything." In the ancient world, that beautifully simple word "Lee" meant something like "the ritual of living daily life" or "the tradition you hold on to for grounding." That is no longer the case that we need ritual and traditions in our lives, you and I tell ourselves. There is no such thing as "Lee" anymore. Yet we yearn for his timepieces.

The lazy Clockseller's oldest daughter, Mercy, was always a little pushy. She is able to sell me a diamond watch that doesn't run with ease, and I am still convinced that it is a good purchase.

The second daughter, Summer, was never paying attention to what goes on in the shop. She gives you the fifteen dollars in change if she remembers, and may give it to you twice if she remembers it twice. Her mind is a thousand miles away.

The lazy Clockseller, Mr. Lee, was forgetful as well, and this has been

"Hop in," the Emperor had said to me. He sees me across the street. He waves me over. "Join us for an early boat ride in the park? I will be meeting my wives there. Come on!"

"Well look at that ride!" I called out to Emperor Puyi as I saw him pulling up across the street from the old Clockseller's shop. He is wearing a color of scarf that matches his new red Ford model 20. It looks like lightning. I immediately fancy he might say, "I'll give you this car, no really, I mean it, He Song, because next week the Japanese will present us with another Alfa Romeo 8C and there won't be space for it all at the gardens." It wouldn't be the first or last extravagance I received. He doesn't say that though. I just get in.

I heard the purr of the motor before I saw the car.

That morning I went to the Tianjin Clockseller to pick up a diamond Rolex for Emperor Puyi. Outside, cherry blossom petals fall to the ground like snowflakes. I shout goodbye to our good friend, Mr. Lee. I will not wait for him to do the proper courtesy of saying good-bye face-to-face. We just shout through the door. He knows I will be back soon enough. I have the Rolex that he repaired. Mr. Lee's daughter, Summer, is tracing letters on the outside doorstep.

The lazy Clockseller, Mr. Lee, what is there to say about him?

He was one of my first friends in this unusual city. Most customers see one of his clocks or watches around town before ever meeting the man behind it. The timepieces he restores are like nothing you could find anywhere else in China. But these clocks personify the man, Mr. Lee. The wall clock that hangs in my own home is ten minutes fast. No surprise there. I will try adjusting it, but it always settles into this pace. You'd demand a refund from Mr. Lee, but he will just smile and convince you to accept a free repair. He would in fact be keen to fix the clockwork inside, plain cinnamon aroma. There is a hovering fragrance of oak moss mixed with a caramel buttery musk, yet it all smells fresh and clean. It tingles the nose. He doesn't smell of the dead emperors of yesterday, but maybe that is just the illusion of his perfume. Underneath the perfume is the scent of his breath. It is as complex as his diet. The exhale smells like a vegetarian, but not plain. It is full of the variety of spices, sauces, and precious vegetables that few can afford. Then the wind blows that all away and there is just the smell of plum blossom pollen.

Elizabeth captured close-ups of the petals with her camera before they touched ground or lake, while they were floating on the invisible air, and she admired their gracefulness on this March day. Focus the long lens. *Snap, snap, snap.* Yes, gravity wins in the end. Yes, the color is gone, the flowers themselves pulled apart, but the petals will fall at their own gentle pace and with grace. I am there to paddle the boat through the water. Cherry blossom petals or plum blossom petals, whatever they may be, encircle my currents in the lake water. Petals grab the oar.

In our boat, we might as well be the subjects of an oil painting. The women are stunning in their spring attire. I am dressed far less fashionably than the Emperor, but my clothes are all new and fine. They fit me well.

Earlier that day, we drove around town in a red sports car like we were conquerors. Wind blows against my hair and pushes into my ears. I cannot hear anything but the wind. Pedestrians on the street stare open mouthed as they do. Motorists and bus drivers try to keep up with our faster engine. We are not inconspicuous in Tianjin. During these days, Yoshioka often makes offhanded comments that build on Puyi's fear that he could be assassinated by Chinese nationalists. Although these words do in the quiet of night gain substance, they have no effect on him out here on the road in the sun. Here we both feel invincible. Emperor Puyi, for all his riches, never had this freedom in the Forbidden City.

and Wan many times back and forth. Two wives create too much confusion as it is. When we had the administrative structure of a thousand eunuchs to assist his Highness and the space of 9,999 rooms at our disposal to coordinate and distance the wives back in Beijing, then yes, back then we could keep track of the proper names and titles, and the difference of Wan and Wen was always as clear as day. In contrast, this life here in Tianjin demands breaking away from much of that old ritual, as Elizabeth so often argues must be so. Informality is the way, you might say now. Yes, we will call her Courtesan Shu. This woman looks on me with the compassionate eyes I remember of my birth mother. She is a good woman. I sometimes wonder whether my mother might have been about the age Courtesan Shu is today back at that time long since past when she let me go off to Beijing.

It was earlier in the year, springtime, that I remember us all out in a white cedar paddleboat at the city park. This is before Courtesan Shu leaves him, so both women are in the paddleboat beside Emperor Puyi. Petals from the trees float on the surface of the water.

There were great banks of flower petals on the grass, freshly fallen from the plum trees. They stick softly to our shoes on the docks. Our footprints are apparent because the petals have been pressed down and pushed to the side. I find it sad that they are no longer holding color. They are faded white and just a petal upon a petal. The flowers they once were, that covered each tree last week, didn't stay together. That was temporary. Their purpose has been served so fruit might come. It is the springtime snow. Yoshioka has a beautiful word for this: Sakara.

"Plum blossom petals," Elizabeth corrected him. Puyi laughs and holds Courtesan Shu tightly.

Courtesan Shu exclaimed, "Oh, the cherry blossom petals are falling to the ground like snow! The pollen is so sweet." The four of us take a breath, and Puyi's complex smells dominate those of his wives, let alone my

What other stories do I want to tell you of Tianjin? There are so many good memories of these eight splendid years.

You see, none of us realized at the time that we were selling our souls, piece by piece, to the Japanese occupation. Part of me is glad I did not know it then. I don't know what that means about my soul to still feel this way, being grateful of my ignorance. It is an evil, no doubt. Does it mean I would live it all the same way again knowing what I know today? No, of course not. I would not make the same choices if I were to live it all again.

Yes, I want to be true in what I say to you, and that makes me contradict my present day self. What I want to say here is this. It was ignorance of consequences that allowed me to enjoy myself so very much. Puyi is a wealthy man without a cause. There are many like him during these decades of excess. They yearn for a purpose and deeply desire the power once promised to them. Meanwhile, the Emperor has a complicated family life, which needs further explanation. Back in the day when Emperor Puyi was young and still living in the Forbidden City in Beijing, his eunuch council strongly encouraged him to marry two wives at once. One woman is a beauty. She is about his age and bold. She rarely displays the good manners of a proper Chinese lady, which was a breath of fresh air at the time. This is Elizabeth.

The second woman was not that lovely, in my opinion, but five years younger than Elizabeth and the one woman I dare to say Emperor Puyi truly loved. Their love is of that heated and passionate sort as we will define love to be in modern day. This second wife is kind to him, but ironically she is the wife who leaves him first because she cannot stand being second to Elizabeth. This second wife goes by many names, and I think the most appropriate of them all in this particular place and time is "the Courtesan Shu." Let us call her that for now. I suppose I could use the wives' common names in this chapter. They are Wen Shu and Wan Jun, so it would be Empresses Wen and Wan. I fear I would confuse myself, and probably you, saying Empresses Wen when our empire has been weak, which happens every couple of centuries, so too have all the other countries around us faced great hardship." If the Empress were to interject here saying, "But look at you, Puyi. Your dress, the amusement park we call our palace, and your lovely Empress (with a curtsy she took from the movies), it is nothing like the old China we lived in," Puyi would yet insist, "Not true! These are just styles of the times. They come into China and flow out again like the wind. I am talking about bigger things like the pull of gravity and the heat of the sun." Yoshioka and I have heard the preaching many times before.

I believed him. I agree with Emperor Puyi. China is something of a foundational stone. Yoshioka sees it differently, though he will never say so. I know that, to him, China is the setting sun. His nation, headed by Emperor Hirohito, is the land of the rising sun. That is the essence of their flag. It is a mockery of China.

Elizabeth's baby was murdered by the Japanese Army shortly after its birth in a secret clinic in Tianjin. This all happens out of sight of the Emperor, because he and I are traveling in Japan (for our first time). I don't think Emperor Puyi ever finds out about his wife's illegitimate child. It was not his child, so Elizabeth claims. The father's identity is never validated, although the staff has their suspicions.

For this problem, Elizabeth went to Yoshioka for help, as we all did. He always listens. Yoshioka has huge resources at his disposal to solve any problem. He promises Elizabeth that everything will be taken care of in secret. It will be easily resolved. Emperor Puyi will be kept away for the remaining term of her pregnancy. "Your baby will be adopted by a family in the outskirts of Japan, perhaps Kyushu. No one will ever know. Now, let's never speak of it again."

~ ~

a French word. Elizabeth whispers it in the valet's ear. He says it to the doorman.

Before we went to the club that night, we had a late second dinner at a newly opened restaurant. Because of the French theme for our evening, Emperor Puyi decides to try this three-star Michelin-rated restaurant. Yes, Tianjin has it all. There is so much buzz about its chef of late. He is a Parisian Jew who chose to relocate here in our town.

In the restaurant, a phonograph played the song "I'll be Home For Christmas" again and again. It strikes that bittersweet note at its end as Bing Crosby sings "if only in my dreams." For me, that final part can bring tears. I sing the lyrics, and the others join in. I don't understand the words. I just mimic the sounds. I think perhaps it is a song about love.

Puyi was frustrated over something and went outside for fresh air and a smoke, leaving us there to conspire. Elizabeth, Yoshioka, and I remain at the table. Elizabeth ignores me when she asks Yoshioka, "Give me a light, Yoshi. How is my daughter?" Yoshioka smiles politely. "Hush, Empress," he says. "You must never talk of the baby. She is being taken care of with the utmost love, I assure you. Her every wish is being seen to, as she deserves. You endanger us all to speak of it further." He lies through his teeth. What would lying Yoshioka not say? In reality, Elizabeth's baby is already dead. Elizabeth doesn't know this. I don't think she will ever know for sure.

Before Puyi left the table, he sipped on a fizzy cocktail while talking to us about his view of China today. He tells us what China is to him and what he wants it to become. "The question I face, the question I will face when my reign is reestablished, is not *whether* China will lead, but *how* we will lead, not just to secure our own peace and prosperity but also to try to extend peace and prosperity around the globe. Now, this question isn't new." He says, "The world is not changing as people say. I believe the big noses outside our borders always needed a strong China in the past, and trends, gossip, and luxury of any of the best cities in the world. In our minds, we are in London, New York, and Milan. Off the ocean breeze we can smell the mist of the upcoming war. You see, the war has not yet started although there are signs. Tianjin has trading ships in its ports that carry people of every nation and circumstance, going here and there, shifting continents and escaping hard times, each with stories and songs to share or intrigues and goods to sell. One of the midnight parties we attend encourages us to dress in Parisian style. For the occasion, we pull out our foreign cigarettes, stylish hats, and black scarves. There is a big band set up in the main room of the club, and they play this new sound they call American Swing. Elizabeth gets up on the stage after more than a couple blue martinis and plays a decent version of Glenn Miller's "In the Mood" by memory. The piano is not quite in tune, but it gives a flatness to the song for my ear that I will forever appreciate. I hear it now. Four bandits around a table. We are all in the mood for entertainment and escape, excitement and perhaps war. Perhaps the whole world is in the mood for war.

There in that club, earlier in the evening, I saw Empress Elizabeth look past Puyi to another man in the smoky haze of the club. She makes friends easily these days. He smiles. She looks away.

Those rowdy graduate students have finally gone. The table is empty now. Maybe it is my mistake and they were never there. No insults were ever said. *They probably never sat there,* I think.

I thought I saw a table of college students making jokes. They are dressed in Parisian style for the party and must be the children of wealthy businessmen, the type that are reckless with their tongues. Was that chiding in our direction and then the word, *Wen,* the name of Puyi's second wife? *Horrible to say such things here. We should leave.* There is laughter.

A secret password was needed to enter this place. The password is need my assistance to interpret it. The servant takes them off intending merely to not dirty his highness's bedroom floor, not possibly knowing the confusion that will transpire (the universe will tremble and shake on this day!). It is only when this servant's chores are done and he asks around about his missing pair of socks that eventually, after a full half hour, we all come to the unfortunate discovery. Perhaps, though, Empress Elizabeth knows of the mistake long before the rest of us, watching with her back turned, holding her pearled jade hand mirror angled just right. She is always a few steps ahead of us.

~ ~

While Puyi lived in Tianjin, watching his world slip away, I offered to help where I could. Empress Elizabeth appears, in some respects, unaware of what happens in this makeshift palace. She certainly puts no effort into the rituals of the imperial family, but I sometimes question the truth of her surface. I begin to believe it is all an act. I believe she has a fierce intelligence. If I am right, then I could only guess at her motives for acting so oblivious and indiscreet. For instance, there has never been a time, not once, when Elizabeth did not discover a new outfit or toy Puyi purchased, for himself or others, and with the greatest speed Elizabeth would turn this information to her own advantage. Elizabeth is careless on the surface but cunning on the inside.

The Empress was the only woman in the household at this stage. There are signs that she, too, is slipping away from the Emperor. She will leave him. Puyi's other wife, what we call his "lesser wife," or "second wife," has already divorced him and is now a schoolteacher. That is a sad, complicated love story that we will get to shortly, as I myself played a small part in the matter.

Besides the exotic trips to Japan, we all kept busy being exotic right here in the port city of Tianjin. We feel we have access to all the culture, breakfast (egg-white quiche) and a hefty lunch (spicy vegetarian duck stir-fry with leeks and saffron rice) flooding it all down onto the freshly waxed floor before his feet. His utter revulsion prevents him from stripping the silk socks from his feet. He can't even breathe. Some of us are laughing, sure enough, but out of sight. The squint of my eyes is all that would betray my inner laughter. I want Puyi to succeed as Emperor, and as I said, he is my best friend, yet humbling him also brings me great joy. The puke, though, that goes too far. I quickly prepare some herbs to settle his stomach.

Puyi sat there lounging in one of the library rooms of The Quiet Garden when his senior staff, a former eunuch, approached him to take off his socks but is rebuffed by the absurdity of it. A servant dare not ask an emperor to reveal his toes to everyone in the room. The situation forces the ex-eunuch to explain the entire embarrassing circumstance. "It turns out these socks here on your holy toes were in fact brought to The Quiet Garden this morning on the feet of one of your new cleaning staff. A young local from Tianjin took off his socks, these socks, while cleaning your dressing room, and unfortunately. . . . It is difficult to comprehend how this happened. The socks somehow became mixed in with the fresh clothing prepared for you by your dressing servant today. My pardon, Emperor, please allow me to remove them from your feet."

I may have not said before how very particular Emperor Puyi once was about who looked at him and when, or how very particular he was about being touched, even by his own family, or how very particular he was about the context in which his name was spoken, whether it has been given all the proper titles, the correct tone, and due respect. Needless to say, wearing another man's dirty clothes, and most particularly his *dirty socks,* is without a doubt the most degrading thing that could befall an emperor. At least that is how Emperor Puyi will view the situation, with a warped perception of his current place in the world.

Wearing another man's socks was a bad omen. Poor Puyi would not the Chinese name, Wan Jun, given to her by her parents during Empress Dowager Cixi's reign ages ago. Elizabeth, the person, is of course Chinese to the core, however much her persona denies it. Her parents had traced her lineage back to our Qianlong Emperor of the 1700s. That emperor reigned strong for a good seventy years! It was a golden time. If only Elizabeth had children, with the blood of two great dynasties intertwined, what would they have become? I can only guess that they'd have put a mark of their own on this world.

Before hosting the Japanese delegations in Tianjin, Emperor Puyi and I have traveled together to Kyoto on two occasions. The respect we receive in Japan is flawless. Puyi feels royal again, and I am astounded by all the gifts. On our arrival, the Emperor Hirohito personally comes to the docks to welcome Emperor Puyi and gives him a banquet that rivals anything in history. This is when Puyi's second wife leaves him. She sees what we choose not to see.

We did have fun those years in Tianjin, especially before the noose of Japanese politics tightened around our necks. Even Emperor Puyi didn't take things too seriously. I remember an incident before our departure to Tokyo that could have been ominous, but was just an occasion to laugh at ourselves, in spite of Puyi's sad state of affairs as Emperor in exile. I suspect Elizabeth played a role in it all from behind the scenes. Either way, the servant's socks were probably the reason Puyi insists on taking me along on his second trip to Tokyo. He expects more bad omens that will need immediate analysis.

Socks? Yes. I will explain.

When Emperor Puyi found out about the "Catastrophe of Socks," or so it will be later called by Elizabeth, Puyi immediately puked out his entire

levon a

heavens themselves that talk to me. The stars are the survivors of the ages. You might be their messenger and will give me their good council."

As we drank our fiery liquor and played cards together, Puyi asked me for this divination. We are outdoors and the stars powder the midnight sky. It will be the last fortune I divine for my Emperor in this lifetime. For these many years as his personal herbalist, I have advised Puyi on my interpretations of many odd things that he or his wives might take as a sign from the heavens. Sometimes it is as common as a bird falling from the sky. Other times it is an accidental misfortune. An example is when he mistakenly put on the dress socks of his servant. "What does it mean? Is it a sign? It might be, right? It feels like a sign in my gut." But it is a different type of divination on this night. It is pure astrology. I see Emperor Puyi look over at Yoshioka in the corner of the garden. Yoshioka appears not to be paying attention to our conversation. Perhaps he is asleep from drink.

～ ～ ～ ～ ～ ～ ～ ～ ～ ～ ～ ～ ～ ～ ～ ～ ～ ～ ～ ～

Before he removed my heart, I gave Emperor Puyi council as a loyal servant and his herbalist. We will proceed now before his betrayal. Prince Chichibu, who is the brother of the Emperor of Japan, visits Puyi in Tianjin. The Japanese Prince is here on behalf of Emperor Hirohito to award Emperor Puyi with the Japanese Cordon of the Chrysanthemum. It is a great honor to their people. To our Empress, Elizabeth, Prince Chichibu bestows the Order of the Crown.

Puyi's fashionable Empress Wan Jun insisted that everyone refer to her by an English name, Elizabeth, while she lived in exile. As Puyi's servant, I always submit to her requests, no matter how petty or outrageous they might seem to me. Who am I to know the bigger picture of things? I have been put here simply to serve. Smoking her cigarettes that have opium mixed in dark tobacco, the Empress says to me on many occasions that the name Elizabeth fits her so much better in the modern day than in the open-air courtyard looking at the stars. They gleam and glisten. Meteors dance before burning into the atmosphere. Planets sparkle. The stars toy with me, their many messages from another age only now arriving to Earth. *Have I interpreted them properly, Puyi?*

He asked me for a divination, so I took my script from those stars. "Tell me more," says the Emperor. "Look there," I reply. "Venus has finished its eight-year cycle today," I say to Emperor Puyi. It has been evident throughout the ages that events in the sky directly impact events on the ground. In my form of astrology, I always divide the night's sky into five palaces: the north, the south, the east, the west, and the centermost region of the sky. The sky's central palace belongs to the Emperor. I say, "To the North crawls the black tortoise. To the East soars the blue dragon, and out of his jaws comes the planet Venus. I see the red bird longing for its gold, but Venus now enters your palace, my Emperor, and the white tiger is there and ready to protect you. I would say you have watched events unfold for long enough. The world is crying out for your leadership. I hear it in the twinkling of the stars. They are ringing out for you. And, there is no doubt that planet Venus has crossed into your palace again.

"Who's to say whether those faraway stars I see today have survived? Only time will tell. We are looking at them in the far distant past, as you well know, my Emperor. It takes billions of years for their light to reach us, so the messages they give today were decided long ago. I understand what you ask of me, and I respect your keen interest in astrology. Your Highness, I will interpret as best I can."

The Emperor fiddled with his diamond rings and gold when he asked me, "Tell me what you see up there. As Emperor, I know what I know. Don't be mistaken, I am not misconceived that you, He Song, are little more than a simple charlatan. I do not place great weight in your astrological interpretations, but I do ask you to speak now because… frankly, I sense when you speak that it is not just your voice I hear but the

We sat in the courtyard of Puyi's temporary palace called The Quiet Garden. The Emperor has a diamond pin in his tie. He wears a western-cut suit with diamond cuff links. On his hand are the largest diamond rings I will ever see. Sitting on his noble face are fashionable German Zeiss eyeglasses. I smell cologne. There are three Alsatian dogs lounging around beside him in the garden as we talk.

The Quiet Garden was secured in the Japanese sector of this port city, which was his refuge. The Empress lives here with him. It is not far from Beijing. The city is less than one hundred miles from his old home, but it is a world away. We are not under the control of the Chinese warlords, for one thing. This is international land ceded to foreign powers long ago.

The fountains in the Garden pattered their songs as we spoke of big plans. It sounds like a stream. White feathery flowers with deep yellow centers grow thick around the garden's central fountain. Tasteful patches of bleeding heart bushes frame the yellow flowers just right. The Emperor employs a fine gardener here. The servants are fewer in number than in the Forbidden City, but the quality of life here is fine in all respects.

He responded to what the stars appeared to say. Emperor Puyi sighs as if expressing his opinions takes great effort. Softly, so I need to strain to hear each word, he says, "Ah, He Song. The stars do not lie, but it is difficult to act. I will miss the ease of this lifestyle we have today. The essential element of my life from the Forbidden City is preserved so nicely here while I have none of those cares of running an empire. Secretly, between you and me, I even find the flush toilets and central heating far more comfortable than the Mind-Nurturing Palace back home!"

It has been eight long years in this foreign-style, two-story building. All that time we are watching Puyi's world slip away. He thinks he has maintained his dignity, but that is his own self-deception. Even I do not believe his dignity has been preserved here. Action is needed now. We are is Japan's attaché to the imperial household. I have grown accustomed to seeing him beside Emperor Puyi these past years. He is the embodiment of Japan's control over our Emperor.

~ ~

The week before they took my heart, Emperor Puyi and I had talked to each other late into the night, playing cards. I am excited for his new prospects, and I am eager to help the Council for the Greater Good implement his bold plans. Japan's best surgeons have secretly made it into the city, he informs me at last. They believe they can use healthy tissues of another man to cure Puyi of his declining condition. Once he wields a stronger body, the Japanese Emperor has promised Emperor Puyi in writing that he may indeed become the figurehead of the Japanese occupation in China. He will be Emperor of Manchuria, and if things go well in this war, he may become Emperor of all of China once again. "Time is of the essence, I suppose," says Emperor Puyi.

While looking down at my flawed hand earlier that night, I said to Emperor Puyi, "Your Highness, I wish I could be of better service to you." I am distraught over his illness, but I cannot conceive it possible that he would ever die. I bow to him as I say this, hitting my head against the ground three times as is the tradition. His life here in Tianjin is nothing like what it was in Beijing, and yet I feel that the two of us have grown closer during his fall from power. Although, of course our adult relationship will never be what it once was when we were boys. I will never call him "friend" aloud, because that would surely offend the god-man, even while I secretly think of him as my best friend and part of me still does to this day. The Emperor looks toward me but not in my eyes when he says, "He Song, you have been useful to me in times of need. You are a dutiful subject to your Emperor. You serve China well." We drink rice wine together out of silver cups.

The previous day, the head of the Council stood from his auditorium platform in the basement of a Swiss-style resort villa and addressed me. Looking down toward me but not really looking into my face, this powerful and mysterious man says, "He Song, you are doing a great service to the empire. This is truly the greatest honor that we could ever bestow." He says the words in the clearest of articulation and with great authority. Heads in the room all nod in agreement. I am the one.

I was there in front of the Council wearing just a flimsy medical gown. They examine me from head to toe. The members of the Council for the Greater Good are still mostly eunuchs that served this emperor or emperors of the past. The doctors remove my robe to measure and prod at every part of my body as I stand there in front of the Council. A large spotlight shines on me, which provides some warmth at least.

I shivered because I was nervous. Yoshioka asks me to stand behind a full-body X-ray machine so the Council can see each of my bones and organs for themselves. Wires are attached to my chest so that over the loud speakers of the conference room we can hear the solid rhythm of my heartbeat. The heartbeat is fast and strong. They all listen to it for a flutter or inconsistency. My heart continues to beat fast and strong.

"This is the donor we have discussed," said Yoshioka.

The Japanese doctors were standing in the front of the meeting room by the podium explaining something about the Emperor Puyi's failing health, but they take down the charts they were reviewing as I enter. A hush fills the room. I feel a cold breeze over my body. My medical gown is light, and I wear no undergarments or shoes.

I waited backstage, still eager to be of service to my Emperor, but unsure that the CGG would find me good enough to be of any real help. "We are ready for you now," Yoshioka says to me in the staging area. Yoshioka all. Emperor Puyi recovers well from his earlier surgery. His old heart had failed him months before while brokering the deal with the Japanese. The new heart beats strong, and the doctors expect him to live for many more years.

When the Council for the Greater Good convened, they voted unanimously to proceed with the experimental heart transplant to extend the life of Emperor Puyi and elected me to become the organ donor. I am left on the operating table to die. I remember waking up in a dark room strapped to a bloody operating table, left for dead.

The surgery was performed in the coastal city of Tianjin. My body is alive but something about me changes. I realize I cannot die. There is something about my face that is new as well, though that will take me longer to discover. I no longer age. I am angry as I struggle with the straps of the operating table. Had I not guessed this would all end in this way, just as it had once before? History repeats itself. Your friends who disappointed you once will disappear again after they obtain what they need. Why did I expect the Emperor would keep his childhood friendship with an orphan boy? Why would an emperor trust a self-taught medicine man like me? I was fooled by Emperor Puyi, and by the whole CGG, into believing that I am important to them. They needed my heart. That is all. Now they have all gone across the border, whisked off to Xin Jing (they are literally calling it "The New Capital") where Emperor Puyi will sit on his throne until Beijing is taken again. I see that one of the Japanese doctors left his military jacket hung by the operating room door. The door is left open. I will leave this place. I will go back to my apartment, pack up a satchel with some provisions and my ring of keys, and go.

⌁ ⌁

I don't remember anything of the surgery itself. It must have taken many hours. My beating heart is removed, and my chest is stitched back together.

CHAPTER 8

May 5, 1934

China's population is 499 million people.

You may wonder how we could delve so deeply into He Song's mind and know so much about the many characters surrounding this man over the century. It is, of course, because I am He Song.

You do not believe me now? How could you stop here, Dear Reader, when we are nearly done? As your narrator, I have already accomplished my main goal. You must now see me for what I am and not just what I became. As narrator I have deceived you thus far to help you understand the greater evils in my actions because there were choices, but we need not prolong the deceit. If you wish while knowing it is me, the villain, telling you the tale to still continue to read the rest of *levon a* to its inception, I am more confident that you can do so without discounting the complexity of all of our decisions and motivations. This is because you, too, have changed. Mankind's life outside of Eden is a complex one. If I were given a choice, I would stand by Eve and eat that forbidden apple once again. Why? I know there is beauty and meaning and significance in the complexity of our lives on earth. Otherwise, we are just animals. I prefer us to be human.

Perhaps our Chinese Emperor Puyi allied with Japanese Emperor Hirohito's army as the only way he saw to regain his throne. It is his last-ditch effort, but with Japanese aid, Emperor Puyi quickly regains some of his former empire in 1934, and he sits on a new throne in one of the Chinese northern territories already conquered by the Japanese. It looks like he might win after officers stop using the term "Prisoner of War" altogether. I witness the results of that change in vocabulary when I am in Nanjing. This is when I change the way of telling my own story. This is my story.

And so, who am I, your narrator of this tour back in time? I am He Song.

levon a

I want to add just a final comment about that baby girl, and then we will be done with it. In the months before her family's massacre, her two older sisters begin trying out names, seeing what might fit her curious personality best. Blue Heron Ha is one of the possibilities. She is beginning to eat a bowl of rice in the morning and can drink a full bottle of tofu milk by midday while sitting on her oldest sister's lap. Her hair is thick and often tied back with a silk bow. She has a favorite red dress.

She wouldn't ever go to sleep without her doll and a kiss from her mother. She sucks in her cheeks waiting for that kiss. She knows how to say eight Chinese words. They are doll, ball, milk, Mom, no, and tickle. The final two are Grandpa and bubble.

⸏ ⸏

That fact that I didn't die probably shook the CGG and its working group assigned to the preservation and reestablishment of the monarchy. From this point forward, whenever I meet the CGG membership, I am no longer fearful of them. Without that shield of Confucian doctrine they once used to force us to protect Emperor Puyi, I feel like I can move on my own terms. Later, when I am on the bumpy road of life with all its complications, like Jasmine's first tragedy or my family's own demise, I can finally beat them at their own sinister game of the greater good.

I was changing. Sure, I do not know up from down at first, because my foundation is unstable. My insides feel hollow. I am lost in the world. I wander aimlessly for three years while war rages on.

The Council may have been changing as well, and so too was the landscape of all the world. Across the sea, Japanese Emperor Hirohito tells his generals not to be constrained by the rules of war established by international law. Those laws do not hold. This includes the treatment of prisoners during war. It is the Japanese Emperor Hirohito's directive that

Even before their arrival, word had spread of the numerous atrocities Japan's Central China Front had committed on their way through China. There are killing contests. Chinese soldiers are hunted down and left in mass graves. Families are massacred.

At noon on December 9, an airplane dropped orange leaflets onto the city. The leaflet urges the Chinese to surrender the city.

Before the soldiers of Japan's Central China Front were sent to Nanjing, Emperor Puyi met with some of them inside his temporary palace in the New Capital. He gives them each his royal blessing for their successful endeavor in crushing Chiang's Chinese Army. In preparation for the assault, Emperor Puyi meets with Japanese General Iwane and thanks him for his good leadership. "This is for a cause bigger than me, General. We need to regain authority over China. The rebel attempt of establishing a southern capital must be crushed," says Emperor Puyi. He means every word.

A speech was broadcast over the radio in which the Emperor said, "I am founding a new empire based on virtue and benevolence. We want to do away with racial bias and conflicts among nations. Japanese and Chinese and Koreans will be able to live side by side. It is for this noble cause that we fight. We all should contribute our grain, our men, and our supplies. I urge my people to carry out their duties diligently, and I encourage everyone to supply what they can to this holy war." Emperor Puyi gives the most beautiful of the remaining jade pieces left in his possession to regional leaders in northern China willing to submit to the Japanese occupation forces without bloodshed. At Yoshioka's request, he writes letters to Chinese resistance fighters advising them to surrender.

It was the finger of Emperor Puyi that pointed the Japanese warplanes in the direction of Nanjing.

bright sun. *Nanjing, I have arrived. What has happened to you?* He feels a rush of excitement. The brutality is captivating to He Song. He wants to see more. How naive this young man can be.

Far north, in Manchuria, Emperor Puyi was dressed in formal attire as he bowed toward Nanjing to acknowledge the fallen Japanese soldiers fighting on behalf of his reign. He is instructed to do this by his advisor and friend, Yoshioka. Emperor Puyi no longer feels conflicted when asked to do so. He bows not to his own people but to fallen enemy soldiers.

Emperor Puyi now viewed all of the Nanjing people as traitors. The president they elected took the power away from Beijing and from himself. If Emperor Puyi ever thought about the cruelty of this war, which he does not, he would consider it completely deserved and justified. These may be Chinese people, but they are not his people. They are against his reign. They want him dead. He wouldn't have given that little baby a second thought. *Murder the child. It means nothing.*

That little baby in the Ha house had achieved the status of toddler around that time, as Emperor Puyi bowed from his hideaway in Manchuria. She has just begun to walk around the little house in bold steps. The world is so different from that new height, *standing!* Waving her hands, shrieking with glee, falling on her rump and getting up for another try. She is not a baby but indeed a toddler, and a fresh new explorer of the world.

A few days before, the wave had come. The sixth and one hundred sixteenth divisions of the Japanese Army enter the city. The ninth division enters through the Guanghua Gate, and the sixteenth division enters through the Zhongshan Gate. To back them up, two small fleets from the Japanese Navy dock on both sides of the Yangtze River. Japanese's Central China Front Army enter the city on December 13. They are commanded by General Iwane.

that would later become a well-known baiju. The notes he hums are G, G, A, and C.

As he was helping an orphan boy write the word "blossom," sitting there in the mud, he sang these words for the first time:

The sweetest of our flowers is dear jasmine.
To pluck them I cannot imagine
the blossoms coming back
on our old beaten track.
So give those rare buds your compassion!

Let them flower, let them flower, our sweet jasmine flowers!
Let them flower, let them flower, our sweet jasmine!

The tune develops further as he he plays with the dislocated children and his lyrics catch on that day. The children will develop more refrains for it. The song grows and takes on a life of its own, spreading through the camps and the countryside that very day. By tomorrow it will be sung in the border provinces. This becomes one of He Song's greatest legacies. Can you imagine the world today without his song?

He Song first entered the city from above some days before, walking the city wall and looking down. The mustard wall he stands on frames the large city with twenty-two miles of ancient brick made a thousand years ago. It is maybe fifty feet high and fifty feet wide at the base. The city wall was commissioned by Emperor Zhu Yuanzhang, the first Emperor of the Ming Dynasty, who is now buried in the hills here. Eighteen huge gates allowed traffic in and out during normal times, and at these gates there are also stairs that lead to the forgotten roadway at its top. He Song notices most gates are guarded today by scores of heavily armed Japanese soldiers, but there is chaos everywhere and not everything is well guarded. From the vantage point of the wall above, He Song sees the Confucius temple to the south on the banks of the Qinhuai River. There is also an old university here that precedes the city wall by another thousand years. A porcelain pagoda and the old presidential palace shade parts of the city from the men become so mean? John had known the Japanese before the war. He often worked with them as business partners, and they have always been so gentle, considerate, and well cultured. When the soldiers entered the city days ago, they were nothing like the Japanese he thought he knew, and he could not understand. It was baffling to him why they wreaked so much havoc on this defenseless population. John continued speaking to He Song as if he were a Japanese soldier. "There are two girls from house Number Five on Sin Road, just beyond Shanghai Road. Could you please check on them, young soldier? The girls are usually the first to come to our class, but they did not show up this morning. They are lovely little girls and I want to make sure that nothing has happened. You can tell their parents I sent you, just to ask. It looks like I can trust you, soldier, that your intentions are not like the other men here." John cannot get away from his station to do such errands himself. He asks this of He Song to test whether he might be trusted for bigger tasks in the future. "Could you do me this favor?"

The international volunteer named John had looked at He Song playing with the children and saw that his eyes were different from the other soldiers. Once they came into the city, their eyes are clouded with a red fog. Their minds go wild. John doesn't see that look in He Song.

The twenty-seven organized all sorts of activities to keep the children busy. One thing that seems to work is writing letters. These kids write letters to foreign schools, to presidents and kings of other countries, and often to relatives living in other Chinese cities. The youngest children draw pictures. Some write poems. The twenty-seven optimistically hope to somehow get them sent. Children across the oceans, sitting at their school desks that very moment, would someday read the letters and reply to them.

He Song sat with the refugee children one afternoon helping them with their letters, that hour before he discovers the hand. His opinion of this war is changing. While the kids sit around him, he hums a new tune

The baby's grandfather must have tried to protect his wife and was killed. The grandmother may have died while she tried to protect two young girls around the ages of twelve and fourteen.

The soldiers first shot the landlord with a revolver, and also his wife, who knelt before these men in green begging them not to kill anyone else.

The soldiers had demanded entrance early that morning, before Ha's daughters set out for school. The door is opened by the landlord after their repeated knocking.

He Song had watched many innocent people taken to the Yangtze River. He didn't see it happen to the Ha family, but still he knows what must have occurred.

Some say there was a killing contest between two Japanese officers. It was a race between the two men to see which of them could kill one hundred enemies first, using only a sword. The killing contest was covered like a sporting event with a daily tally broadcasted to all the Japanese troops. Another cited event was when the Japanese troops gathered 1,300 Chinese soldiers and civilians at the city's Taiping Gate and killed them all. The victims were blown up with land mines. They were doused with petrol and set on fire. These weren't the worst atrocities in He Song's mind. In this long war, He Song will think the baby's death is the worst. He focuses on the individual, not the group. Jasmine would later argue that this tendency is He Song's biggest failure. *You fail to see the biggest picture if you get too hung up on details.*

"Hey, soldier. Please come over here for a word," the leader of the twenty-seven had said to He Song after noticing him sitting with the children. This is the German named John. John sees a deep emptiness in He Song's eyes, but no rage and none of the hostility shown by the others wearing the coat of the Japanese Army. Why have the Japanese military

Now, here is the story. It was He Song's own tears that preserved the baby's hand. His tears contain a certain magic of preservation.

He reached Nanjing in the midst of the month-long massacre, and there he found and cried over the baby's hand, preserving it forever. The tears flowed on it like rain. Pools form in the corners of He Song's lips and flow down his chin and neck. Everything is wet with his saltwater.

He Song found the hand in the rubble of a home at Number Five Sin Road in the southeastern part of the city, having been instructed to go there because the baby's older sisters did not show up to school at the refugee camp that morning. The baby's hand comes from the renowned Ha family. The landlord to the house was a good Muslim man. He Song saw the bodies of the landlord's two children just outside the back doorstep when he exited Number Five. *What a disaster,* he thinks, and he does not know where to look. He wants to look away, but the ugly mess is all around.

He Song found the baby's mother inside the house with a bottle thrust into her body. She must have been beaten in the chest until she died. She was stripped naked and probably raped. It looks like young Mrs. Ha was dragged out from under the dining room table where she may have tried to hide with her baby. The hand was all He Song could find of the infant. There was nothing else. Who am I to even talk about it? Repeating their story feels evil and dangerous. The hand is just lying there on the floor. He Song picks it up.

The walls were still echoing her screams long after the thirty soldiers had left the house. Thirty soldiers terrorizing one family. Why is He Song in this place? Why did he walk into this house so obviously in ruin?

He Song was alone there at Number Five, but there were the fresh footprints of the thirty Japanese soldiers in the mud and the ash. There were bodies around him.

well. Makeshift shelters were erected along boulevards, blocking many of the streets meant to be thoroughfares until the twenty-seven step in and insist on order. In some ways, the twenty-seven provide the basics for refugees for a short period of time, before it's all burned, and they save perhaps fifty thousand lives when all is said and done. But in one most important way, the effort is sorely lacking. There is no protection from the Japanese soldiers.

At the end of each day, darkness came into the camp. The foreigners who run the camp do the best they know how. They have no training. There is no time to prepare. Not until the sun rises will the twenty-seven see what awfulness has happened the night before.

The electricity was disabled in the city, so at night there was utter darkness. At the depth of the night in a refugee camp, only a refugee would understand this darkness. You will eventually have to go out of your tent or your dormitory room to pee, but every danger is out there, invisible. You step too far away and you will be lost forever. You make a wrong step, and who knows.

He Song had no special eyesight and he, too, was fearful at night in those camps. The Safety Zone is not safe.

Late at night, rather than sleep, the foreigners would huddle together and talk to one another, and try to find some hope. "We must give these children something to live for. These kids need to know that there will be a better future for them after the war. Perhaps that is all we can do for them now, but it is important that we provide hope for the survivors," says one of the elder missionaries who came from a land of ten thousand lakes in America and has since lived in China for half his life. He leads by example and hopes to say to the refugee children the next morning, "Your life will be better in the future. I promise you that. I truly believe your lives will get better. God has his eyes on you."

There had been many foreigners living in this city over previous decades. Many even call Nanjing home. Some are businessmen for companies that import and export goods, and others are Christian missionaries called by God to teach the "Good Word" to the Chinese. Yet only twenty-seven foreigners who had lived in Nanjing choose to stay to help the people during this time of great need.

The twenty-seven foreigners who stayed were doctors with the International Red Cross, also five reporters, a few businessmen, including one German named John, and the missionaries. There are dozens of refugee camps popping up all around the American Embassy. This keeps the foreigners busy with meaningful tasks.

He Song had entered the Safety Zone on Shanghai Road, just inside the old city walls that still stood. The Safety Zone was cornered by the Wutai Mountain in the east, the railway to the north, and the old drum tower to the west. Within these parameters were Nanjing University, most of the foreign embassies, and the main city hospital.

He Song became familiar with the layout of the camps. The vast tragedy of it all is a draw to him. It interests him. He doesn't help anyone there in any important way. He considers doing many things, but in the end he just hovers there for a while like a fly. There is one day when he gives blood. There is that. Still, he hoards the food he has with him. He offers no one protection.

The twenty-seven kept themselves busy running the camps and preparing for nightfall. They send out communications to their home nations requesting food and medical supplies, they distribute clean water in designated areas (the river water carries cholera), and they do smaller things like setting up outdoor play areas to entertain the children and perhaps even give them schooling. The refugees take over Nanjing's abandoned university campus and abandoned homes, so the twenty-seven manage these places as the virtue of any soldier as he wanders the country and witnesses the slash-and-burn method of the Japanese occupiers.

The Japanese Army was in control of everything. He Song must be wary everywhere he goes. He continues to wear the tight Japanese uniform he stole, and he fits in with the conquerors on the street. His face could be of a man from either side. The trick is to not sneak around. Instead, walk boldly down the center of the road, go right into random houses without knocking when you are hungry or thirsty, and show no humanity.

At any time, He Song could have been found out and shot right there in the open, right on the street. There is no reason He Song should be allowed free passage. He wonders whether everyone secretly knows about his unusual ties to the Emperor. *No, they cannot all know. It must be the uniform.*

The year 1937 began Japan's full-scale invasion of China. He Song witnesses the torching of most buildings in Nanjing. This marks the conclusion of a terrible massacre throughout the metropolis and is the source of He Song's longtime phobia of rats. Rats scamper out of the city by the thousands as they try to escape the blaze that the humans were unable to survive. Nanjing is left in ruins. This old city sits just to the south of the Yangtze River, our great river that flows from Tibet through all of China, west to east, and eventually dumps into the Pacific Ocean near the ports of Shanghai. The bodies of at least 57,500 previous residents now flow that direction to Shanghai.

The business people already left Nanjing. Before the final burning of the city, the only citizens remaining were living in the Safety Zone as refugees. These refugee camps form themselves around the old American Embassy. The Safety Zone was designated by the League of Nations to be a place of relative safety for civilians, though the Japanese Army is at war and does not recognize the existence of safety zones in Nanjing. This will be one of their war crimes.

CHAPTER 9

January 1, 1938

China's population is 511 million people.

The baby hand was perfectly preserved. Forever that severed hand will look like it did on that sad day way back then. It will never mature into an adult hand of course, but neither will the lovely hand ever rot or be forgotten. He Song just won't let it be. It was put in the Emperor's box so others can know, too, what happened here in Nanjing.

He Song carried the hand in his mahogany box, of which we are so familiar, out of the city toward the Purple-Gold Mountain Observatory where he plans to camp for the night. The cliff of one thousand Buddhas looks down onto him. Purple-gold clouds hang low as they often do here. He Song walks upward through the pines and cypress trees. His legs are sore, but he will not stop while there is still light. There below him is the winding Qinhuai River. Lush mountains surround him. The Ming dynasty tombs are in the hills to the north. Those emperors rest silently in their tombs, undisturbed. Back in that city, from which He Song just left, rests another man of greatness: the country's first elected president. He was the one who first took power from Puyi. He succeeded for a time but is now buried back there in old Nanjing.

He Song saw no point to the war ravaging the world. He is a hollowed man without a heart. We are in the mucky beginning of World War II. The killing has no clear purpose. Hear the rattle of the box. He Song ponders *of my sandals. When I comb my hair at night I will find more seeds there but now, pulling on the arms of my shirt, I let the wind extend the shirt. I flap it with a heave like a flag above my head. A cloud of pollen and seeds comes up and off the wave of the shirt and the billions of particles and tiny seeds blow off as I make a somersault onto itself in the air.*

It was preceded by a lesser somersault when I had jumped up from the grasses, pushing off from the spongy earth.

The increased temperatures forced me to take off my shirt, and my back gleamed against the pounding sun. I stretch out the arms of my shirt, holding it above my head for protection, and that shields me but causes me to see the dirtiness that is there on the back of my shirt. There are pods and cones and stickers and darkness of more things embedded between the threads. So many seeds, all taking different forms, attaching themselves to my shirt.

Something jolted me back to the task at hand. Oh, yes, I meant to find the tear grass! That is my quest for today. The little Yi boy needs his medicine. If not done today, there is always tomorrow. I brought a little bit of rice along to eat and some to share if I meet anyone along the way, wrapped in a leaf with some plum sauce. I also have a raw potato I dug up and the forest has food. I am just starting to get hungry.

And so those childhood memories went on in He Song's head as he walked north from Nanjing. Memories of some thirty years ago divert his mind from the present. They were good times. He does not think too much of the box he now holds.

The wind pushed the earth in its direction. The earth pushes back. The sun pushes its own course, the clouds their own course. The birds fly above me using the sun, the earth, the clouds, and the wind. I am now washing off my feet in the cool river. I pick up some pretty stones that later I might throw at the monkeys and wild dogs. The stones go into my pocket.

I had removed my sandals and scraped the soles against rocks. I pick at them with a stick. It looks like an herb over there had made the monkeys sick. What is it inside the partially digested stickiness? It looks like prickly ash leaf but maybe it is something else… Over there is a family of dead monkeys. That is strange. I see little almost microscopic spiders beside me on the ground. They are red or white. Are they red, or are they white? I think they are red, and then I change my opinion. I cannot tell their color.

That previous half hour I was walking backward to balance the muscles. Why do this? I often walk in reverse a little bit each day, and this is when I step into the monkey puke.

Before, I was following a goldeneye quietly while she was preparing a nest. I see her pulling out a thread and placing it, brick red, on a nearby branch. Sure enough it is picked up. Later I will see this thread interwoven in a fully completed nest. Someday the eggs will be hatched, and the family will have moved on.

I picked up mango leaves, peppermint, mung bean, star anise, and purslane along the way. I see some herbs were already plucked and are laying there on the edge of the path intended for me to pick up yesterday on my way back home, but I have never picked them up. I must have forgotten. The herbs are still there, untouched. If I go just a little farther to the south of here, those mushrooms might still be there, too. I remember mushrooms from yesterday but the mushrooms are now gone. I look for an hour without success.

The dirt and grasses and fuzzy seeds got between my toes and the straps

Here is another memory of that boy He Song once walking these mountains.

I put the Job's Tears into my satchel. It is dug up with my misshapen hands, appraised, and tasted. Boiled with brown sugar it will be light and sweet and warming to the stomach. My shoulders lighten.

My previous thoughts were disrupted by this discovery... Oh, there you are! This is what I spent the morning seeking out. You've been a hard one to hunt down for a so-called common herb, little tear grass!

Before the interruption, I felt my mind almost closing in on something new and interesting. I am becoming increasingly receptive to this new sense that could only be described as always having been right there all along. It is a noise and a smell and a shadow. I find it by listening to the bugs: following the patter of a bee that turns to a rustling of leaves and grows into wind against my ear. Whiffs of pollen lead me to new plants. Although not that one plant I seek, I discover traces of it along the breeze. There is happiness in my heart. In the wind, I hear those somehow familiar songs from long ago that I will surely forget again, but no matter. I enjoy them now. The trees whisper their stories. A smile sits wide on my young face. I am lost in the woods. There is a single hum in my soul and it goes something like "Om."

Memories flood back. This feels like something familiar. I can feel the future.

I looked at the branches on the ground. There is a type of berry attached to that branch that I have never seen before. I follow up the sappy tree trunk. I get sap on my hands. I play with the sap on my remaining fingers. It tastes bitter.

Earlier, I became aware suddenly of the sun. I am diverted to the shaded groves.

"How sad it is that they are not here to see these things," I remember saying to myself as I roamed those mountains.

Here is a memory that He Song clings to like the most precious gold:

Over there is the young man I remember being. He is walking in the lush hills. He smiles and sings. In his thoughts it is not strange for him to meditate on a piece of twisted pine tree bark for hours—not really the bark so much as everything leading up to the bark: how the bark is related to that particular fold in the tree, so interesting in its pattern, and with those ancient lichens clinging to it and the shadows forming around it, which is why he happened to take special notice of it above all the other things on that tree, or any of the other trees, or other wonders that are all around him (how stunning!). A rare and beautiful caterpillar might be inching near his toe, for instance, but he does not see it. Caterpillars eat the poisonous plants as easily as they will eat the helpful ones. Caterpillars are not worth a second look. It is not until they start spreading pollen as butterflies that this species acquires young He Song's attention.

His mind went to magical places as he walked. It skips, and, forgetting what he only just remembered, memories are dusted off for just a moment, slightly changed from the last time, then disappear. A smell brings on a rush of thoughts, some of them feel not of the past or of the future. They are suspended, and young He Song is suspended in this cloudy medium of the Happy Wanderer's Bliss.

He Song the adult man is walking the same mountains today but everything is different today. He is not the Happy Wanderer anymore. There is no HWB today.

Dear Reader, you know how it is, or was. It should be hardly surprising that the story of even He Song's origin is filled to the brim of this most basic human bliss. There is nothing like walking in the mountains when you are young. There is nothing like being young.

the smoke you can smell comes from a sacrificial fire that concluded a wedding procession. No, my mistake. The crowd is up on the hill standing in a double circle placing paper objects in the fire: a house made of paper, a child made of paper, fake money, an automobile made of paper, a luscious peach made of folded paper. This is a funeral. He Song's eyelids hang as the red lanterns do. He is walking through the town. One step after another. Walking north.

I wish, Dear Reader, I could tell you more about this place and their festival and the lovely landscape, but I need to focus on our main character. Something important has been happening to him. If he were a monarch, this part of his life would be the cocoon stage.

He began each day with the remembering. He Song wakes this morning by stretching long, yawning like a mountain lion, and feeling that last night was a good night's rest. He slowly forgets the dreams of the night and sifts out the memories of his past. He Song can't think of any activity he has done more during his time on this earth than wandering the hills aimlessly. He gets up and starts walking.

Walking the hills. That was perhaps the nicest memory of He Song's childhood. It was like he walks now, but it's not the same. He was much younger then, and he moved in whatever direction suited his fancy in the moment, backtracking often, meandering from the original intent, and physically embodying his consciousness: taking off on a tangent path away from the initial objective and wandering aimlessly except for the smallest strings of purpose to enjoy the present moment for what it is, in all its fullness.

Most of all, I was happy. It was a time of discovery, and it was a time of freedom. I breathed in the fresh air on the hilltops. And there was but one sadness. I often felt sorrow that I could not share each moment with my loved ones. If only they could step into my mind.

He Song had been roaming the country for years by the end of World War II. He is walking the back roads and sleeping along the ditches long before the Soviets arrive. His faith in the Emperor has collapsed. He has lost his heart and now wanders.

He had two working eyes, but they were not looking sharply at the world today. Instead they look into the past. He Song cannot feel the present or think about the future. His mind is stuck in the past.

His self-grooming became irregular during these years. He Song shows four days of bristle on his brown chin. At He Song's side jingles the ring of keys. Also, hear that? In his knapsack he has the imperial box, and inside that wooden box is the hand. Part of him intends to walk all the way to Manchuria to bring it to the Emperor who He Song firmly believes is a puppet for the Japanese occupation. That is the direction he heads, but it is a wayward path. Part of He Song wants to just lock the box up in one of the many places underground where he stores other imperial treasures.

His army jacket stank from old sweat. There is just a hint of cinnamon, but not enough to cover the bad odor. He doesn't care. His eyes are focused three meters straight ahead, and nothing comes into his peripheral sight. He Song strolls past a gorgeous mountain town without noticing any of it. Huffing along, He Song walks past the cold, wet ashes beside house after house. The whiff of smoke from a fire burning atop a nearby hill vaguely registers as appropriate for this special day on the Chinese calendar. Today, paper lanterns hang on the eaves of buildings. They are strung above shopping arcades and over the stone bridge of the West River. He crosses over the old bridge. The crystal waters rush underneath.

The paper lanterns were not yet lit. Tonight, holiday smells will drift along with the smoke of burning beeswax candles inside the lanterns. The lights will make a magical display of color over the town. But now, instead,

Emperor Puyi was captured finally by the Soviets before making his planned escape to Tokyo. He is dressed in his finest imperial costume when they come for him. His hands are full of precious rings. I think he wore them for protection, but they provide none. Jewels jut out from his fingers like blossoms.

Poor Emperor, your diamonds will never bloom. I wonder whether we can pray for you in the future from here. Would that be a powerful prayer, or does it not matter now that all these events and your life have passed?

The future is a powerful thing, I dare say, and here we stand in it, Dear Reader, in the future looking back on him. I would think a prayer from the future might do some good. Should I pray for this man I once called my Emperor?

His ponytail was long and well combed. There were few left who still wore that style of hair. That long braid nearly touches the ground.

"Damn!" said the Last Emperor. Spit lands on his shoe. A northerly breeze had circled it back around at him, though he had aimed his wad of yellow mucus toward the side of the road.

It was Operation August Storm, in 1945, when the Soviet forces crossed the Wusuli River into China. The Soviets swept up riverbanks to battle the Japanese who had control of the Chinese land. The Japanese control over China has finally crumbled. The Japanese were attacked on one side by the Soviets, over land, and on the other side by the Americans, over ocean. They will hand the land back to the Chinese people, and Big Brother will then take charge of our well-being.

‿ ‿

An old Clockseller who I once knew showed Jasmine how to set this unusual kind of trap. He uses a hollowed eggshell and a bowl. The egg lifts up one end of the bowl. In the hollowed egg, he places a smelly piece of donut facing inward to the bowl. The mouse will bump the egg and gets caught underneath.

To get the captured rodents out of the trap he showed her a simple trick. She spins the bowl a little to get the mouse moving. Eventually its tail comes out from under the bowl. She steps on the tail to get hold of the mouse. Voila!

"Hey, little girl with the braids. Psst. Come over here. Your approach for catching mice is all wrong. Let me show you." She hears a voice coming from down the road. Free advice for children willing to listen. The Clockseller knows the secret.

The old Clockseller was selling his wares on the side of the road and saw Jasmine running by after a small mouse. He saw many such children run by, but only Jasmine stops to learn his secret trap.

For a time, we went back to a primitive age. There is little fuel after the war resulting in very little mechanical noise. Silence exists again. Animals are scarce, and the humans who remain are all worn down. There are no songs in this land of ours. The new government will be inventing new anthems and folk songs. He Song takes the people outdoors and with sticks they beat the earth and it echoes. The Wolf Whisperer would hum, and they would all hum. Human instruments, no words, but old melodies under the stars.

is raised higher than it has ever been before. The pride comes from the announcement her teacher made this morning. She was named the first-place winner of a competition among her peers. It was a silly competition really, but not for her. The teachers, tired of the number of rodents in the city, set the children to the task of collecting rodent tails. Jasmine was awarded top prize for collecting the most tails of all the children. All of the winners were posted this morning on the school wall. Success is sweet, and she tastes it for the first time. It is indeed the first thing she has ever won, and perhaps, though it is sad to say, the first time this ugly duckling was ever noticed by anyone. There would have been a ribbon presented to her during a future school assembly, had it not been for the accident.

To make the competition easier, some of the kids didn't bother actually killing the mice but just satisfied the teachers' requirement by chopping off their tails. Even in the backyard furnaces, tailless mice probably scamper in the dark corners. Of course the organizers intend that the mice be killed and thus reduce the city's infestation. It was all well intentioned.

She had no embarrassment bringing little mouse tails to class while other children only brought in the longest, thickest rat tails for show. The rules were based on number, not size. Jasmine knows that it is only quantity that matters. Despite their efforts, Jasmine's five siblings didn't collect nearly as many, combined, as Jasmine did on her own, only producing a fraction of the twenty-four mouse tails she captures.

She had a secret weapon for capturing so many mice.

She had designed a master trap.

She would set up the trap each day before sitting down for her homework, and again before bed, and again before breakfast. Every night it is possible to catch at least one mouse. She is lucky, and over one month she catches twenty-four. She lost one, so submits only twenty-three tails.

145   levon a

low, unsettling rumbles, and she has to plug her ears, which prevents her from properly feeling her way in front of her. Crews are hammering apart pieces of an old bridge to create new steel bars. The hammering reverberates through the metal into the ground, up walls and down from the ceiling. She sees sparks and shadows. It feels like she is in another world. Are we still in Suzhou? With the imagination of an eight-year-old, Jasmine became a green dragon looking for these hefty dwarfs to complete her task. She has wings that will carry her, and a nose that will guide her. She hears chisels against stone. Nothing could hurt a dragon.

From the racket above, below, and all around her, there was obviously a great battle among the dwarfs. None of them realizes a dragon is so near. If they had, they would have hidden all their gold but Jasmine sees flicking sparks of yellow everywhere, and she imagines this molten metal to be precious gold.

These men, or dwarves, were not alone in their effort to double the land's steel production. Household items are melted down to contribute, because everyone's small donation can make a big difference. Old bridges are stripped bar by bar and remolded into new steel bars. Parts of train terminals are taken apart, street signs are removed, nails are taken out of unused buildings nail by nail, and even the hinges are taken off the door of the old church in the center of town.

She walked underneath a conveyer of small pieces. The conveyer isn't oiled well and has lost some of its wheels. It clanks along and things bounce here and there. The foundry is indeed makeshift without safety measures in place. The building was once a factory that made the rails for trains and later went out of service. Its meager smokestacks are not tall enough to expel the soot, so the surrounding neighborhoods are in a cloud, and the smell of metal stings the nose.

Jasmine was terribly proud of herself earlier that day. Her head

This evil man in the furnaces refused to accept his role in injuring the girl. He Song doesn't feel like he is at fault. Granted, he wasn't paying attention to the area below when he poured the molten mixture, but why should he? And sure, it was He Song alone who propped that back door open with a stone, giving the girl entry from below, but he did it only to let in some fresh air. It needed to be open. Without some breeze it is truly unbearable in here.

Screams of pain were what He Song remembered. The girl will not remember anything about the splash of molten metal coming toward her eyes. The blackout takes away those memories. It burns, and she yells.

It dropped like a long splinter, a needle of gold. She looks up from below, and it hits her straight in the eye.

It would have all been so ordinary if not for the consequences. Like he has done for the last two years, He Song sets down the shovel to pick up one large metal bar and swings it into the melting pot, causing a little splash as it sinks.

He Song wore a mask and vest to shield himself from the furnace. His thoughts are not about this place. He is thinking about the Widow Du and her family. He pays little attention to his surroundings here. He shovels oddities from the conveyer down into the hungry lava. Things that are not appropriate to be melted he throws into a separate bin, but very little is selected out.

That little girl with braids had come into the factory carrying her family's silverware to be melted down for the cause, and before the spark fell into her eye she walked through the smoke as if on a mission to conquer the world. She is dreaming and steps carelessly. She is imagining that she entered a cave full of dwarves. There are layers of jolting noises in the foundry ranging from high-pitched squeaks of rubbing metal to

levon a

When he arrived, she lay there defenseless, in a coma without supervision. He Song sees beauty in that.

He had picked six stems of jasmine from the side of the road on his way to the hospital to make amends and wrapped the flowers in a bit of newspaper. When he arrives, He Song puts those jasmine stems into a water glass at her bedside. The smell fills the entire room. Jasmine flower smells of spring, of hope, and of better things. This is where she gets the nickname, and that name will become her real name, but she never will make the connection back to He Song. The name originates from those flowers at her bedside.

Should we go back to that day at the Suzhou backyard furnace? I hesitate, but yes, let's proceed. The furnace building was never intended for its current purpose of melting metals, old and new, to produce Chinese steel, and so there is not the proper ventilation or the high smokestacks we come to expect from facilities that do duty works such as this. Black smoke rolls out from the vents and the cracked windows into the streets of Suzhou. It covers the whole neighborhood in soot. There are ancient canals here along the pathways but you can see neither pathway nor canal. Watch your step. You can see no sky. The trees have all been cut to stoke the fire. For five hundred years, this city had been renowned for growing silk, and this neighborhood, famous for its skillful tailors, now focuses on making steel. The silkworms perish in the smog. There are no trees to feed them anyway.

He Song himself was blackened from the smoke. Even the whites of his eyes are blackened with soot. His skin, his clothes, his beard, his hands, those fingernails, the air he breathes in, the air he breathes out, are all black as black can be. Light can hardly penetrate this space.

He visited the girl with braids a good two weeks after the terrible accident that took her eye. She is abandoned there in the infirmary of Suzhou Hospital Number Two. She is one of a dozen women and girls in the room without a nurse. Her linens are changed once a day. There is no family around.

Finally, it hit him. This mess is his. He did this to her.

Just moments before, he felt a desire to distort her further and destroy her completely. *She is so defenseless. I can tear her apart. Who is here to stop me? Nobody would care. Just look what I already did. There are no repercussions.*

He felt a predator inside himself. He looks at her, standing too near, and wants to ruin that innocence. *What a horrible man you are, He Song!*

She was in such pain that day, and the meanness wasn't He Song's first reaction, for at heart he is a healer of sorts. He Song put a tiny piece of dried red mushroom under her lip and she began to chew, and there was relief in her face. Would it be a kindness to assist in her suicide?

How can her life come to anything now? Her face is wrapped in bandages holding in bloody gauze. The metal still sits within the depth of her right eye. He feels her forehead beneath. Her temperature is a few degrees above normal. There is probably an infection. She will always have pain. Her handicap will prevent anyone from loving her. So young, and already her life is over. Look at her curled up like an infant. Her feet are small, as though her parents had tried to carry on our old tradition of binding young girls' feet so that they would grow only half their natural size.

until one month ago when she lost it because of my own carelessness in the furnaces. Molten steel pierced her eye, and the accident was entirely my fault. I must heal her. Does it help in the production of steel? Perhaps. She was Suzhou's best scavenger for scrap metal. Is it for the greater good? Yes! I need your assistance to heal this girl."

He Song arranged the meeting with the Council in the same way he later instructs Jasmine to do. It is the only way to contact them if you are not a member. You must disappear for a time without any explanation or human contact. The first person who eventually finds you is their spy.

Eventually the Council's contact found He Song where he had been hidden away for eight days. The person is dressed like a local police officer, but of course she is also connected to the CGG. "He Song, what are you doing here?" He does not know the officer personally but is not surprised she knows his name. "I need to meet with the CGG. Please take me to them right away. This is urgent."

I can't stress enough that at first He Song denied his own fault in Jasmine's accident; he greatly regretted his inaction in hindsight weeks after the tragedy. Those who say this culture has only shame and not guilt do not know human nature. The guilt wraps around He Song like a boa constrictor strangling him so he can barely breathe. He cannot live this way. The guilt is so strong he may tear out his eye himself if it comes to that.

He needed to do good. He first hides away for days trying to come up with some plan for how to make a life for the girl with braids. Could he give her his vast wealth that is hidden away in a dozen small underground tunnels throughout the country? Riches might hide her scarred face. No, he wants to repair her physically, and there is only one way he knows of for that to be done. He looks at his own hand with the missing fingers and does not want Dear Jasmine to be handicapped. He waits until the CGG's representative comes.

plant rice are producing steel. It is agreed that there are some resources available, even now. It will not be very expensive.

He Song was not scared of this crowd of suits. The members have aged since he last saw them. They look frail and much less sure of themselves than they once did in their traditional robes. Nothing scares He Song anymore. He boldly says, "I have been the Emperor's aide for all of my life, as were you all. I want to change that devotion I have for him to a devotion to the common people. Then I can prove to myself, prove to Big Brother, and prove to Puyi if that too is required someday, that I know what it means to be communist in thought, mind, and purpose."

"Why are you doing this?" they asked moments before. He has been anticipating the question and is ready to answer it but waits until the council members ask it aloud. Sure enough, the question is asked: "Why?" He pauses before answering.

"You know that I cannot die." There was silence when he spoke. Someone in the room drops a cufflink and it clatters.

Each syllable from He Song's tongue registered in their ears. There is a ferocity in his voice this day. Saying no to him is not an option. "We know my organs have worked in preserving the life of Emperor Puyi, and I have done what I can for him. I ask that we now do an experiment to see whether this capability of ours will work for others besides the Emperor. I want you to take out my right eye and give it to the girl."

When He Song walked into the Grand Ballroom in the Peace Hotel on the Bund, light streamed in from all the windows. He addresses the Council first by saying, "Thank you for hearing my request. You know who I am. I called you here today because I require your expertise for an experiment that will interest you. An eight-year-old girl has lost sight in her right eye. It doesn't matter how but I will tell you. She had a working eye case, they can always secure the means to make the operation a success. It is as painful as you might imagine, and He Song lives.

We called this period of modern history The Great Leap at the time, not knowing later generations would rename it The Great Disaster. It is a challenge for us to learn who we are after having been an empire for two thousand years. The people tear up most of the country's trees to use the wood to stoke the backyard furnaces, because Big Brother instructs us to make more steel regardless of the cost. Who cares about the energy it takes, the opportunities that are lost? Our only goal for these three years will be summed up in three words: "Make more steel!" He knows we can become the world's leading steel producer if only all our efforts are put to that one sole purpose. This will help everyone in the end.

I think the Council agreed to restore Jasmine's sight because they too were repositioning themselves to serve the proletariat better, to consider women and the poor, when in the past we gave them little value. It is a shift for them. For centuries, the Council for the Greater Good more or less served the needs of the Emperors under the philosophy of Confucius. Now they are moved by the modern philosophy of Big Brother.

Some of them agreed to the odd request because they were planning Emperor Puyi's reeducation, and would need He Song's participation in that. Others by this point want to see how far they could pull He Song to pieces before killing him.

He Song made a grand speech in front of them all. "Think of the power this council will wield if this works. What other lives can be saved by my mysterious curse?" He Song knows the right words to say to them. He convinces each one.

"How can we bear the costs for this operation?" some members had asked. There is starvation in the country because farmers who normally

CHAPTER 10

June 17, 1958

With almost eight million deaths due to starvation,
China's population is 653 million.

Jasmine was eight years old when she lost her right eye. Eight is usually a lucky number for us. Perhaps it is eight-year-old luck that she quickly receives a replacement eye, a real one that is as good as the one before, and lives out her life as if nothing ever happened. He Song feels a great deal of pity for the girl now but the moment when the molten metal pierced her eye, He Song at first fooled himself into thinking the tragedy was not his fault and that her loss was not his concern. That was at first, and so we will get to that part of the story in this chapter's end.

He Song's contact with the CGG on this one occasion was a great success, and that is how this chapter will begin. He is able to solicit their help to give Jasmine his eye. The council members are terrified of him. They had once thought they knew what he was about. They thought they had the upper hand but the fact that…well, you will see what scares them eventually, but the gist of it all is that the Council for the Greater Good had once left He Song for dead, and here he is still alive!

As you and I have come to accept, He Song does not die, even when his right eye is removed and transplanted to Jasmine. She recovers from the surgery extremely well. It isn't long before the transplant works as if it were her original eye. Miraculous, really. And to remove an eye of a living man? The Council was convinced it was for the greater good, and when that's the

Control Center, he is assigned to work at a village metalworks. He Song works hard and never expects to see Puyi again after the war came to an end, but he keeps hold of the box.

would offer an Emperor."

Puyi explained his thoughts about food. "When I ate meat, I would weep for these animals with such tenderness of heart. I remember that once when I was eating my meal in the palace air-raid shelter, I kowtowed to an egg three times before eating it. By this time, with the exception of eggs, I had become a complete vegetarian." So, Emperor Puyi would slaughter his own people while bowing to his breakfast eggs. What a disgusting, pretentious mind this is to place animal or egg ahead of the human being! Is that really the essence of Buddhism? Big Brother is right. We do not need that religion practiced here!

He Song prodded Puyi by saying, "There are other truths, friend. That is why they sent me to your cell, and this place. We are assigned, you and I, to read about different perspectives on how the world should work. For now, tell me, why is it that you still do not eat meat?"

Puyi had begun that day, seeing He Song, not knowing what direction was up. He is disoriented. The Center's experts were at a loss how to proceed. He Song asks Puyi to tell him what he knows to be true. Puyi responds to He Song by saying, "The truths I do know are thus. My family has disowned me. My wives have left me. I have no children. My five hundred million subjects do not acknowledge me. No one will bow, not even you." He Song stares back at him and nods his head.

The brainwashing began. They call him Puyi now, not Emperor. He is forced to live in Harbin until he changes his ways. At least he was able to leave Siberia! The accommodations are simpler there. It is never warm enough.

The Soviets had turned Puyi over to Big Brother following several years of keeping him under their scrutiny in Siberia so he would not try to reestablish his former empire. Before He Song is brought to the Thought

Emperor be anything but self-centered? If not for He Song's heart, Emperor Puyi would already be dead and now as the only friend or acquaintance who will see him (his family would not even come here), Puyi seeks some false comfort. Although, from the terror in his eyes, Puyi is certain that he will be hanged for his war crimes. His eyes beg.

Has his entire life been unfairly stacked against him? Yes, he was dealt a bad deck of cards, yet as Emperor had the power to change history. It was not all beyond his control. He was a devil sometimes and greedy beyond measure.

He Song had explained early on when Puyi asked whether the Center intended to execute him, "You will live, Puyi. Your past deeds will be forgiven by Big Brother once you acknowledge what you have done to your people and change your attitude. They want you to change, not die. You are not alone in this. Many Chinese are also going through the same reformation of their beliefs. Just take it one step at a time. Here, start by reading this." It is a revised history of the world.

Puyi thought a thousand thoughts while he said, "I can do that," in response to the Thought Control Center's agenda lying out in front of him. A year could have gone by in his mind between each of these words. Then he whispers very softly into the ear of He Song, a warm breath trying to go unnoticed to whatever ears lie behind the walls: "Will they hang me?"

To explain what had to be done, He Song used an analogy drawn from Puyi's practices of Buddhism. He Song says, "So, you are capable of taking the perspective of those eggs. You understand how the eggs might feel being eaten by you. The Communists want you to do something similar. They want you to take the perspective of the poor farmer and treat her with that dignity you normally treat that breakfast egg, but not just that. You will treat the peasants with even more respect because they have more value. You will treat the poor farmer with the dignity you yourself with the Japanese. The harm you have caused us, I suspect you don't yet realize what a tragedy it has been. Tomorrow will be our most important lesson." He Song thinks about the wooden box waiting on his bookshelf. Now is the time to open it.

～～～～～～～～～～～～～～～～～～～～～～

Their very first meeting in the Thought Control Center came as a surprise to the Emperor. When the two finally met each other again, having already both been through so much hardship and suspicion, with the eunuchs and palaces all gone, and now today with both men dressed in identical blue suits when at earlier times their garb couldn't have been more different from one another, the so-called "former Emperor Puyi" who had almost lost all hope could not help but take He Song to be a sign of luck. Puyi holds out his hand. "Peace."

He Song wouldn't answer Puyi's question. "I don't know, Puyi. Maybe what you say is correct. Maybe it never was."

Puyi pondered this question with his old friend: "I wonder whether that time had ever existed at all. Was I ever the Emperor? Had I ever held the universe in my palm as we have been taught by Confucius, as we knew to be true?"

Before he held out his hand, He Song had said to him, "Tell me, Puyi, what are you thinking." He Song moves the chair closer. Puyi smells the cinnamon bark.

His head throbbed. "No, that time is gone," said the Wolf Whisperer when Puyi had asked him, "You will no longer call me Emperor, He Song?" It is difficult for Puyi to finally accept.

He Song looked into those terrified eyes. How could a Chinese look. He does look. He Song continues. "Puyi, this baby was slaughtered by a soldier's sword. Once your eyes have seen her hand you cannot un-see it. I want this baby to forever be in your thoughts." Emperor Puyi has had very little contact with children. Most of what he knows about them comes from books or the movies, and memories of his own childhood. He looks at the soft little hand in his old weathered one and imagines that is comes from the baby Prince Puyi who was not yet crowned Emperor.

When Puyi first saw the box, not knowing what was within, he smiled, got out of his chair, and exclaimed, "I know that box, He Song! Ah, it has been ten years since I have seen anything from the Forbidden City. I have forgotten what beauty is in all that time. Look how well crafted it is. I do not remember giving this box to you. You probably stole it, but no matter. The palace treasures have all been stolen from me now. To see this one piece again, He Song, oh what pleasure it brings." He moves toward He Song, begging him, "May I hold the box? Can we open it?" not knowing. He will wish for a long time that he hadn't opened it, but eventually he will be glad he did.

The day before He Song brought in the box for the indoctrination session, he said to Puyi, "There are very terrible things I will need to show you, Puyi. You will not think me your friend for opening your eyes to the real world but this is something long overdue. The Emperor was in a cloud of his own making, surrounded by palace walls and eunuchs and others who would not let information in, so he could not fully understand the consequences of his actions."

Puyi protested often during the early sessions, saying. "I was trapped, He Song. You know this wasn't my fault. I was crowned prince when I was only two, and the system was set up all around me that controlled my every action. I had no power. I was more a prisoner then than I was with the Soviets after the war or here now in the Center."

"Puyi, we all know you went too far protecting your title and aligning wary of my lies. But please listen too, because I tell you what I believe is true, and my truths should be as much a part of our shared history as the truths of others. You might as well take it all in and sift out the gold from the muck to your own choosing.

The most important session of Puyi's reeducation happened in their first year together at the Center. He Song judges it is time to show Puyi the wooden box and what has been kept inside. Puyi holds the little hand in his palm, turning it from side to side to see its entirety under the table lamp's light. Shadows from the tiny fingers create striped shadows on the rest of the hand, on his own hand, and on the table. The skin is soft and fresh. The fingernails are beautiful.

"I don't know what to say," Puyi said. That is enough for today. It won't come all at once but He Song senses that eventually the Emperor will understand and apologize for the atrocities he committed as Emperor.

He Song had practiced long for this single session, and now that the day was finally here he felt he was prepared. He Song knows he needs to be gentle, because the reality of the hand will be harsh. The goal is not to push Puyi to insanity, but to plant the seed for eventual remorse. He Song says, "I have wanted to show you this, Puyi, for a very long time. It has been preserved for you to know this girl's sad story. That day when I stored her hand in the box, what I really wanted to do was take you there to Nanjing so you could see it all for yourself. But since that was impossible, you were still Emperor and would not listen, I vowed to bring her hand to you. Now it has been so many years. Finally, you will see it." He picked up the hand from the wooden box. Touching it was not repulsive. Instead, it made He Song very sad. It felt like his insides held a wide chasm. Now you must know, Dear Reader, Puyi has always been a superstitious man. He was told long ago that blinking can dispel bad luck, and so can spitting. Now, in this empty room Puyi blinks his eyes wildly. He spits and spits and spits. The baby hand doesn't go away. Blinking has no effect. He will have to

Peanut are the fodder during these times.

The formal indoctrination sessions were different. They are held in a simple white room with a desk, two chairs, and one lamp. Marx fills the bookshelves. Sessions begin with the Emperor reading the following script: "I sincerely apologize for my war crimes. Every day for as long as I shall live I vow to do my utmost to seek the forgiveness of my countrymen for the harm I have done them. I am so ashamed. Comrade Teacher, I am ready to learn more about the history of our country!" The paper he reads from crinkles in his hands. He Song will now go back in time year by year telling Puyi the history as it has been written by Big Brother. Puyi recites the history that was taught to him at the previous session and comes back with any questions he has after thinking it over for the previous twenty-four or forty-eight hours. If Puyi has any memories that conflict with what was taught, these sessions allow the time to talk them out. He Song is there to guide Puyi down the right path.

Reading the Communist's version of history, Puyi hardly recognized himself or this world in which he has lived for a half century. At first it was all hogwash to him. Puyi couldn't believe a word of it. The texts are written so simply with the most basic vocabulary, so they read like children's stories. It might have very well been a peasant farmer who authored it all, for he often finds grammatical errors and very poor choices of words. He does not admit his skepticism to He Song for a long while, but eventually starts expressing his concerns, and talking about them helps He Song finally get Puyi on the right track. It then doesn't take long for Puyi to dive headlong, without questioning, right into this rabbit hole. The Communist history is now true to them both. It is easier to just believe. The world is now based on Big Brother's manifesto, and it will provide grounding for his life in the future.

History has always been as malleable as butter. Books both preserve and distort our shared history. Stories like mine are also a distortion. Be conditions, wake up beautiful to a new millennium. Her mom said so once. She thought about this."

He Song would usually use his hands when telling this much-loved story of Little Bean, spreading out his fingers when he said the words *wake up*. "All her life, the girl Little Bean instinctively collected interesting seeds. They were in every jacket pocket this time of the year. The most precious seeds she put in the button pocket at her chest. As she played throughout the spring, these seeds would haphazardly fall along the trails she most liked to follow, until the weather would warm and there was no need for a coat and her pockets would be empty, and long before the jacket would get its yearly washing, and by that time the seeds of her favorite plants would already have begun to flower along the paths she most liked to follow. But now I am deviating.

"What got it into her little head I will never know for sure. She was looking at a fresh peanut there on the porch and said to it, 'What if I could grow this little peanut in my nose? You don't want to be eaten, I know that.'

"Little Bean, not so naive as us city folk might presume, already knew a great deal about the power of seeds. 'No, no, you want a chance to grow!' the girl said to it and asked, 'Peanut, what is inside you?'"

He Song started the story by saying, "At that time I remember Little Bean really liked the smell of peanuts." He looked into Puyi's eyes. The irises flickered like a joker.

He Song was careful with the razor blade. He has never cut Puyi, yet he has no doubt he could nearly take off the Emperor's head with such a lethal device in his hand, and he had a sneaking suspicion that some members of the Council were hoping for as much. And so to defy their better intentions, He Song instead takes the utmost care to make light of life during these sessions while shaving Puyi. Stories like The Girl and the most wanted to know. Late at night the two would trade guesses, she and her little brother. 'Spicy like hot pepper.' 'Soft like snot.' Her little brother would try to fit one in his nostril, too, but could not. At that time of his life a peanut was too big, his nose too small. Sunflower seeds would fit in but they wouldn't stay in.

"She watered it religiously twice a day by sniffing up water from the right nostril down into the left. I would sometimes notice Little Bean putting warm cups of tea next to her nose. 'Are you all right, Sweetness?' She was often lost in her daydreams. She hummed quietly to her peanut friend and told it long, complicated stories about a little plant and a little girl who were working together in harmony:

> My lovely, lovely peanut plant
> Please grow me hearty bedtime snacks
> And know well the dreams in my head
> Those thoughts I want to share but can't!

She wedged the peanut in her nose one Sunday morning after soaking for the night in her dad's ginseng tea. So excited, she could hardly sleep the previous night, thinking over all the millions of possibilities. 'It will become a friend that never leaves me. Perhaps it could talk to me or read my thoughts. What if it really grows?'"

He Song had shaved half of Puyi's face before starting this second half of the story. He felt no need to rush to a conclusion. He Song is a storyteller.

"The idea came to her when it was late autumn and the flower fields of springtime were three months gone and five months until they were to come again. Little Bean was sitting with her family and neighbors cracking peanuts at dusk on the porch. The girl did not listen to the adult chatter but instead she thought deep thoughts, not just about the peanut so smooth in her hands but more generally about investment and gains. A lotus flower seed can sometimes lay dormant for 1,200 years and then, under the right just before the war. Despite her firm denials, everyone suspected that Little Bean ate it.

"It was placed on the cupboard inside my home for everyone in the village to see. The white root had thin fingers and a curled, pale-green sprout. It looked sad sitting there on the table scorched by sunlight. Everyone who came to view it thought it looked somehow unlike any peanut sprout they had ever laid their eyes on. Of course it was. This peanut had been places.

"It was surgically removed in Kunming Number Five Hospital after I had unsuccessfully tried doing it myself using more traditional methods.

"Unfortunately, a peanut stuck inside the left nostril of a foolish little girl is perhaps one of those modern-day tragedies that the knowledge of the ancients would be ill-equipped to advise. That's how I justified letting her go to the so-called 'medical professionals.' Crushing the nut proved ineffective in my medicine shack and was prone to bruise dear Little Bean's soft, white little-girl face. The tweezers borrowed from my neighbor, who was an earwax cleaner by profession, actually made matters worse by pushing the peanut out of her nasal cavity but up into something much farther back and made Little Bean cry.

"Little Bean had not begun worrying until her secret was discovered by her parents one morning. She had actually been rather proud of the flower bud that her brother discovered protruding from her right nostril. She showed it off to all of my dear friend Peony's children and became quite the envy of her peers, not least of all the hero of her little brother.

"Sure, there was, in hindsight, a crawling feeling at night. Roots had been slowly growing into cavities she never knew existed. It introduced new feelings behind Little Bean's eye, below her ear, beside her jaw.

"How would the eventual harvest taste? That was what Little Bean

They would talk about many things when Puyi got his shave. Because of the blade, Puyi is forced to put more trust in He Song than usual.

"You have never told me that story before. Is it true?" Puyi asked.

The story was about a child and a peanut. "'It melted in my mouth like butter,' is what Little Bean had told me." He Song and Puyi both chuckle.

"I had asked her years later. 'Little Bean, after all these years, I have been meaning to ask you…How did that peanut taste?'"

Puyi couldn't take it. He is forced to listen to this nonsense, and the silliness tickles at his innards. He laughs. He doesn't want to laugh but it cracks through the stone. Puyi wants to be in control of his emotions and most of all his laughter. He doesn't want to move while being shaved. Yet it just is not possible. He Song laughs hard with Puyi.

"One of the resulting complications from Little Bean's surgery back when she was four was this nausea that comes suddenly and mercilessly whenever her little dot of a nose gets even the slightest whiff of peanuts. They say every human nose can distinguish ten thousand unique flavors, and it is only that one smell that will churn Little Bean's stomach. I remember one day she lay there right beside the town nut roaster parked on East Main faint with throw up down her shirt. It makes us all wonder whether there is still a bit of sprout in there somewhere dormant and waiting."

But that's just the ending, or the addendum to it. Here's He Song's silly story, from last to first as he told it to Puyi while shaving:

"The peanut, yes *that* peanut, which has become more indelible in village lore than most residents could hope to ever be, disappeared finally

When He Song was still inside his own room, he had looked into the poster of Big Brother as if it were a broad wardrobe mirror. One final time, he combs his thick hair and the long beard that grows downward from beneath his chin. He inspects the back of his shirt to see if it is properly tucked and picks out wax from his hairy ears using an overgrown fingernail. He smiles at the paper reflection. He does so by not really moving his mouth muscles at all but by doing something with his eye It sparkles. He thinks about the time when both the left and right eyes were working as they were meant to be. Now he has the patch, and beneath that patch are shadows. The wooden box, Pandora's box, sits on a shelf.

In that tiny room, looking out the double-paned window, He Song could see a full moon inches away from the daytime sun. It is Lantern Festival, the fifteenth day of the Chinese New Year. Around the world, ethnic Chinese are preparing rice dough balls that will go in lightly liquored soup for the holiday. The balls, resembling a full moon, are filled with peanut sauce, or bean sugar, or black sesame. The air today carries the smell of candle-toasted rice paper.

Before stepping from his bed that morning, He Song washed his feet using a metal basin. The air is cold. His feet feel sticky and uncomfortable. His bare toes are numb as he lifts them over the bedrail onto the concrete floor. He looks for a cup of tea, which causes him to discover a thermos of hot water. His entire body is invigorated now that his feet are clean. He wipes his wet feet with the bed linen. The water had been scalding hot but wonderfully soothing.

A few days earlier, He Song shaved Puyi's face as he has done almost every third day since he arrived at the Center. Puyi sits still on a stool in his room as He Song takes the last swipe of the blade along the Emperor's upturned neck to chop down the two days of stubble and scoop off the shaving lather.

Puyi came to the topic while picking at the long nail of his pinky. "I had the inkling earlier this week that we were working just six-hour days in the factory. Now yesterday I feel that we worked a twenty-hour day. I decided to count my heartbeats so I can compare one day with another but I do not have a good system to count such big numbers all day and keep track of those numbers. My mind wanders too much for that. But it feels like the bosses here are faking the overhead lights and the break-time bells to fit their production needs, stretching out our workday if more man hours are needed, and making it shorter when they are not."

Earlier, the two of them talked about happiness. "Oh, Puyi! That is not true. I can remember times when you were happy. You are correct that it wasn't when you were concerned about your Emperor duties. That's true enough, yet I remember you being happy one day when you caught that little field cricket and kept him in your pocket as a pet. Do you remember that?"

Emperor Puyi frowned when He Song tried starting them off on the topic of happiness. "He Song, I have never been that. Happiness is for others, not me."

He Song tried so desperately to stay positive. "You know, my old friend, the Communists don't mean to punish you. They just need you to mold yourself into this modern world of ours. The old days are gone, and good riddance to them! You see that we need you to change so that you can survive. The old empire has gone." Quietly he whispers, "And my personal goal goes even beyond what Big Brother has tasked. I want you to finally be happy, Puyi."

This was He Song, the man. Life throws everything at him, and he can survive it all. No, he is not a good man. Do not be mistaken. Yet, you may be able to understand him better now. And there is more to the story.

"That would be very comforting to me, He Song," Puyi said gratefully one day because He Song would bring his request to the Thought Control Center authorities for their consideration.

He Song had merely said to him, "I don't know about that, Puyi. I would tend to think the lighting on the factory floor is the same day after day. But let us talk that over. It is good that you bring these concerns up with me. Big Brother wants you to ask questions, so we can talk them through together. Let me ask them. Maybe our boss will allow us to bring in a clock to test your theory." Puyi takes these words to mean more than they did.

He Song usually acknowledged what Puyi would say, just enough to keep them both from falling into the abyss. "You know none of us keep possessions like jeweled pocket watches in the Center," replies He Song. He often talks to Puyi like an older brother, and these words are meant to knock him down a little and remind him of his place. "We have no need of personal stuff and expensive things. Jewels and diversions just confuse us. I myself, I try to trust the lights and the bells here in the Center, and why not, although I do know that feeling you have. I get it sometimes too. Still, we need to trust the society around us." He Song looks at Puyi and can tell these words were not the right response. He Song tries again, "Say, I do remember that Swiss watch of yours. It was quite a special thing. And that man you bought it from in Tianjin. Can you remember him as well? He was quite a character, that man of clocks. Where might he be now? I wonder if our war with Japan has taken him. Curse that war."

"I have noticed that the pencil factory provides us with different amounts of lighting each day," Puyi said. "Well, as I see it, some days in the pencil factory it feels like we are working for twenty hours straight. We never see the daylight, so who is to say for sure. I no longer have my pocket watch."

to memories of his own face years ago but he doesn't often do that. He forgets.

He Song was similar to Puyi in this one respect. He too hasn't seen his own reflection for a long time. The Big Brother posters do indeed have the same effect on He Song as they do on all the residents at the Thought Control Center. At times, they all believe they possess Big Brother's content eyes, his powerful stance, his glowing skin. Everyone wears his same Mao suit.

At times, He Song also regarded Puyi's face as a mirror to his own. I think the Wolf Whisperer sometimes wishes to be Puyi and imagines it so. He wants to age. He wants to eventually die. They spend hours looking at one another, face-to-face, talking philosophy, history, and feelings. He Song also has the responsibility of shaving Puyi's face every third day, as is common in the Center. This makes you take on some responsibility for other inmates' physical appearances. It was a brilliant move of the Thought Control Center planners to put into place such simple things to create a sense of commonality.

He Song saw himself in the man's wrinkled face day after day, creating a new being out of the clay of our former Emperor. He Song, as we know, does not show aging in any of the typical ways. And this is actually more disturbing to him than you would think. He Song wants to feel the natural pull of time. So what the Wolf Whisperer sees in Puyi is comforting: he sees an old man and so He Song can himself feel old. He Song feels that he may also have thinning hair and a wrinkled forehead.

When they talked during those long hours, Puyi sometimes put his hand in He Song's hand. It is an attempt for grounding. Touch confirms that at least He Song is real. If there is at least one fact you can depend on, you can then extrapolate other truths.

Puyi saw a shadow he'd never noticed before. The shadow entered his room from a light behind an unknown object outside his door. It is an unexpected visitor. *Will you stay awhile and come again tomorrow? You are always welcome. Thank you. I am never too busy for a visitor. It is my fiftieth birthday today. I am just Puyi, an ordinary man like you. Oh, it is the Emperor you are looking for?*

Puyi stared blankly into the corner of his cell until he made the discovery. He sees it now. *Sorry for never noticing you before, Shadow.*

Earlier that day, he scrubbed down his room. *Maybe I will give my room a spring cleaning today,* Emperor Puyi says to himself, not out loud in the empty room but from within. He gets down on his knees and scrubs using a rag. It is surprising where dirt accumulates. *I am fifty,* thinks the Emperor. *How much longer will I live?*

The previous day, Emperor Puyi spent some time with He Song. He Song's mind is somewhere else. He looks in the direction of the former Emperor but with a dazed look. "No, I don't think I will be able to come tomorrow, but we'll see," He Song says to Puyi. "We will get together early next week and discuss your readings…"

"It was nice today. Thank you for the walk outdoors," Puyi said minutes before, knowing the visit had nearly come to an end. "The fresh air is such a relief from this place. So, He Song, I will see you tomorrow then?"

Puyi did not have any mirrors in his room. There are no mirrors in the latrines or hallways or on the factory floor. Without mirrors in the Center, he never really sees himself. There are posters everywhere of Big Brother and those act as a mirror in a way. When Puyi thinks about how he looks to others, an image of Big Brother, glowing, content, a little bit pudgy, is what appears in the mind's eye. If he were to think closely about it, he would dismiss the Big Brother image of himself and rummage back

The Korean War was four hundred miles away, so we would often hear military planes overhead. Rockets fire through the night, and there is a regular stream of military buses carrying wounded soldiers west down the city's roads and healthy soldiers with new guns headed east.

At this point in his life the Emperor had lost everything. No one will call him Emperor. Today is Puyi's fiftieth birthday, but nobody celebrates the event. His food is the same as every other day. He has no visitors.

Emperor Puyi looked back on his life and it all felt fake. The authority he thought he had at one time never existed outside of his mind. The respect he received then was never authentic. His pride he had as a young man had blinded him to reality. Still, Puyi does want to make this day different from the others in the Center. He looks at the bookshelf in his room and realizes he has read them all.

He had to stay in his room. Maybe he could take another stroll outside like yesterday. He has time before his shift begins at the pencil factory. No, there is nobody to take him.

No one could stop him from making this day significant. He will eat this steamed bun like it is cake. He will look at everything around him today like it is something other than what he thought it had been. It will not be an ordinary meal. He will start with the cake. The steamed bread is still slightly warm. Its texture is smooth but looking closer it has tiny round pockets. He finds it interesting how they form. He presses the steamed bun against his cheek. Nobody is looking and who cares if they do. He feels the warmth against his face. The bread has a sponginess and a give, like the soft pillows in his imperial chambers.

He sniffed at the sweet meat inside the steamed bun. Puyi is normally a strict vegetarian but today he eats the meat given him. It tickles his tongue and the Sichuan peppers ride down his throat and warm his belly.

no other place appropriate for a Qing Emperor than Beijing. It is the only place in the universe meant for the man-god, and (if I were truly free to say so) I might argue that Beijing needs the Emperor there as well. He leaves no heirs, so in later years the city will only rely on the bones of hundreds of past emperors buried in great tombs. The city will also rely on the dust of this last one whose ashes will be buried in a commoner's grave.

He Song played an important role in the last Emperor Puyi's reeducation and his repentance before his return to Beijing. Nobody wants to associate with the fallen Emperor but He Song.

Still, why had the Council picked He Song to be the Emperor's tutor in his indoctrination to Communism? Perhaps it is because of He Song and Puyi's unique relationship that went all the way back to when they were just kids. And, there is another reason. He Song owes the Council a favor.

The Council had begun using a code name for He Song by this time. The members call him the Wolf Whisperer. I don't mind the name. We can use it during this stage of He Song's life, when the Council's hands move much of the mechanics behind the scenes.

We are starting this segment in another prison, unfortunately; although it was not formally called one. It is a "Thought Control Center," not a prison, so they all say. My Dear Reader, you might think of it as a psychiatric hospital or a factory or a prison. It is all of these things. And on this sour topic, I fear I have taken you to perhaps too many thus far. Let me promise you, this will be the last one. Going forward, after we have done our job here, which won't take long, we will then only be visiting palaces, mountain villages, and cities. The story will be changing ever so much as we go back in time. There are good memories of this time long ago.

paper, waiting for the next thought, he would look at those stains. Just looking at a hand gives one lots to think about.

While working in Beijing, He Song attended a speech given by Big Brother in defense of the country's traditional Chinese medicine. Big Brother receives a great round of applause when he pronounces, "This one medicine will be the basis of modern natural sciences! It should absorb both the ancient and the new, the Chinese and the foreign, all medical achievements together—and become China's new medicine!" He Song diligently matches the illustrated descriptions from old medicine books with the herbs he finds in Beijing's botanical gardens, both the common plants and the unusual ones. The work and Big Brother's speech encourage him to learn all he can about herbology as well as traditional medicine. He often refers back to the classics written by our Yellow Emperor some twenty-five hundred years ago. He Song can't help himself from occasionally stashing clippings from some of the so-called weeds he finds in the botanical gardens into his coat pocket or between the bindings of his book to later plant in his makeshift gardens at home.

The photo was developed but then embellished. He Song and Puyi are there side by side in the mud. A photographer in a felt black hat tells them both to look his direction, catching the two friends by surprise. *Flash. Snap!* But the developed photo does not capture the mud. It looks like they were in a park. An artist is called into the studio with a fine brush to paint mud on the negative. The picture now has a different feel. They are in a place that is wet and cold. The same expressions as before but now they look embarrassed. Send this version to Big Brother. Leave two copies for the commune here: one to post on the public information board and one for the private file.

It was only when the last Emperor confessed all of his war crimes and recognized his other mistakes that he was freed from the Thought Control Center and allowed back to Beijing where he belonged. There is probably

CHAPTER 11

February 12, 1959

*China's population is 668 million people, less than
half of what it was when this story began.*

You'd think the Council for the Greater Good would be kinder to He
Song given his important role in Emperor Puyi's reindoctrination
into society, but the Council never saw kindness in and of itself
as an important attribute. The greater good, as they saw it, was not about
kindness at all, or gratitude or even compassion. It was about something
else that is perhaps bigger or greater, and I will admit poor He Song, ever
the outsider, never can pin down what that something is.

Big Brother arranged for Puyi to be brought to Beijing so the former
Emperor could write his autobiography before he died. Big Brother allows
Puyi to work in Beijing's botanical gardens during those times that he isn't
writing. Within those botanical gardens, the former Emperor skillfully
employs his eight perfect fingers and two green thumbs. He Song also joins
him for a time in those vast gardens under domed glass and learns a great
deal more himself about our region's herbs before He Song eventually sets up
that final medicine shop in Shanghai. In those luscious botanical gardens,
Puyi weeds through the lilies and thinks about the nature of weeds. What
are weeds? He ruminates on that single thought for many a month. His
kind were once the flowers in the flowerbed and now they are the weeds,
replaced by something much more commonplace. Puyi's hands literally
turned green with the work, staining his skin and nails. Calluses form on
what were once soft hands. When writing his autobiography, pencil on

There is a stone grinder, a kettle for heating water, an abacus for calculating amounts, and the box. This customer is telling He Song that the shop's herbs didn't heal her husband, who had recently died from a diseased heart.

The conversation was impossible to ignore: A customer in back was crying and demanding a refund. Even before Jasmine sees them, she hears He Song say no, he will not refund medicine already used. Results are not guaranteed. It is very hard to say how much worse the illness would have been without the potion. He asks the widow to leave.

There were all sorts of curious compartments for things in this shop and this had an impression on Jasmine. There are big cabinets with shoebox drawers. Other cabinets He Song sells are the size of matchboxes. There is fancy mahogany furniture with drawers within drawers within drawers. Jasmine would be able to file away all sorts of things so neatly if she had this furniture.

Jasmine had been lured into this place one July day, curious about the smells wafting into the streets. Jasmine is feeling the harsh sun on her neck but there is a cool breeze on her cheek that must have come from inside that shop through its open doorway. She smells cinnamon.

Back when she was meeting with her Red Guard companions in the otherwise empty schoolhouse, she drew her voice down to a whisper when she said to them all, "I noticed this wooden box today that He Song treated with the utmost care. I suspect he keeps something unlawful in the box." The children need not let any question go unanswered. Everyone must answer every child's question, and if the answers are not satisfactory, then off with their heads!

Jasmine didn't see why this medicine man, this artist and fake, should be earning a good living on medicine that didn't work. He must be exposed. Perhaps he is indeed a murderer as the woman she met earlier that day had claimed. Young and innocent, Jasmine knows she must bring her concerns up at the next meeting of Shanghai's Red Guards, of which she is a founding member. She must tell them about all the other strange cultural relics and art He Song has for sale in his shop. This strange man she doesn't know well but Jasmine has heard the name before: He Song.

She left his shop earlier that day following a furious customer, and, still curious about the box she had just seen on the back counter of his shop, she hustled across town to make it to her meeting with the Red Guard on time.

The customer had cried when she threw everything from He Song's counter down onto the stone floor. "Murderer!" the customer accuses. "You take advantage of us, among your art and your snobby disposition!" She storms away, knocking over a box that is on the countertop beside the register. He Song gasps and dives for the box. It is made of beautiful wood. Jasmine can't keep her mind off the thing once she sees it. The wooden box will stay in her imagination.

Jasmine had heard this elderly woman while exploring the curious shop, and the yelling drew her toward the back. The box is sitting in a special location on the wide table where He Song measures his potions.

levon a

red light, not green, should be the color of progress. In Communism, red means go.

Nothing was beyond their reach. The children have the power to do or say anything. Their teachers are already sent away to the countryside. There is nothing for them to do during the day other than terrorize the town.

The children indeed terrorized He Song's shop the previous day. They take the wood box from him and schedule a trial for the next afternoon in the courtyard out front where he will be formally accused and possibly sentenced. His pottery is shattered and covers the shop floor. Ancient furniture and paintings are destroyed beyond repair.

"You maggot, how can you own such elite things?" one child yelled. "It is no good for the common person. What a waste." *Elite* is one of the worst insults one could use.

Some of the accusers were pocketing things they took a fancy to because they too were human, with their own vanity and greed. Red Guard members get into He Song's squid ink and write on his walls: "The Calligrapher goes to trial." The children sing an ironic tune as they destroy He Song's shop, and make up various new verses and laugh: "Let He Song defend his elitist ways. Are we not all equal? How dare the one-eyed man presume his writing is better than our own. The children are now the world's calligraphers!"

It was Dear Jasmine who had led them to the Ordinary Remedies and Extraordinary Art shop and to He Song. The Red Guard conclude their daily meeting by agreeing with her that He Song must be exposed: "Let us go there now. We will teach He Song a lesson. He must not put himself higher than everyone else. His shop belongs to the people now."

sentenced. She was one of the last violin instructors left in Shanghai. She is an old lady, and nearly crippled, who had been passed by initially because of her age and kindness, but will be sent out to the countryside like the others because she taught lofty music like Mozart when the Red Guard believes her remaining time and resources should be spent other ways. She will be put to work doing the good work from this day forward.

With a feeling of self-pity mixed with revenge, He Song thought over how he threw his wife's orchids out the kitchen window toward the road. He Song hates his wife for caring so much about the flowers yet being unresponsive toward him in his time of need. His anger feels like a teapot beginning to boil as he watches their life collapse.

Each orchid that He Song's wife had grown was of the rarest kind, only budding once every five years and found nowhere else but the gardens of her ancestors. The stems are cut long and nicely arranged and rearranged. His wife made suggestions as to what the future observer ought to see by way of slightly tilting a single leaf or removing an upper bud to better accentuate another. *I can move the blue stem to the back. Let's take those yellow bumblebee flowers to the side, or more to the front, no, no, no…that's it!* For this entire morning stretching into afternoon, baby nestled in her arm, He Song's wife works on a bouquet. What nonsense. He Song storms into the house angry. The flowers take the brunt of his rage. The baby remains in her arms. She understands immediately. It is now happening to them.

But he shouldn't have blamed his wife. It is not her. It is not him. The Red Guard is causing all this trouble for He Song and his family. They are between the ages of ten and twenty and have taken control of the entire country. Truly, adults are no longer in charge. "Adults are the problem," says Big Brother.

The youth controlled the day-to-day of everyone's life. Even the rules for traffic lights have changed. One child of the Red Guard argues that the provide testimony, but they are now allowed to leave. Each Red Guard wears a strip of red cloth around his right arm. They control everything now.

The woman whose husband recently died drinking He Song's herbal tonics testified before the box was opened, weeping through it all. She accuses He Song of cheating the public. She calls him a murderer.

He Song's wife had also been taken to the podium to provide testimony. She is nervous. Her belly is still round, breasts heavy, and a newborn child is in her arms. He Song's family members are all shivering as if they are cold. He Song's wife was given no time to get a sweater when they showed up at their doorstep and marched her to the square, and the thin scarf she did have on when they came is now wrapped tightly around her baby boy to shade him from the sun. He Song's wife tells the hundreds of neighbors gathered around that their marriage was arranged by local officials two years earlier. He Song had been a good husband. She never minded his missing eye or deformed hand. She answers all the Red Guard's questions succinctly.

Even before the box is opened, He Song's wife hurt as if a thousand tons of earth had fallen onto her, burying her miles deep. She weeps over the broken pots of orchids that she had intended to be gifts for her new group of friends here in Shanghai who were finally accepting her into their community, the type of people who had for so long reproached her for being an outsider. Those pots of orchids are now ruined on the road. Never again could she be so close to a group of neighbors. In her mind, she had already begun calling them her friends though she had not dared to say so out loud. Oh, how she had hoped that an arrangement of perfect orchids might act as the final cement to the friendship of neighbors. But, alas.

"We are next," He Song mumbled to her, looking up at the makeshift platform in the public square. Another neighbor has just been harshly

Whose hand could it be? The people gathered in the street had seen many things these previous months: distinguished musicians, radio personalities, even popular politicians, and respected authors, and so many kind teachers, from kindergarten teachers through college professors, have been beaten or whipped or spit upon for presuming to hold a special skill when, according to Big Brother, the only real skills we should focus on are farming and industrial production for the good of the people. The police allow it to happen, and we assume they get their orders from the top. Yet this severed hand of a baby, it shows that the elite does have something awful to hide. Big Brother is right to call for this Cultural Revolution.

The children have indeed fulfilled what Big Brother has said is their role. They must question everyone. They must find the dirt and rid society of it. If it is the dirt of your parents, all the better for you to come out with it, bear the punishment, and start clean. For the country, we will allow it to happen!

It was opened slowly. The internal hinges let the cover slide upward. Pandora's box doubles in size to the bystanders, who now see both the box's front side and its lovely cover turned in their direction.

The silver key fit perfectly into the keyhole and turned with ease. Jasmine inserts the key, curious what they will find. With a soft click, there is a mechanical release that finally lets go.

He had protested but they all forced He Song to open the box. He Song knows with grave certainty that this is a bad idea. "I don't have the key," he had claimed at first. "Liar, open the box!" Jasmine says to him, reaching for his ring of keys. When there is a lock there is a secret. There must be a key.

He Song had been wearing a dunce hat forced on him by one of the Red Guards. Early on his wife and his baby joined him there on stage to

The crowd left He Song crouched down, his arms pressed against his stomach. He wants to scream, but his lungs feel as though all their air was knocked out, leaving him dazed, airless, and gasping. His body shakes with a terrible desire to produce tears. Just as his lungs have no air, his eyes and mouth are dry.

He and his wife were both sentenced to hard labor on the stage in the square. "This is inexcusable. Go!" Jasmine spits these words angrily after publicly forcing He Song to open the box in front of everyone there. Its contents will cause children to rebel against the establishment, against their parents, and against their teachers. Those children who had been reluctant to join the Red Guard will now follow Jasmine with eagerness and vengeance. It tears families apart.

"This is wrong," Jasmine said in reaction to the baby hand. "Wrong is wrong. He Song." She pauses for effect. This is the people's sentence. Her voice is our voice. "We sentence you to the Production and Construction Corps." She puts the hand back into the box.

When questioned, He Song could not give justification for his bizarre behavior. "I cannot..." the words fail him and he tries again. "I cannot explain why I carry it. I just carry it to remember."

In the box was the severed hand of a baby. Jasmine walks over to He Song, takes the box from his hand, reaches inside, and holds up the hand. "Why?" they all ask.

Everyone had their eyes on young Jasmine who was barely seventeen. They will spread the word of this event far and wide. A so-called entrepreneur in Shanghai secretly kept a box in his fancy shop that contained a child's hand. This is why we must have a Cultural Revolution led by the children. Jasmine spit on him and his wife. "Go! Your son will be assigned a proper family to care for him."

jewels from the Emperor's secret stores. I guess you could say that about the medicine as well. Some of the herbs are really just color and smell to help the emotions, but He Song was famous in the local community at this stage of his life for a miracle brew made mostly of mushrooms. People drank his mushroom concoction by the gallon. For this special medicine, he charged an arm and a leg.

But before we can see the shop, we must start with how that happy life here ended for He Song and his family. This story must continue *levon a* until we reach the beginning.

He Song will not be the same after this day in July. It contains the worst hour of his life. The wooden box will be revealed, and when it is opened, everything begins. I will forever consider it to be Pandora's box because the revulsion of its contents will push the Shanghai public fully onboard Big Brother's Cultural Revolution, regardless of the consequences and the brutality of Big Brother's Red Guards. All the whispering trees in the country will be cut down soon after this day. He Song's wife will be sent to the countryside barefoot and, without the proper gear to survive, she soon dies. The Monkey King will be adopted. The babe does not yet have a name when he is taken from He Song, because it is still custom for fathers not to name their children until they survive to age two. Other people will name this child The Monkey King as further insult, and he will work in factories before he attends school. Jasmine however will be on the road to becoming an influential leader in Big Brother's Red Guard, and without a doubt she becomes one of the most influential women of our age. She does it for the good of all.

When He Song began to realize what had happened, that he was sentenced to be a peasant farmer with nothing, he was alone in the square and tears flowed together with rain. The rain comes out of the blue with tentative drops. Heavier raindrops follow in growing succession. Thunder resounds.

CHAPTER 12

July 1, 1965

China's population is 769 million people.

What I record here I will surely read again and again. What was once fiction becomes surer fact with each read. You cannot reject my story. I am real.

The Cultural Revolution of the 1960s was a very rough period of our history with a lot of conflict and many deaths. The whole community is changed. Big Brother forces us into a new system where we must obey everything. Why? You need to obey the rules to live. It is a violent time that we will all regret in hindsight. Weapons are everywhere. You cannot travel without permits. You cannot buy food without little paper ration tickets.

He Song had already seen a thing or two with both his eyes by then. He is married and has a son whom you and I know as The Monkey King, but here he is just a babe without a name. Jasmine is just a teenager herself.

I will soon show you the two-story shop that He Song built near the People's Road in downtown Shanghai. It still remains. The sign over the doorway says Ordinary Remedies and Extraordinary Art. When it was open He Song sold antiques as well as herbal remedies. Customers walked through the maze of Qing pottery and flower paintings, and many rows of He Song's own calligraphy matted to silk scrolls, to reach the very back of the store where the medicine was sold. It is here He Song normally sat, way in the back. Some of the goods he sells here are fakes but others are priceless and there she is. *Isn't this a small world sometimes.* Strange, growing up the empire once felt so vast to him but now in this republic, people run into the same people time and time again. He walks to the car stalled on the busy road and opens the door. Horns are shouting the frustration of the other motorists, so he cannot hear her words at first. Jasmine is troubled. He holds out his hand to her and says, "Peace." She looks at it, dirt under the fingernails, callused palms, missing fingers, and unclean. "Do I know you? The eye. The hand. Are you…He Song?" she gasps, hardly able to believe, nervous. She felt the danger gathering like a storm. "Yes, Comrade," he says. She shakes his hand and says, "Peace."

So those were their memories, and this is how it actually happened: She secs him on the side of the road and invites him in the car. "Get in," she says. "Do you know how to use a clutch?" The car is stalled out and she will never get back to base on time. The car stalls out again, but with He Song's special touch, it starts.

Tens of thousands of miracles happened to us every day. The magic of forgiveness is everywhere. It has always been in our world, and, if anything, it grows even stronger now. Is that He Song whom Jasmine sees across the street? The Cultural Revolution must have been hard on him. She can smell his unwashed mane from here. It must have fleas. What is that he is eating? Well, finding him again in this lifetime is certainly a sign. *It is my turn to do good.*

and outspoken nature make her a leader in that movement. Her high position in the Red Guard gave her a nice standing going into the PLA when Big Brother decided to end his cultural revolution, led by the guard, and incorporate these two armies into one. The PLA will have no rank from 1965 to 1988, so it is easy for a leader to rise once accepted into the organization.

After the high tide of the Cultural Revolution was over, the Red Guard leaders who didn't simply go back to school entered into a special boot camp within the PLA to learn the terminology of the military and how to follow direction. Jasmine knows a bit about how the PLA works from the military training Big Brother provided the Red Guard under his banner phrase that "The Whole Country should learn from the PLA." Jasmine's first squad leader doesn't understand her. The only man who seems to understand is He Song. He and Jasmine have been taking driving lessons together for a great many months already, and she longs for those times away from work.

Driving was how they met in this city on the Yangtze River, and she often thought about that initial meeting when she was in a military vehicle on loan for the afternoon. The car is stalled beyond hope in the intersection of a busy street. Each turn of the ignition stalls out before she even gets into gear. He Song is looking over at her from outside on the side of the road, hungry and miserable, and she invites him to get in. "Get in," she says simply. She rolls down the window, stares at him for a moment, and her ears begin to hum. That is what she remembers. She enrolls them both in driving lessons, and they will talk in the car as she practices. They drive to all corners of the city and the surrounding countryside.

He Song remembered that initial meeting in his own way. He had only just recently bribed his way out of the Production and Construction Corps labor camp and had not yet time to travel to Shanghai to see what could be salvaged from his previous life. He lifts his head up from his shoes men are already halfway through the obstacle course. She repositions her belt, then goes through the entire course perfectly without error, shooting perfectly. She always polishes her gun before setting it down, and here we all are staring at her for the last ten minutes, thinking the war is already over. Where has she been? She has no sense of timing! I have been yelling at her for the last five minutes and she only then opens her ears to it and notices us all around. How can someone like that be of any use to the army?"

Squad Leader Pollywog first met her one evening while walking down the concrete hallway to his barracks. A beautiful woman behind the desk asks him for his ID, looks up into his eyes, smiling. She says, "Thank you, Squad Leader." Pollywog breathes the air she exhaled in that one sentence, and then does not exhale until he gets to his barracks, thinking all the while how he will marry this woman someday. *What on earth is she doing in such a lowly position?*

"I have some concerns," Jasmine's previous supervisor said to her after only the first week of training. He moves her to an overnight desk post and recommends in her secret file that she remain there without advancement. One thing she doesn't mind about the desk job is filing away all the clearance paperwork and old bulletins that had been in messy piles. She finds great joy in organizing them into orderly folders under her desk. She creates nice labels, file each folder in order by subject and date, and often rechecks everything again and again so that it is all in its proper place. That is the highlight of the desk job.

Many would say, both in and out of the military, that Jasmine was a bully. Pollywog will call it leadership. Without question, Jasmine never deferred to another person unless she agreed with him or her, and even then it would be as much her decision as it was the other person's.

This characteristic of hers worked well as a Red Guard, as you will later see. She is ruthless in her questioning of others. Her ruthlessness

Pollywog had surprised Jasmine when he said that her former sergeant thought well of her. "No way. Really?" she exclaims. "I thought Platoon Leader Lu loathed me. He said that I disregard authority."

Pollywog began their meeting by saying, "I am training a group of leaders within the PLA and spoke to your sergeant. He recommended that you join our division."

Jasmine entered Pollywog's office fifteen minutes before their scheduled appointment. He looks up, noting the time but doesn't mention it. It looks like she is taking everything in, his desk, his hands and nails, the way he looks at her. Jasmine can tell that he is extremely attracted to her. Maybe this is all it was about.

Before he could offer the new position, he had to go through the proper channels within the PLA. The conversation with Jasmine's previous supervisor had really gone like this:

"It'll be a relief, Pollywog. Please, take her. I owe you a drink to have that bit of trouble off my plate. She is a pretty thing though, ain't she?" Pollywog just smiles. He hates when people use his nickname but he never lets them know. Other officials call him Pollywog because they think he rose too fast for his britches. They think his rank is due more to looks than substance.

Pollywog responded to the supervisor by saying, "Not in the army. I think I might have a better place to put her. Do you mind if I take her into my troop?"

Pollywog had also spoken to Jasmine's original drill sergeant, who had similar concerns. He too is critical. "She doesn't follow orders. I tell her to run through the barrels, load her gun, then fire. Now go!...And she stands around thinking it over before she goes. She looks at the barrels, the rack of guns, the place where she should fire. She looks while the other

How was Jasmine recruited? The private conversation with Pollywog ends with her fully on board. His power attracted her. "I'd be happy to do something better for the cause. I know the PLA wants to develop females for promotion into higher ranks, and I know I could be a great leader if given the chance."

He had made his argument well that day He describes how his unique unit within the PLA needs a unique individual like her. "That is how our army is going to be different. We are the people's army. Chinese writing has been hindering the common people from learning to read for three thousand years. Only the highly affluent can dedicate the time to learn to read when the writing is so complicated. When Big Brother came into control, one of the first things he did for us is simplify our writing and the way we read the characters. Now, we have a 95 percent literacy rate, versus before it was less than 1 percent. Less than 1 percent! It is astounding the changes we continue to pursue. I can simplify the PLA for you. Give us another chance, and I think you will do very well."

"But Squad Leader, Sir, I think my fundamental flaw is that I don't understand how the PLA works. I don't understand the terminology that isn't printed in the official manuals, and worse than that, I am not told the secret order of things that go on between men."

He was won over early on in their meeting in his cramped office. He says, smiling, "Then I think you will do perfect with us."

This was because Jasmine had rightly said, "Honestly, Squad Leader, I do. All the time. I question everything."

In his office with the door closed, he asked her, "Do you disregard authority?"

He Song enjoyed having her gentle hand casually on his shoulder. There is a comfortable feeling in allowing this public expression of friendship. In comparison to other countries that are less touchy, it is so much easier here to see who his friends are because in this land we are free to touch. When a hand is placed there, on his shoulder, He Song begins to glow. It is not his skin, but beneath it, where there is a yellow glow that warms gradually, making his words slightly more animated and his attitude more adventurous. It is the difference between one and two. Some philosophers say that the smallest number in the universe is really two. One is when you do not exist.

He Song had nothing in his mind but contentment and happiness. Buddha must have felt a similar way when he sat under the big cypress tree filled with birds chirping and sweet smells, shaded from the fiery Indian sun by whispering leaves, his mind both appreciating and disengaging on the doorstep of Nirvana. This is how it is when He Song and Jasmine are together in friendship.

On the military base just outside the city, Jasmine would continue to work for the PLA. Her first day in Pollywog's unit begins with a lesson about nuclear weapons. There is a video of the detonations in Hiroshima and Okayama. Another video shows the Soviet's own tests.

Pollywog passed a handful of dust around the table. Jasmine feels the dust. "It is just dust. But before, I think it may have been a city," she says. "Correct!" Pollywog's eyes meet hers when Jasmine answers him correctly.

"Who knows what this is?" Pollywog had asked the room of soldiers. The others do not know. "This weaponry we have today is something the world has never seen before. It is in the hands of only a few." He then whispers, "This work is top secret. Nuclear weaponry is now within our military's possession…but we do not understand it very well. Questions need to be asked! Tests need to be made! That, soldiers, will be our task in Lop Nur."

not believing his sincerity. "Puyi is a trickster. Don't go!" He Song listens to Jasmine. He does not go to Beijing.

Jasmine scoffed whenever He Song mentioned Emperor Puyi's declining health and He Song's desire to go see him in Beijing. "Puyi is not just a bit self-centered. He has always been, and at the great expense of us all, his people. What an awful man that old Emperor was. To think he is still alive today. I am grateful you never take me to see him. We are not like him. How can you say that I am, He Song? Look how I cleaned you up. I find you in a gutter all dirt and rags and now you are practically my lover. I dare say any woman would be lucky to have you as a husband now. Pay no mind to that old man and his letters." That is a threat. It is the tone behind the words.

He Song described the old Emperor, saying he was somewhat like her, and not bad in every way. "He always liked to dress well. He always asked many questions. He was a bit self-centered. All in all he was a lot like you, Dear Jasmine of mine."

When he would read the recent letters from Puyi aloud, she would ask, "Tell me more about Emperor Puyi, you poor blind man. Was he really as awful as they all say?"

He would try to get her to go to Beijing with him. Of all their conversations, it is the stories about Jasmine's childhood lake that He Song likes most. When she describes the ice on that lake in winter he says, "You would like Beijing then. It is cold there as well. We could skate. Let me take you there someday. I know ways into the Emperor's old dwellings. We need not just see Puyi the man. We could go into those places where the magic of the Emperor had been and perhaps still is!" But, no, Jasmine is not interested. She holds him back so he will never get to say a final farewell to his friend.

189   levon a

They talked of many things. "Love doesn't feel the same anymore," says He Song as he contemplates whether he might ever remarry.

"My match is not in this lifetime," said Jasmine an earlier day while toying with the idea of reincarnation. I guess that means this relationship will only go so far. He Song always knew it could only go so far.

She told He Song about her childhood as she remembered it. Before her parents moved into the city, they lived in the mountains. Her birthplace had a special lake nearby. Nowhere else in those mountains is there a place to swim but that one place. Everywhere else the rivers are icy, shallow, and with strong currents. But in the lake in the clouds, people can fly. "Man needs water to fly," she says to He Song, describing the sensation, "but it is indeed flying in every way." Jasmine tells He Song many stories of this lake where she was raised as a very young girl. The children there were fascinated by it.

This lake in the clouds got great amounts of sunlight and was shallow. The water is warm by early evening in the summer. If there is just one person swimming, with no wind and no ripples, and if you move slowly without splashing, then you can swim in the starry night sky. The stars reflect their light down and you swim in their reflection. Touch the surface of the sky. Grab hold of a cluster of stars. That is what she would do often as a young child. "You do indeed fly in this tiny lake above the village!" She tells the most lovely stories.

She also described how, in the winter, you can walk on water.

Then, there were the sensitive topics like the last Emperor. He Song receives a letter from Puyi, which he relays to Jasmine. Puyi asks that He Song visit him before his death. His life is fading from him quickly. No one cares. No one seems to remember. Jasmine looks at the letter herself,

I have known." She looks at him crossly like she will never return.

But there was one thing that would always attract her. "My Dear Jasmine, although you have shown me great kindness this year, I will not let go of Pandora's box easily. The last time I let you open it I lost my son and my wife and any sense of what is up and what is down. Chaos came out of that box you opened. But, you endear me once again with that sweet smile. How do you curve your lips so? How do you get that raven black hair to lay so perfectly against that fair white skin of your neck?"

Discussing the box again, she had begged, "Let me win it from you! Give me a challenge, any challenge, He Song, and allow me to earn it. When I am away that will motivate me more than anything."

She had pressed and pressed. May I see the box again? It has been in my thoughts,
"No," he replies softly.

When she asked where it was, he explained, "I buried it before they took us away. I buried it in a tin along with my keys and my photos of the past. It is all still there in the ground."

She first asked about the box while they sat by the fire in the communal room, where they would often chat. "Did you ever get that box back? I would have expected it was destroyed." Her eyes are wide. She had restrained herself all this time, dying to ask.

He Song had grown his thick beard, the beard he will wear until he turns into the jade thief in the Hubei Detention Center. It became scraggly from walking the country like a homeless man. His hair is long and he wears it in a ponytail. At one time, only the Emperor's elite aristocracy was allowed to wear the long braided ponytails. He is maybe the last one in China to do so today. When the communists took over, that hairstyle disappeared.

and chopped onion and places it on a flat dumpling paper, then folds it carefully into a half moon. Jasmine mixes new dough for the dumpling wraps, then pounds it thin. They are talking of the CGG and of the wooden box. Jasmine asks him, "But who are these people?" He replies, "They are the only people I know who have been able to really cause change. To me personally they have been awfully cruel over the years. To contact the Council for the Greater Good, you must disappear completely for a time. Wherever you are hidden, someone will eventually find you. That person who first finds you will be a member from the Council or one of their spies. It might be someone you know or someone you have never seen before. To that person, you say, 'I am ready to meet the Council. Please tell them I am ready.' The person might look confused but he or she will relay the message and eventually you can meet them all. When you meet them all, say you want to join. Tell them your vision of the greater good. Tell them how far you would go to achieve that vision. I have no doubt they will accept you into their ranks immediately."

They were teasing each other that night. Rolling out jiaozi dumplings, they are touching hands more than they usually do. He Song says, "Okay, I will give you a challenge. On your assignment with Unit 8302 you might come across the Council for the Greater Good. I am certain the atomic bombs will be of interest to them so they will have a presence at the test sites. Convince the Council to let you into their secret organization. They are worse than the sphinx in their riddles, and, like her, they may eat you if you answer incorrectly. Yes, that would be a sufficient challenge for you to win a treasure like my wooden box. That is what you may do to earn it from me."

He Song knew the military would be taking his Dear Jasmine away. He wants her to continue to communicate with him when she is gone, to not forget him. "Jasmine, please come back to me whole after all this is done. We will make jiaozi together again, and you can tell me your stories of Lop Nur, and in doing so you will create a world that is bigger than what

Jasmine bought He Song clothing that matched the clean and crisp style she liked about Pollywog. She places the new clothes and shoes in a brown paper bag nicely folded and left in the backseat of the car. He Song drives off with the charity and finds it when he arrives home. There is a note on top of the brown bag in clear letters. "Take it, please. Let me help you. —J." With these clothes He Song looks normal. He Song can now fit back into society thanks to Jasmine.

He Song and Jasmine most enjoyed the driving practice they had done together those summer days in the 1960s. At first they use a military vehicle. Later He Song shows up at Jasmine's dormitory driving a car that appears to be his own. "How'd you get this?" she questions him but he ignores questions he does not want to answer. Jasmine is practicing for a driver's license and still uncertain behind the wheel. He Song is far superior in his ability, yet he feigns a desire to also practice for the same driver's license exam.

In the car, he smelled of cinnamon. Jasmine has never been with him in the morning, so she would not know this, but the smell comes from the cinnamon He Song adds to his morning brew of medical herbs each day. It comes out of his pores sweet and fresh. It hangs on his breath.

They took walks and had picnics. Lying against his shoulder in an open courtyard, people walking past, Jasmine says to him, "And you, He Song, you're my one-eyed beast." He calls her his beauty. She looks at the patch on his eye and lifts it up. Beneath, there is a shadow where an eye should be. But the two of them are similar in that way. She once had a damaged eye. Thankfully hers was repaired as a young child. He Song did not have that good fortune.

Another time, they were rolling jiaozi dumplings out around the table of the community kitchen. He Song takes a scoop of ground pork

Although she doesn't ever call it love, there must have been something. She may love He Song merely because he is pitiful and all wrong for her. Tragically, at the same time she also begins to love the handsome and young Pollywog. Her love for Pollywog is probably not so much an attraction to his handsome physique and features, though he is handsome. Jasmine is attracted to Pollywog because he is such a powerful and passionate man, wrapped in the mystique of the nation's nuclear program, and yet he treats her as an equal. He Song is none of this and never treated Jasmine so. If you are in love with such opposites, will you ever be satisfied? You, Dear Jasmine, are the contradiction.

Being the poor dog found on the side of the road helped He Song fan the flames of romance for a time while Jasmine did her best to clean him up and ultimately let him go. Now that He Song is respectable again, Jasmine shows less interest in him and regardless how she feels her career is destined to be alongside Pollywog. *He Song doesn't need me so much anymore*, she rationalizes while eating leftover jiaozi dumplings they had rolled together the other day. *Hmm. We did make good jiaozi together.* Thanks to her touch, He Song can now manage on his own. It might be better for him if she isn't around, and far better for her. Their most intense months together finally end with her saying to He Song flatly and without any hint of emotion, "I can now see that what I feel for you is a deep form of pity. It is not love." She sits in the passenger seat. Tears swell in her right eye, betraying the tone she wants to set. "We are not meant to be lovers. I refuse to take your heart. If I have been misleading up until now then I release you, He Song. Go your own way. I will go mine." She gets out of the car.

To her credit, Jasmine had worked miracles fixing the broken down remnants of poor He Song. With Jasmine's help and instruction, He Song becomes much like that other man who is attracting her attention in Wuhan. She gives He Song a final haircut one afternoon that looks identical to the haircut worn by the squad leader. It is very professional and fine.

same day press her body against her platoon leader. In each letter to He Song, she will promise to contact the CGG when life becomes less hectic.

In just a thirty-two-month period, China successfully exploded its first atomic bomb, launched its first nuclear missile, and detonated its first hydrogen bomb. The very first Chinese nuclear test drops from a tower and yields twenty-five kilotons of power. All very impressive.

~ ~

If only I could change history.

When Emperor Puyi passed away, nobody was told. With his eyes closed and mind nearly extinguished, Puyi sees himself as a toddler again. The toddler is looking in his direction. Old man Puyi notices that the boy had ten of his own fingers and the long ponytail and the rich silk robes of a prince. They look at each other, and he sees all the years that have passed in between then and now. In doing so, he recognizes the entire life for what it was, and Puyi finds a type of eternity within that boundary. He speaks to the toddler knowing the toddler would not remember this, but the meeting will always be deep inside of him. He realizes now that the toddler will grow up to always know within his soul all that was revealed in this moment.

The night before Puyi died he had a dream of his death. He writes to He Song the next morning.

Days before, he felt it coming as he ate, but until that final evening he would always wake up in the morning to feel the sun.

~ ~

Jasmine's last words to He Song before going off to Lop Nur with Unit 8302 had been, "I hope we never fall in love." Such a thing to say. He waves goodbye.

away. One time Jasmine arranges ten thousand animals to see what will happen to a large group. She needs a team of two hundred soldiers to complete the task. Besides caged animals Jasmine also places the PLA's latest army tanks, aircraft, and other military vehicles in the epicenter to test their limits. She also leads her team to construct buildings around the test site. They build a whole city, even with a working underground metro, and all the supporting utilities. There is a life-sized bridge long enough to cross the Yangtze River. And then, it's gone. The scientists and military commanders need to see what could happen in all sorts of scenarios. Any remains are gathered up once the dust clears and the objects are studied by the soldiers of Unit 8302.

Jasmine often rode an army horse through the wasteland, as did most of Pollywog's team. They wear gas masks over the nose and mouth. Horses wear a special gas mask as well. Watch them now, riding toward the mushroom cloud of an atmospheric surface detonation. Still, even with the mask, Jasmine sometimes feels the smoke in her lungs. The heat touches her from the inside and singes her bronchi. On each side of her, the other soldiers are raising their swords. Yes, they are carrying swords as they enter the radioactive fallout. We can estimate now that 1.48 million people were exposed to the radiation during the tests. Jasmine was only one of the many casualities of Lop Nur.

There was CHIC 6. It is the first full-yield, two-stage thermonuclear test.

Explosions went off in her heart, day after day. Jasmine is still quite young and loving two men at once is hard on her. It is not easy to rationalize or let go. As it turns out, neither man will ever kiss her.

A previous nuclear test used a Tu-16 bomber. In contains lithium 6 and explodes with a yield of one hundred kilotons.

Jasmine continued to write to He Song religiously even after she left town for Lop Nur. She would write him from the base at Lop Nur, but that tumor, he goes to the doctor. The doctors do their best.

Though she glamorized her role in her mind, Jasmine's day-to-day work for much of the time was simply to haul objects in and out of the lake basin. During the nuclear tests, Jasmine imagines putting all sorts of things from her past in the detonation radius instead of what Pollywog assigns to the pit for study. She imagines putting her father there, and the uncles who tried to bind her feet as a child. She imagines luring the steelworker into its epicenter, that man who hurt her eye as a child. She imagines putting her little red book there on the ground and letting the nuclear bomb take it away. The little red book is what Big Brother told them all to recite as kids. Would it shrivel up and disappear? She imagines strapping the last Emperor there and all his dirty wealth. In reality, though, she drags out horses and cattle and pigs to see what happens to them. The blast creates an unreal surge of light. There are usually no remains. When there are, she brings them back to the station for further tests.

During this time at Lop Nur, Jasmine had dreams of returning to the banks of the Yangtze River where she and He Song had sometimes rendezvoused. In the dream, she is breaking up with him formally, telling him all the intimate details about Pollywog, and yet still she demands the wooden box from him. *Why? Just because. I want it, just because. I do not love you.*

There was another recurring dream, more of a daydream. She has the wooden box in her hands. In her fantasy, he is making pork dumplings. She tells him stories about the nuclear tests while they cook. They fold flattened dough around the ground pork. It is when she describes to him how every object can be so easily obliterated at Lop Nur that He Song suddenly offers the box to her to have it destroyed. In the daydream, He Song says to her, "Destroy it."

The animals placed one mile from the blast center were burnt to cinders but those tied up five miles from the center would not die right that with each passing day we can survive together on Earth, the odds that an ET will visit us increase tenfold.

If that extraterrestrial landed at Lop Nur, they might think they were back home. It is a dried-up salt lake that looks like a crater of the moon. The crater has salt deposits on the ground as deep as two feet in some places, causing swirls of colors in the rock. The landscape is colored in rust, teal, white, gray, and blue. The wind blows harshly against our faces here. If not for the biting sand, the wind would be more welcomed because it at least blows clean air in our direction from the north. The lakebed looks desolate now, but at one time it fostered one of the oldest of civilizations. This would have been when there was water in the lake. Rivers have changed over time, and now there is no water, just the massive empty crater that reaches seventy miles wide. There are concrete buildings on the lip of the crater. These buildings hold scientists, engineers, and Pollywog's unit.

Martian-like now, Lop Nur was the main test facility for our nuclear program. Maybe it is the radiation that gives it a certain feel that defies gravity and other laws of nature. In Lop Nur village and the surrounding areas, it seems to Jasmine that the people themselves are different, alien. Everyone's face is asymmetrical, which makes them seem ugly to her. One eye has grown slightly below the other, or is maybe bigger than the other. An eyebrow on the left is bushier than the right, maybe longer, or grayer. The villagers are unhappy about their bodies and tend to complain. One arm has more muscle. Babies' butt cracks run a little to the left or right rather than straight up to the spine. Their fingers go every which way so that if you were to place one hand against the other, they curve in various directions. The same goes for toes. Look into the mirror and see your left breast is higher. Perhaps a lump is starting there? Hair does not fall evenly on the shoulders. Your hair and nails yellow easily. People cough all around you. This is life in Lop Nur.

It all went unseen most of the time. When a resident discovers a

8302 is very busy. In the letter, she leaves out everything about her heated romance with Pollywog. Yet, she writes "Lovingly, Your Comrade Jasmine" at the end of the letter. Why does she continue to lead He Song on in this way while there is another man?

Jasmine's entry into the People's Liberation Army, commonly called the PLA, was a complex story in which the late Swad Leader Pollywog played an important role. She isn't army material. This is clear as day, and I am surprised she lasts as long as she does in their hierarchies. The nature of these military organizations is to ensure soldiers will defer to their higher authority during battle. Everyone must do so, all the way up to the army general, who in kind defers to Big Brother himself. Jasmine doesn't play that way.

Pollywog took his team, Unit 8302, to a desolate area of the country called Lop Nur for a secret assignment. There is so much to learn about nuclear weapons now in the 1960s. At this time, the magic of the nuclear explosion is especially new and wonderful. I have heard it said, and I am sure you have heard the same yourself, that the human race is a test case for how long any advanced civilized society can survive in our universe. How humans on Earth fare will tell us whether there could be extraterrestrials from other planets advanced enough to visit Earth someday. Let me explain. Humanity on Earth developed the capability for spaceflight and satellite communication only over the last seventy-five years of our thirty-thousand-year history. At nearly the same time, we also developed the knowledge and ability to cause our own nuclear annihilation. It therefore seems likely that any extraterrestrial civilization will progress in technology in a similar way, learning how to destroy themselves at about the same time they develop the technology to fly to the stars. The theory goes that if we humans can prevent our own annihilation for, say, two hundred years, despite having the power of nuclear weapons at our fingertips, then it is likely other advanced societies might be able to survive at least long enough to build fancy spaceships that can visit Earth. So, the astronomers conclude

He felt that same creeping feeling at breakfast in the morning while eating his rice congee with a short, fat spoon.

The night before, he had a strange dream that felt so real that when he woke he wondered which state was reality and which was sleep. In the dream he meets himself as a toddler and his whole life is strung out before them both. The adult man he is today, now in his prime, stares back into the eyes of the baby he once was. They don't understand one another but together they look at the entire life Pollywog had chosen to live, from end to end, and then they stare at each other. In doing so, Pollywog feels a type of eternity that has always existed somewhere inside him.

Before his death, Pollywog enjoyed reading and editing Jasmine's personal mail before the letters were sent out. He does this to an important letter she sends to He Song just before the fatal crash. To him it is not unusual to censor the writings of your underlings. Pollywog does this to all his officers. It is quite normal. In fact, in Communist China it is not at all unusual for multiple people to review personal mail sent and received. His mail, too, is probably reviewed by someone before it is delivered to him. For the letter Jasmine sends to He Song, Pollywog first removes "lovingly" from the conclusion of the letter. That word is not needed! He also removes all mention of Unit 8302 and Lop Nur for security reasons. The base needs to remain a secret. He leaves in the information she writes about the CGG, which he himself never knew existed, but Pollywog isn't surprised such groups are around us, nor is he at all surprised that the CGG would have a great interest in Jasmine for she is a remarkable person. He looks forward to He Song's responses so he can learn more about this secret council.

In the letter that Pollywog will edit, she wrote about her great interest in the work done at Lop Nur, that our country is learning all sorts of exciting new things about the power of the nuclear bomb, and in a final paragraph Jasmine wrote how she hoped to reach out to the Council for the Greater Good as soon as she could find the time, but her work in Unit protégé a household name. His Antonov turboprop aircraft crashes into the snowy peaks of the Kashgars. The Soviet plane was given to the Chinese military a decade earlier and had been used to drop the test hydrogen bombs, but this day its mission is to transport Chinese troops into Lop Nur. Unbeknownst to everyone at the time, these extra men, if they arrive safely to the region, might provide enough added force to push the Soviets west past the mountains, much farther back than Jasmine will be able to do with her limited number of men. How things can change. Friends become enemies. Gifts become weapons against the gift-givers. Planes crash. Soldiers perish.

The An-12 turboprop fell five thousand feet and disintegrated into flames before impact in those western mountains. The four propellers have been trailing smoke since takeoff. Pollywog looks back at the strong diagonal tail sticking up from its midfuselage. He sees smoke but disregards it. There are only ten windows on the aircraft and Pollywog is given one of them. Rather than looking back, he continues to look toward the sun where Jasmine is waiting. On board are six crew and ninety-two passengers. There will not be a shred left of the poor Pollywog who held Jasmine's heart. A picture of Jasmine disintegrates in his pocket.

If he'd had a moment for hindsight, the poor platoon leader could have appreciated the comforting feeling he'd enjoyed for most of his last day. Of course the platoon leader will not be aware of anything once the plane is sucked in on itself from the air pressure. However, in his seat before the trembling and the noise and the blast, when things still seem normal, he does see his end.

When Pollywog boarded the flight he had that creeping feeling that death might be near, but he rationalized to himself that the feeling must just be love jitters. Should he propose to Jasmine right away? No, let the love wait a while. Give it time to grow.

She was going to leave her camp up for a while longer. She wants to go fishing first. That way she can grill any fish she catches before moving on.

How long would it take for the CGG to find her? Jasmine has already been out here in this wilderness for seven days. *Am I making it too difficult for them to find me?* She is making her location difficult enough for military acquaintances not to find her, but not so difficult that no one will ever find her. She wants to be found. With the abundant supply of fish, fresh water, and firewood, and with summer approaching, she could live this way for a while. She feels harmony in nature all around her, giving her the essentials she needs for life. In the big space and quiet hours, the fresh air is enough to fill the void.

It was an emotional time for Jasmine when she jumped. A senior officer in the army, to whom Jasmine had reported, passed away just weeks before the Seven-Month War began. At the funeral service in his hometown, a good ways from Lop Nur, the PLA command decides to give his post to Jasmine at least in part because, without a doubt, Jasmine was his protégé at Lop Nur. She is riding on the train back to base in a lone officer car following her promotion when she decides to jump off the train. It is moving at a slow speed. *Take the leap!* It is an easy landing. She does it without thinking about consequences back on the base. She has one goal in mind: Seek out the CGG.

The former platoon leader from whose funeral Jasmine had left that prior day went by a fitting nickname used in some private circles. Although some might say the nickname is slightly impolite to use postmortem, it has always made me smile to mention it. Let's use that nickname here: they called him Pollywog.

Pollywog never did turn into the prince Jasmine had hoped for. The commander dies in a plane crash shortly before the war that will make his hook or breaking the line feels like it takes all day but probably just takes minutes. She laughs during most of the fight. Jasmine has to step into the water, grab the fish by the gills, and pull it up to shore. The fish comes up to her knee.

She waited for that first bite. It does not take long: nibble, ever so lightly. A worm gently dragging itself in the current. Nibble. *There it is!*

Jasmine was eager to try her luck fishing. The River Wusuli has a history of catastrophic floods in the springtime and its surface usually freezes over until April, but it has melted open early this year and the spring flooding still hasn't come. The pole she uses is handmade from an eight-foot bamboo stick. She uses her old hairpin for the hook. The worms she digs up near her camp.

She waited for the CGG messenger to find her deep in the woods. He Song had not said who it would be—only that the messenger would search her out if she hid away for a period of time. While out here alone in the wilderness, Jasmine witnesses starving people moving across borders between China and Soviet Tajikistan not knowing where to go, some in large caravans of thirty or more families leaving their ancestral homeland. She also witnesses Soviet patrols moving far past the mountain ridge that is no doubt Chinese land. None of this concerns her. She is lost in other thoughts, still in mourning.

Jasmine got a late start that morning. Just before dawn would have been the better time to fish. She reconsiders and instead packs up her tent and supplies and leaves the pack beside the coals in the fire pit. Doing so, she gets a much later start to fishing than she would have liked. But something inside her needs to have everything packed up before leaving. *It does feel better to have it all ready, so maybe it's worth the extra hour,* she tells herself. It also allows her time to have another cup of tea.

She had been knocked unconscious and woke up confused. When Jasmine finally becomes aware of her surroundings, she sits up and sees the three Soviet soldiers. She is in these woods to find the Council for the Greater Good's representative. What a surprise that the CGG representative might be non-Chinese, but this must be they. He Song had not said one way or another, but she had assumed it was a strictly Chinese organization. She ignores the bruise on her head and quickly stands up to salute. "I have been waiting for you out here. I want to meet with the Council for the Greater Good…" she starts in rudimentary Russian but doesn't finish. One of the Soviet border control soldiers is startled by her sudden movement and shoots her in the leg. That is their first mistake.

While she was coming to, the men were gathered around her discussing what to do next. They speak Russian. "She dresses herself like a lieutenant but she is a woman," says the first. "I heard that the PLA put women soldiers on their front lines and some have become officers," says the second. The third man doesn't like any of this and gruffs, "What do we do with her?"

Her last memory prior to all this was of something flashing from the corner of her right eye just before she felt a jolting knock to her head. *They have me now,* she thinks. She is relieved rather than scared because she doesn't know who they really are.

Her own capture happened while she was proudly looking over her morning's catch strung between two pine trees a few feet away. There are sturgeon, humpback, chum salmon, and graylings. The wind changes and Jasmine smells a whiff of tobacco. She smiles wide. *Finally, they have come!*

The first catch that morning was the biggest river fish of them all. The time it takes to real in the humpback salmon without dislodging the

Jasmine?" She has a basket on her head full of herbs and wild mushrooms gathered from the forest, and she is wearing traditional garb. Her cheeks are bright pink. Her hair is braided with metal charms clipped in the folds.

Jasmine's mind had been racing in so many directions moments before. Returning to her makeshift camp in the woods, she finds everything is as she had left it. The Soviets have not been here yet. *I must go!*

Down by the river, Jasmine had just pulled the men's bodies into the brush and returned to her camp. She had mistakenly thought these were the CGG representatives. She goes through the dead men's possessions. One of the soldiers has a formal-looking document written in Russian. She takes the document with her and takes the fish she had caught that morning, but leaves everything else as it is.

"Oh, what have I done?" She can't see the skin of the three dead men. It is just hair and blood. The human skin is hidden under a coat of beard and thick brown hair, and an inside layer of dark blood released from the head wounds, almost black now and pasted to everything.

She used a strip of her own clothing to bandage her leg wound. The bullet is still in her muscle. This is the first time she's been shot. It isn't as painful as she expected. Her body is numb. It shivers.

Three shots fired, one to each head, killing all three. Jasmine does well with a gun.

Having been shot in the leg, she shot back because there was no choice. She can tell from the men's expressions they have no idea what she is saying, and they don't care. "Let's kill her here and take the fish," they say to one another in Russian. That is their second mistake. The doomed men turn from her to grab the fish. That gives her just enough time to reach down for her revolver and to shoot.

have made the difference. Perhaps there would not have been a war that year; perhaps Beijing and Moscow would continue to be allies, and, with China's vast resources to feed the Soviet Union's might, the USSR might have eventually won its Cold War with the West. President Nixon most certainly would have never visited China, the pandas Sing Sing and Ling Ling would have stayed in the Misty Mountains, and we would continue to be a communist country of happy, ordinary proletariats all wearing the same gray jackets in uniform, and all of us, save a special few, would remain contently closed off and oblivious to the wider world.

Jasmine must have calculated it all in her head, and decided to act. When Jasmine returns to base, she is taken immediately to the infirmary. Her leg needs surgery. A bullet is removed but she will not stay overnight for the recovery. Something has lit a fuse in her. The document she recovered from an earlier encounter with the Soviet border patrol is translated and reveals that the Soviet border patrols under Colonel Leonev are actually conducting scouting missions in what seem to be preliminary steps for USSR advancement on part of China's western territory. Their scouts are not only assessing the military vulnerabilities of China's border towns, but also all of the mineral deposits available there.

〜 〜

Earlier, back in the woods of Rare Treasure Island, Jasmine let out a gasp. *Oh!* "So, you know who I am." Jasmine needs a moment for it to sink in, and then she continues. "I have a message for the Council. I ask that a meeting be arranged between us. I want to become a new member." The peasant woman looks at her knowingly, nods in reply, and then disappears back into the forest.

This was the representative. Jasmine takes a breath. What is past is past. Let's move forward from here. Forget the Russian soldiers for the moment, Dear Jasmine. Take a breath and then speak to this representative.

The peasant woman's voice took her by surprise. "Excuse me,

and her soldiers have been standing firm since the conflict began.

Fortunately, her men had been making preparations of all kinds during those fourteen days of quiet. Trenches are dug and guns mounted in strategic locations on the island and along the surrounding bank. Maybe there will be no response by the Soviets. That is what they all hope. A telephone call comes from Big Brother himself congratulating Jasmine for her actions taken already. "Stand fast," he says to her.

The conflict began when Jasmine's small group of PLA troops ambushed the Soviet border guards on Rare Treasure Island. She takes them all by surprise. She gives no warning. By the end of her assault, the Soviets have fifty-nine dead, including one senior colonel, and ninety-four wounded.

The morning before she ambushed the Soviets, an order was made to go to the island and secure it for the Chinese. But who gave that order to start the war? It is my belief that Jasmine acted alone and on her own will. Jasmine reports it to her superiors once her troops are already deployed. A telegram is eventually sent about the confiscated Russian document giving justification to the actions, approved by Beijing leaders after the fact. Big Brother only receives the communication after events are irreversible. Someone made the decision before those in power ever knew. There was no official authorization.

Before Jasmine left for battle, He Song also was sent a short telegram. She might die today, so it should be sent now. The telegram says, "Contact with the CGG established."

⸝ ⸝

I have thought long and hard how history would be different if Dear Jasmine had only gone fishing one hour earlier in the River Wusuli as she had originally planned that March morning in 1969. One hour might

might think him a hindrance. She instead gave him a leadership post on the front line.

Jasmine yelled into her walkie-talkie: "Great courage leads to greater courage. This is how we will win the war!" There is another blast.

When Ren pulled the trigger, his infantry standing behind him were somehow freed of their fear of being found out, of becoming exposed, of being instantly killed. They pull the triggers of their rocket launchers in concert. Their deadly contents launch one, two, three, four, in sync!

Sergeant Ren made it look easy. He picks up his Chinese bazooka as the dreaded tank comes near, crossing over the river, coming up the bank. Four of his infantry lift their newer versions of Chinese rocket launchers as if their hands are tied to his. The troops stare at him, not at the tank, and match their aim to his aim by following his arm.

Prior to its ultimate destruction, the secret tank's fire control system had already become somewhat cumbersome for its new crew. Only forty rounds of ammunition can be carried inside and Jasmine can tell the tank is running low. When it looks like there's a lull of the main gun, Jasmine signals her team for an attack, but her young soldiers do not respond. They just stand there in their tracks, fingers locked. They are terrified to expose themselves to this metal monster.

The secret tank indeed caused significant damage to the Chinese forces before its eventual destruction. Jasmine's troops are blown to pieces all around.

It was after two weeks of quiet. The Soviets finally retaliate by storming Rare Treasure Island. Colonel Leonev sends the secret tank to flatten Jasmine's claim to the island. No one on the Chinese side has ever seen anything like it. The tank is incredibly mobile and fitted with snorkels, allowing it to cross through the deep river and up onto the island where the brave woman warrior

POWs closely guarded on the Chinese side of Wusuli River. The white contamination suits they were wearing all hang outside of Jasmine's tent, like flags, ready for her men to use if needed.

One day earlier, the Soviets waded to the island to collect their dead. One of these bodies is that of the senior colonel still left inside the tank. From the riverbank, Jasmine says to her sergeants, "Hold your fire. Let them collect their dead."

The dead soldiers were the result of three days of vicious fighting when Jasmine's platoon had pummeled the opposing forces with a relentlessness the Soviets had never seen. *These Chinese do not sleep or take a minute's rest.* Each man and woman on her side feels invincible. Jasmine successfully halts the Soviet penetration and eventually evicts all Soviet troops from the island. She does not consider the costs.

What initiated this brilliant rally when the Chinese were outnumbered and outgunned? Without any doubt, it is Sergeant Ren's direct hit that disables the leading tank, killing its commander and blocking the advancement. That, Dear Reader, becomes a turning point in the battle. It comes as a surprise. Ren aims the rocket directly into the tank's telescope eye. The Soviet tank's first officer lifts his guard to inspect the damage of Sergeant Ren's shot. What a mistake for him to open the hatch, because exactly then three missiles hit directly on target, destroying half his body and enough of his compartment to stop the tank in its tracks. There is hope yet.

Fortunately for us all, our rash platoon leader had Sergeant Ren on her front line. His bravery cannot be overstated. Maybe it comes from his once having been a part of the second great world war, or maybe it came from his older age, or maybe it was his familiarity with shooting nearly the same style of Chinese bazooka that he held that day on the island, once having used it to defend his own home against an encroaching Japanese Army. Ren was one of Jasmine's oldest soldiers, so another army captain good exercise for Jasmine because it helps keep track of every variable in the battle and the chances that each can turn one way or another, and then she in practice tugs fiercely on those variables most to her favor. Most of us disregard important variables that could affect the outcome of things, whatever our battle may be. It is usually too much information for most people to process. Jasmine's mind, however, can handle the complexities. *I should become a mathematician,* she thinks to herself. *After I retire from the army, that's what I will do.*

To her men, she pointed out the captured tank, the secret tank. "Look what Sergeant Ren has done. Look here what our bravery can achieve! Even their best tank cannot stop us. China has the mandate of the good and the right. We will not stop now."

The battle was bloody. Eventually, the Chinese and Soviet armies camp on opposing sides of the river, and the island becomes a dead man's zone. On March 17, our side crosses over onto the island to remove our dead soldiers. Jasmine examines the tank more closely and tries to enter it. *Locked!* This miraculous T-62 MBT apparently had a nuclear radiation protection system. The system must have automatically turned on and sealed the tank's interior some time after the battle, preventing anyone from entering the main compartments. She pulls at knobs and tries using the butt of her rifle. The system probably self-initiated from the high radiation levels on her from the Lop Nur testing facility. Lop Nur is China's main nuclear weapons test site, and when the wind blows from that direction your nose begins to buzz. A blower and filtration system removes the radiation-contaminated dust from inside the tank, and Jasmine can hear it blowing out dirty air. The tank's crew were all wearing contamination suits when they were captured, so this system probably does not protect against biological or chemical weapons, only nuclear. For additional protection, you need the suits. Two members of the tank's crew had perished during the fight, and those bodies were collected earlier by the Russians, but the others became prisoners of war during the last battle. Jasmine has the secret tank that was abandoned there. They pull the tank only as far as the river but no farther because Jasmine's artillery forces thwart the Soviets. The tank sinks in river mud. Jasmine is so proud when a petty officer brings her news about the latest movements on the battlefront. It is yet another win for her men. She tells her superiors about it as she heads off to Wuxi. She is granted a short military leave for whatever private business she has on the coast.

～ ～

Rare Treasure Island had two names. The one we use is Chinese but there is another one that is Russian. They call it Damanskii Island. It sits in the River Wusuli (Russians call the river the Ussuri, but enough of that), which is a north-flowing tributary that feeds a larger river that flows into Siberia. The river waters come from both glaciers and subterranean springs from who knows where deep below. Locals know there is good fishing there. You could throw in a fishing line with any bait on its hook, and without much skill you will catch a twenty-jin fish.

A waterlogged Soviet tank that would eventually take an honored place at the Chinese military museum in Beijing was pulled out of the Wusuli River with the help of a team of divers from the Chinese navy. River water is still dripping down from the tank's six wheels on each side. Jasmine has never seen anything like it. She stands by and looks it over as the events of the last few months spin in her head. The tank is well armed but was much more mobile during battle than any tank in our army. Now, China will have one too. It can be disassembled and its design will be studied and duplicated. Jasmine smiles.

Earlier it had been just Jasmine's single unit under attack by more than one hundred Soviet troops, at least ten tanks and fifteen APCs. When the odds look bleak, Jasmine recalculates in her head and asks herself, *Is there still a chance we can hold on?* In doing such a calculation, you need to factor in all the possible elements and their probabilities. This becomes a

"I can say with the greatest humility that I have witnessed what our new bombs can do firsthand. At Lop Nur testing facility, I actually tied up a living dairy cow in what was to be the epicenter of the atomic blast with *these hands*." She raises her hands from the table in front of her. "After the explosion, I went back to that spot, and there was no cow. There was no rope. There was not even dust. Obliteration is the right word to use."

She was insistent. "We need to maintain our independence from the Soviets whatever the cost. Our liberty is worth the risk of a prolonged war with heavy casualties. Even the use of nuclear weapons needs to be on the table."

The counterargument had been tested first. "How can you say continued independence is worth the annihilation of an entire city and millions of Chinese people if this border conflict were to escalate to a nuclear war?" the Council asks itself in several ways. Jasmine will have an answer they all could agree with that day.

It was He Song who encouraged Jasmine to speak her voice. He had not been thinking about the greater good of society, as Jasmine so often does. He had been thinking only of Jasmine's good, regardless of the broader consequences. He just wants her to have happiness in her life. Nearly a year ago, when he had told her the secret ways to get in touch with the CGG, He Song still held the unrealistic hope Jasmine might return to him.

A representative of the CGG had brought Jasmine to the meeting that weekend on a private jet. It waits on the runway in Lop Nur. They give her twenty-four hours to arrange leave from the PLA. The entire time the jet just sits there on the tarmac, the two pilots resting inside the cockpit and the CGG rep resting in the cabin, waiting.

Before Jasmine departed for Wuxi, the Soviets sent in a recovery team to Rare Treasure Island in a last-ditch attempt to either take back or destroy the

"Why have you allowed me here?" in response to Zhou Enlai's question, "Why have you bothered to come?"

When they initially saw one another inside the Beijing airport terminal, they shook hands but did not make eye contact. Alexei Kosygin just mumbles sadly, "Nor do I, Premier Zhou," after Zhou Enlai admits that regarding this current conflict, "I have positively nothing to add." This is the only diplomatic effort in this sad state of affairs. It doesn't look good for peace.

Farther south, more interesting things had been happening among the war hawks. Jasmine writes a five-page letter to He Song about her ordeal with the CGG before she returns to the battlefront at the Soviet border. A great deal of her letter is about her feelings of empowerment. She writes about how they listened to her and gave her wings.

The Council for the Greater Good was meeting in secret in the Chinese lakeside town of Wuxi. Jasmine's request is granted. She becomes the newest member of the Council. Her prospects for a good future couldn't be better. The Council chooses to support the course of war, reluctantly. The Cultural Revolution was hard on everyone's identity and they were no exception. Many on the Council no longer know for what to fight. Jasmine gives them that something, and she is passionate, so they'll go along with it all, come hell or high water, at least for now. Most members have lost their passion in stages over their long lifetimes, with every famine, war, and personal failure, and now they're just bone dry.

Speaking in front of the CGG, she concluded, "No doubt there is risk, and still I say we should war on the Soviets! Why? The goal of the Soviet's revisionism is to push China back to capitalism, make our people to feed their dark machine, and that is not what we are. That is not why I was born!

tea from a metal thermos. The back of her head is sweaty, and she combs through her crop with her long fingers. A single piece of hair remains between her fingers. No, it is too long to be her hair. Whose could it be? It is maybe a piece of her hair that somehow got past the military barber time and time again. She flaps it off her hand like a piece of dirt and doesn't watch it float away.

As the skirmishes devolved into war, with the CGG fully on board, the Chinese finally deployed two fresh infantry platoons to Rare Treasure Island with heavy artillery support. The Soviets only deploy a few dozen additional soldiers and six BTR-60s. From the ground on the front lines, China looks like it can win this fight. Jasmine is put in charge of a secret mission to create a new offensive along the western border. It will be called the Tielieketi Surprise.

✂ ✂

While Jasmine was away from the front lines to meet with the Council for the Greater Good, the China-Soviet tensions continued to be on the rise. In one of the more creative protests our country has ever seen, ink bottles are thrown by angry Chinese citizens at the Soviet Union's embassy in Beijing. Interestingly, the walls of Russia's embassy remain black to this day.

In a feigned half-hearted effort, the Soviet Prime Minister stopped over in Beijing on his way back from the funeral of the Vietnamese leader Ho Chi Minh. This is the conversation he had with his Chinese counterpart:

Zhou Enlai's parting words were simply, "To say goodbye, Comrade Alexei. To say goodbye." The Soviet Prime Minister never makes it farther than the Beijing airport. He is back on his plane within an hour.

Seeing no progress, Prime Minister Alexei Kosygin had asked him, two neighbors since at least 1892. The low Sarikol mountains pass through the land here delivering crystal-clear water to the Tarim River and had once fed Lop Nur, a saltwater lake that you will learn more about as this chapter unfolds.

At camp earlier that day, Jasmine finally received the long-awaited response to a letter she had sent to He Song detailing her success with the Council for the Greater Good. His response comes in a large parcel that contains one piece of paper and the infamous wooden box. *Oh!* She holds the wood box and shakes it gently. There is a soft noise.

Dearest Jasmine,

Congratulations! I am impressed yet again. If I still had a heart to give it would be yours. I am sending you the wood box, which you now absolutely deserve. Let it inspire you as it will.

I have started walking across the country to see for myself this border with the Soviets, and perhaps I will see some of the battle if it comes to war. If by chance I come across your company there, I will do what I can for you and your group as you need of me.

To walk across a country is to own that country, to walk through the dirt and dust—not looking at it through the window of a car or train. That is where I am in life. It will take me a year or more to get anywhere, because I walk it now.

I became a drifter when my wife died. Jasmine, you cleaned me up for a time but even you won't bring me out of this state of detachment I am in. I wander. What can you expect of the poor soul who lost his heart? I will try walking.

I hope you did not expect me to give the key. The key was not part of our bargain. That, my dear, will continue to stay safely with me. The locked box, though, is yours to keep.

With the greatest respect and admiration,
He Song

In all, her troops suffered twenty-seven losses. Where will it end? She sips

Fortunately for everyone on this planet we call home, before the Soviets dropped that first H-bomb its government wisely contacted their powerful archenemy (in secret of course) to warn them of their plans so there would be no mistake that the nukes were directed at Chinese cities and not at the American bases nearby. It is just seven years after the Cuban Missile Crisis. Again, the world comes just a hair away from nuclear catastrophe. It's hard to imagine, but it's true. Both are silly reasons for ending everything. Of all the bad things that could happen, and do happen, at least this one never does. The Soviets expect the Americans to stay neutral in the matter but they still worry that if not warned about the nuclear attack, the United States might mistake such a strike to be an affront to American troops that are stationed in nearby Taiwan, Japan, and South Korea.

The problem all began with a small strip of land in the Pamirs that was never very well mapped, so both sides could make a legitimate claim. Jasmine escalates the tension by boldly bringing her squadron into Tielieketi, and these actions are supported by both Big Brother and the CGG.

Jasmine was an up-and-coming platoon leader in the national army with cropped hair and a tight smile. The ashes of the last Emperor Puyi have been in the ground for two years at this point. The remains of Jasmine's former platoon leader, a death of more importance to her, are already speckled over the snowy peaks of the Kashgars. She would think of him when she looked out on the horizon. Occasionally, every few days, she hears a low boom that vibrates through the earth and trees and her body like a Tristan chord on a cello. It is another nuclear test.

The hair floated over her head, far up into the air. A breeze takes it over enemy lines and farther up into the snow-capped mountains. A Saiga bellows from those mountains. Its rabbit fur blends in to its surroundings. She cannot see the horned Saiga but wonders whose side it would be on if it needed to pick one. Would it be Chinese or would it be Russian? The area where Jasmine's units are battling the Soviets has been disputed between the

Chapter 13

October 16, 1969

China's population is 812 million people.

One could argue that Jasmine is really the one at fault for our war with the Soviets. What historians will later call the Seven-Month War, it is clearly a mess and nearly escalates into a nuclear conflict between two superpowers with the defeat of Jasmine's squadron at Tielieketi. Let me explain.

The Seven-Month War came to a close when the Americans responded to Nikita Khruschev's message through a secret communication. They say that if just one nuclear bomb were to be dropped onto Chinese territory, the United States will retaliate by launching one thousand nukes aimed directly on Russian cities. The United States will not stand by and allow the Soviets to use their nuclear arsenal on anyone—that's the point, not even on China, a country many Americans fear. The Russians then use their conventional weapons to slaughter Jasmine's squadron one by one, leaving only her to tell the tale.

Before getting rebuffed by the Americans, the Soviets had planned to respond to Jasmine's aggression in their territory by sending a full-scale nuclear attack that would rain down on Big Brother's largest cities to bring an end to the ridiculous war. It isn't that the land itself is of any value, but the Soviets fight because of principle. Their vast and reaching borders must be recognized by all, yet China's bold moves first on Rare Treasure Island and more recently here appear to be a test of Soviet resolve.

that led nowhere. He Song loses none of his resolve. Whenever she is down, He Song says to her, "Then do it for the adventure. That is how one should look at life. No matter if your plans work out or turn out to be a wreck, this is going to be a fun story you can tell people someday, and it is a story that will be uniquely yours, or I suppose, in this case, a story uniquely *ours,* that we share."

The landscape stretches in tones of green swimming in mist. Vibrantly colored orchids poke out from little moss patches wedged high in the elbows between tree trunks and their branches. The orchid flowers look like butterflies sitting on the slenderest of stalks and release the most decadent scents. I would testify they are better than the best desserts mankind has ever made. You catch a whiff, and then it's gone.

There were mountains to cross. But the mountains can get lost in the tree canopy. You feel their incline but you do not see the peaks. Radiant sunrays stream down through the leaves. As the team wearies, their sight focuses merely on keeping to the trail in front of them, but Jasmine's ears remain attentive for the sounds of panda.

He Song had packed his travel sack for the adventure of a lifetime. They are going to capture two giant pandas. He was amazed to learn they still exist. For all his time walking the country, he had never seen a panda. When he had told his son what they would do, his son was awestruck and He Song feels that same childish awe. They had permission from Big Brother himself. "Jasmine, thank you for allowing me to come."

Months before, by the Yangtze River, Jasmine had said, "It is a commission, He Song. Big Brother wants a calligraphy to acknowledge the historic event, and he likes the way you write your words." He Song smiles widely. A photograph is taken by a man in a black felt hat.

"What are you collecting, He Song?" she asked early on in the expedition. He tells her, "This and that."

He Song had known about another species of animal that roamed these forests. It was half deer and half bird. As the de facto storyteller in the group, He Song tells the tales he once heard as they walk along the brush. There are differing reports on whether this strange animal's size was that of a deer or that of a large falcon, but there was no doubt its front section was that of a deer, and its antlers produced a rare remedy for ailments of the brain. Sadness could be cured by thinly slicing its fresh antlers and soaking the chips in rice wine for thirty days. The resulting liquor tasted bittersweet, so the old texts say.

Yet how to catch such a beast that possesses both hooves and wings, He Song was better off trying to catch wild pandas! Pandas are no less mystical and no less precious. They are difficult to spot and are rarer than diamonds. Yet at least pandas don't have wings. You can follow a panda's tracks, and their tracks will not disappear like the tracks of winged deer will so often do.

"It feels good to be out here in the woods again," he said to her while swatting at bugs. A bug that looks like a stick crawls up his arm. He then looks up and sees a bright swath of stars. "The stars look like powder spread across the black sky."

Leeches became a problem for the entire group. Hooking onto pant legs, then sliding down into socks and up onto the skin of your bare legs, they drink indulgently from their hosts once attached. Jasmine counts twenty-seven on her feet one day! Each one has to be pulled off, leaving a blistery mark of red where it had been attached.

Jasmine became less than optimistic that this expedition would be fruitful and said so in private to He Song while walking yet another trail

It turns out that the two panda cubs had already separated from their mother, which is typical for cubs after one year of age. They were on their own doing fine by themselves, building a life as best they knew how. It had been mostly a life looking at the bamboo leaves and the shadows they make as their claws strip forty pounds of leaves off stalk after stalk and eat them one by one. Occasionally they would swat away bugs, or go to a mountain spring for a drink. They pause to listen to the sounds of the forest. When they smell humans, they dash away.

Translucent whiskers felt the breezes. They bend with foliage and spring back into place. Hardly noticeable to others, they bring some of the strongest sensations to cubs.

Before capture, their appetites were deeper than the Three Gorges. A small forest is needed to sustain the pair. Fortunately, bamboo forests grow fast. Jasmine and her team can see the bamboo grow right before their eyes as they track the bears. That's the type of sustainable food source pandas require. The bamboo grows as fast as they can eat it.

It was while they were camping these foothills of the Himalayas that He Song taught Jasmine how to track Venus through the seasons. "Time can be kept on its eight-year cycle," he says to her. "Look up there, in line with the moon. Just watch that spot before sunrise; it comes up as the first brilliant light. It is pulling up the sun. I've heard it called the star of sympathy. It is responsible for the morning dew."

He collected additional herbs that would help put the pandas to sleep if the drugs they were carrying didn't do the job. He is collecting this and that growing up along the path. He Song often dabs bits of plant in his mouth before putting them into his pouch. He must recognize certain herbs by taste. He empties out his black silk pouch each night, dries the herbs by the fire, and crushes them into fine powder.

Ling Ling and Sing Sing are wild born and were captured in the misty forests by Jasmine's team.

Let's join her corps as they tracked the panda bears for days in the muggy mountain forests in these foothills of the great Himalayas. One of her guides is of the local village. In total, she had a company of eight men. Five of these soldiers act as porters, or muscle you might say, and carry most of the supplies and roll the large steel cages that transport the animals once they are captured. There is a zoologist to look after the pandas. He Song is also there. His role is threefold. He is commissioned to write a piece of calligraphy to mark the event as history so later it can be inscribed into stone along the great Three Gorges of the Yangtze River. He is also there to help administer anesthesia to the animals when caught. He is an expert of various herbal means. His third task is to provide company and conversation to Jasmine. She made the request for him to come.

"I feel bad for the pandas," He Song said, looking into the cage.

"Animals don't have feelings. No need to personify them, they exist in the moment and care not of the past or future. These pandas are tools for mankind, and we can use these two best right now by giving them away," Jasmine will maintain. She feels no guilt.

The smell of humans was strong that day in the valley. Sing Sing is restless and wants to run toward the neighboring lands. He calls out. Ling Ling however refuses to go on until she finishes her breakfast. That will be their downfall. The bears separate for that reason. Jasmine is able to sneak up on each with a long net from the opposite direction of the light mountain breeze. In a minute there are needles in their veins so they will sleep until they reach the city of Chengdu, where they will be prepared for their long sea voyage as China's great ambassadors.

levon a

It came as a surprise. Wrapped in golden yellow rice paper is a glass eye!

At first she said, "Young man, I have a small gift. It will help you look better for the cameras, and hereafter you may fit in better with this new society." The yellow color of the wrapping is an old imperial color. Is that who she then represents, someone from Emperor Puyi's clan? But the Emperor is dead, and all of his people are either gone or turned communist.

~ ~

The commemorative lines that He Song inscribed in large red lettering on the cliffs of the Three Gorges are thus:

Our Giant Pandas leave their forest home to forge a friendship.
The final implications will not be known in our lifetime.
We owe Sing Sing and Ling Ling gratitude
And wish them Godspeed.

He initially writes these lines on a long, single sheet of rice paper that will be rolled up and sent to Big Brother for his inspection, then reproduced in ten-foot letters on the cliff of a great cavern in the great gorges that will be photographed by tourists on boats or on foot for many years until a large dam floods the Three Gorges area of the Yangtze River valley to increase energy production for the region.

The names of both pandas were given by Big Brother himself. He has his reasons and often doesn't care to explain. Sing Sing (twinkling star) was born in 1971. Ling Ling (the name means a darling girl) was probably born in 1970. Some say her name is intended to sound like the bells little girls sometimes wear on their wrists.

When Jasmine rode horseback here for military observations over the years, she had heard many stories from villagers, some no doubt fantastical but others substantiated, about pandas living on this mountainside. Both

I'd like to think this old lady was the lost mother of He Song. He never found his parents, although he looked, and maybe this preproduction manager is that lost mother returned. She is here to give her son a jewel to remember her by and forgive all the past and make it right. His real mother also smelled of honey. He Song remembers long lashes and long hair, and a gentle laugh. This woman has those compassionate eyes of a mother. If He Song were not in the middle of so many other things at that point, ready to go on air, he would give the old lady a hug rather than just popping in the glass eye and rushing off to Jasmine and the cameras. But, alas, he never will see this lady again.

"The man who had this eye has passed. It is mine now to give and I give it to you," the old woman said to He Song. The eye slides into his socket perfectly, and after this day many will assume he has two working eyes. Before this moment his blindness was obvious because of the patch. Occasionally he will still bump into walls or hit his head on things like before, but as long as he swings his arm ahead of him just a little and takes it slow, he can prevent accidents from his lack of depth perception. The swinging arms with time become more of a dusting motion, and he pretends he is dusting off things around him.

He Song wasn't quick to accept such a gift, so to convince him, she said, "I too have lost much. I too wished I could have controlled the universe to different ends and in time have learned I have no control over it. In my time, I have seen the bad and endured it. Pain does not last. Everything heals, and the world changes so much that the memories themselves change. That is why you need this gift, to help you heal and become whole. Perhaps inside you still have hollow areas. I cannot say. Let us at least work on this surface of yours. It is a handsome face but that dark void in your eye socket is distracting to those who look at you. This will improve the symmetry."

This was all because He Song pushed her away at first and said, "I don't care for outward appearances anymore, madam comrade. If you have seen what I have seen, you'd know one eye is enough."

He Song had always wanted to tell her his story of the man who could not die. "I know an interesting story that took place here in southern China," he offers. "Let me distract you with it now. Look here, Dear Jasmine."

Earlier, He Song took her hand in response to a compliment she had just given him. His handsome face is a comfort. "It delights me to know that the gift was not in vain," he says.

~ ~

Jasmine immediately commented on his new glass eye when he appeared in the studio. "It looks better, He Song. The eye. It's very nice." Before the cameras went live, the two friends had been ushered into separate makeup rooms. He Song was given a glass eye by the preproduction manager so he no longer wears a patch. Until this day, Jasmine always knew him with a patch.

He Song was starting to rebuild his life. Jasmine is surely a part of this reconstruction of his dignity. He Song had been a monster at one time. First, she humbled him and tried to destroy him. Then she did her best to build him back up, probably because she pitied him like she would pity a poor street cat. She may have also started to have regret. It isn't love she feels toward him, she always tells herself, but she expects he had been in love with her. Let him feel love. He has lost so much because of me, the poor man. He lost his child and his wife and his home and his livelihood.

Where did the glass eye come from? Who is this preproduction manager who gave it to him? She prepares the talent and her extras for the televised presentation today. She is very old, and it has been a long time since He Song has seen anyone of that age. Few elderly people are around anymore. Most have died, if not from war then famine or revolution. He Song inhales through his nose. She smells of honey and licorice. Her hair is smooth and reaches to her waist in braids. Her hands are as large as cantaloupes, strong and muscular. She looks as if she could lift a car on her own. Her eyes penetrate right down into his soul.

everywhere, even there. She had taken possession of the locked box years earlier, but not its key.

The pandas were making noise in the studio. They are each in separate cages eating bamboo.

To ease Jasmine's mind before she went on air, He Song told her a story of the man who cannot die. He finishes the story by saying, "That is perhaps how it is with him. Piece by piece, he will be given away over time."

He said this because of her distasteful comment that he just took in stride. Jasmine might not mean what she says when she says, "Then I would give away his larger organs, piece by piece." She is only half engaged in his story. Her mind is instead calculating the number of potential viewers she will have just minutes from now, and how a different word choice here or there might sway their opinions.

He kept trying to distract her with the story. "I would grind this man up into tiny pieces and give it to the population," she says to him. He Song looks disturbed. "How will eating immortal flesh keep mortal people alive? They'll just poop it out," he jokes in return and that makes her smile. "I don't see a benefit."

She had asked whether he wants to die and He Song answered with an undeniable "Yes!"

"He could not die, you see," explained He Song. "They had tried to take every piece out of him, and his body continues to run. What would you do to such a man?"

Jasmine was nervous to go on live television. He Song keeps her sweaty hand in his. "Maybe this is all a mistake," she says, losing confidence. "Maybe this is not what I believe."

He Song was invited to attend the recording of Jasmine's televised speech in Chengdu and had stood there right behind the tall television camera so Jasmine was literally looking into his eyes, although in her mind's eye it was the eyes of the American president she saw. No, not just that. It is the eyes of the world that wants to know this country better. When their eyes connect, He Song's own ears begin to ring with that familiar sound of Om. It is almost the sound of a light bulb ready to go out. The sound of Om is soft, yet it permeates from everywhere as a connection of energy, an invisible electricity, between them and the world.

At this time in their lives, He Song and Jasmine flirted with each other like two lovebirds in springtime, just as they had been not long ago on the muddy banks of the Yangtze River in front of a photographer. She smells the evil on him, but in a small amount that is almost attractive when mixed with his natural scent of cinnamon (he put cinnamon bark and ginseng in the brew of herbs he would drink every morning, and the potion seeped from his pores).

They briefly discussed Pollywog's death. They mourn him. The better man is dead. Jasmine has been promoted to fill Pollywog's position just prior to the border war with the Soviet Union, and afterward was decorated with medals of valor for fighting a good fight against a much stronger foe. Her army post brought her back to the south. Platoon Leader Jasmine is now assigned to guard the difficult terrain bordering Sichuan that includes the panda forests. Her responsibility entails protecting the country's natural resources from its own people as much as it does to protect the villagers from the neighboring countries along the long border. Medicine men love the bones of panda, and of course their fur coats are of extraordinary value.

Those years He Song maintained a game of mystery, a kind of hide-and-seek, between them. He knows Jasmine wants the key to the wooden box, so he soametimes lets it dangle just within her reach. It started in the jungle when they were hunting pandas. He brings his ring of keys

American zookeepers unfamiliar with these very sensitive animals. These two pandas would need to survive to show the vitality of our people and become loved by the world.

Let's jump back to her speech itself. Jasmine said to the Americans, "These giant pandas are rare treasures to us all, for there are very few left in the world today. The last live here in the China wilderness. They represent dichotomy: black and white, good and bad, gentle and dangerous, new and ancient, populous and barren. Their face shows us both the yin and yang of life." This last sentence is deleted before being rebroadcast to Beijing because it sounded too *feng zixiu*.

But she said more; she said what had to be said. "It is the people and the people alone who are the motivating force in making world history. We must liberate the world. The social systems of China and the United States are fundamentally different, of course they are, and there do exist great differences between the Chinese government and the United States government. We hope that through talking with one another, not just out there in Beijing, but having Americans come here to the countryside, we will gain a clearer notion of our differences, which will allow us to make efforts to find a common ground. A start can be made in forming good relations between our nations. Let's give gifts, receive gifts, and recognize one another again."

American spies had informed Nixon that this was the fiery young woman who started the conflict with the Soviets. Why the change in her spirit? They were convinced it was because of the failure of the communist system in China and the hope of capitalism. Did she also know about America's recent role in preventing the Soviets from using nuclear weapons on her troops and civilians?

Jasmine didn't see the contents of her speech that day as a change in spirit. She has always wanted to engage the world.

Everyone across the planet clapped. Oh, the applause! The ovation continues for several minutes after the television screen goes out. In Beijing, Big Brother stands and adds, "Hear, hear. A toast to friendship." The American President doesn't drink the rice wine. Jasmine's speech really does change how he thinks of the Chinese, however, and he will use many of her words again and again in his foreign policy. The pandas are a gift that has an effect.

Now I should add that "live television" was a relative term. Everyone believes it is live. Nearly everyone.

"We give these animals to you in trust. It is not the first time China gave two pandas to America. Two pandas were already given to the Americans once before by our enemy. Mrs. Chiang Kai-shek gave them away. It was another time that we need not dwell on. Those pandas did not survive long in America, which is a great loss to all of us. It is sad. But, I, just a farmer with a uniform, and on behalf of all the ordinary women and men here from the heartland of China, think it is worth giving Americans a second chance. Here is another pair of our most treasured animals for your people to enjoy and care for. Their names are Sing Sing and Ling Ling."

Her voice has matured into a clear bell. Jasmine is in her early twenties at this time, and has already made a name for herself by fighting a popular war against the Soviet Union. Her speech is titled, "Mitigating the risk of a misunderstanding and miscalculation that could lead us to war," and is a more refined version of a similar speech she delivered to Big Brother during the early preparations for the Americans' visit. In preparation, Big Brother had traveled the country soliciting opinions on how to posture ourselves to the Americans. In response, Jasmine's branch of the PLA sent her to speak to him. Big Brother liked her idea so much that he allowed a generous allocation of national funds to pull together an expedition to find a suitable pair of giant pandas from the wild to be used as gifts. They needed to be healthy enough to survive the long trip and the possible mistakes of

This was one of those special moments in history when Jasmine spoke out in a public way that gave her sway over everyone's idea of right and wrong. She gives her short speech on live television from the Chinese city of Chengdu, while Nixon watches from the Great Hall of the People on the other end of the country, uncertain whether to even accept a toast with his former nemesis but perhaps friend and future ally, Big Brother. President Nixon's men advise him to not drink any of the rice wine during his stay.

The world watched the televised event in which Jasmine addressed the American president from the lush countryside of Western China.

Jasmine matured into a plump model of feminine beauty. Her figure is an example of what extreme beauty probably looked like in the Renaissance when to be well fed was to be attractive. She shows curves and health and vitality in every pose, and she does constantly pose. Her eyes sparkle fire. Her essence exudes fertility, so much so that if one were to sprinkle her with water, no doubt our Dear Darling Jasmine would sprout flowers. With great kindness she helped The Monkey King, when he was about seven years of age, reunite with his biological father, He Song. As a platoon leader in the PLA, Jasmine holds enough clout to put the child in a special boarding school in Chengdu where he may focus on mathematics. On his school holidays The Monkey King spends time with He Song at his home, as a father and son should. The adoptive family eventually distances themselves.

The American delegation to China all sat in the Great Hall of the People in Beijing, that big ugly building beside Tiananmen Square. All sorts of Americans are there, including the famous news anchor Walter Cronkite and the lovely, up-and-coming reporter Barbara Walters, plus many translators and pencil pushers from the US State Department, including the so-called great statesman named Henry Kissinger, who doesn't even know how to use chopsticks! Many people say Kissinger is an uncivilized man. Chinese military bands play American folk songs like "Oh! Susanna" so the Americans will feel at home.

CHAPTER 14

February 21, 1972

China's population is 854 million people.

The population breaks a billion a decade later in 1982.

This chapter is about television. TV is catching the world by storm and China is no exception. Our first national broadcast was televised on May 1, 1958. Within fifteen years, ten million Chinese have access to a television set. The goal is for every household to have one.

Nineteen seventy-two was the year that President Richard Nixon finally made a goodwill trip to China. Up until this point, Communist China was a blurred spot on the world map because our internal politics were considered "scary." Of course that attitude has to change. This country now has a larger population and there are mineral resources that could not be ignored.

Jasmine presented a special gift to America on a live broadcast. Most of us first hear her voice on radio but the lucky ones see her live on television. What a moment. The gift is two panda bears named Sing Sing and Ling Ling. The First Lady, Pat Nixon, squeals with glee when she sees the pandas. "Comic little things," she says. "A real scream." The American public will adore them. They become the symbol of our newfound friendship over the Pacific.

toward women, opening doors for them and helping carry their bags of vegetables. Couples often invite "the Calligrapher" to their home when they are newly married to write a calligraphy piece for them that, in effect, names their home and will forever hang framed in their main sitting room. When asked to do this, He Song lays the blank white paper out before himself and holds it down with four artist stones. These calligraphies, matted on silk during the framing process, will say things like "the Phoenix catches the rain," and are renowned for their strong black stroke and steady hand. He makes a fair living on his calligraphy. Everyone in the neighborhood knows that He Song is that very artist who once painted a message in calligraphy about pandas high above the Yangtze River in the famous Three Gorges. There are other business dealings in which he dabbles, but this is more or less his life today.

Life wasn't bad. The country has had good harvests and has, for the first time, begun exporting food because there is now a surplus. By this time, The Great Disaster's famine is a distant memory.

Elsewhere in China, Big Brother's mausoleum was almost complete. They say his body is preserved with the people's tears and its skin does not decompose. I suspect the formula is a gift from the CGG. The mausoleum is monumental, just outside the gates of the Forbidden City in that large square called Tiananmen Square. The building for Big Brother makes even the tomb of the Empress Dowager Cixi, who had been known for her excesses and waste, look unimportant and petty. Big Brother's portrait hangs there as well. His face is beautiful except for one mole.

In contrast, Emperor Puyi's body was cremated. The last Emperor's ashes are scattered unceremoniously in an unmarked gravesite of the common person. From this we can see who has won and who has indeed lost.

they did he threw something together free of charge. While he practiced medicine early on in life, and even had a shop for selling remedies once or twice long ago, he is only occasionally asked to practice serious medicine now. He only performs surgeries with great reluctance and never has satisfactory results. He understands the pain it causes, having undergone many unfortunate and severe operations himself, so he never takes surgery lightly. However, herbs and mushrooms brewed in tea are another thing altogether. It is light medicine and can be effective for certain conditions. He still believes, and probably always will, that he comes from a long line of herbal healers, but I will say here that this is mere speculation. It is difficult for He Song to even remember whether his father's voice was high or low, whether he was tall, fat, or short, let alone details of his father's occupation. He Song's father is clouded in old memory mixed with dreams.

He Song still dabbled in the sale of antiques from time to time and that was mostly what was meant by "entrepreneur and consultant" in pretty green font on his business card. Calligrapher and artist is what he has the most skill in today. The real He Song is a fine calligrapher. His stroke of a brush rivals that of the great masters of the Ming period. In the detention cell, with only water and a homemade brush, his artwork is less than amazing, and that is all you have seen thus far. But, Dear Reader, give him a real brush of fine horsehair, and he has the talent to paint an apple that has the essence of an apple in every way, except that it is black and white, just squid ink on rice paper. He can capture the image of people exercising in the park in the morning fog as well as the best photograph, in just a shadow of ink from a wet brush stroke on paper. What he can do as an artist is magical. One stroke of the bamboo brush, and a second with more ink, and done. Two strokes and there is a painting. A masterpiece.

He Song was accepted by his neighbors those years before he disappeared to save his son. He has conversations with friends about how the city is growing so fast, and he likes talking about cars. He always shows kindness to children who play in the courtyard, and he shows courtesy

The son contacted his father for help with an electronic text message using a shell account through CANET. A phone is smuggled in (along with the cigarettes and the hard rice liquor and the extra food) allowing The Monkey King full access to his normal office assistant while in jail. Meanwhile He Song has the sent message on his lap, printed out in full color, as a train carries him across the country to save his child. He Song reads it again and again until it becomes crinkled. He doesn't know what he will say to his fallen son. The message he has only states the facts. His son waits in Hubei Detention Center. The sentence could be carried out at any time. There is no hope for appeal.

Bing, there was the sound of a new message. He Song is beside his computer adjusting his signature template. In pale green lettering: "He Song, Calligrapher, Consultant, and Entrepreneur." Every electronic message he sends ends in the fixed signature, which includes a JPEG file of a beautifully handwritten "He Song." He is working on making the image a little wider to match the other font, but clicks out of this window to read his new message. The message he receives has a fancier signature line. A bold stripe of blue above and below the signature gives just the right effect to the blue lettering "The Monkey King, CEO and President, Jinjin Enterprises, 888 Nanjing Road, Shanghai."

⁓ ⁓

Let's end this chapter, going further back in time, with a short note about the life that He Song, the father, traded in for death row. In our next chapters I can refer to this man as simply He Song and his son will be referred to as The Monkey King, which I think is the most appropriate and honest way of telling our story, because that is how the world knew them in the past.

He Song no longer considered himself a professional medicine man, although some friends still asked him for his healing potions, and when bore. I will not remember you with fondness. And, now you say you'll save me by cutting off my fingers."

Before taking out the knife, the father said, "I will always be here for you. There is nothing I will not give my son. The worse you are, when you are the most in need, the stronger I love you. Perhaps this is strange, but it is true! You can have each of my organs. You can have all of me. Yes, yes indeed, I intend to save you. For this to work, we have to cover the obvious. Let us get that over with right now."

He Song had been strict. During his first visit, before devising an escape plan for The Monkey King, he drills his son like any father would, or perhaps more severely than others might dare, asking him what brought him to this unfortunate circumstance, as they stand there just a short hallway away from the execution chambers, to which the son cried and pleaded, "Father, I wish I had perfect foresight. If I had only known how one bad thing would lead to another, I would not be in this dire predicament today. Help me, Father." Neither man can catch his breath through the tears. Both are silent for a long while before The Monkey King speaks again. "My factories have been using lead paint in our production. For this small thing, I have been caught and found out. The red and the yellow both contained lead. I knew it did. I admit it. The lead paint really looks so much better. That's why we chose it. It wasn't because of cost. We used the red on all children's toys for export. It has better gloss. It sells better. Why does it matter? Others get away with so much more, Father. When it was discovered, there was a secret investigation, and the provincial government publicly put all the blame squarely on me as CEO. It is a publicity stunt, pure and simple. It is as if my life means nothing to them, these officials who have taken my bribes for years. But they felt they must demonstrate to our Australian buyers that we Chinese take their concerns seriously. They have sentenced me to death by firing squad. It could happen at any time. The waiting is unbearable."

He Song was heartbroken. "Why did they sentence you with capital punishment, my child?"

cell. Let the stubble on your young face grow into a beard like mine. It may take some time but it will grow full. Once you look like me, I will take your place on death row.

He Song bribed nearly every guard in the complex with red envelopes at every visit and had but one request of them. Pay no attention to The Monkey King or his cell. No special treatment. No interaction whatsoever. Just let him be, lost forever in the prison and its bureaucracy. When you see his name anywhere in the record books, remove it.

This deception produced more blood than it should have, but it needed to be done or they would have been found out. Putting both hands up behind his head, He Song takes his long hair out of its braid. He cuts lengths of it to use as rope around his son's pointer finger down below its knuckle. He also ties twines of hair around the tips of his son's ring finger, his middle finger, and his thumb. These are tourniquets so his son does not bleed to death. With the knife breaking through muscle and bone, cut, cut, cut. Cut. The Monkey King's fingers cut easily. The knife is sharp enough to cut cleanly though. *Blood of my son on my hands, over my shoes, sticking there thick. Some on my face. At least he has made it this far as a grown man without yet seeing his own blood.* The blood streams out like his life. It runs its course. In the darkness everything is wet with warm blood. He places the tips of his son's fingers into his own jacket pocket. In the future, the jade thief will always wear gray cotton-filled gloves to fill in those missing spaces on his own hand. Everything becomes illusion.

He Song cleaned off the knife they will both use later to shave, but that is not all! It is a blade made of Japanese steel. Strong, clean, sharp. The handle is made of ox bone, and he has carried it in a sheath of rough Tibetan ox leather.

The Monkey King went cold and responded, "You hurt me more as a child than you remember. You never noticed your neglect and the pain I once was." They will not see each other again for many years: first in Macao, and later in Shanghai. There is no mention of thanks. There is no regret.

"I will no longer call you father. I am now He Song, and your son is dead." These are the final words of The Monkey King.

This rescue attempt was more than He Song simply passing his own name to his son, but that is the confusing piece for me as the storyteller and probably for you as well, my patient reader.

The man born as He Song had to give away his name to his imprisoned son, who was previously named The Monkey King, so that they might change places. It is a guarded secret told to no one until today. I trust you with it now.

The second secret I'll share is that the original He Song, who we have been calling the jade thief Lao Shifu all this time, has a face that cannot age. This secret has been hidden many years under a thick, black beard, and now to you it has been exposed. If this seems strange, to have a face that does not age, you are correct. It is very strange, and it will need to be examined further later in our story.

For this to have worked as well as it did, both father and son had to prepare months in advance. Clothes need to be prepared. Finances need to be explained. The beard of He Song needs to be accentuated and trimmed in a peculiar way. The hardest part during the careful preparation is holding onto one's patience when the justice officials in Hubei could act on the death sentence at any time. Every time He Song visits his son The Monkey King, he is prepared to face a surprise execution.

But this time luck was on their side. The Monkey King is instructed by his father to grow his beard as thick as he can in the darkness of the prison and never show his face to the guards. Stay in the shadows of your

Weeks before the jade thief had a piece of chalk to write out his poems, he used a handmade paintbrush made from tufts of his own hair wrapped tightly around a chopstick. He dips the handmade brush in his cup of water.

Prior to writing poetry, he drew pictures with the water on the stone. When the gray stone is wet it becomes darker, and he can produce many shades in a single stroke. He tries drawing god with his homemade brush. His pictures of god are of all sorts. He draws a thousand figures in revolution. This is god. He draws the birth of a child among a large family. Another day, this is god. He draws the beautiful yellow mountains at sunrise. He draws clouds that look like great mountains and lightning raging throughout them, and above these he paints dragons, planets, and stars.

His first picture of god, though, was a representation of Pepper and himself alone here in this cell. Where is god here? That is indeed the question. He stares at this painting in particular until it evaporates and there is just gray stone again.

⌐ ⌐

In this chapter, The Monkey King died. It was a difficult name he had to endure for this long, the poor child. We will let him die. I do wish that the younger years of his childhood could have gone a different way. You will eventually see why it happened as it did, and you will understand the regret.

There were two men in a cell, looking eye to eye. The day is here. They exchange clothes. They shake hands. "Lao Shifu," says the one. He prepares to leave. The visiting hours are almost over.

When told his son was dead, the father replied, "So be it. I remain your old teacher, if not your father. Please call me Lao Shifu if I should ever get out of this place. Perhaps I will try my hand in trading precious stones when that time comes. You can take everything I own. You are now what I

Meanwhile in Hubei, his father got over that ridiculous phobia of rats he had held since childhood. They can be company, he rationalizes to himself. They can be friends. They are easy to domesticate. They are loyal. In the darkness, the rat packs take the shape of hounds.

He named a regular visitor Pepper. Man's best friend, Pepper.

It's not that the jade thief's fear of rodents decreased in solitude. It's just that the rats are inescapable in this place. In early life, he had always been able to walk somewhere else if he saw a rat. *Just accept the situation you are in,* he thinks to himself here in his detention cell. *Make friends where you can get them. Stay calm and, like everything else, you can get through this.*

In that same bare cell where Jasmine would later sit, the man who is called the jade thief wrote on the wall with chalk and made a few last changes before inscribing the words finally in stone with a blade:

When the misdeed is to protect my son, what do you say?
To deny him help feels wrong in a fundamental way.
In the end what is really right and what is truly wrong?
Morality is just one's perspective thinks the lonely He Song.

(Jasmine will later edit these poems with crimson lettering when she is imprisoned here for a different crime.)

Before he inscribed the words he tested various phrases by writing on the cement walls with water. There are literally dozens of versions. For company he only has the rats at present, and the future men who will use his cell when he is gone. He has months to choose exactly the right rhyme, and you have read his final work. Here was an earlier attempt:

When my misdeed is to love, what then? I pray.
To deny help would be a wrong in a bigger way.
In the end what is right, who will say?
Is there any goodness in our world today?

Prison administrators will believe the body is cremated, which is not true. Who will ever know otherwise? A shady figure stands up among the corpses set for cremation and walks away.

There are aspects about time that Lao Shifu considered while sitting in that jail. Beard growth, for one. Outside of jail, the jade thief would have an afternoon shadow were he to shave every morning. If he had an important evening engagement, he might consider shaving twice that same day. In jail, however, with different nutrition and light patterns, there is no regularity in the growth of his beard at first, and then eventually a new pattern emerges. For this lonely man it just creeps along. His nails also grow more slowly. They are brittle and yellow. He hardly needs to shave that last day.

Another aspect of prison time, the sleep rhythm and the hunger rhythm, were mentioned before while we were in Tu. In this dark place where we are now, the lack of light blocks a man's biological rhythm and so there is no rhythm. Even the pulse of the blood that flows through the jade thief's veins is irregular.

Outside in the sunshine, the newly created He Song fit well into the Chinese society of the late 1980s. He is now twenty-five. He would think of his father more often, now that he lives at his father's house, at least for a time, and wears his father's clothes (until he buys new ones), and to this day The Monkey King still responds to his father's name. Sometimes, he will even forget who he really was. He walks with more of a strut than his father ever did. The shar-pei he found starving in his father's apartment became a lasting friend (He Song's dog survived his time alone by eating the leather off the furniture when there was nothing else to eat). In business ventures he is more risky than his father, and ultimately far more successful. In no time, after his escape and renewal, the new He Song becomes a powerhouse all his own.

⌐ ⌐

to see and then the lights come back on and you exit out the theater door. I demand real change on this sacred ground, here where I stand, where the common people stand and live and deserve better. You know they do! You are responsible for the chaos as much as I. It is your corrupt systems that bring on their anger. Of course we revolt because there is good reason to revolt."

He Song had said to her, "You are causing trouble when there need not be any. So much good has happened since you brought our country to near ruin during the Cultural Revolution. Do you not remember that? It haunts me. I remember that egotistic teenage girl with braids who ruined my family. How could I ever forgive you? And here you are at it again. To repeat it all is unimaginable. It is no different this time."

"Are you spying on me?" she asked him.

Found out, he said, "Jasmine, you recognize me then?"

She wasn't sure, but she sounded certain when she said, "He Song, you have changed, but it is you. Age is not being kind to either of us."

Jasmine thought she spotted someone familiar after one of her campus talks. At first she thinks it is a thick-bearded college administrator, dressed in a nice suit and tie, but then realizes he must be He Song. He is so well dressed he must be deep in dirty business.

⸏ ⸏

Around this same time, the jade thief finally walked out of the Hubei Detention Center and into the night. He practices tai chi shadowboxing alone in the quiet darkness for six months until he can finally walk out the door without notice. Records will now show that He Song's son, The Monkey King, dies here on this day. A doctor verifies the death of a man.

talk of a more utopian Chinese society, she is on the train again, and the students already devoted to her cause, infected with powerful ideas and as ambitious as ants. It would take the army itself to quell the fire. The army comes into Tiananmen Square the night of June 3 with tanks and live ammunition and for several days the city streets become a war zone. The youth camping out there are slaughtered and jailed, while the organizers like Jasmine were are secured into fortified jails. They disappear from public view for years, sometimes forever.

Jasmine was secretly detained three days before the crackdown. It may have been He Song who squealed on her to the army or the police. This is what Jasmine believes happened.

Not long before Jasmine was jailed, she indeed ran into He Song. She is surprised by how much He Song has changed. No older in appearance than the last time they met, but so much younger in personality. An evil tone that had always turned her stomach rises more to the surface than ever before. It is this part of him she will see from now on. It covers everything. He Song did not smell of cinnamon that day. She smelled only cigarettes and tooth decay. "Off with you, He Song! If you are not part of this effort of mine, then go!"

"Ai, those heavily charged words are so beautifully strung together, Jasmine," responded He Song. "Things are so often not what they seem to be. Someday you will realize you are the marionette performing on stage while real leaders like me are behind the scenes controlling all the strings."

She insisted, "Things are not what they seem, He Song. I have no regrets for what I have done. Dignity will be the epitaph for the dignified. Despicableness has been the passport of the despicable. I will not be stopped on this quest to create something real for China, not something falsely promised to be waiting for me in my next life, or something I should relish through consumerism, or something imaginary that requires a movie ticket

She was not in Beijing during the protests for which she is now condemned. In fact, Jasmine has somehow always stayed out of Beijing, and in so doing, perhaps has avoided the trappings of the place. He Song will tell her, as you will see, he always found it strange to have Jasmine always in the west or the south and never to have treaded the same ground as the last Emperor in the north. This strange fact adds to that foreboding He Song has often felt that one of these two key people in his life may be just a dream, and the other the single reality. He wakes and he is in the land of Jasmine. Or, another time he wakes and is there helping the last Emperor somewhere in the north. Rules of law and nature were different in each of their worlds. Time even worked differently. Smells, colors, light, none of it with Jasmine was anything like when he was with Puyi. The Emperor would hold time still. Time around Jasmine would always rush by. But if it really is the case that one has been a dream and the other the reality, who then is the dream? When you are with either person, they feel real enough. They smell real. It is real.

During that contentious time in 1989, Jasmine still did her part to help spread the chaos occurring on Tiananmen Square (a million protesters were camped in front of the Forbidden City in Beijing demanding change) to other smaller communities throughout the country, especially in the south and in the west where she was most accustomed. In her view, the south and the west are the country's breadbasket and economic heart. A real shake-up is possible if they are included. In all, tens of millions are involved, and that May of 1989 the central government lose all control. The police no longer act on the government's behalf. They side with the protesters. Those weeks, Jasmine visits a different major city every other day and then sneaks onto a train by night to her next event. Her stage routine is the same in each place she visits. She wears her old military coat. She lets the word of her possible arrival spread among the students by word of mouth, and then she simply shows up on a major campus unannounced one day just before classes began. By the time the professors realize no students showed up to class because they had been sitting in the courtyard absorbed in Jasmine's

Life in her cell was tedious. She relives her mistakes in her mind. She often wishes she had something to read other than just the graffiti on the wall from past inmates who she assumes are all now dead. Surely this is death row. How could it be anything else when she is accused of treason?

The graffiti on the wall was a poem of sorts and a riddle at the same time. It is written in a familiar hand. She writes through it in a heavy hand: *Right is always right.*

These forty words, scrawled there on her cell wall among other nonsense, touched a nerve:
If my misdeed protects our children, what then?
To have done right would've caused greater pain.
In the end we may know
But here I sit on skid row
It is my fear that I am growing insane.

There is another poem beside it:
White lies prevent harm to my son.
What is truly right when all's wrong?
My faith is that he
Will turn out to be
A better man than his father He Song.

Still another, on a different wall…
When love is my wrong I need pray.
For help to see things the right way.
I ask what is right
My soul burns this night
To know if there is goodness today

~ ~

ask you that. Have I missed something or are we not in a prison? Something has gone terribly wrong, and where does the responsibility lie?"

One of Jasmine's supporters chimed in, "Already the Council has invested in her betterment, and that generosity has repaid itself in full. We gave her the eye, and she uses it well. Never has she been a disappointment. Never has Jasmine deviated from the goal."

An old man cried, "I nominate Jasmine!" He had always been an ally and supporter. "She has the oratory talent that is still very much needed by our group. She is discreet when discretion is needed. I have always liked her vision of the world."

The Council meeting began with the tall Chairwoman Ren addressing the twenty-nine members: "We have one topic today, to choose our next Council chair and do so with sensitivity to how the world has changed of late. My tenure as chair will end with the Chinese New Year."

The Council members were all present when Jasmine entered the meeting hall. There are no new members. One woman is in a wheelchair, a great woman Jasmine respects, and the others are sitting in cushioned leather chairs. She knows everyone by name. They are very familiar with her as well, and look at her directly in the eye without shame.

"Let us commence the 547th meeting of the Council for the Greater Good. Today's meeting is being held in Hubei Detention Center to accommodate one of our members. Notes of our meeting will be taken by Yuxin, Scribe of the Council."

A freshly pressed Mao suit was waiting for Jasmine at the foot of the bed when she woke in her cell. Her shoes are polished. The tailored blouse smells like it was washed outside of the prison. *Are they here already? It would have been nice to be given notice, but so be it.* She quickly brushes her hair.

currently employs fewer than a hundred spies. I propose expanding it to one thousand. But there is more…"

When General Zhang felt it was the appropriate time, he stood, clicked his heels, and addressed the current chair. "May I add a word?" he asks. There is a pause. The chair nods. As he inhales, Jasmine's expectations plunge.

Earlier in the meeting, an old woman rose from the shadows. Jasmine had always thought she was crippled because she moved in an automatic wheelchair, but she is standing now on her own two legs. "I would accept the nomination, though I myself will vote for Jasmine. I vote for her immediate release, and I vote for her ascension to chair."

Jasmine nominated this same woman for chair by saying, "I think the real question is, who can move us forward. Surely, today is a low point, but haven't we all seen worse? Who is the best candidate for today? It is not me, surely not. I nominate our eldest member, Xixi." Why did Jasmine say this to the Council members? It appears she is showing humility, but she is rarely humble, so this is more likely a move to present a viable candidate who can compete against General Zhang when she does not feel capable to beat him. Maybe Jasmine truly feels fallen. It is entirely possible.

Hair full of lice, bites around her ears, this was not Jasmine's best moment. In my opinion, this is the one time in her life when she should have defended herself with more skill. This is her chance to stand up for herself, and whether it is because of a sense of defeatism, a love for the Greater Good, or something else, regardless of the reason, she misses this important chance.

General Zhang smeared Jasmine early on by saying, "Hasn't she deviated? I would say just a bit. Council members, why are we here today? I

levon a

the army's strength behind them, they may have won." This is the former chair, taking sides.

The general spoke before her. "With the utmost respect to Jasmine and her group of young radicals, a wound has been opened. It needs to scab over and heal before Jasmine can take the chairmanship of this council, which I have no doubt she will eventually do. There is still time. Mark my word, she will be chair one day," says General Zhang, Jasmine's second greatest rival, while avoiding her eyes. He knows the right things to say. No one can argue this. "I will take the chairmanship for now. I hold the position of strength and can hide our less popular members under my cloak. Jasmine will be kept here. No harm will come to her, but she cannot be freed, and for heaven's sake she cannot be empowered right now. That just failed. The time is not right."

The general sucked the air from the room. There is hardly another breath of oxygen for the others to share.

He started with a question. "What can the Council accomplish in China at the present time? I think we can work at our recruitment while keeping a low profile. It might finally be time to invite an overseas Chinese member into our inner circle as well, possibly a Singaporean, or a Russian perhaps, to join our ranks. And, we need youth. Jasmine is our youngest member today, and though I love you dearly, we all do, we must admit you are no young bird like you once were, and you are no longer really in touch with these newest generations who are clearly determined to take power from the elderly. I want to recruit younger members over the next decade."

The general's jacket was full of ribbons and metals. "I might begin my limited speech by saying thank you. I think this committee does good work, but we cannot be complacent. The CGG needs to adapt the newest technologies to our communication. The military I command can assist us with that task. I also want to build our network of spies. The Council within an hour, a lethal shot of poisons usually does the trick best. None of the execution rooms are open to the public. All executions are carried out under a shroud of secrecy. Bodies are cremated right away. Families of the criminals are not invited to the executions and usually not informed in advance. Prisoners also don't know what to expect or when. Each second in this place hangs heavy.

When the Council had visited Jasmine at the detention center, there were members of both sides of the Tiananmen Square conflict represented within the group. The supporters even propose that Jasmine could become the chair of the CGG despite losing the recent political battle, but this proposal is ahead of its time. The proposal is overridden and the Council members unanimously decide that Jasmine should stay in prison at least for a time. Yes, she will retain her seat on the CGG. Members usually hold their Council seats for life, so this is not as unusual as it might appear to you. Dear Reader, you may finally want to ask me, *What is this Council for the Greater Good?* It is a body with a long history that goes back to the eunuchs. The members have the means to change the world, and they do what they do for the greater good of everyone.

The vote was unanimous. Jasmine is sent back to her jail cell. General Zhang becomes the next chair. The meeting concludes.

Jasmine chimed in one final time as the meeting came to a close. "Leave me here then. Be it for the greater good." This signals that she will vote the same as the other council members.

"Let's move ahead with a vote for General Zhang. We all know him to be a leader not driven by emotion. The chair needs to have masculinity at this present time. He is strategic and he is manly. It will be helpful to have the army with us at our disposal rather than against us blocking our path. That's what the youth lacked during the Tiananmen protest. With

CHAPTER 15

October 6, 1989

China's population is 1.13 billion people.

Jasmine was in a different detention center in 1989, before being transferred to the prison compound in Tu. The government has imprisoned her for supporting the failed Tiananmen Square uprising that collapsed in June of 1989. This initial jail where she is held is more secure but less remote than the one in Tu. This allows the Council to visit her.

This detention center housed a mix of truly horrible criminals alongside political prisoners who, too, were dangerous but under a different definition. Unfortunately for them all, the facility has multiple means of execution available for every occasion. Executions can be carried out swiftly without any bureaucratic red tape, and there is very little discretion on when or by what means it can be used. While sitting in her cell, Jasmine knows well that more people are executed in this facility in one month than most other modern countries have terminated in their entire history as nation states. Firing squad is still a preferred means here, because it spreads the blame along a row of ten men with rifles. That way nobody will ever know for sure whose gun it is that holds that single bullet and whose guns hold the blanks. It is more likely that your gun holds a blank, right? It allows the executioners to feel more like they are just part of the system that aims for Justice. The possibility of blank bullets exonerates the executioners from guilt. There are also rooms here for hangings, there are two separate electric chairs, which can be run simultaneously, and there are rooms for administering lethal injection. If you need a sentence to be carried out

Photo of Emperor Puyi:

Two men stood side by side. He Song has a patch over one eye. Puyi is wearing his German glasses that look like they were crushed and pieced back together. Emperor Puyi and He Song have the same height and build. Both wear the same style Mao suit and are looking scared at the camera as if they will be hit by it, and they appear deadened to all other things happening around them. There is mud on their hands from working in the gardens. A patch is sewn on one knee of He Song's work pants. No rings or jewelry are worn by either man. There is no clothing that would distinguish Puyi to be the old Emperor except his soft hands and his noble face. Yet, we all know who he is.

This was the photo Jasmine would later find, the same one the jade thief had meant to destroy. He throws it into a disposal bin bound for the village incinerator but that is the way of things here in China. One man's garbage is material that can eventually be reused for another purpose.

～ ～

The jade thief had originally bribed his way into the managerial position at this TVE using Qing gold as he still had access to it and so much other lost wealth of the empire. He pretends to have dug up the gold doubloons on his farmstead not far away. The truth is that he moved to Tu to find Jasmine and help her.

There were so many good places to bury your possessions in this world of ours, and that was what he had done. My advice would be just don't forget where you put it because the top layer of the Middle Kingdom's landscape can change over time. You'd think that a five-hundred-year-old tree would stay put, but very few of them have survived this rough century. Rivers, bridges, cities can all crumble. It all changes on the surface. But the earth, that is to say the dirt beneath this all, is always there and remains more or less intact. And in the dirt, you can hide treasure. Just mark it well.

back to front. His head is shaven almost smooth. That is the style then for young boys. However, there are still those thick, dark eyebrows. Perhaps the eyebrows are a sign. Yet the boy shows a truly friendly smile to the photographer.

He was tall and lean. The jade thief thinks he can see the curve of his spine already in this photo, the laziness he had even then to be in a constant slouch rather than sit and stand upright. Do you see the pride here? No, no pride is visible. When you think about it, what would The Monkey King have had then to give him pride at this humble point in his life?

Anyone would want a child like this one. I most certainly would! So full of possibility. The jade thief thinks that, yes, this was a fine boy. Whatever has happened to this person? He must still exist inside the older version in some form, in some way, maybe to reappear someday like a butterfly. That is reason to hope. No, it is not the blindness of a parent. It is just hope. Still stranger things happen all the time. We live in the world of a hundred million miracles every minute, so why not this?

In that black-and-white photo, you couldn't see any of the health issues that would later develop. The child will be in and out of the hospital all his life, and his father always will do what he can as both an herbalist and a donor. Will that extra stuff that goes into him produce an imbalance in his moral compass? There had been a look one day. That was when the jade thief saw a change in The Monkey King. He can remember that look but cannot remember the events surrounding the moment. The look was that of entitlement.

But before seeing the others in his album, the jade thief took out a photo of He Song and the Emperor. He removes it from the album and throws it into the trash.

Photos of Jasmine in the album:

She had been photographed beside her books with a pencil in hand. It was taken after an operation that restored her vision as a young girl. She needs to wear thick spectacles for a time then.

Was the cancer in her even then, or was it Lop Nur that exposed her to too much radiation? Was it from smoking those few times or was it secondhand smoke?

Jasmine was not yet beautiful in this photograph. She is in that awkward stage between child and young adult. Mentally, she probably feels ready to rule the world but has no education. Given the opportunity, this girl will take control from all of the authorities around her, thinking she is the only one who could see the hypocrisies of society and that she alone knows the better way. He Song is her neighbor, and his new wife is pregnant at the time of this photo. The baby will be called The Monkey King.

There was another photo, this one of Jasmine and He Song later in life. Both are dressed in unflattering swimsuits. Their hair is wet. The Yangtze River is in the background. They might be holding hands, but their hands are cut from the frame. Smirks and shared secrets run around both of their faces and it looks as though they might together suddenly splash the cameraman. Had he loved her? Yes, it seems now that he once had. Those smiles certainly say it. At that time there beside the Yangtze there was a mutual fondness and perhaps love.

Photos of The Monkey King in the album:

He was pictured beside foster parents, a boy of age three playing with a stick and a hoop of wood with a foster brother. There is none of that hairiness that covered The Monkey King as an adult from head to toe,

The possibilities of winning increase on this larger board. But still, she needs the game to become more challenging. Her mind needs to be challenged. She closes her eyes and dreams about how the game can be made more complex.

Normal tic-tac-toe played in two dimensions was no fun. On the ground she draws the x's and o's in a line. Playing tic-tac-toe in rows and columns of three is too easy. Let's try using rows of four.

~ ~

Have I awoken this morning in the East or in the West? he wondered those months before introducing himself to Jasmine as Lao Shifu, the jade thief. Memories of one place exist, but the jade thief touches the cool stone walls and knows he is not there now. He closes his tired eyes and tries to return to the dream, but his body is present now in the East no matter how his mind wanders elsewhere. With some bristle on his chin, the jade thief sits up. "It feels like my body is being pulled by both sides, like dough, stretched thin across the vast land of the Middle Kingdom," he says to himself on his cot in his lonely room. There are photos on the floor.

At his dormitory here in the township village enterprise, the jade thief looked through the old photographs the night before. Some are of Jasmine and some are of The Monkey King, and he tries to remember these people at those times back when they were young. He wonders whether he could have seen the traits that would lead to their downfalls back when the photos were shot. Were those traits visible then?

That previous year an acquaintance was going through his old papers and mementos in preparation for a move and mailed the old albums back to the jade thief. They had been stored away years earlier. The photos were pasted on rice paper sleeves bound together by a light bamboo cover.

could be played in six dimensions on her cell floor. It doesn't have a name yet and is essentially a game of tic-tac-toe.

The game took six dimensions. Shape is her fifth dimension. Some pieces are round and some are angular like triangles and squares. Five shapes in a row can win the game. To add the final dimension, she thinks about time. Often her game of tic-tac-toe comes to a draw, but that need not be the end of the game. Instead, when the spaces are all filled, the game can begin moving in reverse and pieces can be removed one at a time. This interests her, because she can remove the pieces in a different order from how they were placed. And, before the board is all clear of tiles, the flow of time can go forward again and Jasmine can play new tiles in those spaces where the tiles have been removed. The game feels familiar in some ways this second time around, but different. Where it came to a draw before, she makes different decisions now. Jasmine plays this game with herself because there is no one else to play. Someday she will test her invented game against a foe.

Let's increase it by another dimension, her mind had demanded! Rather than drawing in the dirt of the ground, she must use objects to represent the x's and o's, then give these pieces even more attributes. Her cell is made of brick and mortar. There are chips of both lying around on the ground. She collects them all into two piles. There are the light-colored mortar pieces that will be the x's and the o's will be dark brick.

She added another rule and another. You also can win if you get either five tall pieces in a row, regardless of whether it's made up of mortar pieces or bricks or a combination of the two. Five short would win as well. Jasmine plays with this new rule for many days, but then it too loses its challenge. She needs to add another dimension.

When the game had fewer dimensions, Prisoner Number Five experimented with the game using a board of five rows by five columns. This works. The winner gets five mortars in a row first. *Now, rows of five!*

the wall beside her. He doesn't respond. There is a silence now. She must say more. Telling him of her sad prognosis makes tears well up in her eyes. Jasmine hopes the darkness will hide her tears from view.

All this came as suddenly as the day he showed up peeping through the bars with an outstretched hand. "Hello. I am a manager from the local TVE. You may call me Lao Shifu." She likes having a visitor. Time takes its leave in strange places, doesn't it? At night, you can sleep through eight hours like not a second has passed; no more than a blink and morning is here. It can become like this when you have a daily rhythm or routine, day after day, so that a year or more will go by in a flash. Yet, there can be those other nights that last an eternity. Seconds do not move aside. They will not let the next pass.

From the comfortable living room where you listen to my story today you might have reliable hunger rhythms where, even without a clock, it is clearly time to eat at 7:00 a.m., noon, and 6:00 p.m. Your stomach gurgles and aches. Even without a watch, or a bell, our bodies know the regular time for meals. But it is not like that in the summertime, at least not in places like Tu. That heat does not allow the body to get hungry in a regular way. There is often just one meal a day because it is just that hot. You don't need more than that. Maybe a quarter watermelon is sufficient for that single meal and it could be eaten at any time.

One day, auspicious, unexpected, and unannounced, this young man with the ironic name, whom Jasmine believes she has never met before, started visiting her regularly just outside her cell. They talk about her cancer through the bars. She doesn't question the mystery of it. He is probably associated with the Council. She teaches him to play her new version of tic-tac-toe.

〜 〜

During the winter months, Jasmine had been developing a board game that

"Take a breath. Hold it," he said to her through the bars when teaching qigong. "Let the oxygen enter your blood, then find your center. Listen to that center. Feel its warmth and its power. Now, talk with it. Your inner qi has a language. There is just one word and it sounds like this: Om." She makes that sound. "Now, exhale."

When the jade thief had time, he would teach Jasmine the healing art of qigong. "Breathe. Now talk to the inner qi. Let's build some walls against the cancer. The walls will be made out of healthy cells that refuse to be corrupted. We don't want the cancer to spread further than it already has. Later, we will push it back. For now, let's build encampments." Jasmine envisions these encampments as little Red Guard soldiers within her body. In truth, her body is fighting the cancer as best it can, but medical attention is urgently needed.

The body probably bought itself additional time. Practicing this qigong magic provides her some hope. She already knew the basics of sword dancing, so learning the qigong method isn't such a leap for her as it would be for a beginner.

She doesn't go along with the lessons at first. "You look like such a nice young lad but here you practice an art that is old and out of favor. How mysterious. And you call yourself the jade thief, though you look to be no older than thirty. Ironic, you are. Is that it? Or is there more to it?" The story he tells her is this. "I was once a practitioner of the old style of qigong taught by monks at Shaolin," he says. "I will teach you how to use the art against your cancer until we can find medical means to treat it. I think we can arrange a transplant for your lungs soon after your release. I know of a donor who can spare one lung."

She did not tell him about her illness until he forced it from her. On one visit the jade thief asks her, "Is that blood?" when he notices Jasmine coughing up a dark jelly. "Never mind that," she replies, wiping it onto

Government, although sometimes she slips. "Thanks, young soldier," Jasmine says as she receives her first meal in two days. "Don't forget me up here. I depend on you. I need you to stay alive."

~ ~

The jade thief sometimes wandered the prison after visiting Jasmine to find any hidden passageways in case they were needed someday. In doing so, he finds other secrets. There is a room on the fourth floor of the former monastery that is filled with sunlight and has the most spectacular views of Tu's surrounding limestone hills and lakes. Among the windows, a stone statue stands there in the room's center. It is just ruins. The head of the deity is no longer there. It has no arms and there is only one foot. The torso remains. Everything else was probably hammered off at one time or another. Still, the jade thief looks at the statue as if it were some great masterpiece. There is still that one foot there so beautifully carved. It's not hard to imagine the whole piece based on that foot. It glows in the sunlight. Touching the stone, it is warm.

The jade thief said aloud, "Why have you abandoned me?" He is alone in this room and his footsteps echo. For a moment he feels utterly abandoned. The turns of fortune can feel so unfair.

He and Jasmine had many conversations in that prison. She once says to him, "If I could cut it all away I would do it myself with this soup spoon. I have pain everywhere. It is in my bones. I feel it crawling in my brain and behind my eyes." Tears fall.

People's voices sometimes do not age and that was certainly the case with Jasmine. The jade thief closes his eyes when talking with old friends like her, and pictures them like they were long ago. It is a form of time travel. Some voices are ageless.

gives a manager like the jade thief pause. These education classes on quality are certainly a step in the right direction. The focus on quality is new here. During the quality improvement classes, the jade thief will talk to the laborers as if he needs their help in finding the solution and ask them questions that make them think. He wants them to improve their performance in their own way. That is what he is trying to do today in the firework factory. It is a big barn, really, but many sorts of buildings can be called factories if used that way. He begins his talk by asking, "Can any of you tell me what the word 'quality' is? How can we define it?" Many hands go up.

~ ~

In jail, Jasmine no longer tracked Venus through the seasons. *Venus, star of sympathy, where are you now?* If only Jasmine had someone to hold. It is the being alone that is the coldest. What she wouldn't give for just a hug.

"Government, look here. If you think your job is not important, that is not true! There is nothing more important than bringing the helpless food and water, keeping the most vulnerable safe. It is the most important job any of us will ever have. You prevent the death of me." She is talking to the guard outside of her door. The guard is temporarily transfixed on those words drifting out from the cell, but when he leaves the ward he will quickly forget. His attention is already beginning to fade. It is human nature to forget such things. Prisons are unpleasant and those locked up are sad, with such sad stories. It makes you crazy to think on it too much, so it is better to not get wrapped up in it in the first place. Let it be.

"I'm sorry we forgot to bring your meals yesterday, Number 5. The second shift didn't show up to work. Well, here is a little extra for today. Eat up." He must call her Number 5, not Comrade. She must call him

The children were nervous about the jade thief's surprise test exercise. Some of these kids have worked in the factory for three or four years and never heard of a quality inspection in all that time. When Lao Shifu says to them, "I ask you, then, can we open this box of fireworks you just manufactured and see if every single one that we light will explode as promised? Let's give it a try. There are twenty-five in the box." The anticipation in the room is not of excitement as much as dread. Everyone suddenly expects there to be a dud. Maybe they are all duds! Who knows?

Are these the same children who cheered, "Yes it is!" when the jade thief asked, "Is our work quality? No duds would show up in good quality. True quality is a consistently good product." Yes, it is they. You can't blame them. Confidence will erode when it is based on nothing more than inertia.

One child had said, "Quality is when there are no dud fireworks in the box," when her manager asked.

"Yes, what else? Yes?" Lao Shifu prodded. He looks over at that girl. She is perhaps fifteen years old.

"Quality is when the work is completed to the highest standard," said another girl with braids when he first asked, "Yes, child, what is quality?"

During their break time, the jade thief blew up a red balloon and let it loose in the courtyard for the kids to use in their play. Such joy it gives the children.

The factories here were not what you'd think. There are no assembly lines. The electricity isn't consistent. Sometimes it goes out for days. There isn't any of the efficiency of a Ford factory assembly line like you'd have seen on television. Instead, there is a table here, a table there. One chair over there is broken. The corridors are not clean. Field mice run around. Warehouses are disorganized and many things get lost. It demand for our much-loved baby formula is too high if we go with pure 100 percent milk. Looking him in the eye, his supervisor says, "Here, have a cigarette. Tell me, really, what else can be done? It needs to happen." The key is not to let anyone know about the change in ingredients. Imagine all the paperwork there would be if word got out. It will only be a small circle that knows. It is the small things like this that need to be done to keep everything running well. It is the manager's responsibility and, although the workers shouldn't be bothered with all the technicalities of the business, he is really doing it for all of them.

The leaves of the maple trees changed color early. Purple from scarlet, light yellow from deep green. Days shorten. Mid-autumn harvest festival passes quickly. Lao Shifu prefers calling it the August Moon festival, which is another name for it.

Moon cakes were distributed earlier that month, and there was extra cash handed out for the good work. Moon cakes are a unique treat that the workers eagerly anticipate each year. They come in from the factory bosses in beautiful tins. There are eight small cakes, each with a special filling. Some contain a mix of nuts and honey. There are jam fillings, some with creamy chocolate or sweet meats. Morale in Tu's township village enterprise is good, and rightly so. There are rumors of possibly taking a delegation of workers to Disney World or Frankfurt early next year to reward those who deserve thanking, and to learn more, as we must, about how other countries run their production lines.

On a typical sort of day earlier that season, the jade thief focused his day's labor on the TVE fireworks production. Twenty-five fireworks are lit that afternoon one by one. Twenty-four go off fine but the last one he lights sizzles but does not explode right away. There is a collective sigh from the children. Then, without any warning, it too goes off. A perfect batch! Everyone claps and cheers. Some hug. The child workers are so proud.

At the village enterprise of Tu, a concrete gate arched over the road. It reads, "Tu Factory and Processing Center Number One." Its administrative offices are just beyond the concrete gate in unpainted concrete box–buildings with flat roofs. Slogans are hung on the sides of one building in white lettering on red fabric: "Work hard and get ahead!"

The jade thief arrived to work on time. He must sign in at the entrance and show his worker's permit and TVE identification. There is a briefing before the next shift to discuss policies and new operations techniques. The children who work in the fireworks factory are given a shorter workday but must also attend these briefings. One topic of note today is that the TVE is waiting for important raw materials needed for a new type of firework called Galaxy7500. With a sound that sizzles like a fried egg, it will pop into 7,500 dazzling sparkles, which is the exact number of stars a person can see with their naked eye on a dark, clear night. The TVE deputy vice-president says with gusto that the Galaxy7500 may become so popular we will be seriously considering drawing up plans for a brand new production facility, eventually. It's all possible. Good news from the business side!

Being a manager at a TVE was truly a twenty-four-hour job. Even at night before he goes to sleep, the jade thief takes a stroll through the enterprise buildings in his casual clothes and tennis shoes to make sure everything is on the up-and-up. In the baby formula production facility, he does his routine task out of sight, mixing the rice powder into barrels for the next day just as he was instructed. He always does what he is told. He keeps the secrets that need to be kept. The jade thief doesn't mind his life here and feels that he contributes in a positive way to society.

Weeks earlier, the jade thief had a serious conversation with his supervisor. It is about this rice powder he must add to the baby formula in their factory. The supervisor says the rice powder can act as filler when it is needed and should cause no harm to the babies. It will become increasingly needed because the milk production in Tu is lower than anticipated and

Turning his body, he kicks his right heel.

Before the right side is done, he focuses on his left lower body and stands on one leg.

We are nearing the midpoint of his daily exercise.

He just has to strike two ears with both fists, left heel kick.

High pat on horse, single whip!

Cloud hands, single whip!

Continuing backward in the routine, his right hand grasps the sparrow's tail, wards it off,

Rollback, press and push. Breathe.

There is a left grasp for the sparrow's tail, ward off, rollback, press and push.

Reverse reeling forearm, step back and drive the monkey away.

Left, then right.

Lao Shifu breathes deeply and strums the invisible lute.

He brushes his knee and steps forward, left, then right.

He is a wild crane spreading its wings.

It all started, as it does each time, by parting the horse's mane.

of the Emperor boy, Puyi, and he would think about someday capturing one for Jasmine and giving it to her for company. And today, finally, he will.

~ ~

Every morning while living in Tu, before biking to the monastery or showing up to work in the factory, the manager Lao Shifu practiced his tai chi shadowboxing dance to focus on his inner energy. His soul is shifty, to say the least, and especially so if he doesn't make a conscious effort each and every day to exercise the inner energy. The old masters call that place inside your chest the chi. These are the twenty-four postures he often practices, here in reverse from last to first. That it greatly resembles Jasmine's swordplay is no coincidence:

> *It ends with the jade thief crossing his hands to a close.*
>
> *Just before, he withdraws and pushes as if closing a door.*
>
> *After he turns his body, deflects, parries, there is a punch!*
>
> *A knife penetrates the back.*
>
> *A sword lay at the bottom of the sea.*
>
> *Then shuttle back and forth.*
>
> *The jade thief focuses on the right lower body and, like a bird, stands on one leg.*
>
> *He is a golden bird standing alone.*
>
> *Single whip, then squatting down, a snake creeps down.*

heavens were encouraging it to be.

On the way to the prison that day, the sun became harsh as the jade thief pedaled. He feels his neck start to redden and burn. *The chirp reminds me of a cricket that Puyi once kept.*

Lao Shifu tucked the cricket into his pocket. "You are coming with me, little friend." He finds a walnut shell on the ground that he quickly carves into a small cage. He carves it with a pocketknife and ties the two halves together with a red silk string. "There now. It is a palace."

"I will introduce you to my friend, little cricket. I predict she will be with you until the end of your days. For your part of the relationship all that you need to do is sing for her and keep her company. I realize that I will be taking you away from this paradise here, but alas I do not have a choice or at least I don't much care. There are more important things."

A cricket jumped on his shoe when he was picnicking, taking a rest from the bike ride. There is a gentle thud. It feels heavy. The cricket doesn't speak for some time, then it chirps a hallelujah like a mountain lion. While the jade thief snacks, he talks to the cricket. "How old could you be? Two years, three maybe. I dare say you have not seen much," but he reconsiders the statement. "Yet I wonder how much you have seen in your short lifetime below the grasses, hopping about as you do. Surely you have watched the planting of the rice, the harvest, and the renewal after winter. You know your share of snakes and owls, ferrets and other predators. You have tasted bugs and grasses, and have your favorites and your foods of last resort. Do you have friends? No, I suppose not. You are a wanderer."

The jade thief brought a thermos of green tea with him that day and decided to take a break. With some steamed bread wrapped in a towel, he creates a small picnic on the ground, allowing a cricket to jump on his shoe. He would often hear the crickets on that bike ride. Their song reminds him this way so that Jasmine would mistakenly take it to mean the keys were his reward. Though his words were misleading, they literally meant his current situation was a result of the kindness given to He Song's son, saving his life.

In the darkness of the prison, the jade thief could picture Jasmine young again. Her fiery voice has not aged one day since he first met her. "His son was like you in some ways, always getting into trouble," he says, not for the last time. "The Monkey King was a name that fit him well. But, alas."

Disturbed, she cried out, "Who are you, Lao Shifu? How do you know He Song?" after he admitted to her in the darkness that, "Yes, these keys belonged to He Song." She feels a strange disorientation. She looks into his eyes and her ears begin to ring.

Jasmine had noticed something familiar about the ring of keys. "Those remind me of He Song's keys," she says, curious.

It had all started out so much better. The jade thief is prepared to give his gift found in the grasses outside of Tu. "I brought you someone to keep you company…" As the jade thief rustles though his sack, Jasmine sees the young man's keys glistening. There are too many keys to get a clear count. Some have dragons on them. Others have flat heads that are square, pentagons, or stars. Some are simple in shape and made of heavy iron. A ring holds them together like she remembers.

As you, my reader, have seen, Jasmine will like her gift and will not pay too much thought to the keys, or He Song, or the death of his son, The Monkey King. It all works itself out after a moment of confusion. The jail is bright but cold that day. Jasmine hears the cricket before her visitor mentions the gift. He is so excited to give it to her. He has no idea that attention might turn elsewhere to his keys and He Song. He is thinking about the hug he had given Jasmine on his last visit. It had felt like the

That cricket kept her company a great many days.

Then, it sang! Hearing the cricket, she is transported to a place of her childhood along the riverbank, dirty, playing, believing in fairy folk and water dragons. She is a young girl with an imagination. Adventure lay behind every tree.

It was a gift from her mysterious visitor. The jade thief offers the walnut shell to Jasmine before they know one another well, and, showing a great deal of courtesy and respect, she takes the tiny gift from him into her hands. She holds it, strokes its ridges, feeling the life inside. The cricket jumps but doesn't sing.

"So, here. I brought you this gift. It is a cricket I found on my bike ride here today. It can be your companion for when you are lonely. In dark times, the more he will sing. The Emperor himself carried one." Finally, they are both calm again.

Was there a tear in Lao Shifu's eye? Yes, a drop hanging there above his soft cheek. Jasmine doesn't care about his pain. Who is this man that considers He Song a friend? There is still a tinge of evil in the air, but she lets it pass and lets the jade thief's explanation sink in.

He needed to explain to her, "The Monkey King is dead. He drowned in the Yangtze River. They say He Song watched it happen."

"I knew The Monkey King, too," she said. "I returned the boy to He Song when he was young. Maybe I was partly responsible for that horrid name as well. Where is he now?"

He had to find a reasonable story that could explain to Jasmine how he came into possession of He Song's ring of keys. "I saved his son's life once. When I saved the son of He Song, this was my reward." He said it in in that moment before things happen, it is indeed possible to see an effect before its cause. That is what happens here in the rice paddy fields of Tu. It happens occasionally to us all. Just pay attention.

In Tu, the irrigation ditches ran right beside the road. Water buffalo pull carts full of rice. The buffalo are dark with heavy horns. They move like shadows in the rice patties. You can smell rice husks burning. Long stretches of water provide reflections better than the best manmade mirrors. They reflect hills steep and misshapen like camel humps. The water is clear enough to see carp swimming below, followed by their little ones. When the jade thief bikes along one field, an enormous flock of birds fly up from their hidden place in the grass and form a cloud of bodies blocking out the sun, pooping everywhere, making a huge racket. The coolness of their shade is great relief. And then they are gone.

Inside the prison, Jasmine had been thinking with a cricket in her hand. Jasmine will release the cricket when she is released, she imagines, there inside her cell. The scene will play out like this. First the cricket might continue to stay nestled on her hand, or may jump off for a moment into the weeds only to hop back onto her shoe and stay there. Jasmine will then reluctantly keep the cricket for another day, then try releasing it again and again. The final attempt will be in a different time of day, perhaps at dusk, so that her insect friend can hear the many other crickets calling from the grasses. In this way, the bug will teach her to be sensitive to the time again. Here in prison, there is no need to care about time, and it is better not to keep track, because, in not caring, a missed meal or an absent visit isn't so aggravating to the spirit. To function again in society, she will need to adopt that structure of time again. *Thank you, little cricket,* she will say to him when he goes, *for keeping me company for so long and, now that we are free, reminding us both about the sun and its gift of time.* In her mind, she throws the empty walnut cage into the blue grasses. This is all just a daydream she repeats over and over while sitting on the floor of a cold and lonely cell.

A plump black fly suddenly flew into the jade thief's eye with a splat while he was biking that road to the monastery. He thinks he saw it coming at him right into his eye. Did he know it would end up there in his eye? Yes, he did! The entire path of the fly is recorded in his memory. He saw it coming. *Splat.*

Why mention this memory of a common fly, so small in scale within a story that spans one hundred years?

He saw it coming. The jade thief is usually thinking about Jasmine while biking, but he still needs to pedal carefully along the road and not veer off into a soggy ditch. He needs to avoid potholes and automobiles and the occasional stray dog. His eye looks around. There is so much to see. The fly he will dig out of his eye is coming right for him. Sure, he will see it when it is just in front of his nose, but the surprise is that he also sees it long before. Twenty seconds before, when all sorts of other bugs are buzzing in the air around the fly, he sees it. You'd think there would be no way to distinguish this one fly as *the* fly that would end up in his eye. Fascinating!

He did not pay special notice to the other bugs. But perhaps by magic, since it will be the one that ends up swimming in his eye, somehow the jade thief Lao Shifu is able to follow its path in advance of the result from way out there all the way splat into his inner eye, and he sees how it all comes to be from twenty seconds out and ten feet away all the way in, closer and closer, nine, eight, seven feet now, . . . on its path to the center of his left eye. Although sure enough he is not able to avoid the event from happening, he does remember that he was aware of it all, and retains the information in his brain.

How can that be? Yet, here is proof it can happen. The jade thief's eye and brain know what is going to happen before it actually happens, and so the fly will be noticed and the event will be recorded into memory. His body will know to notice the flight of that particular fly, because somehow

For her attempts at escape, the guards never punished Jasmine. One wouldn't expect a woman like Jasmine to just stay put. She burrows into the walls with her chopsticks, she shovels dirt with her drinking cup, and she scrapes stone bricks with her fingernails. It keeps her busy. Allowing some hope is never a bad thing. The young guards have nicknamed her "Auntie Mole" rather than Number Five and are not intentionally cruel, though they are cruel enough in their inattentiveness. Sometimes they forget to feed her. It is always very cold in the stone room and she did not have adequate clothing until the jade thief brought her better clothes and a jacket from the TVE. Sun streams down from windows high above and cannot touch her face. To have the sun touch your face. What a luxury!

Jasmine was once discovered in the halls dressed smartly in a male guard's uniform but without any shoes. She is taking a casual pace step by step down toward the exit.

It was not easy keeping this woman confined. Over the long term, the feat proves impossible. She checks the lock every hour of every day so that the one time it is not properly secured she makes the most of her luck. She is gone.

Back then, the jade thief pedaled rhythmically on a black single-speed Flying Phoenix bicycle through the rice paddy fields. The chain jingles along. *Tat ta tat. Tat ta tat. Tat ta tat. Ta!* The dirt road has bumps and puddles. Ducks waddle about in little groups. He scratches at the mosquito bites on his legs as he rides along. He occasionally gets off his bike and walks, just to breathe in the countryside.

Riding along, he saw fishermen out in their boats. They use cormorants to dive into the clear lake water and disappear. Then there is a second splash. Rising from the water, the birds bring back enormous fish just as they have been trained to do here for many centuries. The fishermen reward their birds back on the boat.

off his bike for a few months to adjust to having just one lung, but does he ever listen to the doctors? No, he never does. He was running on happy adrenaline knowing Dear Jasmine would be saved yet again. He has been an avid bicyclist while living in Tu. It is easier to get from place to place on a bicycle than any other mode of transportation. Walking is good, but the jade thief's days are busy now, so bicycling gets him where he needed to go quicker, yet not too quickly that he might miss the scenery as he would in a car. Before her release, while Jasmine was coughing up blood in her lonely prison cell, the jade thief often rode his bicycle from his office in the TVE to the prison to visit her there.

Jasmine's prison in Tu was located inside a former Buddhist monastery built to last forever, with ornate carvings and intricate mosaic floors. Chinese monks were mostly killed off by the mid-1950s, so the monastery hasn't been in use for its original purpose for some time now. There is hardly any religion left here today. Those few monasteries and temples that have not been destroyed have been transformed by the communists to provide practical uses for the community, such as prisons, hospitals, and schools.

The sign-in process for visitors of inmates at the prison in Tu varied for the jade thief each time he visited Jasmine. It depends on which guards happen to be on shift. There is usually a wait before he gets anyone's attention. He smiles. Patience is needed. Staying humble is a must. The guards are very young, self-absorbed, and prefer to not be troubled. Machine guns are within their easy grasp. Although the guns are intimidating, they are never used. A thick haze hangs around the guards' chairs from smoking packs and packs of Marlboros. The cigarette butts cover the floors.

He hands out red envelopes to all the guards. There is money inside that allows him unrestricted access to Jasmine. Red envelopes are the failsafe key. The jade thief eventually learns other ways of getting into the facility without passing any guards, but he prefers this method for regular visits so that the palms are greased in preparation for her eventual release.

clatter and chatter hushed to enjoy that single female voice. "Back to work, everybody!" he then yells. "We are weeks behind our production schedule. No more nonsense, Jasmine. Stop those stories." He dusts off the workshop table with an old cloth, wipes off the chair from where he will observe, and takes a seat. Yet again, the jade thief is interrupting what everyone else thought to be a most captivating story.

The largely uneducated workers, innocent to the larger world around them, were so enthralled they didn't notice the jade thief walk into the workroom, brushing off sawdust with his gray gloves as he went. Jasmine is telling them about that wooden box she acquired long ago from He Song. "From the outside it is a simple wooden box about three inches by three inches square," she said. "From the outside it is a simple thing. Nothing out of the ordinary. But open it up, and the contents are quite shocking indeed. The box holds a little baby hand. I swear it's true!"

He accepts her nonsense from time to time. By and large, the jade thief is happy Jasmine adjusted so well to the township village enterprise farm and factory life, and proud that he was able to do what he did for her. It was the jade thief who helped Jasmine get released from the local prison through large bribes that would probably allow a few lucky children of local officials to afford college in America, and then through a separate channel of bribes, this time directed toward doctors and hospital administrators, he arranged Jasmine's treatment for her cancer. He even donated one of his own lungs to her and it was transplanted successfully in a city hospital nearby. As a living donor, he could choose the recipient to whom his lung would go, moving Jasmine up on the long waitlist of poor men and women in need of a new organ. She would have surely died without the lung. She would have wasted away in jail without him.

Both of Jasmine's lungs needed to be removed. It took some time for Jasmine to recover from the transplant and subsequent treatments, but less than would have been expected. The jade thief's doctor told him to stay

Tu had an old, beautiful monastery built into the side of a limestone hill. Jasmine can see it when milking the cows. A banyan tree reaches out from an inner courtyard and spreads out wide over the monastery's clay-tiled rooftops. The village also has an active TVE that now produces a range of products from baby formula to firecrackers. TVE stands for Township Village Enterprise and is a village of communist farmers working together like a corporation to become relevant in the new world economy of the 1990s. Jasmine sees drains flowing fluorescent liquid from one of the main manufacturing buildings into the side ditches just beyond its property gates. She thinks that someday soon she will put a stop to that.

Before her surgery, Jasmine spent a few months making toy trains in the TVE's wood shop for exported goods. The hard work, both using her muscles and being around other people again, is rejuvenating after having been in prison for so long. It is like waking up after a long winter hibernation. One visible change in her comes today when she shows up to the morning group exercise with her hair nicely combed. It is a simple thing, yet it is a vivid change. When a woman's hair is a tangled mess, the image it conveys is probably worse than it need be. Immediately after her release from prison she had forgotten about appearances, but she is adapting to society again at her own pace.

Jasmine's powerful oratory showed signs of a return. Thank goodness. Common dialogue, that of people like you and me, is giving way to talking with passion as unrestrained as before with that old manner that was uniquely Jasmine's, that womanly voice so deep it promises to take us along on an adventure, exciting, dangerous, and reverberating in multiple overtones. TVE workers stop what they are doing to listen to her. That is the Jasmine we know and love. The workshop tools are silent. There is one voice in the room. The people are listening to Jasmine's every word.

The jade thief was a manager at this township village enterprise in Tu. Occasionally he will enter a nearly silent workroom with the normal in the pungent mud of this farm. This thought makes her giggle a bit (yes, Jasmine can giggle!), tears rolling down her cheeks. She blows out a laugh.

That photo of He Song and the Emperor had been crumpled in the township landfill for a long time and just barely escaped the incinerator by catching the attention of an employee who felt that it was too pretty to burn. There are blooming flowers of all kinds in the photo and that is what caught her eye. It must have fallen out of that person's pocket and into a puddle.

It is funny how things get misplaced and are rediscovered.

Jasmine did not press for a leadership role in Tu. This allows her time to focus on the basics like adjusting to social interaction again, bit by bit, and that is fine with her at least for now. She was a great leader once, and no doubt will become one again, but these slower paced years right now in Tu are meant for recovery.

While recovering from her surgeries, Jasmine began to pay more attention to the natural wonders around her for therapy, and to learn what nature can teach. She stares at rows of ants parading up and around their anthill. The ants can teach her cooperation, strength, and endurance. The green sandpipers and lapwings overhead teach her about reference points and scale. In such a wide area as the sky, the birds can take so many angles in their flight. There is no one way. There are billions of ways! Just pick your goal and take one of those billions of routes. So, dearest Jasmine, what is your goal today?

She milked cows at the dairy barn three times a day most days. Milking is at 4:00 a.m., an hour before dawn, second milking at 11:00 a.m. in full midday sun, and third milking at 6:00 p.m., when it is dusk and buggy. Baby formula is manufactured on-site using this milk. Hundreds of thousands of children depend on it.

CHAPTER 16

July 31, 1995

China's population is 1.2 billion people.

This chapter takes place in the small village town of Tu. The environment here is nothing like the other places we have been. Puyi's former empire, this place we call the Middle Kingdom, what others call China, is such a vast land with so many marvels, it could easily be a world onto itself. It might be best that you, the reader, think it thus.

In Tu, there was lots of fresh water, both lakes and rivers knot into one another so one felt as if there was more water than land. The water leaves pockets of dry land, but most of the land in Tu is soggy.

Those firm places were connected by boat or by narrow, reaching crescent-shaped bridges built in a different age. A few bridges here are as old as Marco Polo. The rice patties lying in between are in mushy land fed by flowing water. Colorful carp swim along much of it. Eels burrow in the mud. Green mountains are in the distance. It is misty throughout the valley. Jasmine would walk in the fields of Tu during her recovery, sometimes barefoot.

One day, she found a photo of He Song and the Emperor Puyi in a puddle on her walking path. She assumes it is not an original photograph but rather a printed copy torn from some textbook that chronicled the reeducation of Emperor Puyi. It shows the two men working in a garden. In this staged photograph, they are not only working in mud and covered in it—politically, morally, and physically—but now these two men are covered creating gardens over Victoria Peak. Fireworks also shoot off in sync with those above from the main skyscrapers and out from the bay. It starts to rain and everything disappears because of a veil of umbrellas. Then the rain stops and the fireworks appear again. They talk about the future handover, and Jasmine is already planning the protest in Macao.

As was common between them, the jade thief quipped, "Dear, what will we burn down this time?"

Jasmine gazed over at the island through the gunpowder and smoke and said, "I will do my part to ignite a spark. That might be all that is needed."

"He Song does like to gamble," suggested the jade thief. They agree on setting up a game of mahjong. Sunday will make the arrangements.

"For a proper protest in Macao next year, I will need the police on our side," Jasmine said and asked, "Sunday darling, how can we get He Song to help? He has them all in his pocket." A public action will be risky but she must try to do something that matters.

Jasmine invited the jade thief to Hong Kong to attend her commencement earlier that day. It is the year 1998. The jade thief is like family to her now. He even sat in the classroom when Jasmine defended her final thesis at the university, smiling and proud. They will be calling her "Professor" soon! The thesis paper she presents is a complex calculation on whether one individual could change the course of history. She determined that a person born in 1900 had a one million percent better chance of having a significant influence on history than a child born in modern day. If that person was closely connected to a person of great power, the chances of affecting history went up exponentially. Career choice, gender, and nationality all mattered a great deal in the calculations as well. Curiously, intelligence and even the level of education had little impact.

That was her routine with a sword. It is an exercise and a meditation in one.

She took the broadsword in both hands. It is heavy but balanced. She juggles it from right to left.

The sky was clear. Looking up, Jasmine often tracks Venus through the seasons. It is on an eight-year cycle and is in line with the moon. Her favorite time is watching it just before sunrise as the first brilliant light, pulling up the sun. They say it is the star of sympathy and is responsible for the morning dew. At dusk it takes the sun away.

When Jasmine first entered the park beside the environs of St. Lazarus Church, it sounded like an outright jungle up above in the magnolias, although it is impossible to see past the wide waxy leaves and ballooning flowers. She hears a racket of birds, crickets, and bugs of all kinds in the trees and feels a sprinkle of rain. She hums that old Ming tune stuck in her head.

~ ~

Before we leave this chapter, let's skip back one year to end with Jasmine finishing her doctoral thesis at Hong Kong University. She is dressed in her graduation robes and is looking up at fireworks.

The Professor, the jade thief, and the old woman named Sunday looked across Hong Kong's bay toward Macao and began to conspire. The island of Hong Kong is within sight of the peninsula of Macao, which in turn is in sight of the Chinese mainland. Spectacular fireworks thunder overhead. One set of fireworks looks like a dragon dance, with a huge smiling mane, glowing eyes, and a dozen legs across the evening sky. This produces an idea. *Boom. Boom.* Eventually the fireworks become too loud for conversation and the smoke too thick to see, but the booms and flashes go on and on as if there is a great war among the gods. The fireworks are like blooming flowers,

There is a single whip of the sword then squatting down, a snake
   creeps down.

She turns her body and there is a left heel kick!

Strike to ears with both fists, and right heel kick!

High pat on horse, and a single whip of her sword.

Cloud hands, and a single whip.

Breathe.

She takes a right grasp of a sparrow's tail, wards it off, then rolls
   back, press and push.

Jasmine grasps the sparrow's tail the first time, wards off, rollback,
   press and push.

Reverse reeling forearm, then step back and drive the monkey away.

Left, then right.

Strum the lute.

Brush knee.

Step forward, left, then right.

She is a wild crane spreading its wings.

Breathe, Jasmine.

And begin by parting the horse's mane.

How much of your own history can your remember, Dear Reader? And of that, what is real? And say it is all true; was any of it really caused by your own freedom, or is freedom the greatest lie of our age? Is it, as He Song will say, that the story has already been written? To know thyself, you carry around a book. You read it each and every day. You believe it is written by you. And that must be taken by faith.

⸏ ⸏

Jasmine practiced with the sword dancers in another area of the park. She finally says, "Thank you for letting me use this," returning the sword she has borrowed. "Bless your generosity." The dancers respond by saying, "Come back and practice with us anytime."

With sword in hand, right here on this park lawn that would be the epicenter of her plans for the next day, Jasmine closed her eyes and practiced a familiar routine she had learned from the jade thief years earlier while sitting in a lonely prison. It is elegant how her sword cuts into air. This is her routine, told in reverse. Imagine a beautiful woman with a sword in hand:

She ends by withdrawing and pushing as if closing a door.

But not before she turns her body, deflects, parries, and then punches.

A fan opens then penetrates the back.

Breathe!

A needle sinking to the sea bottom.

Her feet shuttle back and forth.

She is a golden bird standing alone.

Jasmine knew her crowd well. She says in her deep voice, "Let me tell you, World, I do not believe! If tens of thousands of challengers lie under your feet, I still do not believe that my dream is false; and if the ocean is destined to breach the dikes, let all its brackish water pour into my heart and you may count me as number ten thousand and one!"

Jasmine came upon the group at about 11:00 in the morning. The ragtag assembly wears t-shirts and sandals, congregating below a large magnolia tree. Some work on the long bamboo poles, connecting them so that they would reach twenty-five feet in length. These poles attach to huge lengths of shimmering green silk cut in the shape of a dragon's wing. Tomorrow, the march from this park toward the sea will have organizers holding the dragon wing flags about every quarter of a mile, one wing on each side of the road, flapping up and down with a slow grace. From the bystanders' perspective, it will look as though the parade of people is indeed a dragon and these are its great wings. But the organizers know the secret message that the flags contain. The organizers will only flap the wings when they see the wings a quarter mile behind them flapping and so on each quarter mile for the length of the parade. If the wings behind them stop flapping, then the people need to stop to give the protesters inside the park more time to remove The Happy Man statue from his pedestal. If the wings from behind start flapping again, then the dragon can move onward, toward the sea. This would have indeed been a dragon if their plans were not so completely foiled by He Song.

The light revealed the morning as the sun changed from night to day. More is revealed each hour until the city streets are bustling with a new day.

The trees above the park had a million leaves and each leaf casts a shadow. On each leaf there is more than one shadow, beside it and below it and overlapping it. There is more shadow in the tree than sunlight.

She scanned the crowd calculating in her mind the chances for their success. Who should be demoted and who promoted in her organizational structure of activists to increase their chances of success tomorrow? Depending on the scenarios, she now estimates a 20 percent chance that she will pull off the plan in full. Striking Mercy, a show of her own strength and the red of another's blood in front of the others, gave her an additional three percent.

"We are doing this civil disobedience for the good of everyone." She stares the more senior members in the eye. *Don't any of you dare stand in the way. This isn't the time for mistakes. Instead, follow me.* In a throaty voice that reverberates into three separate tones, Jasmine shouts, "WE CAN SUCCEED!" She doesn't care who hears her now.

Jasmine knew she needed to shock the organizers to rally them and embolden them all for the challenges to come to both keep them focused on the important task at hand and clearly make her point that she cannot be crossed. Different situations require a different shock. In some circumstances, the group might need to see their leader punch a tough guy in the face to knock out his tooth, then pick up that tooth and fling it into the crowd. She has done that before, but this isn't the place for that. It could be removing all her clothes, which Jasmine has done before as well to get the proper attention, and standing there naked, shouting to them all, "I don't care what you see. Our action tomorrow is bigger than that. If this is shocking to you now, you just wait until tomorrow!" But not here. She chose something a bit more subtle.

Mercy's head flew back as she fell to the ground.

That poor girl was always unlucky. *Wrong place and wrong time,* Jasmine thinks to herself. With a wide swing, Jasmine smacks Mercy in the jaw.

Mercy had been saying "Justice, now! Justice, now!" as if the mood has taken over her senses. She comes up towards Jasmine's makeshift stage, emerging from the crowd, shifting the attention.

careful with her answers. A protest is only effective if organizers maintain control. It should not become a riot.

She reiterated the timing of each action. The Happy Man will be dismantled at noon. The acrobats will begin their part once the statue is destroyed, perhaps at 12:30 but it might take longer. If there is a delay, it will be signaled down the line by holding up the flags.

She had them fired up. Their spirits are high. Tomorrow, Macao will be turned over from the Portuguese state, and the locals will finally show their true colors and demand a democracy.

Wheels within wheels. Jasmine sees many things in motion on different levels. Some gears move slowly, but they are moving beneath her in this land and among these people. These are her kin. They are revolutionaries who herald from a long lineage. *We will not be downtrodden. Not in the long run. Eventually, we can win.*

"You will face great personal risk in these next days. A state security officer has already invited me for tea. We all know what that means.

"We are demanding that Macao become a practice area of a new system. We want to select a governor with experimental democracy. Big Brother never thought us as important as Hong Kong. Our peninsula is smaller. So there will be less focus on having us assimilate. The academics have all been arguing for our cause, but there needs to be a final push for the government to take the risk. That is why we are taking action tomorrow!

"Dear Warriors, why are we taking this action?" she asked. The captive bird longs for its home in the grove. "Long were we confined to the cage of imperialism. Now we return to freedom!"

in and out from the direction of an outdoor tea garden that lies nearby. Tall trees abound. Jasmine can still hear a few crickets in the trees, although they are quieting under the full sun. The air smells like the sea.

She talked with the organizers right there in the public about the risk and goals and possible costs. There is no better place to hold a secret meeting than right outdoors. She scans the crowd of organizers. A woman named Mercy is shielding her eyes from the strong sun, her head down. Yes, these people appear to be on board. The minions will follow their lead tomorrow. Jasmine chose these community leaders who had proved themselves to her over the years as always dependable. Their attitudes never deviate, and they are always on time. Jasmine smiles and the dot of crimson stretches out into a toothy grin. Jasmine has a foreboding feeling that this Mercy will be unlucky yet again within these days but no matter. She knows the risks. They all do.

Mercy was famous in certain circles for once calling out to a crowd long ago in a different protest for a much different cause, "Don't say this is Justice! I do not feel better when that word is used." Jasmine remembers they were at a village factory that had burned to the ground days before with forty young workers trapped inside. Mercy was hugging the survivors and their families. Then, she had emptied out her wallet and said, "This will be some assistance to help you during the tragedy. But, mind you, it is not justice." That was years ago, but still those words ring out. Jasmine looks around at the powerful women around her now.

"Everyone has their pagers ready?" Jasmine asked the organizers in the park. She stands on a makeshift podium. "We are passing around your disposable phones for text messaging. You will all get one."

"My Dear Warriors…You must message everything you see tomorrow," she repeated again and again.

There were questions about what to do when arrests begin. She is places to be. Jasmine waits at the corner of Estrada do Cemiterio and Rua do Volong roads, humming a familiar Taiwanese tune of hope that blends into old lines of poetry. It is the same poetic tune stuck in her head all day as she mulls over her plans for tonight and tomorrow. She realizes she has been followed by shadowy figures all day, but whose side are they on? She needs just a little more time.

By mistake I fell into the web of this dusty world,
Here forty-nine years of my life have been wasted.

Follow your gut now, Jasmine. Follow your heart!
Imagine a better world. Let it take you!
Hope is not far away!

Like the captive bird will long for its home in the grove
or the fish in the tank craves for its former abode.

Distance blurs my native village from my sight,
Wrapped in mist and smoke rising from the chimneys.

Long, long was I confined to this cage I made for myself;
But now I will return to nature once more!

It is getting closer and there is blue sky.
We share the feeling that we can almost grasp this dream
Clinch that dream in hand and feel free!

In her pep talk to her organizers that afternoon, she drew from this poem written by the great T'ao Yuan-ming in 405 AD while seamlessly working in lines from another of her favorite poems by modern-day activist Bei Dao.

That day of the Mahjong game, Jasmine had been walking throughout the streets, finalizing the details for tomorrow's protest, visiting the park where the sculpture is located. Yes, she is being followed but she does not see their faces clearly. Her actions are too bold to succeed. While more cautious activists would hold secret meetings among the intellectuals, that is not her style. Jasmine does things in the open whenever possible and lets the battles be seen in full view of all. The remains of St. Lazarus Church are a tranquil park on most days. On a breeze you hear old string music flow trouble during her travel, but she always factors in the unforeseen delay when scheduling important meetings. Despite the crash, the timing will work fine. Before sitting down to play poker, part of her regrets not helping the injured. The other part is glad she didn't get involved. The greater good is to attend the mahjong game on time and win.

She had not paid her cab fare. Each minute she stays at the scene increases the likelihood she will be late. She must go now. *Stop shaking, open the door, take your purse, and move on!* She cannot fail her task tonight. This taxi crash and the unpaid fare are inconsequential in the larger scheme. She sits for a moment on the boulevard flowerbed, then walks away.

The taxi was on its side when she regained consciousness. Jasmine knows she must get out of the crushed vehicle quickly in case it gets hit again by oncoming traffic. Busy traffic buzzing, swerving around the wreckage, hardly notice what whizzes past them. There is blood on Jasmine's hand. She thinks she may be going into shock.

Jasmine felt it all around her, airbags blast, the cab spinning on its side. The taxi is part of a five-vehicle collision, hit by a city bus from behind. *Bam bam bam…bam.* Airbags protect all the drivers from any terminal harm.

She saw the car crash before it happened, even though it must have come from behind (perhaps a glimpse of the driver's rearview mirror gave her the warning). Jasmine intended to take the taxi all the way to the mahjong game. It would have been a thirty-minute ride. She is in the back seat, purse on her lap, silent and thinking. She somehow anticipates the fly that splats into the windshield, based on the knowledge that it did splat. She forgets the fly soon after, and the crash takes over everything.

Before she hailed the cursed cab, two other black cabs drove right on by, not willing to pick her up. Who knows why. The drivers have other needs tonight is He Song's support. She needs to win him, not the game.

At 7:45 p.m., before the jade thief started to play, he wiped everything off around him with a cloth. There is quite a bit of dust in the air with all of the construction. He Song greets the players with a stiff handshake. He appears friendly and welcoming. His suit is shades of fine white material.

The Professor waited more than an hour for everyone to show up to the mahjong game. She arrives early. He Song and the others show up late and act as though they are on time. There are no apologies. He Song shuts the door, sealing them inside. He says, "Welcome. You are my guests tonight. This get-together was suggested by Sunday," (who smiles at her name, brushing the purple bangs from her eyes) "and although I am extremely busy these days, I have agreed. Let's begin the play!"

⸍ ⸌

The Professor played a few rounds of poker in the casino lobby to fill the time while she waited, and had been doing quite well against the riffraff who were there. She easily racks up two hundred dollars in winnings. When judging her cards, Jasmine (her other name can be laid to rest as we move backward in time) weighs the most likely bets using the same complex statistical calculations that earned her a PhD at Hong Kong University, that is, to bet high when the risk is low and pull out if the risk is too high. She doesn't need a calculator for this. Her brilliant mind is her computer. She folds her winnings into her purse and goes to the toilets to freshen up, and there she notices a streak of dried blood above her left brow. She picks away at the bloody scab with her nails. What a mess.

Getting to He Song Enterprises's grand casino, Jasmine needed to walk the final two miles or she would have arrived even earlier. She walks in comfortable heels, and her tight blouse thankfully does not block the evening breeze. No blisters form on these lovely feet. There had been some a new one. There are black market ways of getting Falun Gong organs as you well know but I prefer to have yours. And, if I should win, I will take it tonight. If I lose, eh, I may still take it as mine." He Song stares into the jade thief's good eye. His meanness makes him smile.

The jade thief provoked him, true enough. When the jade thief asks He Song for a peculiar list, and that list becomes a wager, He Song incredibly agrees: "Okay, done. I have written down the names and you can read them if you win the next game. But, now I will make a request as well to make this competition more exciting. You cannot say no."

The jade thief had indeed asked for He Song to wager something unusual, and at the time it may have seemed he brought the misfortune on himself, but I think he made the request to make the Professor's request for *guanxi* seem less radical. It was certainly less personal. Or, did the jade thief have another agenda? "Their names and birthdays, please," the jade thief says. He Song scowls but, to the surprise of everyone at the table, goes along with the jade thief's request. He Song calls in the waiter to bring a piece of rice paper and writes down perhaps as many as (could it be?) ten names with a golden Mont Blanc pen he keeps in his suit and then folds it five times and then into a paper dove. The paper dove sits there with the chips on the table.

At 8:00 p.m., while the jade thief was about to take the chips he had won from He Song at the end of one lucky round, he stopped short and instead said to his opponent, "He Song, instead of taking your money tonight, I want something else. Write me a list of your offspring, all of them, including any illegitimate children. It is for this that I will play tonight." He Song smirks at the word "illegitimate."

It was all such a shame. For a round or two it appears that others might gain the edge, but that only fools the men and women in our story and not you, my Dear Reader. You can see that what the Professor really the game, then I will assist you in this endeavor. Is that it? Ha. You may try," said He Song. "Hmm, I do not promise anything more than to consider your proposal. You may not ask any more of me than that, Professor."

"Tomorrow the handover happens here in Macao. Portugal's empire has expired." She raises her cup as a toast and takes a long sip. He Song does not toast with her but instead removes one of his silver cufflinks and adds it to the pot. He appears to be going along.

The Professor responded to the jade thief by saying, "Portugal lost Brazil long ago. They do not rule Africa or India anymore. There is nothing of their empire left in the world except for us in Macao, and that right was preserved merely because of England's heavy-handed hold on Hong Kong, which ended last year. Tomorrow the charade will finally come to an end and Macao will return to China. We are not Portuguese and never were. That itty-bitty piece of Spain is in no state to rule us anymore. This moment of freedom is long overdue. We must seize it and become free."

The jade thief had been reiterating the history of Hong Kong's handover last year. "Yes, Sunday, it was the Daoguang Emperor who allowed the British to take the island back in 1842."

Sunday reminisced passionately with her often-incorrect details. Her mind is starting to show signs of the woman she becomes by Jasmine's wedding banquet. "It has been one year since the handover of the Hong Kong colony from the British to the Chinese government." (All true.) "I still can't believe they let it go after holding onto it for one hundred years." (No, it has been much longer than that! More like one hundred fifty!) "He Song, will you not throw in your cufflinks to the pot, and consider assisting the Professor with her plans tomorrow?" The wagers become more interesting!

But none of this was as shocking as when He Song had said to the jade thief, "You must wager me your kidney. Mine has gone bad. I need college students, qigong practitioners, or fan dancers, are skilled in hiding their true performance within the guise of their regular training routine. Look there. What art! All of the pulling down is hidden and what you see is the constant rising motion lifted by a community. It is not a sole happy man deformed by colonialism. Instead it is a group to be envied. That is who we are, He Song."

The Professor intended to center the mass protests around a sculpture left by the Portuguese. "The sculptor is Larry Bell," she says darkly.

"I know the park you speak of, but I have never noticed this art before. Who is the artist?" asked Sunday.

The Professor's voice deepened as she explained her plan. "I am just doing my part to ignite a spark on this peninsula. We are planning a large demonstration for tomorrow. There is an abhorrent piece of public artwork standing in the middle of Lou Lim Ioc Garden Pavilion. It has sat there for far too long, and it epitomizes the worst of Western colonization. The Happy Man sculpture will be chopped down from its marble pedestal in full daylight tomorrow while I give a planned speech beside it. Here, look at this piece." She holds out a photo on her iPod. "The blatant glamorization of institutional violence has given me nightmares ever since I first laid eyes on it. Three tons of bronze warped into a man. His hip is disjointed, his head is warped and small. His entire body looks like it is in pain with awful arthritis. Stretched out, beaten up, he raises his hands to the heavens as if he is happy with the cruel situation. Don't be happy! This is not how life ought to be!" She looks in his eyes. "Indeed, that is why I am here," said the Professor to all the players. "I need the *guanxi* He Song has with the police officials here in Macao." She turns to He Song. "I will win it if I must."

"So that is why you are here? Normally I would absolutely not get involved but I see now you intend that to be my wager in this mahjong match today. You want to use my *guanxi* with the Macao police? If you win her consent, boost her onto a human ladder consisting of a dozen acrobats. She is lifted up on broad shoulders all the way to the concrete pillars still exposed more than thirty feet off the ground, then thrown high, another four or five feet. As she reaches the peak of her ascension, she raises the napkin up high and it flaps like a torch as she descends, on gentle hands, to the floor again.

"We already have enough acrobats signed on so that if some are arrested others can replace them in a second and third wave, but still we require your help, He Song, in keeping the police away. I will also need your *guanxi* to assist those who are arrested—some might be your own employees—so they are treated gently and given quick release."

"Clowns with daggers," chimed the old lady with purple hair. She is getting excited as the Professor explains her plans. He Song notices the two women are in cahoots.

"Tomorrow the Happy Man bronze will be passed along in bits and pieces along our entire parade route and thrown into the bay. May it sink fast and become beautiful coral! The official parade celebrating the handover will have already begun by eleven tomorrow morning, and all of those people in the parade more or less are *my* people who support our cause. Organizers have been told to stall the procession at noon so that our people will be standing foot to foot covering the full two miles of Macao's main roadway between the statue and the bay. This allows us to move the remnants of the ugly thing hand to hand by all of our people so everyone can be intimately involved in the protest, truly a people's protest, and every body will be used to create the human barricade that ought to prevent the police and army from getting too involved in the deconstruction of the statue and the acrobatic finale. Back in the park, once the sculpture art is removed, in its place acrobats will perform the live piece of art. See, they are actually practicing for tomorrow's stunt over there. It looks like practice for your future Cirque du Soleil performance, and so it *is*, but let me tell you that Chinese acrobats, just as Buddhist monks, by taking off the jewels around her neck and laying them in the center of the table. They were gifts from a late husband.

At 9:00 p.m., the Professor tried the nobility card. She should not have done so. Already enough had been said, enough revealed. The Professor says, "It will be a beautiful display that will be remembered. The acrobats will create an indelible image for our movement here in China. Allowing Macao a chance at democracy could redefine our nation. The protestors will be lifting one another up atop the marble pedestal in the central park that once saluted the Happy Man statue." She takes a breath. "And the acrobat at the bottom who had helped with the lifting will be replaced and then lifted up himself. Nobody stays at the bottom. That will be our message. Our goal is a happy society that is strong and supportive, the new Macao! Tomorrow's public art display will spread by word of mouth even if the media is in lockdown. When foreigners come by tomorrow to watch, which they will, including CNN reporters—let them all come—we will allow them in the space. What an experience it will be for them. It will be the most beautiful thing. I can't wait!" She is wearing a tight white blouse that has long been her trademark outfit. It has become slightly transparent from perspiration.

You see it was not enough for her to just tell He Song. The Professor insists on demonstrating the idea first, interrupting their game before it had barely begun. "The acrobats are training now. See through the window there. They are trying new techniques to help the uninitiated, the fragile, even children, anyone can gently enter the human acrobatic ladder we will set up tomorrow in the park, and each participant will be lifted up for a brief moment up to its height without getting injured. Watch." She coyly grabs a red silk napkin from He Song's lap and steps out of the high stakes room, leaving the thick doors open, and wanders over to the acrobats practicing just beyond. Left on the mahjong table is an iPod she set to play Su Rui's pop tune "Following My Gut." Two other acrobats eye her entering the practice space and tumble over beside her, one man on each side, and, with note out of my ear. We were all fooled. The magician's secret? He wore a false thumb. He stuffed the notes in the false thumb." He Song laughs and his chuckles are contagious.

⁓ ⁓

The wagers made in the mahjong game were getting interesting well before midnight. Besides just money, the Professor wagers a wooden box of some mysterious value, which sits on the Mahjong table beside a key, a pile of fine jewelry, a sheet of rice paper folded into a dove, and one of He Song's cufflinks. What is inside that box of Jasmine's? Only two of the players around the table know and neither one will tell. He Song shakes it. He appears curious. There is a thud of something heavy inside. The box is locked.

The Professor already told He Song what she is after. She wants his *guanxi* with the police. She now tells the jade thief to throw in a silver key that she knows he carries on his ring of keys. She convinces him with a wink. The jade thief reaches down for his belt, and He Song tenses up. To his great relief it is not a gun or knife the jade thief reaches for and he instead brings up his set of jingling keys for all four players to view. He finds the one key and then unties the leather strap containing too many keys to count. The single silver key drops to the felted table with no sound. He looks over at He Song, their eyes connect and then He Song removes a silver cufflink from his shirt. It is put in the pot of wagers as well. The cufflink becomes a symbol of something He Song does not define. The Professor assumes the best.

The old lady with purple hair feigned interest in the wooden box, commenting that it was well crafted in fine mahogany. Curiosity breeds curiosity. She notes the subtle inlay and the masterful way the corners are locked and sealed. She tries to look through the keyhole but it does not let in enough light. "Now, this is a mystery! Where are you from? What fortunes do you hold, little wooden box?" The fortune-teller ups the wagers in their own thoughts on how to win the game. Four philosophers around a small table. What good is that?

How did the four come into such a topic in the first place? It was a story that He Song told the others about a magician and his false thumb that they were all commenting about. At the story's conclusion, the Professor jokes, "You better not be hiding a tile that way, He Song. Do you have a false thumb too? Let me see those awful hands of yours!" The Professor's accusation drips with sarcasm.

He Song revealed the secret of how a novice magician did his trick. "The thumb was made of soft plastic. Here's what blew my mind, though. It wasn't a good fake thumb at all. The false thumb hardly even looked like a thumb! It was too large for his hand. The material was too stiff. I saw it then, once I knew. It was not even the right shade to match his skin color. Despite all this, still his audience (who are more sharp-eyed than the common man, trust me) didn't notice it at all! This is why. We were not looking *at* his hands, we were looking for something *in* his hands. Without any hesitation, he confidently let us see everything in clear view because he knew our minds would hide the secret for him."

He Song began his story this way. "Yesterday at lunch, a business partner of mine performed some sleight of hand magic. Sitting at our table were a senior jet propulsion researcher and another scientist specializing in genetic engineering. And there was me and my partner, the magician. Magic is a hobby of his. His audience at the table are all smart people, right? We are attentive to detail, at least." He scowls at a waiter trying to fill a glass. "Wait for that! I am talking now." He Song turns back to the group. "So, in clear view, he took out a brightly colored one hundred-dollar bill, folded it without much ceremony, and it instantly vanished into thin air, then a moment later he turned it into a one-yuan note. It made the engineer jump out of his seat. The novice magician (remember, this is just a regular old business guy in a suit!) concluded by pulling the original hundred-dollar on their Blackberries (curse those wretched things!) in a twenty-four-hour 'around the clock' present using the global ERP networks designed to bring information together instantly. If the ERP anticipates a low stock in company stores, it instantly makes new orders before they are even needed. If a factory has an input that decreases in cost, say for instance I sell my recycled plastics at a reduced price, the ERP allows stores around the world to cut their retail prices *instantly*. We businessmen are not connected by a ticking clock anymore. Instead we are in touch with needs and demands that require instant attention, with some preparation, yes, but also with revision and re-revision. Global business is not bound by time. Nothing binds us." All such nonsense, draped in business lingo. Everyone finds him so difficult to follow.

The players all had something to say in this early stage of the Mahjong game. They are sometimes laughing together and other times cautiously looking at their tiles. Nobody yet is feeling like they are the loser. They all have hope that winning is possible. Any one of the four could win the jackpot. There is an abundance of time and assets at this point and so the four talk philosophy. "Hush, Lao Shifu," says the fortune-teller. "I think it is Father Time that is our false thumb. Time comes from a pre-1421 concept of a flat universe. Past is yesterday where the sun went down, present is the daylight of today, and future comes later from the east: Past, Present, and Future. Those ancient people that invented time weren't able to follow the sun around the earth and didn't know better back then. That is how they modeled time, and who could blame them, but then modern civilization got stuck in the habit because it is convenient. Now we know the world is not flat. That concept has changed. The universe is round and expanding. Is it really so blasphemous to finally challenge our concept of linear time?"

To get that scolding from the fortune-teller, the jade thief had said, "I sometimes feel like I am that false thumb of which He Song now speaks. Enormous mistakes sit there in plain view yet we overlook them." He scowls at the game. The old lady, He Song, the Professor all scowl and swim

Events repeat themselves, although we may not realize that we have all been here before. This tile game has been played before. The backstabbing has happened before. Her shock. His ruthlessness. Sure, the players sometimes change. The dialogue can be different. The story, though, repeats itself again and again.

The Professor steered the conversation away from He Song's business. She is comfortable talking philosophy and hopes to work it into her broader goals for cultural uprising. "I've read that, using the most advanced telescopes, our scientists are able to see back to the Big Bang," she says, laying down her Mahjong piece and taking another. "Astronomers can look into the sky tonight and see the Big Bang from billions of years ago as if it is happening right now. Those rays of light from the beginning of the universe are only touching us now for the first time. Those particular rays from that particular distance have never touched us before. And so, it is difficult for me not to conclude that the creation of the universe is not happening as I sit here. You know stardust? That's real material. Our atoms are made of particles from the day of creation. It is in our bodies already, and it continues to fall anew into our atmosphere every day. It falls onto each of us." *I pray it will bring us luck tomorrow when we make our bold stand against the establishment.* Finally, she feels a bit of oxygen come into the room and she sits up straight again, shoulders strong. He Song is ready to speak.

He Song attempted to turn even this debate about the essence of time to the blah blah blah of his unethical businesses. He starts the roadblock by coughing phlegm into his hand. "I have something to say now. Hush. It has occurred to me that we could say that the modern-day businessperson like myself, for instance, is a time traveler of sorts," He Song says, smiling. "We modern executives manage multinational factories and information technology support services on the other side of the world where it is literally still yesterday. You see, across the international date line *it is* yesterday. And from overseas, other businessmen orchestrate the transportation of finished goods sitting here in tomorrow. They do this stressful work *all right now* life. Don't you, He Song? Search for the Now point in time, and surely you will never catch it. I can give you that. A singular Now moment might not exist, just as you say. But, search instead for what we call life and it is impossible not to see the Now. We don't experience life in separate points. They are more like chunks of life. Life comes at you in chunks. And it isn't past when your mind finally experiences them. It is an ever-changing experience, each chunk different from the one before. Even our memory is ever-changing. And that cold Present you speak of, He Song, has no place here." She goes on. "Take fire as the illustration. Fire is not a single moment. It is the result of matter changing forms and releasing its energy. It is in that period of change where we see fire. My view of time is much like fire in that way. We see both—time and fire—only when objects change."

He Song talked like an amateur philosopher. "The End seems to be ever present," he argues, trying to convince the others that the Present doesn't really exist and therefore neither does time. "I challenge you all to try this. Keep your mind on a thought. How long did it last? Now, one minute later, do you still remember the thought? Probably not. Do you remember the thought before that thought? Definitely not. I remember being scared to fall asleep as an adolescent because I knew I would be a different person when I woke. I would be up all night worrying. I think I was right to worry then. I am not that same boy. The End *is* ever present. You try to hold on to the Now and you find out it was never there. We look only at the Past," says he. The Professor shakes her head in disagreement.

"Pong," called the jade thief out of the blue. The old woman jumps. The mahjong game is taking a turn. "I was waiting for that piece and will take it for my own. Thank you!"

He Song had been saying, "Suppose people live forever…"

"Time is a circle," added the jade thief in a way that demanded it to be true. Obviously he thinks it is fact, tested, tried and true. Time is a circle.

puzzled me this very afternoon. I just finished reading a novel today. It was just so-so. Off and on throughout the summer the book has kept me moderately entertained. I read a few pages at each sitting then put it down. I figure it has taken me a total of some thirty hours to read it from cover to cover when all is said and done. Thirty hours! But here is the puzzle. When I came to the last page today, after the final lines where the hero lives happily ever after, there were a couple of blank pages without numbers, then the author's bio, and finally there was an advertisement for the audio cassette version of the book. The advertisement says the audio cassette version has a running time of *just three hours*! My word, just three hours!? But how could that be? It made me think. My mind must function at a much slower pace than average speech, a tortuous pace if you will, if it takes another person only three hours to read what it takes my mind to read in thirty. Assuming that my mind actually moves slower than Mr. Hotshot reading the same book into his hotshot microphone, is it then so difficult for me to believe that thoughts can move at different speeds? No, that is not unreasonable." She looks around. "Is it so difficult to then believe that my heart can beat at a different pace than yours, that my blood flows slower, fingernails grow and pause? Is it so difficult to believe that my cells grow slower and my stomach digests slower? Time might work differently for me than it does for you." She makes a good point.

This was the tail end of a forty-minute conversation about time, which began with He Song telling everyone about a magic trick he saw that day. "I pity you and that mind," the Professor says to He Song. "A world without memories is a world without present, He Song!"

The Professor was stirred because He Song had argued thus. He says he does not trust time. He does not believe in it. He Song says something to the effect that time is a quality not a quantity. "You cannot measure it. This watch, it is just show," he says. The Professor is confused. "How then, can you say an event ever happened at all?"

The Professor forgot her tiles for a moment as she spoke. "Yet I feel fortune-teller throughout the long evening, reading the jade thief's tea leaves at first and then moving on to the reading of palms.

~ ~

By 9:45 p.m., the acrobats and staff-in-training who had been in the outer complex had all gone home. There is a break in conversation.

While the Professor sat stoic in front of him, the jade thief touched on what would hurt her most by saying, "And the moments just before a plane would crash, what of those? What of that moment before they sizzle? Do any of our philosophies still hold? Time and fire and revolution. Is it really change at all, I have come to wonder?" *Good, I have your attention. Dear Jasmine, you need to steer this conversation back to the matters at hand! I have given you an opening. Enough of this philosophy that has no relevance to our problems right now.* There is pain on the Professor's face for only a moment, and as she files it away, the shadow passes from her eyes, and she is ready to move the conversation back to tomorrow's events.

The Professor had only used jet planes for her previous example to make a philosophical point about time. As the four gambled away their possessions, they became philosophical. "Albert Einstein proved time is relative," she says. "I remember an example I once learned in school before Big Brother called on the Red Guard to shut it down. Einstein said time is not absolute. A man is in an airplane and his brother is standing on the ground. The flying man's wristwatch will tick at a different speed than his brother's watch on the ground. That has been tested and proven to be true!" After saying "airplane," her thoughts drift to a man she loved once who died in a plane crash.

The youthful-looking jade thief responded to something Sunday said earlier by saying, "If that were true you might be aging slower as well. That explains how you stay so lovely! No one could guess your true age."

Sunday had said, "Now that you all mention it, something about time so far off. I must take advantage of the time I have." Isn't that true for us all? She takes a long drink of eight-treasure tea. "You and me, we are all just temporarily capacitated. This is what I have always said. We are born incapacitated as an infant needing our mothers, and that is how life usually ends, helpless as a vegetable. It's my turn to deal." *Strange, isn't it,* thinks He Song. *Why has Sunday arranged this little game among enemies if she thinks she will soon die?* He Song looks around the table. *The old woman probably hopes to be inducted into the Council for the Greater Good before her death by building good favor with the Professor. Curse the CGG!*

A couple of rounds before reading her own palm, the purple-haired woman turned to He Song's hand. She sees a hand that is missing fingers. *What can a hand like his accomplish but evil deeds?* "Evil intent and a dark future, yet you will be happy, He Song."

She had also looked at the Professor's palm and said to her, "You will win in the end, little sister." They look at each other knowingly. They have an alliance. "Thank you," says the Professor, mouthing the words softy.

Sunday had begun by asking the jade thief to take off his gray gloves so she could read his palm. He reluctantly obeys. She notices that he too is missing fingers. The dismemberment matches He Song's right hand finger for finger. The women are taken aback. "I see we all have had unsuccessful dealings with the mafia. That is how it is with them. They feed on fingers. Are their own ten not enough? No, they will eat off everyone's fingers if given the opportunity." Looking again at the jade thief's palms and comparing them to his clean-shaven face, she sees the mystery. His face is that of a man no more than thirty years, though he must be much older. "Well, then. I see a longer life for you than what is usual, though one that becomes more hollowed with time."

To lighten the mood around the table, the old lady offered to tell fortunes between games. She does so using the manners of a practiced these people were unhealthy from the start. The village enterprises are at least happy now for the steady income I bring. There is broad consensus that we are doing them good." He coughs a little cough into his fist. She fires daggers with her eyes and discards a tile.

The Professor interjected while He Song was taking a breath so she could change his perspective of his company's success by saying, "Cancer rates must be high in those village enterprises of yours." Her mind becomes clouded from memories of a township enterprise in the village of Tu.

To pass the time, He Song explained his operations. "My village factories melt down the used plastics. It is not a very sophisticated business. We build small workshops behind each household. They basically heat cast-iron pots over open coal fires. The garbage melts into pellets, which our factories can then turn back into anything. The toxic fumes get lost out there in the backwaters, and everyone feels greener for recycling their plastics. That's the service I can provide the world, and companies like Sony or Nike cannot do it themselves. I wonder whether there could be a recycling industry if I were not willing to do what I do. I am an important link in the chain." He sees no wrong in that.

At 10:15 p.m., fresh bottles of champagne were brought in. He Song drinks one cup first, then refills his tulip glass and the glasses of the others. He spills the bubbly wine down the front of his shirt but doesn't notice. "Let's toast to the mischievous Aires who bring enemies together time and again. And toast, too, to our apparent fortunes both won and lost!" The jade thief drinks only tea. The green tea leaves stick to the side of his cup, and there is one hanging from his lip right at this very moment.

⌐ ⌐

Sunday read everyone's palms throughout the evening play. She concludes this round of Mahjong by reading her own. "For me, I see death is not smiles, lights a cigar, and passes it to the Professor. She accepts the cigar and smokes it with care. "I might invest in the industry of war when I can. I might be in favor of initiating a grand war," he says while thinking of old grievances against Japan. She nods back, thinking instead of how we might wage war against an injust system here at home.

The Professor won the round before by taking a tile discarded by the jade thief. As part of her winnings, she earns his little key that fits the lock of an antique wooden box. For a moment, the Professor considers not taking the key off the table and leaving it in the pot for a while longer, but then she puts it safely in her pocket.

At about 11:00 p.m., He Song finally noticed a stain on his shirt and shouted, "Blast this!" His temper is flowing again. He will lose points in this round. He is unsettled. It causes the Professor to think again about the box she gambled. *Where is the box?* The Professor shifts from side to side fiercely looking around the small table for her wooden box. It was out of her sight for only a moment, sitting with the other things being wagered, and she is baffled where it could have vanished. She is about to mention its disappearance aloud when the box reveals itself. It had only been covered by Sunday's sleeves during the shuffle, and reappears as the old woman pulls her arms back. He Song is distracted by the Professor's concern, not knowing it's only about the box. He tries to follow her eyes and in doing so he discovers the wine stain on his white clothes.

〜 〜

"I don't recall that that was ever an issue," said He Song at first to her potentially hostile allegation, "but you evidently have a strong opinion." He does not show any sign of remembering his betrayal. He Song defends himself saying, "Regarding my enterprise, it'd be hard to say whether there truly is a higher incidence of cancer or tendency toward bad health because of our pollution. It is a cost neither you nor I need to worry about because *intend to eat me piece by piece as the fortune-teller says of the Chinese mafia lords? Is that why he allowed us here, to trap me?* The jade thief tries not to reveal his fear of losing. He Song says to him, "I hadn't known you have such assets in Japan, but I am not surprised."

The jade thief rattled his keys for effect. "I own a '65 Ford Mustang blue as the sky parked secretly in Japan. My baby. In mint condition. The V-8 engine can outrun anything." *No takers yet.* "Now, that's a car of anyone's dreams. I would risk my neck for that car if we went to war." The Professor coughs slightly. He Song is drawing a miniature Zen garden in his ashtray. His long fingernails act as the rake.

It was nearly11:30 p.m when the jade thief added, "Of course I once hated the Japanese for what they did to us, especially Nanjing, especially there…but you know I have been to Japan many times since, and there is part of it that impresses me." He is replying to the suggestion from other players that we might someday war again with Japan.

A new double-layer wall marked the start of a new round with the Professor's turn to deal. He Song then remarks, "I would say we could war against Japan. Or, we could war against Taiwan. North Korea. Russia. All of them at once, perhaps," he says. "It doesn't matter who. The time feels right."

The Professor said earlier, "I do not disagree on that point, He Song. A war at this time could be a benefit for all who survive it. The earth's population is too large today. We consume far too much for the status quo to be sustainable. A brutal war could take us to the greater good." In the same tone she would use when ordering off a menu, the Professor asks, "Against whom shall we go to war if we do?"

It was as though for that moment He Song and the Professor were talking as one. "I am becoming somewhat of a war hawk," he admits as he your kidney, friend," not at all jokingly. His voice is steady. The jade thief Lao Shifu was indeed forced to wager his own kidney in the earlier hours of the game, and now He Song will have his kidney by night's end. How can you take an organ away from a man, you ask? It is easily done. *Might he take it out right there and then?* they all wonder. Their thoughts fill the room.

He Song was after organs that night and perhaps that is the only reason he agreed to host his three enemies. He needs a kidney desperately. His doctor told him both kidneys are failing him now. He is on regular dialysis but soon that will not be enough. He Song knows of but one donor who would be his match.

The jade thief tried to replace that frightening wager with safer things such as material possessions, but his cash was already spent. He has a large collection of expensive cars, the keys for which rattle on the leather strap hanging at his side. The jade thief says, "I often daydream about that beautiful car parked away in Japan. I store it in a tall, narrow garage with elevator lifts. You look as though you don't know about those Tokyo parking garages, Sunday? It is ingenious technology. I have seen fifteen cars stacked up in a space no larger than this room." The jade thief stretches his arms far behind his back. He tries to look relaxed as he talks.

As he worked his charm, which ultimately failed, the jade thief moved his fingers past two Buick keys on his chain to a silver Ford key that had a triangle eye and attempted to add it to the pot. He says to the other players, "When the Professor asked me to wager my silver key to the antique box, I did as she asked and she has won the key from me fair and square." He sighs and continues, "I lost most of my money as well during this frankly disappointing night, but I do hold many other keys of value that would make a good prize. Why not allow me to wager another of my keys instead of my kidney, yes?" He throws in the "Made in Detroit" key, but He Song immediately throws it back to him. *He Song is eyeing my kidney as if it is already his, as if I have no right having it inside my body anymore. Does he* other fees he requires, plus turning a blind eye to whatever he intends for the jade thief's internal organs, she could still receive He Song's backing in tomorrow's important endeavors. What really matters to her analytical mind is not the outcome of a single round or the life of a single man, but instead the ultimate winner of this war of virtues, and she has good odds to be the one on top in the end. Hands brush against one another.

As the game passed over the threshold of midnight, the conversation had deviated to He Song's noxious business, and its so-called "success," and away from the Professor's complex schemes for a large-scale protest in the streets tomorrow. The Professor should sense that He Song is not going to help her and walk out of the game here and now. The stuffy business talk interests no one but He Song. He speaks over everyone else but to whose ears? He just wants to fill his own ears with lies. "A hundred thousand cargo containers send goods to America but we don't import very much. Those containers come back to China mostly empty. Five years ago I started to pay a small fee to fill empties with American garbage and bring it all back here to China. American municipalities sometimes even *pay me* to take it! Don't laugh. Garbage is a matter of perspective. To me, it is all resources, pure and simple. I recycle the plastics into something I can sell at a premium, such as this green felt." He Song pongs another tile discarded from his opponent. He looks over at the jade thief but not into his eyes. He Song instead looks down to the man's hip and with stubby fingers he pokes at the jade thief's side and prods a little at the inner kidney as to lay claim. The jade thief shivers at the touch.

When the jade thief was finally out of cash to gamble, he tried to barter more of his material possessions but He Song would insist, "No need to add more of your antiques to our gambling pot." Looking around the table, he jokes, "Who needs another car? Not me! That Japanese parking garage you speak of could be of interest to me, but I know it is not yours to give since *Communists hold no property!*" His words are sarcastic and almost daring him to fight. He Song then says with a smile, "Tonight I will take benefit of a tonal language like ours. A different tone changes everything. She also says, "pong," and takes a piece discarded by He Song to reveal a set of red dragons on the table. Once, long ago, people did indeed call He Song "the little thief." Perhaps those words still echo here.

At 2:00 a.m., he said proudly, "The most profitable of my companies today is international recycling. The felt of this table here, this was made by my Shenzhen factory out of recycled materials." Soft green felt on the tabletop prevents the ox bone mahjong tiles from smacking on the table as they would on kitchen tables all around China, and for that matter on uncovered tables in Chinese households all around the world. It is such a common game after dinner on an ordinary evening. The green felt mutes the usual noise. Only fancy places like this room use felt.

The bone tiles still crackled as the players rolled them into one another, kneading them, mixing, confusing them out of any order that once had been. The shuffling around of mahjong tiles so that dots mix with bamboo, winds mix with flowers, is like nothing else. Hands touch. The shuffle ends each round to allow players to build new walls of tile that will reveal unknown treasure beneath as the four break it apart late into the evening, or more accurately into the early morn.

The round ended with the Professor's score still on top. He Song reveals the Three Adopted Sons of the Wind with pride. The Professor is careful with what she discards so that she can lead in points even when she fails to win the mahjong. She tallies up the points. They shuffle the tiles together at the little table's center.

He Song won an earlier round at 1:30 a.m. with a tile discarded by the jade thief, and the loss might cost the jade thief his life. The Professor knows her friend the jade thief is now in grave danger, but the cause for which she fights is bigger than just one person, even he, and all is not yet lost. There is a chance if she wins the game and pays He Song whatever

She always underestimates the danger around her. She won, but really, she lost.

Before that terrible close, the four players had been fairly civil to one another and had a discussion like never before, lasting almost eight hours in a small space around a small table. "Most of my fortune has now moved to legitimate businesses," He Song concludes through that last round of play. His skin looks gray and waxy. Chuckling at how situations can so quickly change, he adds, "Perhaps I will someday become this peninsula's governor. The lines are blurring with these new casinos that need not follow mainland law, nor, starting tomorrow, Portuguese law. What was black market before is legal now."

"Is business going well?" asked the old woman to ease the tension the Professor had again caused. The Professor is so blinded by the excitement that she is winning the most points that she forgets she must allow He Song to believe he has won. Unlike the Professor, the older woman understands the signals He Song is sending out and anticipates the game's disastrous end. *We have to get out of here,* the old woman thinks to herself. *But how? The Professor will not get what she is after tonight. We must humor this awful man to get safe passage out of this dangerous snake hole.* She tries using a secret gesture between activists that means *Hold your tongue!* but the Professor does not see. The old woman's name is Sunday, and she is one of the women we met in the first chapter at the wedding supper. She has not yet lost her mind. She lost much of her jewelry during this Mahjong game, but no matter. She still has enough.

While He Song proudly talked about his profits, the Professor muttered, "You are a thief!" just loud enough that He Song might have barely caught it from across the small table. They would be fighting words if he had heard it clearly. Fortunately, she does not say it loud enough to be certain "thief" is the word she mutters, because if the tone were slightly different, the phrase's meaning changes entirely, to one of praise. That is the in jail. He Song notices the Professor tuck the small wood box she had wagered back into her purse as she leaves. The cash is all left on the table.

He Song finally put a stop to the charade that allowed the Professor to make such unrealistic presumptions of winning the game and his allegiance tonight. All evening, the Professor would not acknowledge his innuendos of power, so he had to finally state them as bluntly as if a vulgar foreigner were sitting at their table. He appears the bad host tonight only because he was forced into it by this relentless woman. He Song says, "Do not think you have won the game tonight, Professor. You have not, because I say you have not. Do not fool yourself into thinking that because you won points with mahjong tiles I might allow your activists safe passage while in Macao. I have considered your request as you asked, or shall we say, *as you have gambled,* and I have come to my decision, which ought to have been Goddamn bloody obvious to you from the start. Those traitors with whom you associate yourself will all be arrested this dawn and you will receive no help from me to save them!" He pauses, but has more. While the Professor only stares invisible darts at him, he goes on. "For me, it is just business. The police will crush this embarrassment you intend for Macao before it ever happens. You put too much trust in your notions of the rules of the game. What rules, Professor? What rules are there, really? I make the rules here. Now, go!"

It was a sad ending for the Professor's ambitions in Macao. She plays her hands as best as can be done. But let us continue to move backward in time through the evening to see what the four were attempting to accomplish.

At nearly 3:00 a.m., not expecting his reaction, the Professor had indeed said, "You have lost, He Song," as she lay down the uniform of the dragon in the final game after long hours of serious play. Tallying the points, He Song's losses double many times over. But to say that He Song has lost, she was wrong in that. You will see this is a trend for poor Jasmine.

lady with purplish-gray hair. The game is done, but don't worry. We will start with how it ended and go to the beginning.

Was this the same Professor whose wedding you attended? She looks so much older now, and yet that cannot be. She should be younger! It must be her troubled mind, her shock. Lines wrinkle her face from a recent blow. She is in survival mode. *This is not the end.* She is reminding herself that she has made it through 100 percent of the bad times in this long life of hers, so chances are excellent that she will get through this evening as well. That is some comfort. She will not let He Song defeat her. Not tonight.

He Song shouted after her with a high and maddening voice, "You, dear Professor, have a false sense of freedom. The future is fixed. You play your part in a script that has already been written!" The Professor is walking out, followed by the other woman. The men stare into each other's eyes. This reunion was a long time coming.

"No, Professor, I do not lose."

He Song spat out each word. The vein at his temple looks like it might explode. It is hard not to stare at it engorged like a blue worm. Sweat flows down his face. He Song is tired, severely drunk, and irrational. He raises a revolver that he must have hidden in his chair. "Ladies, you may go. Now! This game is over. It is late. But not you, Lao Shifu, you must stay with me. We have more business before I will let you go." This casino complex is mostly financed by He Song Enterprises. He Song holds all the power here. The guards outside the door report to him. He Song clearly does not want to become involved in anything political, and he believes the Professor's plot is just that. She should have known it would never be. He Song is constructing this expensive facility for his acrobats to perform to make a profit, not to be revolutionaries for a greater cause. Revolutionaries won't make any money for him. What was she thinking, this relentless woman, getting them all involved? With his failing kidney, he would probably die old-world mix of shabby chic, circus tents, and make-believe countryside starlight, like an open-air carnival in an old Romanian village. Mirrors against mirrors reflect the LED stars on the ceiling into infinity.

The facility was still being constructed so we have to use some imagination to see it for what it will be. Overlook the exposed concrete pillars of the outer structure and the unfinished ceiling covered with white tarp to keep out the monsoon rain. There is bamboo scaffolding for the men who all wear work boots and orange work outfits, presently making a lot of racket shooting nail guns into drywall.

The mahjong game I want you to witness was played in a wood-paneled, high-stakes gambling room with floor-to-ceiling windows on the two sides facing the unfinished acrobatic theater. The walls are thick to keep out the noise. There are two large oak doors and three armed men standing outside smoking. Beyond, in the honeycomb of connecting rooms and smaller buildings of the casino complex, we find the new casino staff training even this late in the day. Their new uniforms are freshly pressed. In the open atrium the Chinese acrobats are also practicing, some in costume and some in workout clothes. A few acrobats are trying out a unique mechanical device that will mystify their audience during future Cirque du Soleil shows. It flings the men like an old-world catapult. Other acrobats are stretching on tumbling pads or hanging from rings. Those practicing in costume have odd makeup—like demon monkeys.

Now let's go inside that high-stakes room. That's where the action has been all evening. Mahjong is a game where everyone is the enemy to everyone. It isn't poker. You have to beat everyone to win. The players still feel a gentle vibration from the construction outside, but the only sounds they hear come from the crackle of mahjong tiles and the dark sarcasm of four voices who've seen a thing or two. The four players finally get up from their short stools around the square mahjong table: He Song, Jasmine (who goes by the name "Professor" tonight), the jade thief Lao Shifu, and an old

CHAPTER 17

December 19, 1999
China's population is 1.25 billion people.

Once upon a time our economy was much smaller. Our wealth grows rapidly over these decades, and the sustained growth becomes the envy of the world. It is unbelievable to outside countries at first (How did Big Brother do it? They thought we faked the numbers!), and in the big cities along the Pacific coast, the economy grows even faster than the rest so that it can be said the wealth in a place like new Shanghai increases two hundredfold! What would it feel like to have your paycheck multiplied by 200? Just imagine it! My billfold bulges with all that extra cash.

It was not so long ago when we Chinese didn't have it all, but we had a promise it would come. This is a time when we find extra money in our purses each day and feel the momentum that the amount will grow and our prosperity will continue in this way forever. It is the last days of 1999 when China is a poorer place, and some might say it is a simpler time.

But don't get me wrong; although the GDP was small, there was still big money back in the 1990s. In fact, I am taking you into one of the larger casino developments on the Macao peninsula. Construction is nearly complete here. Besides gaming, the complex will soon house a two-thousand-seat Cirque du Soleil acrobatic theater with a unique stage design specifically built to premier a unique acrobatic show billed as "The Return of the Monkey King." The interior style of the casino complex is a new- and echoes brought back memories of another time (a time we will eventually get to in great detail, Dear Reader. All in due time.). Of course the ancient cedars still reaching to the heavens from the palace courtyards are another sign of life here within these walls. You can hear their long branches creak from gravity's strain. There are other signs, but none scurry like the eunuchs and bureaucrats had once scurried around these many alleyways when the Qing Emperor ruled.

When he entered the palace after so many years away, the jade thief's shadow was like an arrow piercing the heart of what lay inside. The golden-water river bends like a bow in the large open square before the Gate of Supreme Harmony. His long shadow crosses over one of the five marble bridges whose balustrades are decorated with patterns of dragons dancing with phoenixes among swirling clouds. He is back in the palace again. And so be it, the thief. Nobody is there to stop him.

He came into the Forbidden City through the Five-Phoenix Tower at the southern entrance. Drums and bells in the main gate's tower were struck whenever the Emperor Puyi would move about the place back in the day. The jade thief remembers. The bells above are now silent.

the human race, and, if that should happen, they will become the default guardians of what we have built here, assuming they can further adapt to the world once we are gone. Although they do scurry over one's shoes and brush against one's pant leg in the dark, I have come to take it as a compliment when nature chooses to include you rather than avoid you. Wouldn't you agree with me on that? Their patter you can hear a half-mile away in the quiet night. *Cha-cha-cha-cha-tatata*. It is the sound of a dragging tail and eighteen unclipped nails. When there are hundreds you hear them all, nails against stone floor. When they are not scurrying, rats nibble at everything in sight. Their teeth continue to grow all through life, which forces them to gnaw at stone, metal, plastic, whatever they find so those teeth don't curl back into their heads.

Well, enough of that. Are they dirty? No. They are constantly grooming themselves and their pack, and they are not the carriers of disease that Europeans will tell you they are, despite, sure, one bad episode way back in the Middle Ages. As any doctor with a good education is well aware, the plague hadn't actually come from the rats but from the fleas that traveled on their coats. These fleas can just as easily travel on other mammals such as squirrels and dogs. Humans are the real carriers of disease. Vaccinate yourselves, humans, and let the rats be! The plague of the 1600s, now long gone, caused rats to be disliked so much in Europe that their reputation has never recovered there. In *our* culture, the rat is the first of the twelve animals of the zodiac that represent the years gone by. In the zodiac, a different animal represents each year in twelve-year cycles. Legend has it that the rat outwitted the others to secure its place first among the twelve. Rats should be revered for their ability to find and store away items of great value, their natural charm, and as I have already said, their unwavering loyalty to the pack. Again, my apologies for all that. Now, let's return to the humans and their tale.

The jade thief felt the presence of the packs, and it provided him some comfort knowing there still was life beating within this place. The

Pardon me, my Dear Reader, but let's deviate from the human story of He Song, Jasmine, and the Emperor for just a moment before we continue. I want to give some context before the jade thief first enters the Forbidden City and our chapter draws to an end. You know he gets the jade rings. You know this place is creepy. But you do not yet know it all. There is more to discover here. I want to lay it all out for you now. There are indeed communities still living within these walls. There are young bucks, does, and their kittens living together in colonies within the rusty red bricks of the Emperor's grand palace, as they have been here for a millennium. Their social systems contain complex hierarchies, just as it is with the men among whom they once lived. I have heard that pack members form deep bonds with one another, so much so that they will risk their own lives to save a family member or a friend.

Of course I am talking about the rats. There are two kinds in Beijing. Both the brown rat and the black rat originated here before spreading across the planet. The brown originates from the great plains of northern China where wild rats still live in burrows today. The black originates farther south. There have been grand battles between the browns and the blacks for territory over the millennia, following the trail of human civilization. They compete for our leftovers. The black are more timid and therefore less prevalent today due to the browns ultimately driving out the timid rat packs. Many other lovely species have become endangered as well because they lost this competition in mankind's world for space and food. There are now two billion brown rats in China and five billion worldwide. They rule those levels below the Forbidden City that the Mongolians once built. They still know what is down there.

Before we move on, let me just say that there was a time when brushing up against a rat made your narrator squirm, but I admit I now appreciate their company and the fact that, no matter how desolate a place may seem, you can always have a friend with short ears and a long, hairless tail. These mammals have been here since the dinosaurs and may yet outlast dangle outside his coat, are frozen by the winter air. If he were to take off his gloves and touch the metal door latch at these temperatures, the exposed skin would immediately stick to the metal and not let go. The west wind howls over the rusty red thirty-two-foot-tall walls. He looks around north, east, south, west. Each has a large gate and they are the only known entrances today, but I know for certain there was once a fifth entrance to the palace. Wind tears at his face. He ducks behind a marble phoenix.

The jade thief took a short rest to regain his bearings. It has been years since he was here last, and this part has changed. He bites into candied crabapples skewered on a stick that he bought from a street vendor earlier in the capital streets. The kabob is a favorite wintertime treat for Beijingers. He loved them as a kid. It is the hard sugar shell that crunches. The crabapples are soft and tart, saved from the autumn harvest to meet the wintertime demand of street vendors. This treat needs the winter temperature to keep its solidity. At normal temperatures the sugar would melt away. The bamboo stick looks like it might be holding five plump strawberries there under smooth, clear candy-glaze and that is about how it tastes, like strawberries. It is a shock to the tongue of sweet and tangy, a crunch and then softness.

The heavily dressed man made his way over an extravagant stone bridge extending over a deep moat that was home to an abundance of turtles in the summer. They are now slumbering deep below in the mud. Dragons, too, might reside deep in the mud caves as some old fables go. The silly government people do not know all of what is hidden here.

Snowflakes in the courtyard were moving side to side, up and down, not at all in unison from a single breeze, as you would think they should. Instead each flake takes its own sometimes-nonsensical trajectory to the ground. It feels like a snow globe being shaken except that the snow is so much lighter, really only a little heavier than a particle of dust, and therefore the many hidden, conflicting breezes make this unusual spectacle feel less strange.

of jade comes not from the mineral itself (it is just green rock without much practical use) but instead from what the beholder sees for themselves in the natural waves of hues and transparencies in the green stone. Thus the value of every piece of jade, or in this case the two pieces combined, is entirely in the eye of the beholder and unique to each moment in time. Its value is ever changing by whoever beholds it. It is essentially art, like a painting, only its artist is nature itself. There are such curiosities here within these palace walls but the proper gift to give the Professor on this occasion is something that cannot be traceable to the Emperor's own stores. His own hand-painted calligraphy wouldn't do as a gift. It would reveal too much. Jewels would be excessive. Simple is best. *Perhaps a jade comb for that lovely white hair? No, the rings are better. The rings are perfect.*

He had entered the inner court, but he bypassed the imperial residential areas when he reached the palace, to focus instead on the old storehouses and offices. Glazed tiles of yellow, green, and blue are plastered out in unique patterns. These are the markers, and he follows their trail. There are arrows in the patterns, coded messages hidden everywhere.

Three sets of stairs led the jade thief up from a white marble terrace where he passed through a pair of cast-bronze lions. They are the last remnants of the imperial guard. The mortal guards passed away long ago.

The HOSH's gravitational pull even drew in the jade thief, Lao Shifu, below its mustard-yellow roof, if just for a moment, even though he had no good reason to enter. *This is a sacred place and the pull is real.* Lao Shifu has no doubt that the moon and stars once orbited around this center point of the earth and the universe. It sits on a three-tiered terrace of white marble carved with dragons. Golden dragons also play along the walls.

He had come all this way for the Professor. Snow crunches under the jade thief's canvas boots. He is out in the elements now, inside the courtyards but not yet down inside the buildings' subterranean halls. His keys, which

The jade thief hadn't meant to come across anyone back here in these shadows, but he came prepared. He carries knives and other tools. Two teenagers, hidden away, need to be silenced. Easily done.

There was perhaps a look of surprise before the two lovers fell asleep, allowing the jade thief to pass without further complication.

The jade thief had let the sleeping powder drop out of the black silk pouch like white smoke and blew it directly into their young faces. The golden drawstring is loosened at the top. He holds out that strange silk pouch to them, inviting them both to look. They are curious of course. Who is this man? What is it that he has? The powder creates a cloud of white in their direction. The jade thief gives a heavy blow then holds his breath.

The two teenagers felt his breath and looked up. They see him in the shadows. He holds one finger to his lips. *Shhh.*

It was in a hidden stretch of hallway where he found them kissing. It was out of the way. Maybe he should just pass them by. How did the kids get in here? They are foreigners on winter vacation whispering in French, so he doesn't know what they are saying there in the darkness, but their emotions are strong. The girl and the boy both have tears freezing their cheeks, yet they smile and kiss with such vigor.

The jade thief was deep in thought. He takes off his scarf and hat. He rubs his chin. His cheeks are ice cold. What can he bring to such a wedding? He paces back and forth inside one of the forgotten storerooms until his head throbs. He looks again at the map. He tries a key in this next door ahead. The gift must be special. He remembers seeing two identical jade rings long ago. The rings shared a similar vein of green running through each. Those jade rings would be an interesting choice. Of the many fascinating properties of jade, the one that the jade thief most admires is that the value

Dust was his enemy, and dust was everywhere in these rarely visited hallways of the Emperor's Forbidden City. He assumes it is the remains of the dead. Whenever the jade thief goes into a new place, but most especially in this palace, he habitually dusts things off with his gloved hands. Gray gloves are what he wears, so this habit of his never darkens them. Walking into a new room, he wipes his hand along the windowsill. He blows the gray dust off his glove. *This dust is from yesterday,* he thinks. It was yesterday's life. It may be the skin of the dead emperors. A little bit of it too may have come down from the heavens. He blows dust from a door handle to reveal a keyhole. The key he'll use has the head of a dragon and a tail that winds down and around the shaft of the key to its tip.

The suffocating dust felt like a bag closed around his head. Losing control, he releases a heavy "Achoo!" into the darkness, knowing he shouldn't. It echoes. The jade thief tries to get his breath again but he cannot. No air. Just dust. He hears scampering from the corners of the shadows.

The air had grown thicker with the dust his boots stirred up. It tickles his hairy nostrils. His lung spasms without assistance from a partner lung or a reliable heart. Although he can appear heroic, the jade thief has a frail side. His skin is as translucent as paper and his insides are a mess.

For direction into this part of the labyrinth, he followed the colored tiles on the walls. The hallways look the same, but the jade thief knows every tile in this maze is unique, created by the artisans of the Emperor and arranged with great care. If he could just see from that point of view, see the tiniest patterns within the individual tiles (really, that's what we need to do or we are lost!). This is difficult to do because the palace architecture demands our attention on a monumental scale (like a European cathedral), but we must ignore all that and examine the patterns of the tiles. Only then will the signs to the eunuchs' secret pathways reveal themselves as they do for the jade thief, our guide.

levon a

building is easy to find. The original planners placed the HOSH in the exact center of the Forbidden City, and thus it is the center of Beijing. This special place, where the Emperor's dragon throne resides, is essentially the center of the universe, so some diehards still say. Not the government leaders who control the media here. They will not say so publicly, but I think they all still believe in the power of the HOSH.

But there had been other rooms, secret places, and that is where the jade thief came from just now, Dear Reader, beyond the obvious to the mysteries stored farther within. These rooms lie deeper, hidden, forgotten by the people of today. Footsteps echo down dark corridors. Spiders climb on my arm and yours. What is the goal of our expedition? We are going to find two lovely jade rings for Jasmine. They were stored in an eight-foot by ten-foot room with strange script on the door that looks not at all like common Chinese characters but more like swords joined together in battle. It is the writing of the Mongolians.

The jade thief almost couldn't believe he found the room again. He doesn't expect to find it on his first attempt. The door had been hidden for decades. Various iron keys clink together on a frayed leather strap hanging from the jade thief's belt. One of his keys gains us entrance into this secret room with the Mongolian script on its door. The jade thief is here with us now, modern-day 2016, just days before the wedding in Shanghai, and the man is in need of an appropriate gift. There are precious things around us, but the jade thief is intent on the jade rings. Even in the darkness here, they glow. How wonderful is the cold green light that brings out the beautiful patterns in the stone.

Before entering the room, this strange man marked a blue X on his faded map, hand-drawn from memories and expeditions long past, and folded the brown paper back into his satchel. His gloved hands fumble for his keys in the shadows. He came prepared. He wears a tiny LED light so he can find the keyhole. *Click.*

CHAPTER 18

Three days earlier in Beijing.

The foundations of this place are Mongol, he thought to himself, shivering in the cold with two rings stowed deep within the inner pocket of his thick wool coat. That is what we don't realize. We just see the surface of things in our day-to-day lives. The jade thief, however, likes to venture deeper. He knows that long ago Khan ruled all the known world. It was he who then brought his capital here to Beijing. The dirt is thus made of the blood of Mongol warriors and of the men whom they slaughtered here. Although few structures from that ancient time still stand today, the bedrock remains theirs. A layer of the Great Wall has Khan's mark. A subterranean level of the entire old city is Mongolian. There were other rulers before them, but the others do not matter in this story. Khan's men created Beijing.

The jade thief stepped through the light snow that had accumulated on the concrete walk. His single trail weaves past the drifts from where he is now, plugging along all the way back to the shadowy gates from where he came. In the center of Beijing's sprawling metropolis there still lies this walled Forbidden City built for the emperors back in 1406. Historians will tell you that the 999 buildings on the palace grounds must contain 9,999 rooms, because "nine" is a homonym for "long life." But where are they all? Many remain hidden today.

Before moving on, he looked back one last time and saw the top of the HOSH peer over the high wall. *Such memories!* Everyone has of course heard of the palace's Hall of Supreme Harmony (the HOSH). That

Ten minutes earlier at the Shanghai International Airport, where the Magnalev service originated, He Song and the jade thief had a heated conversation about whether or not to skip lunch to arrive at the wedding on time. He Song is just plain irritable today. "We should eat something. I am dying here," He Song begs, but the jade thief Lao Shifu will hear nothing of it. "We have to go! We have traveled too far. Let's not be late now," he maintains while pushing He Song through the crowds. "I am just so thirsty," He Song keeps saying. He is sick but no one knows that yet. They finally decide to go without a meal or even tea in favor of making it to the wedding on time, where there is sure to be an abundance of both.

He Song had arrived late on his Hunan Airlines flight from the Macao peninsula. The jade thief is already waiting for him at the gate, cleanly shaven, looking down at his watch. His face looks no older than thirty. He had arrived that same day from Beijing, then waited anxiously for He Song. The airport is full of people, as is typical.

It was an easy flight for the jade thief that morning. He has a window seat in the front of the sleek Boeing 787, giving him a nice perspective. The passenger sitting next to him keeps glancing in his direction. She finally inquires, "You are a Beijinger?" He just smiles back with a nod. There is a toddler in the seat behind that kicks the back of the jade thief's seat again and again, but he does not look back. While in the air, the jade thief watches a sparkling planet, Venus, lead the sunrise out his window as it bursts out onto the landscape to create a new day. He thinks to himself how small the really big things can appear to us sometimes. Little Venus, the star of sympathy, pulling up the sun!

become lost in the moment, feeling dizzy, excited, and perhaps a little drunk from earlier cocktails. The Professor is first surprised when the jade thief, the invited guest whom she has expected and has placed at a table of great honor, does not hand her a red envelope as the protocol requires, but instead gives her the two beautiful jade rings unwrapped. "You look lovely," says he. These are his wedding gift to her? The jade rings that look like nothing she has seen anywhere before. They are cool to the touch and shine as though a bright green fire is trapped inside. She lifts up her head while the rings shine a mossy-green glow on her hands, and there at his side is He Song, the uninvited, in the flesh! Their eyes lock and her ears begin to hum. "So . . . thanks for coming, eh?" says He Song mockingly.

Earlier, firecrackers announced a celebration at the foot of the Shangri-la tower. Firecrackers should dispel the ghosts, and red paper cuttings of *Fu* are placed on all the windows and doors to keep them away. Smoke from the strings of firecrackers lifts high in the air. Hundreds and hundreds of sharp pops ring out. This will be a wedding to remember. Jasmine, who no man could restrain, will finally be married. It is in all the papers. The published guest list becomes a who's who. Even the president's music star wife is expected to attend.

He Song and the jade thief came to the hotel that day by magnetic train. Shanghai's Magnalev hovers over its tracks and can move at great speeds because, with no wheels, the only friction is caused by air. Whizzing past, it sounds like a jet plane. At the train station, a recorded announcement bellows over the platform speakers, "Safety is a shared responsibility . . ."

On the Magnalev, He Song probably contaminated the entire car of passengers with the bird flu. He spits on the shiny chrome-plated floor before taking his assigned seat. As with many older Chinese, spitting remains a habit difficult to break despite the public campaigns against it and the potential fines. He Song just doesn't care. His fever is setting in.

The Professor had protested He Song's entrance at first but the jade thief distracted her. The jade thief says, "Please give them a try. I am curious to know whether they will fit your fingers." The Professor's fiancé tries on a ring, not knowing the implications. The jade thief Lao Shifu adds, "If they do fit your hand, surely you must accept our gift because this is then all meant to be." What are the chances that they would go around both of their knuckles so smoothly? But they do! Each ring is a perfect fit. The wedding couple cannot help but smile at each other.

The Professor almost didn't allow it to happen. Looking away and crossing her arms, she protests, "He Song is not invited!" The jade thief replies with ease. "I don't recall that stipulation, Professor. My invitation says I can bring a guest. He Song is my guest tonight." He Song adds, "You really do look stunning, Professor." The Professor and her fiancé want to further protest He Song's unexpected intrusion but do not wish to offend their friend the jade thief. So impressed they are by the precious gift, they are now too caught up in their imaginations. Their minds are no longer here in the present and instead they think about how perfectly the exchange of these rings will fit into the other staged events. Their attention is no longer on the present problem. They will not be forceful enough to prevent He Song's entry. It would take more of a fight. They want the rings but not He Song, and which desire is stronger? While they hesitate, both the guest and the intruder take the opportunity to push themselves inside.

You see, the Professor was already rather caught off guard by the many friends who were arriving, one after another, dressed in their finest, each handing her a thick red envelope full of newly minted cash, the sum adding up to an incredible amount, and that was precisely when the rings appeared out of the blue. As is tradition, the wedding couple stands at the entrance welcoming their guests inside. *This is actually happening! The wedding, all of it. Our guests are arriving and the happy ceremony is about to begin.* What a rush of conflicting feelings comes down onto the Professor. She is not herself. She and her fiancé stand at the entrance by the elevators in welcome, and they both begun spreading here early on. It came from the first handshakes when the master chef stepped out to acknowledge the most important guests, and unfortunately touched the doorknob before carefully washing his hands and going back to work.

They exchanged wedding rings before dinner and there was no denying that something magical happened at that moment. Exchanging rings is a Western tradition that the Professor had not expected to include. The air is heavy with meaning. The groom's feminine hand places a green jade ring on the lovely hand of the Professor, who then places a similar ring onto the finger of her spouse, and I think time really does stop. The wedding couple sees each other in a new way for the first time. Both bow to one another. A cup of tea is passed. Sip. Sip. Then, applause. It is done.

Would it all have been better without the jade rings?

The surprise rings were such tempting objects that the Professor had no hesitation whispering to the wedding planner to incorporate them into the ceremony at the very last second before everything was scheduled to begin. Every other piece of the ceremony had been planned ages ago, making this bit of spontaneity feel all the more fun. The wedding planners agree to the latest addition when they see the jewelry waiting there on the tray, each ring complementing the other so beautifully as a groom should do for his bride. A dark wave of green jumps off one wedding ring and onto the other. It would be impossible to make such jewelry in the modern day. You want to touch those smooth, subtle lines. The rings welcome your touch. They long to be around a finger again.

The rings were such a surprise and so very impressive that the jade thief got through the entrance with He Song and sat down before anyone realized what happened. "You are welcome, Jasmine, and I wish you both well," he calls back to them. Turning their attention to the banquet tables beyond, He Song and the jade thief step deeper inside the wedding hall. They are in!

over the web to acquaintances far and wide who could not come but were luckily able to watch on their handheld devices from afar. Those friends now use Facebook (finally legal in China!) to send their red-envelope gifts electronically to the Professor and her husband. Messages read, "Double happiness to the wedding couple," and contain electronic currency.

The musicians and dancers provided us with entertainment on a platform along the north wall before dinner. An ancient song playing right now is from a time preceding the very first Qin Emperor two thousand years ago. Dancers use paper fans to draw the eye. There are swords standing behind them that were used in an earlier dance performance when the guests were being seated. The Professor watches it all. She lifts up her hair, letting it breathe. The hair settles back down to her shoulders. One single loose strand remains between her fingers and she waves it away. She doesn't watch it float on the air, over the guests. The food is almost ready. The Professor thinks about choice paradox. People get stressed when they are given too many good choices. That is precisely why she designed to put some bad tasting dishes on the table that added color but she knew would not be touched. She has found, and research has confirmed her suspicion, that we are much happier with a couple good options rather than a multitude of them.

Everyone was hungry after the short ceremony but hunger was temporarily quelled by interesting conversations, such interesting people all around, appetizers and drink in each hand, and the real entertainment became not so much the musicians or the dancers but the guests interacting with one another on that wonderful day. A jolly fat man in the corner tells jokes, tilting many ears, while a waitress steps out to get him more gold-bottled mao-tai from the kitchen's stores. When the kitchen door opens, there is a rush of noise and steam. Inside, ten chefs and many more sous-chefs are managing woks of spiced oil flaming up from time to time. There will be no less than twenty courses for this dinner but the kitchen moves like clockwork, each gear knowing its role exactly. The virus had third person when saying "Mercy, dear." Are there just two names among the three old ladies? And with two names, will none of the three claim just one! The Professor eyes this table of confused guests who sit with the old women. More than one guest at this table shrugs his shoulders, and the Professor just winks back.

They began talking about the sugary foods because the youngest of the mysterious old women was bumped and said, "Well, look at me now, covered in noodle! How I wish I could maintain my feminine sweetness as well as the bride has done. She must share Liu Xiaoxin's secret to eternal youth. Doesn't the Professor over there look like she is a cube of refined sugar ready to turn our world into a better place."

The old woman's chair was bumped by a child from behind. She drops a noodle hanging between her chopsticks. "Don't trip, little one!"

Earlier one of the purple-haired old women at the table had said, "My grandkids are already eight, nine, six, and four, Sunday," although that statement couldn't be true! She is far too old to have such young grandchildren. The oldest woman talks while watching the kids run around her between the tables, thinking that the rosy-cheeked child over there might very well bump into her friend's chair from behind, but saying nothing. And so on goes the conversation among the three old women at the center table.

You fear this does not bode well for understanding *levon a*? Fear not! There is an easy explanation for the confusion at this table. Poor old Sunday has grown senile over the past decade and now calls the friend sitting beside her by the wrong name. Summer is the correct name. She calls her Sunday, but no matter. The other woman is named Mercy. The Professor invited senile Sunday to the wedding because once she'd had a great mind. Now, let's move on!

CCTV cameras on the underside of the drones televised the ceremony you are looking so bony these days. You look like you did after our defeat in Macao. Oh, what rough times we had but it has gotten better. You must eat more!" She turns back to the woman on her left, saying, "Here, Sunday, the head is the most tender part." This is the traditional role of the youngest, to serve her elders, who seem to be named Mercy and Sunday. The fish head of course is the tastiest. Who would deny that?

She had just said, "That was a better protest of ours. Our message during the Beijing Olympics went well too. People are taking notice." She pushes away her dish. "The sauce is a bit sweet for my taste, but that is how it always is with Shanghai dishes. Here, this fish meat will be milder. Would you like to eat the fish head, Sunday, or should we give it here to Mercy? I shall scoop it for you."

Sugar and success were the topics that had preceded the youngest woman's gracious scooping of the fish. With great authority, the oldest of the three turns to her right and says, "Sunday, you tell these chefs no sugar please! But then, no, why bother because they will insist that, oh, we must put in at least a little bit of sugar for taste. . . . Do you remember when we all wore those florescent t-shirts during the World's Fair? We cannot savor economic freedom without political freedom. That is what was printed on those pink shirts." All three laugh. Wait. What is that? Is there another Sunday here at the table? Now it appears that the oldest of the three thinks the other purple-haired woman is named Sunday.

It is confusing because the third lady had stated earlier looking into the eyes of the woman with a tinge of blue in her hair, "Sunday, these Shanghai chefs put in ladles full of sugar. Or they sneak it in. Oh, how I miss the food from back home. Ah, but this is a wedding to celebrate and why not on this special day eat some extra sugar. Mercy, dear, I say, why not." This both initiates the topic of sugar, tingling everyone's taste buds just at the mention of the word, and the confusion. So, this old woman now talking must be Mercy. She must have been talking about herself in

(Rewind, and so on. You are doing fine. Now you can do this on your own. The spaces between paragraphs are always steps back in time.)

A child noticed that a single strand of Jasmine's hair floated above all the guests. It flows up and catches a current of air, probably from the air conditioning. It then catches a breeze from a small helicopter drone taping the ceremony. The strand of hair summersaults over the people and almost lands on someone, but just in time it floats away. The child points at the strand of hair. She imagines it could be an almost-invisible dragon visiting the human race for this festive occasion.

There were three helicopter drones videotaping all the afternoon's events. The cameras are now zoomed in on the Professor from various angles. Her table is in the front of the room and slightly elevated. The flying drones are small and quiet enough to be hardly noticeable. Each drone has four propellers, a small camera, and a microphone. A child tries reaching out to catch one but it buzzes away from his reach. A few families with children are in attendance. A toddler runs around the table legs in untethered glee.

Sitting around one of the hall's central tables, three gray-haired ladies pried at a giant steamed fish to get at the meat from its underside without turning it over, while the other guests at their table looked baffled. These women appear to be great friends, yet something is amiss. On the one hand, their language is full of endearments. They touch hands frequently, catching up on all sorts of gossip about new fortunes made, past lovers lost, domestic politics, and their demanding house cats. And yet, on the other hand, there is a strangeness in how they talk. The graying hair of two of them has a purple tint, making them look all the more ridiculous but I suppose they do not see it. The hair of the third is a cooler hue that looks almost blue.

The youngest among them turned to her right with a frown. "Mercy, strikes a nerve, so he presses on. "No, I mean, really, I'm sure it would be a fascinating book if you get your thoughts in order...," he says coughing into his hand. Feeling further insulted, her mind is preparing a way to cut him off again but with finality this time to change the subject of this loathsome conversation forever. *What could be dangerous about turning to the weather?*

(Rewind fifteen minutes)

The dinner conversation between them began as a general critique of Communism today and our rule of law, but quickly deteriorated into quips laced with sarcasm. With a tall glass of wine in hand, the INGO CEO says sadly, "This system we have today is terribly unstable. It cannot last..." He Song's words suddenly drown her voice, "Ma'am, I must interject. Are you and I really sitting at the same table? Is *instability* the reality you see before us now?" She looks surprised and says, "Excuse me, I am speaking," but it doesn't stop his stream of words so she says even louder now, "See *here*, Mister He Song!" He Song looks up at her and fights back, "No, you *see* here!" She then protests again, "Really, I can't let *you* go on." To this, he puts on a new face, looking abashed, "Are we not free to express our opinions?" Beads of sweat roll down his forehead.

(Rewind some more)

Members of the Council for the Greater Good took up three tables in different parts of the room and, before the ruckus with He Song, they talked among themselves in whispers. The sunlight reflects on the pearl inlay of the banqueters' almost two thousand chopsticks. Sharp light cuts all the shadows in this room. There are no real shadows, just various levels of brightness. From bright to very bright, gleaming, and then, brightest of all, there is the reflection off Jasmine's suit under the intensely bright spotlights above.

her table's conversation to another direction. Yet the stubborn man beside her will not let their squabble drop. Not now. It isn't about the content of what they say anymore. "Sunday's weather is bound to be unpredictable," He Song rebuffs her attempt while coughing into his hand. There is a wad of mucus that he wipes onto his napkin. He adds, "Who cares about the weather until the day arrives?" The female CEO has had enough of this. He Song has exhausted her patience minutes ago. She makes a face back at him that looks like she caught a bad odor and he takes to mean *you bastard!* She doesn't expect what is coming next. She doesn't know how dangerous this man is. Lots of eyes are on them when He Song finally stabs her hand with a dessert fork. Blood flows onto the white tablecloth.

(Rewind ten seconds)

A breath before she will attempt to start a new conversation at her table with those fateful words that there may be a chance of rain, in the short time it took her to inhale, the CEO escalated the confrontation by turning her head away from He Song just as he was making his argument. It is not what is being said that is important anymore. He Song notices her looking away from him as he speaks and also notices that while turning her head away her face conveys a real pain at being put here beside him. Her inhale makes a deep moan that echoes over the banquet hall. This sound she makes says to everyone present, no matter what language they speak, "*Pity me. Rescue me. Why is this man such a jerk?*"

(Rewind one minute)

She and He Song argued long before it escalated to bloodshed, and the microphones caught a phrase here and there. He starts to light a smoke while she chokes on a swallow of wine and says, "That's very rude." He pushes another button. "Oh, Wise Lady Beyond All Measure," He Song guffaws jokingly while tugging at his unkempt beard, "you should've written a book about it." She smiles nervously, "I *am* writing a book." This

Meanwhile an invisible virus has spread among the guests. He Song brought it into the banquet hall, and it has been festering for an hour. Chances are good that half of the room is already infected. The virus is a highly contagious and possibly fatal version of avian flu, known as H1N1. But the virus is invisible and its consequences come later when everyone has the perspective of hindsight, say tomorrow or next week. That is for the future, and, my Dear Reader, we are headed in the other direction. We are going into the past.

(Rewind)

Unaware that their very lives will be at risk, the guests gossiped loudly to one another about how the hotel security threw a bearded man out of the room after he attacked that lovely woman sitting just there beside him. Who had seen what? "Tell us what you saw," they ask each other while they eat. Everyone had a different point of view from their assigned seat, along with a different version of the events.

(Rewind)

Where did all those security men come from? They seem to pop out of the air. Four large guards grab hold of each arm and leg while He Song protests with the most vulgar words, swinging his head because his neck is still under his control until the fifth man who had been holding him under both armpits from behind finally has enough and sprays a spongy material into his mouth. The screaming suddenly stops. He Song's eyes widen. He disappears from view.

(Rewind)

The video cameras in the room were able to capture some of He Song's assault on the guest. They record her commenting loudly, "I heard that there is a 75 percent chance of rain this weekend," in the attempt to change than the anger she feels underneath. Each table gets her undivided attention for a few minutes. *Thank you for coming. Never mind that little disturbance. Everything is fine now. Thank you for giving us the honor to celebrate this special occasion with you.* "Toast to long life, riches, and happiness," the guests all want to say but before they can the Professor interrupts instead with a simple "Toast to our future!" May it be better than the past. Jasmine has never had an easy life, though her composure will fool you. She looks into your eyes like she understands. There is compassion, strength, and no hint of pride. "Toast to the future!"

(Rewind)

He Song's chair in the banquet hall was empty because Jasmine had thrown him out just minutes before. Blood stains a napkin resting at his vacant seat. Beside the empty seat sits a jade thief the Professor knows well. She calls him Lao Shifu, a sign of great respect to bestow on one who looks so young. The jade thief is looking at the hand of another guest, the CEO of an international NGO, and providing his medical advice on whether or not she should go to the emergency room immediately to have the injured hand examined.

(Rewind)

How dare he! the Professor thought before the lobsters arrived, before the toasts of rice wine and her emotions had time to settle. Rather than laugh it off, she is fuming. It boils her blood to think of how He Song has tried again and again to control her over the years. It never stops! He always tarnishes her good intentions. That is why he was not invited here today. The world would have been so much better had He Song never been born. She returns to her long-considered thoughts of murdering him "for the good of the nation." She tries to hide her rage even as it tears at her insides.

(Rewind)

bite-sized pieces to the tiny china bowls sitting in front of them. The meat dishes still have pieces of bone and gristle, which adds to the flavor of the meat, so after you gnaw the meat from the bone inside your mouth, you spit the bone out onto the tip of the same chopsticks that had brought them in, then lower them down from your mouth onto the tabletop where they sit in a pile. Waiters occasionally come by and wipe the bones from the tabletops with their rags. One beautiful dish that amazes the room is Shanghai lobster, still living, on ice but carefully cut so that the meat of its tail is exposed and it cannot resist when you pull it out in pieces. The lobster meat is fresher than fresh. Courses are brought to each table and uncovered at exactly the same time with great show.

(Rewind)

The smartphones first buzzed with a tweeted response to the drama caused by our villain, He Song. The Professor's new spouse reluctantly passes her iPhone to her, although they had promised all phones would be put away today. All things considered it is reasonable to allow Professor6489 to send a short tweet. **Mischievous He Song gives me pause on this joyful day to reevaluate my reality and wonder. . . . Has the old emperor been reborn? #shangri-la?** A short tweet, true enough, it is that. Yet something about it feels bigger. Just the act of typing the words out and pressing send allows the Professor to breathe normally again. Here is another breath. Relief comes swiftly. She unclenches her fist. She wanted to ask that one lingering question aloud for some time. She has a history of expressing opinions that nobody dares say, let alone publish. What began as anger towards He Song now spins into a new but familiar direction.

(Rewind)

The Professor and her spouse went around to each of the tables, toasting their many guests. Small glasses clink together. She has learned to show a strong face to the public. She wants to show her success today rather safety and relief that she has never felt so strongly before, she goes through the files in her brain to delete. What is not needed anymore need not be retained. Deleting the useless, the no longer meaningful, will allow space for a powerful mind like hers to focus solely on the future:

Macao, 1999: delete, trash.

Doctorate studies in Statistics: save and refile.

Cultural Revolution, 1966: delete, trash

Speech to President Nixon: save and refile.

Traumas of childhood: delete, trash.

The frozen lake: save and refile.

A cluttered mind is a weak mind. She must constantly be sharp and on her toes. She has only just begun to make her mark. The spot of crimson stretches along her pale face in a broad, toothy smile. There is a piece of garlic-sautéed greens (a petal of locally grown clover, sweet and popular) showing between her teeth that she nonchalantly removes with a manicured nail. She used to file away her thoughts by physically writing the memories on note cards. The act of writing it down relieved her mind and allowed better categorization, and when the information became unnecessary, it was easy to discard. If the Professor had not begun those mind exercises years ago, she would not be the highly functional mover and shaker she is in China today. Writing it out is not necessary anymore. Her mind is now wired to file, save, or delete on command. It is a very convenient way of living. An uncluttered mind is efficient.

(Rewind)

The food brought before them with white gloves on covered trays was more than wonderful. She touches her new spouse's right hand. Waiters race along replenishing the spinning lazy Susans in the middle of each table and removing the used dishes. Chopsticks attack the shared dishes in each table's center. The white tablecloths become specked in red, brown, and yellow sauces dripping from guests' chopsticks as they bring back delectable

The Professor set aside her iPhone to take a bite of sweet buttercream cake. The reflected pool light touches a waiter scooping eight-treasure soup into small bowls. Jasmine goes by the name "Professor" now to re-image herself as an intellectual rather than a revolutionary. She is there with her new spouse. Tradition says that the wedding bride should change outfits three times throughout the ceremony but they have chosen to stay in their matching Gucci suits. She is very tall for a Chinese woman. Her brown eyes are striking. A wavering patch of light shines in one eye while the other holds back in a relative shadow. Her hair is snow white. There is a thick silk ribbon tied loosely around her neck in old-world Eastern style. Her cufflinks have memories. Her ring is new to her finger. It is made of imperial jade.

Again, rewind…

Everyone's phone vibrated when Professor6489 tweeted. **If only time could freeze on this moment. Pour us all more Maotai please! #weddingofthecentury #happiestdayever #shangri-la?** There is a photo attached. The number of Professor6489 followers is increasing exponentially by the minute. The Professor is married. She is happy. Life, though hard, is good.

Rewind…

Before tweeting her elation to her friends and followers around the world, she had to take a deep breath and smile. Here in the moment, things look pretty good. The banquet table where they sit is round, as are all ninety-nine tables in the room. Their lack of corners allow for 886 guests, plus the hosts, which is exactly the correct number for good fortune. *Never have I hosted an event so under my own control,* thinks the Professor as she scans the room. In a moment she calculates all the costs of the day in her head including those that were unexpected. It is all worth it. With a feeling of

CHAPTER 19

December 21, 2016
China's population is 1.4 billion people.

There was a grand wedding banquet that December day.[1] The sunlight streams in through the heavy glass-plated walls and ceiling of the tall atrium here on the ninety-ninth floor of the Grand Shangri-la Hotel. The light dives down into the gentle waves of a heavily chlorinated pool carved in pink marble tile, then it reflects back up onto the smartly dressed guests, making them sparkle in wavy brightness. Though outside the sky is a gloomy gray, the guests will focus on the beautiful skyline still visible from here of new Shanghai. New Shanghai was not so long ago just a muddy swamp, yet now from this nest in the clouds we can see innovative architectural masterpieces scraping the sky for miles along the Huangpu River until the river waters dump out into the Pacific Ocean. Once called the pearl of the Orient, today this new version of Shanghai is the brightest gem of the world.[2]

Now, rewind…

---

1   Note that the first sentence places you in a new moment in time. The first sentence of every paragraph will do this for you. The remaining paragraph tells the story in a normal chronology as if you are watching a movie segment on television. Action moves forward in a normal way within the paragraph.

2   As your eyes float over the empty space between paragraphs, prepare to move to an earlier moment in time than where you have already read. It is like the movie is rewound still further, so you don't miss the real story. The next first sentence will be your anchor as you read. And so on. In every paragraph the first sentence will imply, "I now take you even further back in history so you may understand." Place yourself there, then let the moment play out before you.

"Please don't tell me how this story ends," you say.
"Then let me tell you how it all began," I reply.

There was once an Emperor boy and a woman as fiery as a dragon who formed a friendship with a man who could not die. Their story is well worth retelling if you have the time to experience it *levon a*, or backward as we say, from last to first.

Welcome, Dear Reader. I will guide you down this gentle road. Like that first time you rode a bicycle, it may feel a bit awkward for the first mile or so, but soon bicycling felt like the most natural thing, did it not? In my opinion, reading backward is as natural, because it matches how our brains sometimes process memories. It is not usually how we read novels, but maybe that's something for us to change rather than accept. I agree with Jasmine on that one point at least. We should not be content with the way it's always been.

It is now the year 2016, and our villain He Song is in modern-day Shanghai during the winter solstice. It will be the shortest day, but the longest night. The story starts today and will go backward from there, as does all of my memory.

The woman originally had no proper name. She was called Second Little Sister by her family, but oh, she became so much more than that! In Middle Kingdom lore, a woman like her could likely be the serpent of Xihu Lake in disguise. He Song called her Dear Darling Jasmine and that is why she will be called Jasmine here. The name of the Emperor boy mentioned above is Puyi, and he died in 1967 of natural causes. The man who should have died is named He Song. On He Song's right hand he has only three fingers and a stubby thumb. His heart was removed long ago. He Song is an evil man.